He's her best friend . . .
or maybe something more?

Suddenly, I want to touch him.

Not a push, or a shove, or even a friendly hug. I want to feel the creases in his skin, connect his freckles with invisible lines, brush my fingers across the inside of his wrist. He shifts. I have the strangest feeling that he's as aware of me as I am of him. I can't concentrate.

St. Clair coughs and shifts again. His leg brushes against mine. It stays there. I'm paralyzed. I should move it; it feels too unnatural. How can he not notice his leg is touching my leg? From the corner of my eye, I see the profile of his chin and nose, and—oh, dear God—the curve of his lips.

There. He glanced at me. I know he did.

I bore my eyes into the screen, trying my best to prove that I am Really Interested in this movie. St. Clair stiffens but doesn't move his leg.

Again. Another glance. This time I turn, automatically, just as he's turning away. It's a dance, and now there's a feeling in the air like one of us should say something. Focus, Anna. Focus. "Do you like it?" I whisper.

He pauses. "The film?"

I'm thankful the shadows hide my blush.

"I like it very much," he says.

I risk a glance, and St. Clair stares back. Deeply. He has not looked at me like this before. I turn away first, then feel him turn a few beats later.

I know he is smiling, and my heart races.

OTHER BOOKS YOU MAY ENJOY

ANNA
and the
FRENCH
♥KISS

STEPHANIE PERKINS

speak

SPEAK
An imprint of Penguin Random House LLC
375 Hudson Street
New York, New York 10014

First published in the United States of America by Dutton Books,
a member of Penguin Group (USA) Inc., 2010
Published by Speak, an imprint of Penguin Group (USA) Inc., 2011
Reissued in this Speak edition, 2013

THE LIBRARY OF CONGRESS HAS CATALOGED THE DUTTON BOOKS EDITION AS FOLLOWS:
Perkins, Stephanie.
Anna and the French kiss / Stephanie Perkins.
p. cm.
Summary: When Anna's romance-novelist father sends her to an elite American boarding school
in Paris for her senior year of high school, she reluctantly goes, and meets an amazing boy
who becomes her best friend, in spite of the fact that they both want something more.
ISBN 9878-0-525-42327-0 (hardcover)
[1. Interpersonal relations—Fiction. 2. Boarding school—Fiction. 3. Foreign study—Fiction.
4. Paris (France) —Fiction. 5. France—Fiction.] I. Title. PZ7.P4317 An 2010
[Fic]—dc22 2009053290

Speak ISBN 978-0-14-241940-3

Designed by Irene Vandervoort

Printed in the United States of America

13 15 17 19 20 18 16 14 12

For Jarrod, best friend & true love

chapter one

Here is everything I know about France: *Madeline* and *Amélie* and *Moulin Rouge*. The Eiffel Tower and the Arc de Triomphe, although I have no idea what the function of either actually is. Napoleon, Marie Antoinette, and a lot of kings named Louis. I'm not sure what they did either, but I think it has something to do with the French Revolution, which has something to do with Bastille Day. The art museum is called the Louvre and it's shaped like a pyramid and the *Mona Lisa* lives there along with that statue of the woman missing her arms. And there are cafés or bistros or whatever they call them on every street corner. And mimes. The food is supposed to be good, and the people drink a lot of wine and smoke a lot of cigarettes.

I've heard they don't like Americans, and they don't like white sneakers.

A few months ago, my father enrolled me in boarding school. His air quotes practically crackled over the phone line as he declared living abroad to be a "good learning experience" and a "keepsake I'd treasure forever." Yeah. Keepsake. And I would've pointed out his misuse of the word had I not already been freaking out.

Since his announcement, I've tried yelling, begging, pleading, and crying, but nothing has convinced him otherwise. And now I have a new student visa and a passport, each declaring me: Anna Oliphant, citizen of the United States of America. And now I'm here with my parents—unpacking my belongings in a room smaller than my suitcase—the newest senior at the School of America in Paris.

It's not that I'm ungrateful. I mean, it's *Paris*. The City of Light! The most romantic city in the world! I'm not immune to that. It's just this whole international boarding school thing is a lot more about my father than it is about me. Ever since he sold out and started writing lame books that were turned into even lamer movies, he's been trying to impress his big-shot New York friends with how cultured and rich he is.

My father isn't cultured. But he is rich.

It wasn't always like this. When my parents were still married, we were strictly lower middle class. It was around the time of the divorce that all traces of decency vanished, and his dream of being the next great Southern writer was replaced by his desire to be the next *published* writer. So he started writing these novels set in Small Town Georgia about folks with Good American

Values who Fall in Love and then contract Life-Threatening Diseases and Die.

I'm serious.

And it totally depresses me, but the ladies eat it up. They love my father's books and they love his cable-knit sweaters and they love his bleachy smile and orangey tan. And they have turned him into a bestseller and a total dick.

Two of his books have been made into movies and three more are in production, which is where his real money comes from. Hollywood. And, somehow, this extra cash and pseudo-prestige have warped his brain into thinking that I should live in France. For a year. Alone. I don't understand why he couldn't send me to Australia or Ireland or anywhere else where English is the native language. The only French word I know is *oui*, which means "yes," and only recently did I learn it's spelled o-u-i and not w-e-e.

At least the people in my new school speak English. It was founded for pretentious Americans who don't like the company of their own children. I mean, really. Who sends their kid to boarding school? It's so Hogwarts. Only mine doesn't have cute boy wizards or magic candy or flying lessons.

Instead, I'm stuck with ninety-nine other students. There are twenty-five people in my *entire senior class,* as opposed to the six hundred I had back in Atlanta. And I'm studying the same things I studied at Clairemont High except now I'm registered in beginning French.

Oh, yeah. Beginning French. No doubt with the freshmen. I totally rock.

Mom says I need to lose the bitter factor, pronto, but she's not the one leaving behind her fabulous best friend, Bridgette. Or her fabulous job at the Royal Midtown 14 multiplex. Or Toph, the fabulous boy at the Royal Midtown 14 multiplex.

And I still can't believe she's separating me from my brother, Sean, who is only seven and way too young to be left home alone after school. Without me, he'll probably be kidnapped by that creepy guy down the road who has dirty Coca-Cola towels hanging in his windows. Or Seany will accidentally eat something containing Red Dye #40 and his throat will swell up and no one will be there to drive him to the hospital. He might even die. And I bet they wouldn't let me fly home for his funeral and I'd have to visit the cemetery alone next year and Dad will have picked out some god-awful granite cherub to go over his grave.

And I hope Dad doesn't expect me to fill out college applications to Russia or Romania now. My dream is to study film theory in California. I want to be our nation's greatest female film critic. Someday I'll be invited to every festival, and I'll have a major newspaper column and a cool television show and a ridiculously popular website. So far I only have the website, and it's not so popular. Yet.

I just need a little more time to work on it, that's all.

"Anna, it's time."

"What?" I glance up from folding my shirts into perfect squares.

Mom stares at me and twiddles the turtle charm on her necklace. My father, bedecked in a peach polo shirt and white boating shoes, is gazing out my dormitory window. It's late, but across the street a woman belts out something operatic.

My parents need to return to their hotel rooms. They both have early morning flights.

"Oh." I grip the shirt in my hands a little tighter.

Dad steps away from the window, and I'm alarmed to discover his eyes are wet. Something about the idea of my father—even if it is *my father*—on the brink of tears raises a lump in my throat.

"Well, kiddo. Guess you're all grown up now."

My body is frozen. He pulls my stiff limbs into a bear hug. His grip is frightening. "Take care of yourself. Study hard and make some friends. And watch out for pickpockets," he adds. "Sometimes they work in pairs."

I nod into his shoulder, and he releases me. And then he's gone.

My mother lingers behind. "You'll have a wonderful year here," she says. "I just know it." I bite my lip to keep it from quivering, and she sweeps me into her arms. I try to breathe. Inhale. Count to three. Exhale. Her skin smells like grapefruit body lotion. "I'll call you the moment I get home," she says.

Home. Atlanta isn't my home anymore.

"I love you, Anna."

I'm crying now. "I love you, too. Take care of Seany for me."

"Of course."

"And Captain Jack," I say. "Make sure Sean feeds him and changes his bedding and fills his water bottle. And make sure he doesn't give him too many treats because they make him fat and

then he can't get out of his igloo. But make sure he gives him at least a few every day, because he still needs the vitamin C and he won't drink the water when I use those vitamin drops—"

She pulls back and tucks my bleached stripe behind my ear. "I love you," she says again.

And then my mother does something that, even after all of the paperwork and plane tickets and presentations, I don't see coming. Something that would've happened in a year anyway, once I left for college, but that no matter how many days or months or years I've yearned for it, I am still not prepared for when it actually happens.

My mother leaves. I am alone.

chapter two

$\mathcal{I}$ feel it coming, but I can't stop it.

PANIC.

They left me. My parents actually left me! IN FRANCE!

Meanwhile, Paris is oddly silent. Even the opera singer has packed it in for the night. I *cannot* lose it. The walls here are thinner than Band-Aids, so if I break down, my neighbors—my new classmates—will hear everything. I'm going to be sick. I'm going to vomit that weird eggplant tapenade I had for dinner, and everyone will hear, and no one will invite me to watch the mimes escape from their invisible boxes, or whatever it is people do here in their spare time.

I race to my pedestal sink to splash water on my face, but it explodes out and sprays my shirt instead. And now I'm crying harder, because I haven't unpacked my towels, and wet clothing reminds me of those stupid water rides Bridgette and Matt used to drag me on at Six Flags where the water is the wrong color and it smells like paint and it has a billion trillion bacterial microbes in it. Oh God. What if there are bacterial microbes in the water? Is French water even safe to drink?

Pathetic. I'm pathetic.

How many seventeen-year-olds would kill to leave home? My neighbors aren't experiencing any meltdowns. No crying coming from behind *their* bedroom walls. I grab a shirt off the bed to blot myself dry, when the solution strikes. *My pillow.* I collapse face-first into the sound barrier and sob and sob and sob.

Someone is knocking on my door.

No. Surely that's not my door.

There it is again!

"Hello?" a girl calls from the hallway. "Hello? Are you okay?"

No, I'm not okay. GO AWAY. But she calls again, and I'm obligated to crawl off my bed and answer the door. A blonde with long, tight curls waits on the other side. She's tall and big, but not overweight-big. Volleyball player big. A diamondlike nose ring sparkles in the hall light. "Are you all right?" Her voice is gentle. "I'm Meredith; I live next door. Were those your parents who just left?"

My puffy eyes signal the affirmative.

"I cried the first night, too." She tilts her head, thinks for a moment, and then nods. "Come on. *Chocolat chaud.*"

"A chocolate show?" Why would I want to see a chocolate show? My mother has abandoned me and I'm terrified to leave my room and—

"No." She smiles. "*Chaud*. Hot. Hot chocolate, I can make some in my room."

Oh.

Despite myself, I follow. Meredith stops me with her hand like a crossing guard. She's wearing rings on all five fingers. "Don't forget your key. The doors automatically lock behind you."

"I know." And I tug the necklace out from underneath my shirt to prove it. I slipped my key onto it during this weekend's required Life Skills Seminars for new students, when they told us how easy it is to get locked out.

We enter her room. I gasp. It's the same impossible size as mine, seven by ten feet, with the same mini-desk, mini-dresser, mini-bed, mini-fridge, mini-sink, and mini-shower. (No mini-toilet, those are shared down the hall.) But . . . unlike my own sterile cage, every inch of wall and ceiling is covered with posters and pictures and shiny wrapping paper and brightly colored flyers written in French.

"How long have you *been* here?" I ask.

Meredith hands me a tissue and I blow my nose, a terrible honk like an angry goose, but she doesn't flinch or make a face. "I arrived yesterday. This is my fourth year here, so I didn't have to go to the seminars. I flew in alone, so I've just been hanging out, waiting for my friends to show up." She looks around with her hands on her hips, admiring her handiwork. I spot a pile of magazines, scissors, and tape on her floor and realize it's a work in progress. "Not bad, eh? White walls don't do it for me."

I circle her room, examining everything. I quickly discover that most of the faces are the same five people: John, Paul, George, Ringo, and some soccer guy I don't recognize.

"The Beatles are all I listen to. My friends tease me, but—"

"Who's this?" I point to Soccer Guy. He's wearing red and white, and he's all dark eyebrows and dark hair. Quite good-looking, actually.

"Cesc Fàbregas. God, he's the most incredible passer. Plays for Arsenal. The English football club? No?"

I shake my head. I don't keep up with sports, but maybe I should. "Nice legs, though."

"I know, right? You could hammer nails with those thighs."

While Meredith brews *chocolat chaud* on her hot plate, I learn she's also a senior, and that she only plays soccer during the summer because our school doesn't have a program, but that she used to rank All-State in Massachusetts. That's where she's from, Boston. And she reminds me I should call it "football" here, which—when I think about it—really does make more sense. And she doesn't seem to mind when I badger her with questions or paw through her things.

Her room is amazing. In addition to the paraphernalia taped to her walls, she has a dozen china teacups filled with plastic glitter rings, and silver rings with amber stones, and glass rings with pressed flowers. It already looks as if she's lived here for years.

I try on a ring with a rubber dinosaur attached. The T-rex flashes red and yellow and blue lights when I squeeze him. "I wish I could have a room like this." I love it, but I'm too much of a neat freak to have something like it for myself. I need clean walls and a clean desktop and everything put away in its right place at all times.

Meredith looks pleased with the compliment.

"Are these your friends?" I place the dinosaur back into its teacup and point to a picture tucked in her mirror. It's gray and shadowy and printed on thick, glossy paper. Clearly the product of a school photography class. Four people stand before a giant hollow cube, and the abundance of stylish black clothing and deliberately mussed hair reveals Meredith belongs to the resident art clique. For some reason, I'm surprised. I know her room is artsy, and she has all of those rings on her fingers and in her nose, but the rest is clean-cut—lilac sweater, pressed jeans, soft voice. Then there's the soccer thing, but she's not a tomboy either.

She breaks into a wide smile, and her nose ring winks. "Yeah. Ellie took that at La Défense. That's Josh and St. Clair and me and Rashmi. You'll meet them tomorrow at breakfast. Well, everyone but Ellie. She graduated last year."

The pit of my stomach begins to unclench. Was that an invitation to sit with her?

"But I'm sure you'll meet her soon enough, because she's dating St. Clair. She's at Parsons Paris now for photography."

I've never heard of it, but I nod as if I've considered going there myself someday.

"She's *really* talented." The edge in her voice suggests otherwise, but I don't push it. "Josh and Rashmi are dating, too," she adds.

Ah. Meredith must be single.

Unfortunately, I can relate. Back home I'd dated my friend Matt for five months. He was tall-ish and funny-ish and had decent-ish hair. It was one of those "since no one better is around, do you wanna make out?" situations. All we'd ever done was kiss, and it wasn't even that great. Too much spit. I always had to wipe off my chin.

We broke up when I learned about France, but it wasn't a big deal. I didn't cry or send him weepy emails or key his mom's station wagon. Now he's going out with Cherrie Milliken, who is in chorus and has shiny shampoo-commercial hair. It doesn't even bother me.

Not really.

Besides, the breakup freed me to lust after Toph, multiplex coworker babe extraordinaire. Not that I didn't lust after him when I was with Matt, but still. It did make me feel guilty. And things were starting to happen with Toph—they really were— when summer ended. But Matt's the only guy I've ever gone out with, and he barely counts. I once told him I'd dated this guy named Stuart Thistleback at summer camp. Stuart Thistleback had auburn hair and played the stand-up bass, and we were totally in love, but he lived in Chattanooga and we didn't have our driver's licenses yet.

Matt knew I made it up, but he was too nice to say so.

I'm about to ask Meredith what classes she's taking, when her phone chirps the first few bars of "Strawberry Fields Forever." She rolls her eyes and answers. "Mom, it's midnight here. Six-hour time difference, remember?"

I glance at her alarm clock, shaped like a yellow submarine, and I'm surprised to find she's right. I set my long-empty mug of *chocolat chaud* on her dresser. "I should get going," I whisper. "Sorry I stayed so long."

"Hold on a sec." Meredith covers the mouthpiece. "It was nice meeting you. See you at breakfast?"

"Yeah. See ya." I try to say this casually, but I'm so thrilled that I skip from her room and promptly slam into a wall.

Whoops. Not a wall. A boy.

"Oof." He staggers backward.

"Sorry! I'm so sorry, I didn't know you were there."

He shakes his head, a little dazed. The first thing I notice is his hair—it's the first thing I notice about everyone. It's dark brown and messy and somehow both long and short at the same time. I think of the Beatles, since I've just seen them in Meredith's room. It's artist hair. Musician hair. I-pretend-I-don't-care-but-I-really-do hair.

Beautiful hair.

"It's okay, I didn't see you either. Are you all right, then?"

Oh my. He's English.

"Er. Does Mer live here?"

Seriously, I don't know any American girl who can resist an English accent.

The boy clears his throat. "Meredith Chevalier? Tall girl? Big, curly hair?" Then he looks at me like I'm crazy or half deaf, like my Nanna Oliphant. Nanna just smiles and shakes her head whenever I ask, "What kind of salad dressing would you like?" or "Where did you put Granddad's false teeth?"

"I'm sorry." He takes the smallest step away from me. "You were going to bed."

"Yes! Meredith lives there. I've just spent two hours with her." I announce this proudly like my brother, Seany, whenever he finds something disgusting in the yard. "I'm Anna! I'm new here!" *Oh God. What. Is with. The scary enthusiasm?* My cheeks catch fire, and it's all so humiliating.

The beautiful boy gives an amused grin. His teeth are lovely—straight on top and crooked on the bottom, with a touch of overbite. I'm a sucker for smiles like this, due to my own lack of orthodontia. I have a gap between my front teeth the size of a raisin.

"Étienne," he says. "I live one floor up."

"I live here." I point dumbly at my room while my mind whirs: French name, English accent, American school. Anna confused.

He raps twice on Meredith's door. "Well. I'll see you around then, Anna."

Eh-t-yen says my name like this: *Ah-na.*

My heart *thump thump thumps* in my chest.

Meredith opens her door. "St. Clair!" she shrieks. She's still on the phone. They laugh and hug and talk over each other. "Come in! How was your flight? When'd you get here? Have you seen Josh? Mom, I've gotta go."

Meredith's phone and door snap shut simultaneously.

I fumble with the key on my necklace. Two girls in matching pink bathrobes strut behind me, giggling and gossiping. A crowd of guys across the hall snicker and catcall. Meredith and her friend laugh through the thin walls. My heart sinks, and my stomach tightens back up.

I'm still the new girl. I'm still alone.

chapter three

The next morning, I consider stopping by Meredith's, but I chicken out and walk to breakfast by myself. At least I know where the cafeteria is (Day Two: Life Skills Seminars). I double-check for my meal card and pop open my Hello Kitty umbrella. It's drizzling. The weather doesn't give a crap that it's my first day of school.

I cross the road with a group of chattering students. They don't notice me, but together we dodge the puddles. An automobile, small enough to be one of my brother's toys, whizzes past and sprays a girl in glasses. She swears, and her friends tease her.

I drop behind.

The city is pearl gray. The overcast sky and the stone buildings emit the same cold elegance, but ahead of me, the Panthéon shimmers. Its massive dome and impressive columns rise up to crown the top of the neighborhood. Every time I see it, it's difficult to pull away. It's as if it were stolen from ancient Rome or, at the very least, Capitol Hill. Nothing I should be able to view from a classroom window.

I don't know its purpose, but I assume someone will tell me soon.

My new neighborhood is the Latin Quarter, or the fifth arrondissement. According to my pocket dictionary, that means district, and the buildings in my *arrondissement* blend one into another, curving around corners with the sumptuousness of wedding cakes. The sidewalks are crowded with students and tourists, and they're lined with identical benches and ornate lampposts, bushy trees ringed in metal grates, Gothic cathedrals and tiny *crêperies*, postcard racks, and curlicue wrought iron balconies.

If this were a vacation, I'm sure I'd be charmed. I'd buy an Eiffel Tower key chain, take pictures of the cobblestones, and order a platter of escargot. But I'm not on vacation. I am here to live, and I feel small.

The School of America's main building is only a two-minute walk from Résidence Lambert, the junior and senior dormitory. The entrance is through a grand archway, set back in a courtyard with manicured trees. Geraniums and ivy trail down from window boxes on each floor, and majestic lion's heads are carved into the center of the dark green doors, which are three times my height. On either side of the doors hangs a red, white, and blue flag—one American, the other French.

It looks like a film set. *A Little Princess*, if it took place in Paris. How can such a school really exist? And how is it possible that I'm enrolled? My father is insane to believe I belong here. I'm struggling to close my umbrella and nudge open one of the heavy wooden doors with my butt, when a preppy guy with faux-surfer hair barges past. He smacks into my umbrella and then shoots me the stink-eye as if: (1) it's my fault he has the patience of a toddler and (2) he wasn't already soaked from the rain.

Two-point deduction for Paris. Suck on that, Preppy Guy.

The ceiling on the first floor is impossibly high, dripping with chandeliers and frescoed with flirting nymphs and lusting satyrs. It smells faintly of orange cleaning products and dry-erase markers. I follow the squeak of rubber soles toward the cafeteria. Beneath our feet is a marbled mosaic of interlocking sparrows. Mounted on the wall, at the far end of the hall, is a gilded clock that's chiming the hour.

The whole school is as intimidating as it is impressive. It should be reserved for students with personal bodyguards and Shetland ponies, not someone who buys the majority of her wardrobe at Target.

Even though I saw it on the school tour, the cafeteria stops me dead. I used to eat lunch in a converted gymnasium that reeked of bleach and jockstraps. It had long tables with preattached benches, and paper cups and plastic straws. The hairnetted ladies who ran the cash registers served frozen pizza and frozen fries and frozen nuggets, and the soda fountains and vending machines provided the rest of my so-called nourishment.

But this. This could be a restaurant.

Unlike the historic opulence of the hall, the cafeteria is sleek and modern. It's packed with round birch tables and plants in hanging baskets. The walls are tangerine and lime, and there's a dapper Frenchman in a white chef's hat serving a variety of food that looks suspiciously fresh. There are several cases of bottled drinks, but instead of high-sugar, high-caf colas, they're filled with juice and a dozen types of mineral water. There's even a table set up for coffee. *Coffee*. I know some Starbucks-starved students at Clairemont who'd kill for in-school coffee.

The chairs are already filled with people gossiping with their friends over the shouting of the chefs and the clattering of the dishes (real china, not plastic). I stall in the doorway. Students brush past me, spiraling out in all directions. My chest squeezes. Should I find a table or should I find breakfast first? And how am I even supposed to order when the menu is in freaking *French*?

I'm startled when a voice calls out my name. Oh please oh please oh please . . .

A scan through the crowd reveals a five-ringed hand waving from across the room. Meredith points to an empty chair beside her, and I weave my way there, grateful and almost painfully relieved.

"I thought about knocking on your door so we could walk together, but I didn't know if you were a late sleeper." Meredith's eyebrows pinch together with worry. "I'm sorry, I should have knocked. You look so lost."

"Thanks for saving me a spot." I set down my stuff and take a seat. There are two others at the table and, as promised the night before, they're from the photograph on her mirror. I'm nervous again and readjust my backpack at my feet.

"This is Anna, the girl I was telling you about," Meredith says.

A lanky guy with short hair and a long nose salutes me with his coffee cup. "Josh," he says. "And Rashmi." He nods to the girl next to him, who holds his other hand inside the front pocket of his hoodie. Rashmi has blue-framed glasses and thick black hair that hangs all the way down her back. She gives me only the barest of acknowledgments.

That's okay. No big deal.

"Everyone's here except for St. Clair." Meredith cranes her neck around the cafeteria. "He's usually running late."

"Always," Josh corrects. "Always running late."

I clear my throat. "I think I met him last night. In the hallway."

"Good hair and an English accent?" Meredith asks.

"Um. Yeah. I guess." I try to keep my voice casual.

Josh smirks. "Everyone's in luuurve with St. Clair."

"Oh, shut up," Meredith says.

"I'm not." Rashmi looks at me for the first time, calculating whether or not I might fall in love with her own boyfriend.

He lets go of her hand and gives an exaggerated sigh. "Well, I am. I'm asking him to prom. This is our year, I just know it."

"This school has a prom?" I ask.

"God no," Rashmi says. "Yeah, Josh. You and St. Clair would look really cute in matching tuxes."

"Tails." The English accent makes Meredith and me jump in our seats. Hallway boy. Beautiful boy. His hair is damp from the rain. "I insist the tuxes have tails, or I'm giving your corsage to Steve Carver instead."

"St. Clair!" Josh springs from his seat, and they give each other the classic two-thumps-on-the-back guy hug.

"No kiss? I'm crushed, mate."

"Thought it might miff the ol' ball and chain. She doesn't know about us yet."

"Whatever," Rashmi says, but she's smiling now. It's a good look for her. She should utilize the corners of her mouth more often.

Beautiful Hallway Boy (Am I supposed to call him Étienne or St. Clair?) drops his bag and slides into the remaining seat between Rashmi and me. "Anna." He's surprised to see me, and I'm startled, too. He remembers me.

"Nice umbrella. Could've used that this morning." He shakes a hand through his hair, and a drop lands on my bare arm. Words fail me. Unfortunately, my stomach speaks for itself. His eyes pop at the rumble, and I'm alarmed by how big and brown they are. As if he needed any further weapons against the female race.

Josh must be right. Every girl in school must be in love with him.

"Sounds terrible. You ought to feed that thing. Unless . . ." He pretends to examine me, then comes in close with a whisper. "Unless you're one of those girls who never eats. Can't tolerate that, I'm afraid. Have to give you a lifetime table ban."

I'm determined to speak rationally in his presence. "I'm not sure how to order."

"Easy," Josh says. "Stand in line. Tell them what you want. Accept delicious goodies. And then give them your meal card and two pints of blood."

"I heard they raised it to three pints this year," Rashmi says.

"Bone marrow," Beautiful Hallway Boy says. "Or your left earlobe."

"I meant the menu, thank you very much." I gesture to the chalkboard above one of the chefs. An exquisite, cursive hand has written out the morning's menu in pink and yellow and white. In French. "Not exactly my first language."

"You don't speak French?" Meredith asks.

"I've taken Spanish for three years. It's not like I ever thought I'd be moving to Paris."

"It's okay," Meredith says quickly. "A lot of people here don't speak French."

"But most of them do," Josh adds.

"But most of them not very well." Rashmi looks pointedly at him.

"You'll learn the language of food first. The language of love." Josh rubs his belly like a skinny Buddha. "*Oeuf*. Egg. *Pomme*. Apple. *Lapin*. Rabbit."

"Not funny." Rashmi punches him in the arm. "No wonder Isis bites you. Jerk."

I glance at the chalkboard again. It's still in French. "And, um, until then?"

"Right." Beautiful Hallway Boy pushes back his chair. "Come along, then. I haven't eaten either." I can't help but notice several girls gaping at him as we wind our way through the crowd. A blonde with a beaky nose and a teeny tank top coos as soon as we get in line. "*Hey*, St. Clair. How was your summer?"

"Hallo, Amanda. Fine."

"Did you stay here, or did you go back to *London?*" She leans over her friend, a short girl with a severe ponytail, and positions herself for maximum cleavage exposure.

"I stayed with me mum in San Francisco. Did you have a good holiday?" He asks this politely, but I'm pleased to hear the indifference in his voice.

Amanda flips her hair, and suddenly she's Cherrie Milliken. Cherrie loves to swish her hair and shake it out and twirl it around her fingers. Bridgette is convinced she spends her weekends standing before oscillating fans, pretending to be a supermodel, but I think she's too busy soaking her locks in seaweed papaya mud wraps in that never-ending quest for perfect sheen.

"It was *fabulous*." Flip, goes her hair. "I went to *Greece* for a month, then spent the rest of my summer in Manhattan. My father has an *amazing* penthouse that overlooks Central Park."

Every *sentence* she says has a *word* that's *emphasized*. I snort to keep from laughing, and Beautiful Hallway Boy gets a strange coughing fit.

"But I *missed* you. Didn't you get my *emails?*"

"Er, no. Must have the wrong address. Hey." He nudges me. "It's almost our turn." He turns his back on Amanda, and she and her friend exchange frowns. "Time for your first French lesson. Breakfast here is simple and consists primarily of breads—croissants being the most famous, of course. This means no sausage, no scrambled eggs."

"Bacon?" I ask hopefully.

"Definitely not." He laughs. "Second lesson, the words on the chalkboard. Listen carefully and repeat after me. *Granola.*" I narrow my eyes as he widens his in mock innocence. "Means 'granola,' you see. And this one? *Yaourt?*"

"Gee, I dunno. Yogurt?"

"A natural! You say you've never lived in France before?"

"Har. Bloody. Har."

He smiles. "Oh, I see. Known me less than a day and teasing me about my accent. What's next? Care to discuss the state of my hair? My height? My trousers?"

Trousers. Honestly.

The Frenchman behind the counter barks at us. Sorry, Chef Pierre. I'm a little distracted by this English French American Boy Masterpiece. Said boy asks rapidly, "Yogurt with granola and honey, soft-boiled egg, or pears on brioche?"

I have no idea what brioche is. "Yogurt," I say.

He places our orders in perfect French. At least, it sounds impeccable to my virgin ears, and it relaxes Chef Pierre. He loses the glower and stirs the granola and honey into my yogurt. A sprinkling of blueberries is added to the top before he hands it over.

"*Merci*, Monsieur Boutin."

I grab our tray. "No Pop-Tarts? No Cocoa Puffs? I'm, like, totally offended."

"Pop-Tarts are Tuesdays, Eggo waffles are Wednesdays, but they never, ever serve Cocoa Puffs. You shall have to settle for Froot Loops Fridays instead."

"You know a lot about American junk food for a British dude."

"Orange juice? Grapefruit? Cranberry?" I point to the orange, and he pulls two out of the case. "I'm not British. I'm American."

I smile. "Sure you are."

"I am. You have to be an American to attend SOAP, remember?"

"Soap?"

"School of America in Paris," he explains. "SOAP."

Nice. My father sent me here to be cleansed.

We get in line to pay, and I'm surprised by how efficiently it runs. My old school was all about cutting ahead and incensing the lunch ladies, but here everyone waits patiently. I turn back just in time to catch his eyes flicker up and down my body. My breath catches. The beautiful boy is checking *me* out. He doesn't realize I've caught him. "My mum is American," he continues smoothly. "My father is French. I was born in San Francisco, and I was raised in London."

Miraculously, I find my voice. "A true international."

He laughs. "That's right. I'm not a poseur like the rest of you."

I'm about to tease him back when I remember: *He has a girlfriend.* Something evil pokes the pink folds of my brain,

forcing me to recall my conversation with Meredith last night. It's time to change the subject. "What's your real name? Last night you introduced yourself as—"

"St. Clair is my last name. Étienne is my first."

"Étienne St. Clair." I try to pronounce it like him, all foreign and posh.

"Terrible, isn't it?"

I'm laughing now. "Étienne is nice. Why don't people call you that?"

"Oh, 'Étienne is nice.' How generous of you."

Another person gets in line behind us, a tiny boy with brown skin, acne, and a thick mat of black hair. The boy is excited to see him, and he smiles back. "Hey, Nikhil. Did you have a nice holiday?" It's the same question he asked Amanda, but this time his tone is sincere.

That's all it takes for the boy to launch into a story about his trip to Delhi, about the markets and temples and monsoons. (He went on a day trip to the Taj Mahal. I went to Panama City Beach with the rest of Georgia.) Another boy runs up, this one skinny and pale with sticky-uppy hair. Nikhil forgets us and greets his friend with the same enthusiastic babble.

St. Clair—I'm determined to call him this before I embarrass myself—turns back to me. "Nikhil is Rashmi's brother. He's a freshman this year. She also has a younger sister, Sanjita, who's a junior, and an older sister, Leela, who graduated two years ago."

"Do you have any brothers or sisters?"

"No. You?"

"One brother, but he's back home. In Atlanta. That's in Georgia. In the South?"

He raises an eyebrow. "I know where Atlanta is."

"Oh. Right." I hand my meal card to the man behind the register. Like Monsieur Boutin, he wears a pressed white uniform and starched hat. He also has a handlebar mustache. Huh. Didn't know they had those over here. Chef Handlebar swipes my card and zips it back to me with a quick *merci*.

Thank you. Another word I already knew. Excellent.

On the way back to our table, Amanda watches St. Clair from inside her posse of Pretty Preppy People. I'm not surprised to see the faux-surfer hair stink-eye guy sitting with her. St. Clair is talking about classes—what to expect my first day, who my teachers are—but I've stopped listening. All I know is his crooked-teeth smile and his confident swaggery walk.

I'm just as big a fool as the rest of them.

chapter four

The H-through-P line moves slowly. The guy ahead of me is arguing with the guidance counselor. I glance at A-through-G, and see Meredith (Chevalier) and Rashmi (Devi) have already received their class schedules and exchanged them for comparison.

"But I didn't ask for theater, I asked for computer science."

The squat counselor is patient. "I know, but computer science didn't fit with your schedule, and your alternate did. Maybe you can take computer science next—"

"My *alternate* was computer programming."

Hold it. My attention snaps back. Can they do that? Put us in a class we didn't ask for? I will die—DIE—if I have to take gym again.

"Actually, David." The counselor sifts through her papers. "You neglected to fill out your alternate form, so we had to select the class for you. But I think you'll find—"

The angry boy snatches his schedule from her hands and stalks off. Yikes. It's not like it's her fault. I step forward and say my name as kindly as possible, to make up for the jerk who just left. She gives a dimpled smile back. "I remember you, sweetie. Have a nice first day." And she hands me a half sheet of yellow paper.

I hold my breath while I scan it. Phew. No surprises. Senior English, calculus, beginning French, physics, European history, and something dubiously called "La Vie."

When I registered, the counselor described "Life" as a senior-only class, similar to a study hall but with occasional guest speakers who will lecture us about balancing checkbooks and renting apartments and baking quiches. Or whatever. I'm just relieved Mom let me take it. One of the decent things about this school is that math, science, and history aren't required for seniors. Unfortunately, Mom is a purist and refused to let me graduate without another year of all three. "You'll never get into the right college if you take ceramics," she warned, frowning over my orientation packet.

Thanks, Mom. Send me away for some culture in a *city known for its art* and make me suffer through another math class. I shuffle toward Meredith and Rashmi, feeling like the third wheel but praying for some shared classes. I'm in luck. "Three with me and four with Rash!" Meredith beams and hands back my schedule. Her rainbow-colored plastic rings click against each other.

Rash. What an unfortunate nickname. They gossip about people I don't know, and my mind wanders to the other side of the courtyard, where St. Clair waits with Josh in Q-through-Z. I wonder if I have any classes with him.

I mean, *them.* Classes with them.

The rain has stopped, and Josh kicks a puddle in St. Clair's direction. St. Clair laughs and says something that makes them both laugh even harder. Suddenly I register that St. Clair is shorter than Josh. Much shorter. It's odd I didn't notice earlier, but he doesn't carry himself like a short guy. Most are shy or defensive, or some messed-up combination of the two, but St. Clair is confident and friendly and—

"Jeez, stare much?"

"What?" I jerk my head back, but Rashmi's not talking to me. She's shaking her head at Meredith, who looks as sheepish as I feel.

"You're burning holes into St. Clair's head. It's not attractive."

"Shut up." But Meredith smiles at me and shrugs.

Well. That settles that. As if I needed another reason not to lust. Boy Wonder is officially off-limits. "Don't say anything to him," she says. "Please."

"Of course," I say.

"Because we're obviously just friends."

"Obviously."

We mill around until the head of school arrives for her welcome speech. The head is graceful and carries herself like a ballerina. She has a long neck, and her snow-white hair is pulled into a tidy knot that makes her look distinguished rather than elderly. The overall effect is Parisian, although I know from my acceptance letter she's from Chicago. Her gaze glides across us, her one hundred handpicked pupils. "Welcome to another exciting year at the School of America in Paris. I'm pleased to see so many familiar faces, and I'm even happier to see the new ones."

Apparently school speeches are one thing France can't improve.

"To the students who attended last year, I invite you all to give a warm welcome to your new freshman class and to the new upperclassmen, as well."

A smattering of polite applause. I glance around, and I'm startled to find St. Clair looking at me. He claps and lifts his hands in my direction. I blush and jerk away.

The head keeps talking. Focus, Anna. Focus. But I feel his stare as if it were the heat of the sun. My skin grows moist with sweat. I slide underneath one of the immaculately pruned trees. Why is he staring? Is he still staring? I think he is. Why why why? Is it a good stare or a bad stare or an indifferent stare?

But when I finally look, he's not staring at me at all. He's biting his pinkie nail.

The head wraps up, and Rashmi bounds off to join the guys. Meredith leads me inside for English. The *professeur* hasn't arrived yet, so we choose seats in the back. The classroom is smaller than what I'm used to, and it has dark, gleaming trim

and tall windows that look like doors. But the desks are the same, and the whiteboard and the wall-mounted pencil sharpener. I concentrate on these familiar items to ease my nerves.

"You'll like Professeur Cole," Meredith says. "She's hilarious, and she always assigns the best books."

"My dad is a novelist." I blurt this without thinking and immediately regret it.

"Really? Who?"

"James Ashley." That's his pen name. I guess Oliphant wasn't romantic enough.

"Who?"

The humiliation factor multiplies. "*The Decision? The Entrance?* They were made into movies. Forget it, they all have vague names like that—"

She leans forward, excited. "No, my mom loves *The Entrance!*"

I wrinkle my nose.

"They aren't *that* bad. I watched *The Entrance* with her once and totally cried when that girl died of leukemia."

"Who died of leukemia?" Rashmi plops her backpack down next to me. St. Clair trails in behind her and takes the seat in front of Meredith.

"Anna's dad wrote *The Entrance*," Meredith says.

I cough. "Not something I'm proud of."

"I'm sorry, what's *The Entrance?*" Rashmi asks.

"It's that movie about the boy who helps deliver the baby girl in the elevator, and then he grows up to fall in love with her," Meredith says as St. Clair leans back in his chair and nabs her schedule. "But the day after their engagement, she's diagnosed with leukemia."

"Her father pushes her down the aisle in a wheelchair," I continue. "And then she dies on the honeymoon."

"Ugh," Rashmi and St. Clair say together.

Enough embarrassment. "Where's Josh?" I ask.

"He's a junior," Rashmi says, as if I should have known this already. "We dropped him off at pre-calc."

"Oh." Our conversation hits a dead end. Lovely.

"Three classes together, Mer. Give us yours." St. Clair leans back again and steals my half sheet. "Ooo, beginning French."

"Told you."

"It's not so bad." He hands back my schedule and smiles. "You'll be reading the breakfast menu without me before you know it."

Hmm, maybe I don't want to learn French.

Argh! Boys turn girls into such idiots.

"Bonjour à tous." A woman wearing a bold turquoise dress strides in and smacks her coffee cup down on the podium. She's youngish, and she has the blondest hair I've ever seen on a teacher. "For the—" Her eyes scan the room until they land on me.

What? What did I do?

"For the singular person who doesn't know me, *je m'appelle Professeur Cole.*" She gives an exaggerated curtsy, and the class laughs. They swivel around to stare.

"Hello," I say in a tiny voice.

Suspicions confirmed. Out of the twenty-five people

present—the entire senior class—I'm the only new student. This means my classmates have yet another advantage over me, because every one of them is familiar with the teachers. The school is so small that each subject is taught by the same *professeur* in all four grades.

I wonder what student left to vacate my position? Probably someone cooler than me. Someone with dreadlocks and pinup girl tattoos and connections in the music industry.

"I see the janitorial staff has ignored my wishes once again," Professeur Cole says. "Everyone up. You know the drill."

I don't, but I push my desk when everyone else starts pushing theirs. We arrange them in a big circle. It's odd to see all of my classmates at the same time. I take the opportunity to size them up. I don't *think* I stand out, but their jeans and shoes and backpacks are more expensive than mine. They look cleaner, shinier.

No surprise there. My mom is a high school biology teacher, which doesn't give us a lot of extra spending money. Dad pays for the mortgage and helps with the bills, but it's not enough, and Mom is too proud to ask for more. She says he'd refuse her anyway and just go buy another elliptical machine.

There may be some truth to that.

The rest of the morning passes in a blur. I like Professeur Cole, and my math teacher, Professeur Babineaux, is nice enough. He's Parisian, and he waggles his eyebrows and spits when he talks. To be fair, I don't think the spitting is a French thing. I think he just has a lisp. It's hard to tell with the accent.

After that, I have beginning French. Professeur Gillet turns out to be another Parisian. Figures. They always send in native speakers for foreign language classes. My Spanish teachers were always rolling their eyes and exclaiming, *"¡Aye, dios mio!"* whenever I raised my hand. They got frustrated when I couldn't grasp a concept that seemed obvious to them.

I stopped raising my hand.

As predicted, the class is a bunch of freshmen. And me. Oh, and one junior, the angry scheduling guy from this morning. He introduces himself enthusiastically as Dave, and I can tell he's as relieved as I am to not be the only upperclassman.

Maybe Dave is pretty cool after all.

At noon, I follow the stampede to the cafeteria. I avoid the main line and go straight to the counter with the choose-your-own fruit and bread, even though the pasta smells amazing. I'm such a wuss. I'd rather starve than try to order in French. *"Oui, oui!"* I'd say, pointing at random words on the chalkboard. Then Chef Handlebar would present me with something revolting, and I'd have to buy it out of shame. *Of course I meant to order the roasted pigeon! Mmm! Just like Nanna's.*

Meredith and her friends are lounging at the same table as this morning. I take a deep breath and join them. To my relief, no one looks surprised. Meredith asks St. Clair if he's seen his girlfriend yet. He relaxes into his chair. "No, but we're meeting tonight."

"Did you see her this summer? Have her classes started? What's she taking this semester?" She keeps asking questions

about Ellie to which he gives short replies. Josh and Rashmi are making out—I can actually see tongue—so I turn to my bread and grapes. How biblical of me.

The grapes are smaller than I'm used to, and the skin is slightly textured. Is that dirt? I dip my napkin in water and dab at the tiny purple globes. It helps, but they're still sort of rough. Hmm. St. Clair and Meredith stop talking. I glance up to find them staring at me in matching bemusement. "What?"

"Nothing," he says. "Continue your grape bath."

"They were dirty."

"Have you tried one?" she asks.

"No, they've still got these little mud flecks." I hold one up to show them. St. Clair plucks it from my fingers and pops it into his mouth. I'm hypnotized by his lips, his throat, as he swallows.

I hesitate. Would I rather have clean food or his good opinion?

He picks up another and smiles. "Open up."

I open up.

The grape brushes my lower lip as he slides it in. It explodes in my mouth, and I'm so startled by the juice that I nearly spit it out. The flavor is intense, more like grape candy than actual fruit. To say I've tasted nothing like it before is an understatement. Meredith and St. Clair laugh. "Wait until you try them as wine," she says.

St. Clair twirls a forkful of pasta. "So. How was French class?"

The abrupt subject change makes me shudder. "Professeur Gillet is scary. She's all frown lines." I tear off a piece of baguette. The crust crackles, and the inside is light and springy. Oh, *man.* I shove another hunk into my mouth.

 38

Meredith looks thoughtful. "She can be intimidating at first, but she's really nice once you get to know her."

"Mer is her star pupil," St. Clair says.

Rashmi breaks apart from Josh, who looks dazed by the fresh air. "She's taking advanced French *and* advanced Spanish," she adds.

"Maybe you can be my tutor," I say to Meredith. "I stink at foreign languages. The only reason this place overlooked my Spanish grades was because the head reads my father's dumb novels."

"How do you know?" she asks.

I roll my eyes. "She mentioned it once or twice in my phone interview." She kept asking questions about casting decisions for *The Lighthouse*. Like Dad has any say in that. Or like I care. She didn't realize my cinematic tastes are a bit more sophisticated.

"I'd like to learn Italian," Meredith says. "But they don't offer it here. I want to go to college in Rome next year. Or maybe London. I could study it there, too."

"Surely Rome is a better place to study Italian?" I ask.

"Yeah, well." She steals a glance at St. Clair. "I've always liked London."

Poor Mer. She's got it bad.

"What do you want to do?" I ask him. "Where are you going?"

St. Clair shrugs. It's slow and full-bodied, surprisingly French. The same shrug the waiter at the restaurant last night gave me when I asked if they served pizza. "Don't know. It depends, though I'd like to study history." He leans forward, like

39

he's about to share a naughty secret. "I've always wanted to be one of those blokes they interview on BBC or PBS specials. You know, with the crazy eyebrows and suede elbow patches."

Just like me! Sort of. "I want to be on the classic movies channel and discuss Hitchcock and Capra with Robert Osborne. He hosts most of their programs. I mean I know he's an old dude, but he's so freaking cool. He knows *everything* about film."

"Really?" He sounds genuinely interested.

"St. Clair's head is always in history books the size of dictionaries," Meredith interrupts. "It's hard to get him out of his room."

"That's because Ellie's always in there," Rashmi says drily.

"You're one to talk." He gestures toward Josh. "Not to mention . . . Henri."

"Henri!" Meredith says, and she and St. Clair burst into laughter.

"One frigging afternoon, and you'll never let me forget it." Rashmi glances at Josh, who stabs his pasta.

"Who's Henri?" I trip over the pronunciation. *En-ree.*

"This tour guide on a field trip to Versailles sophomore year," St. Clair says. "Skinny little bugger, but Rashmi ditched us in the Hall of Mirrors and threw herself at him—"

"I did not!"

Meredith shakes her head. "They groped, like, all afternoon. Full public display."

"The whole school waited on the bus for two hours, because she forgot what time we were supposed to meet back," he says.

"It was NOT two hours—"

Meredith continues. "Professeur Hansen finally tracked her

down behind some shrubbery in the formal gardens, and she had teeth marks all over her neck."

"Teeth marks!" St. Clair snorts.

Rashmi fumes. "Shut up, English Tongue."

"Huh?"

"English Tongue," she says. "That's what we all called you after your and Ellie's *breathtaking* display at the street fair last spring." St. Clair tries to protest, but he's laughing too hard. Meredith and Rashmi continue jabbing back and forth, but . . . I'm lost again. I wonder if Matt is a better kisser now that he has someone more experienced to practice on. He was probably a bad kisser because of me.

Oh, no.

I'm a bad kisser. I am, I must be.

Someday I'll be awarded a statue shaped like a pair of lips, and it'll be engraved with the words WORLD'S WORST KISSER. And Matt will give a speech about how he only dated me because he was desperate, but I didn't put out, so I was a waste of time because Cherrie Milliken liked him all along and she totally puts out. Everyone knows it.

Oh God. Does *Toph* think I'm a bad kisser?

It only happened once. My last night at the movie theater was also the last night before I left for France. It was slow, and we'd been alone in the lobby for most of the evening. Maybe because it was my final shift, maybe because we wouldn't see each other again for four months, maybe because it felt like a last chance—whatever the reason, we were reckless. We were brave. The flirting escalated all night long, and by the time we were told to go home, we couldn't walk away. We just kept . . . drawing out the conversation.

And then, finally, he said he would miss me.

And then, finally, he kissed me under the buzzing marquee.

And then I left.

"Anna? Are you all right?" someone asks.

The whole table is staring at me.

Don't cry. Don't cry. Don't cry. "Um. Where's the bathroom?" The bathroom is my favorite excuse for any situation. No one ever inquires further once you mention it.

"The toilets are down the hall." St. Clair looks concerned but doesn't dare ask. He's probably afraid I'll talk about tampon absorbency or mention the dreaded P-word.

I spend the rest of lunch in a stall. I miss home so much that it physically hurts. My head throbs, my stomach is nauseous, and it's all so unfair. I never asked to be sent here. I had my own friends and my own inside jokes and my own stolen kisses. I wish my parents had offered me the choice: "Would you like to spend your senior year in Atlanta or Paris?"

Who knows? Maybe I would have picked Paris.

What my parents never considered is that I just wanted a choice.

chapter five

To: Anna Oliphant <bananaelephant@femmefilmfreak.net>
From: Bridgette Saunderwick <bridgesandwich@freebiemail.com>
Subject: Don't look now but . . .

. . . the bottom right corner of your bed is untucked. HA! Made you look. Now stop smoothing out invisible wrinkles. Seriously. How's Le Academe du Fraunch? Any hotties I should know about? Speaking of, guess who's in my calc class?? Drew! He dyed his hair black and got a lip ring. And he's totally callipygian (look it up, lazy ass). I sat with the usual at lunch, but it wasn't the same without you. Not to mention freaking Cherrie showed up. She kept flipping her hair around, and I

swear I heard you humming that TRESemmé commercial.
I'll gouge out my eyes with Sean's Darth Maul action
figure if she sits with us every day. By the way, your
mom hired me to babysit him after school, so I'd better
go. Don't want him to die on my watch.

You suck. Come home.
Bridge

P.S. Tomorrow they're announcing section leaders in
band. Wish me luck. If they give my spot to Kevin
Quiggley, I'll gouge out HIS eyes with Darth Maul.

Callipygian. Having shapely buttocks. Nice one, Bridge.

My best friend is a word fiend. One of her most prized
possessions is her *OED*, which she bought for practically nothing
at a yard sale two years ago. *The Oxford English Dictionary* is a
twenty-volume set that not only provides definitions of words
but their histories as well. Bridge is always throwing big words
into conversations, because she loves to watch people squirm
and bluff their way around them. I learned a long time ago not
to pretend to know what she was talking about. She'd call me on
it every time.

So Bridgette collects words and, apparently, my life.

I can't believe Mom hired her to watch Sean. I know she's
the best choice, since we were always watching him together,
but still. It's weird she's there without me. And it's weird that

she's talking to my mom while I'm stuck here on the other side of the world. Next she'll tell me she got a second job at the movie theater.

Speaking of, Toph hasn't emailed me in two days. It's not like I expected him to write every day, or even every week, but . . . there was an undeniable *something* between us. I mean, we *kissed*. Will this thing—whatever it is—end now that I'm here?

His real name is Christopher, but he hates being called Chris, so he goes by Toph instead. He has shocking green eyes and wicked sideburns. We're both left-handed, we both love the fake nacho cheese at the concession stand, and we both hate Cuba Gooding Jr. I've crushed on Toph since my first day on the job, when he stuck his head under the ICEE machine and guzzled it straight from the tap to make me laugh. He had Blue Raspberry Mouth for the rest of his shift.

Not many people can pull off blue teeth. But believe me, Toph can.

I refresh my inbox—just in case—but nothing new appears. I've been planted in front of my computer for several hours, waiting for Bridge to get out of school. I'm glad she emailed me. For some reason, I wanted her to write first. Maybe because I wanted her to think I was so happy and busy that I didn't have time to talk. When, in reality, I'm sad and alone.

And hungry. My mini-fridge is empty.

I had dinner in the cafeteria but avoided the main food line again, stuffing myself with more bread, which only lasts so long.

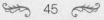

Maybe St. Clair will order breakfast for me again in the morning. Or Meredith; I bet she'd do it.

I reply to Bridge, telling her about my new sort-of-friends, the crazy cafeteria with restaurant-quality food, and the giant Panthéon down the road. Despite myself, I describe St. Clair, and mention how in physics he leaned over Meredith to borrow a pen from me, right when Professeur Wakefield was assigning lab partners. So the teacher thought he was sitting next to me, and now St. Clair is my lab partner for the WHOLE YEAR.

Which was the best thing that happened all day.

I also tell Bridge about the mysterious Life class, La Vie, because she and I spent the entire summer speculating. (Me: "I bet we'll debate the Big Bang and the Meaning of Life." Bridge: "Dude, they'll probably teach you breathing techniques and how to convert food into energy.") All we did today was sit quietly and work on homework.

What a pity.

I spent the period reading the first novel assigned for English. And, wow. If I hadn't realized I was in France yet, I do now. Because *Like Water for Chocolate* has sex in it. LOTS of sex. A woman's desire literally lights a building on fire, and then a soldier throws her naked body onto a horse, and they totally do it while galloping away. There's no way they would have let me read this back in the Bible Belt. The sexiest we ever got was *The Scarlet Letter*.

I must tell Bridge about this book.

———

It's almost midnight when I finish the email, but the hallway is still noisy. The juniors and seniors have a lot of freedom because, supposedly, we're mature enough to handle it. I am, but I have serious doubts as to my classmates. The guy across the hall already has a pyramid of beer bottles stacked outside his door because, in Paris, sixteen-year-olds are allowed to drink wine and beer. You have to be eighteen to get hard liquor.

Not that I haven't seen *that* around here, too.

I wonder if my mother had any idea it'd be legal for me to get wasted when she agreed to this. She looked pretty surprised when they mentioned it at the Life Skills Seminars, and I got a long lecture on responsibility that night at dinner. But I don't plan on getting drunk. I've always thought beer smells like urine.

There are a few part-timers who work the front desk, but only one live-in Résidence Director. His name is Nate, and his apartment is on the first floor. He's in graduate school at some university around here. SOAP must pay him a lot to live with us.

Nate is in his twenties, and he's short and pale and has a shaved head. Which sounds strange but is actually attractive. He's soft-spoken and seems like the kind of guy who'd be a good listener, but his tone exudes responsibility and a don't-mess-with-me attitude. My parents loved him. He also has a bowl of condoms next to his door.

I wonder if my parents saw that.

The freshmen and sophomores are in another dormitory. They have to share rooms, and their floors are divided by sex, and they have tons of supervision. They also have enforced curfews.

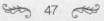

We don't. We just have to sign a log whenever we come and go at night so Nate knows we're still alive. Yeah. I'm sure no one ever takes advantage of this high security.

I drag myself down the hall to use the bathroom. I take my place in line—there's always a line, even at midnight—behind Amanda, the girl who attacked St. Clair at breakfast. She smirks at my faded jeans and my vintage Orange Crush T-shirt.

I didn't know she lived on my floor. Super.

We don't speak. I trace the floral pattern on the wallpaper with my fingers. Résidence Lambert is a peculiar mix of Parisian refinement and teenage practicality. Crystal light fixtures give the dormitory halls a golden glow, but fluorescent bulbs hum inside our bedrooms. The floors are glossy hardwood but lined with industrial-grade rugs. Fresh flowers and Tiffany lamps grace the lobby, but the chairs are ratty love seats, and the tables are carved with initials and rude words.

"So you're the new *Brandon*," Amanda says.

"Excuse me?"

"Brandon. Number twenty-five. He was expelled from school last year; one of the teachers found *coke* in his backpack." She looks me over again and frowns. "Where are you *from*, anyway?" But I know what she's really asking. She wants to know why they picked someone like me to take his place.

"Atlanta."

"*Oh*," she says. As if that explains my complete and utter hickness. Screw her. It's one of the largest cities in America.

"So you and St. Clair seemed pretty *friendly* at breakfast."

"Um." Is she threatened by me?

"I wouldn't get any ideas if I were you," she continues. "Not even *you're* pretty enough to steal him from his girlfriend. They've been together *forever*."

Was that a compliment? Or not? Her emphasizing thing is really getting on my nerves. (My *nerves*.)

Amanda gives a fake, bored yawn. "Interesting *hair*."

I touch it self-consciously. "Thanks. My friend bleached it." Bridge added the thick band to my dark brown hair just last week. Normally, I keep the stripe tucked behind my right ear, but tonight it's back in a ponytail.

"Do you like it?" she asks. Universal bitch-speak for *I think it's hideous.*

I drop my hand. "Yeah. That's why I did it."

"You know, I wouldn't pull it back like that. You kinda look like a *skunk*."

"At least she doesn't reek like one." Rashmi appears behind me. She'd been visiting Meredith; I'd heard their muffled voices through my walls. "Delightful perfume, Amanda. Use a little more next time. I don't know if they can smell you in London."

Amanda snarls. "Nice *glasses*."

"Good one," Rashmi deadpans, but I notice she adjusts them anyway. Her nails are electric blue, the same shade as her frames. She turns to me. "I live two floors up, room six-o-one, if you need anything. See you at breakfast."

So she doesn't dislike me! Or maybe she just hates Amanda more. Either way, I'm thankful, and I call goodbye to her retreating figure. She waves a hand and moves into the stairwell as Nate comes out of it. He approaches us in his quiet, friendly manner.

"Going to bed soon, ladies?"

Amanda smiles sweetly. "Of course."

"Great. Did you have a nice first day, Anna?"

It's so peculiar how everyone here already knows my name. "Yeah. Thanks, Nate."

He nods as if I've said something worth thinking about, and then says good night and moves on to the guys hanging out at the other end of the hallway.

"I *hate* it when he does that," Amanda says.

"Does what?"

"Check up on us. What an *asshole*." The bathroom door opens, and a tiny redhead maneuvers around Amanda, who just stands there like she's Queen of the Threshold. The girl must be a junior. I don't recognize her from the circle of desks in senior English. "God, did you fall in?" Amanda asks. The girl's pale skin turns pink.

"She was just using the restroom," I say.

Amanda sashays onto the tile, her fuzzy purple slippers slapping against her heels. She yanks the door shut. "Does it look like I care? *Skunk Girl?*"

chapter six

One week into school, and I'm knee-deep in Fancy International Education.

Professeur Cole's syllabus is free of the usual Shakespeare and Steinbeck, and instead, we're focusing on translated works. Every morning she hosts the discussion of *Like Water for Chocolate* as if we were a book club and not some boring, required class.

So English is excellent.

On the other hand, my French teacher is clearly illiterate. How else to explain the fact that despite the name of our textbook—*Level One French*—Professeur Gillet insists on speaking in French only? She also calls on me a dozen times a day. I never know the answer.

Dave calls her Madame Guillotine. This is also excellent.

He's taken the class before, which is helpful but obviously not *really* helpful, as he failed it the first go-round. Dave has shaggy hair and pouty lips, and the peculiar combination of tan skin and freckles. Several girls have a crush on him. He's also in my history class. I'm with the juniors, because the seniors take government, and I've already studied it. So I sit between Dave and Josh.

Josh is quiet and reserved in class, but outside of it, his sense of humor is similar to St. Clair's. It's easy to understand why they're such good friends. Meredith says they idolize each other, Josh because of St. Clair's innate charisma, and St. Clair because Josh is an astounding artist. I rarely see Josh without his brush pen or sketchbook. His work is incredible—thick bold strokes and teeny exquisite details—and his fingers are always stained with ink.

But the most notable aspect of my new education is the one that takes place outside of class. The one never mentioned in the glossy brochures. And that is this: attending boarding school is like *living inside* a high school. I can't get away. Even when I'm in my bedroom, my ears are blasted by pop music, fistfights over washing machines, and drunk dancing in the stairwell. Meredith claims it'll settle down once the novelty wears off for the juniors, but I'm not holding my breath.

However.

It's Friday night, and Résidence Lambert has cleared out. My classmates are hitting the bars, and I have peace for the first time. If I close my eyes, I can almost believe I'm back home.

Except for the opera. The Opera Diva sings most evenings at the restaurant across the street. For someone with such a huge voice, she's surprisingly small. She's also one of those people who shaves her eyebrows and draws them back on with a pencil. She looks like an extra from *The Rocky Horror Picture Show*.

Bridge calls as I'm watching *Rushmore* from the comfort of my mini-bed. It's the film that launched Wes Anderson. Wes is amazing, a true auteur involved in every aspect of production, with a trademark style recognizable in any frame—wistful and quirky, deadpan and dark. *Rushmore* is one of my favorites. It's about a guy named Max Fischer who is obsessed with, among many things, the private school that kicked him out. What would my life be like if I were as passionate about SOAP as Max is about Rushmore Academy? For starters, I probably wouldn't be alone in my bedroom covered in white pimple cream.

"Annnnn-uhhhhhh," Bridge says. "I haaaaate themmmm."

She didn't get section leader in band. Which is lame, because everyone knows she's the most talented drummer in school. The percussion instructor gave it to Kevin Quiggley, because he thought the guys on the drumline wouldn't respect Bridge as a leader—because she's a girl.

Yeah, well, now they won't. Jerk.

So Bridge hates band and hates the instructor and hates Kevin, who is a twerp with a disproportionately large ego. "Just wait," I say. "Soon you'll be the next Meg White or Sheila E., and Kevin Quiggley will brag about how he *knew you back when*. And then when he approaches you after some big show, expecting special treatment and a backstage pass? You can sashay right past him without so much as a backward glance."

I hear the weary smile in her voice. "Why'd you move away again, Banana?"

"Because my father is made of suck."

"The purest strain, dude."

We talk until three a.m., so I don't wake up until early afternoon. I scramble to get dressed before the cafeteria closes. It's only open for brunch on Saturdays and Sundays. It's quiet when I arrive, but Rashmi and Josh and St. Clair are seated at their usual table.

The pressure is on. They've teased me all week, because I've avoided anything that requires ordering. I've made excuses ("I'm allergic to beef," "Nothing tastes better than bread," "Ravioli is overrated"), but I can't avoid it forever. Monsieur Boutin is working the counter again. I grab a tray and take a deep breath.

"*Bonjour*, uh . . . soup? *Sopa? S'il vous plaît?*"

"Hello" and "please." I've learned the polite words first, in hopes that the French will forgive me for butchering the remainder of their beautiful language. I point to the vat of orangey-red soup. Butternut squash, I think. The smell is extraordinary, like sage and autumn. It's early September, and the weather is still warm. When does fall come to Paris?

"Ah! *Soupe,*" he gently corrects.

"*Sí, soupe*. I mean, *oui. Oui!*" My cheeks burn. "And, um, the uh—chicken-salad-green-bean thingy?"

Monsieur Boutin laughs. It's a jolly, bowl-full-of-jelly, Santa

Claus laugh. "Chicken and *haricots verts*, *oui*. You know, you may speek Ingleesh to me. I understand eet vairy well."

My blush deepens. Of course he'd speak English in an American school. And I've been living on stupid pears and baguettes for five days. He hands me a bowl of soup and a small plate of chicken salad, and my stomach rumbles at the sight of hot food.

"*Merci*," I say.

"*De rien*. You're welcome. And I 'ope you don't skeep meals to avoid me anymore!" He places his hand on his chest, as if brokenhearted. I smile and shake my head no. I can do this. I can do this. I can—

"NOW THAT WASN'T SO TERRIBLE, WAS IT, ANNA?" St. Clair hollers from the other side of the cafeteria.

I spin around and give him the finger down low, hoping Monsieur Boutin can't see. St. Clair responds by grinning and giving me the British version, the V-sign with his first two fingers. Monsieur Boutin tuts behind me with good nature. I pay for my meal and take the seat next to St. Clair. "Thanks. I forgot how to flip off the English. I'll use the correct hand gesture next time."

"My pleasure. Always happy to educate." He's wearing the same clothing as yesterday, jeans and a ratty T-shirt with Napoleon's silhouette on it. When I asked him about it, he said Napoleon was his hero. "Not because he was a decent bloke, mind you. He was an arse. But he was a short arse, like meself."

I wonder if he slept at Ellie's. That's probably why he hasn't changed his clothes. He rides the *métro* to her college every night, and they hang out there. Rashmi and Mer have been worked up, like maybe Ellie thinks she's too good for them now.

"You know, Anna," Rashmi says, "most Parisians understand English. You don't have to be so shy."

Yeah. Thanks for pointing that out now.

Josh puts his hands behind his head and tilts back his chair. His shirtsleeves roll up to expose a skull-and-crossbones tattoo on his upper right arm. I can tell by the thick strokes that it's his own design. The black ink is dark against his pale skin. It's an awesome tattoo, though sort of comical on his long, skinny arm. "That's true," he says. "I barely speak a word, and I get by."

"That's not something I'd brag about." Rashmi wrinkles her nose, and Josh snaps forward in his chair to kiss it.

"Christ, there they go again." St. Clair scratches his head and looks away.

"Have they always been this bad?" I ask, lowering my voice.

"No. Last year they were worse."

"Yikes. Been together long, then?"

"Er, last winter?"

"That's quite a while."

He shrugs and I pause, debating whether I want to know the answer to my next question. Probably not, but I ask anyway. "How long have you and Ellie been dating?"

St. Clair thinks for a moment. "About a year now, I suppose." He takes a sip of coffee—everyone here seems to drink it—then slams down the cup with a loud CLUNK that startles Rashmi and Josh. "Oh, I'm sorry," he says. "Did that bother you?"

He turns to me and opens his brown eyes wide in exasperation. I suck in my breath. Even when he's annoyed, he's beautiful. Comparing him to Toph isn't even possible. St. Clair is a different kind of attractive, a different species altogether.

"Change of subject." He points a finger at me. "I thought southern belles were supposed to have southern accents."

I shake my head. "Only when I talk to my mom. Then it slips out because she has one. Most people in Atlanta don't have an accent. It's pretty urban. A lot of people speak gangsta, though," I add jokingly.

"Fo' shiz," he replies in his polite English accent.

I spurt orangey-red soup across the table. St. Clair gives a surprised ha-HA kind of laugh, and I'm laughing, too, the painful kind like abdominal crunches. He hands me a napkin to wipe my chin. "Fo'. Shiz." He repeats it solemnly.

Cough cough. "Please don't ever stop saying that. It's too—" I gasp. "Much."

"You oughtn't to have said that. Now I shall have to save it for special occasions."

"My birthday is in February." Cough choke wheeze. "Please don't forget."

"And mine was yesterday," he says.

"No, it wasn't."

"Yes. It was." He mops the remainder of my spewed lunch from the tabletop. I try to take the napkins to clean it myself, but he waves my hand away.

"It's the truth," Josh says. "I forgot, man. Happy belated birthday."

"It wasn't really your birthday, was it? You would've said something."

"I'm serious. Yesterday was my eighteenth birthday." He shrugs and tosses the napkins onto his empty tray. "My family isn't one for cakes and party hats."

"But you have to have cake on your birthday," I say. "It's the rules. It's the best part." I remember the *Star Wars* cake Mom and Bridge and I made for Seany last summer. It was lime green and shaped like Yoda's head. Bridge even bought cotton candy for his ear hair.

"This is exactly why I never bring it up, you know."

"But you did something special last night, right? I mean, Ellie took you out?"

He picks up his coffee, and then sets it back down again without drinking. "My birthday is just another day. And I'm fine with that. I don't need the cake, I promise."

"Okay, okay. Fine." I raise my hands in surrender. "I won't wish you happy birthday. Or even a belated happy Friday."

"Oh, you can wish me happy Friday." He smiles again. "I have no objection to Fridays."

"Speaking of," Rashmi says to me. "Why didn't you go out with us last night?"

"I had plans. With my friend. Bridgette."

All three of them stare, waiting for further explanation.

"Phone plans."

"But you've been out this week?" St. Clair asks. "You've actually left campus?"

"Sure." Because I have. To get to other parts of campus.

St. Clair raises his eyebrows. "You are such a liar."

"Let me get this straight." Josh places his hands in prayer position. His fingers are slender, like the rest of his body, and he has a black ink splotch on one index finger. "You've been in Paris for an entire week and have yet to see the city? Any part of it?"

"I went out with my parents last weekend. I saw the Eiffel Tower." From a distance.

"With your parents, brilliant. And your plans for tonight?" St. Clair asks. "Washing some laundry, perhaps? Scrubbing the shower?"

"Hey. Scrubbing is underrated."

Rashmi furrows her brow. "What are you gonna eat? The cafeteria will be closed." Her concern is touching, but I notice she's not inviting me to join her and Josh. Not that I'd want to go out with them anyway. As for dinner, I'd planned on cruising the dorm's vending machine. It's not well stocked, but I can make it work.

"That's what I thought," St. Clair says when I don't respond. He shakes his head. His dark messy hair has a few curls in it today. It's quite breathtaking, really. If there were an Olympics competition in hair, St. Clair would totally win, hands down. Ten-point-oh. Gold medal.

I shrug. "It's only been a week. It's not a big deal."

"Let's go over the facts one more time," Josh says. "This is your first weekend away from home?"

"Yes."

"Your first weekend without parental supervision?"

"Yes."

"Your first weekend without parental supervision *in Paris*? And you want to spend it in your bedroom? Alone?" He and Rashmi exchange pitying glances. I look at St. Clair for help, but find him staring at me with his head tilted to the side.

"What?" I ask, irritated. "Soup on my chin? Green bean between my teeth?"

St. Clair smiles to himself. "I like your stripe," he finally says. He reaches out and touches it lightly. "You have perfect hair."

chapter seven

The party people have left the dorm. I munch on vending machine snacks and update my website. So far I've tried: a Bounty bar, which turned out to be the same thing as a Mounds, and a package of madeleines, shell-shaped cakes that were stale and made me thirsty. Together they've raised my blood sugar to a sufficient working level.

Since I have no new movies to review for Femme Film Freak (as I'm severed from everything good and pure and wonderful about America—the cinema), I fiddle with the layout. Create a new banner. Edit an old review. In the evening, Bridge emails me:

Went with Matt and Cherrie M (for meretricious) to the
movies last night. And guess what? Toph asked about

you!! I told him you're great BUT you're REALLY looking forward to your December visit. I think he got the hint. We talked about his band for a minute (still no shows, of course) but Matt was making faces the whole time, so we had to go. You know how he feels about Toph. OH! And Cherrie tried to talk us into seeing your dad's latest tearjerker. I KNOW.

You suck. Come home.
Bridge

Meretricious. Showily attractive but cheap or insincere. Yes! That is so Cherrie. I just hope Bridge didn't make me sound too desperate, despite my longing for Toph to email me. And I can't believe Matt is still weird around him, even though we're not dating anymore. Everyone likes Toph. Well, sometimes he annoys the managers, but that's because he tends to forget his work schedule. And call in sick.

I read her email again, hoping for the words *Toph says he's madly in love with you, and he'll wait for all eternity* to appear. No such luck. So I browse my favorite message board to see what they're saying about Dad's new film. The reviews for *The Decision* aren't great, despite what it's raking in at the box office. One regular, clockworkorange88, said this: *It sucked balls. Dirty balls. Like I-ran-a-mile-in-July-while-wearing-leather-pants balls.*

Sounds about right.

After a while I get bored and do a search for *Like Water for Chocolate*. I want to make sure I haven't missed any themes before writing my essay. It's not due for two weeks, but I have a lot of time on my hands right now. Like, all night.

Blah blah blah. Nothing interesting. And I'm just about to recheck my email when this passage leaps from the screen: *Throughout the novel, heat is a symbol for sexual desire. Tita can control the heat inside her kitchen, but the fire inside of her own body is a force of both strength and destruction.*

"Anna?" Someone knocks on my door, and it startles me out of my seat.

No. Not *someone*. St. Clair.

I'm wearing an old Mayfield Dairy T-shirt, complete with yellow-and-brown cow logo, and hot pink flannel pajama bottoms covered in giant strawberries. I am not even wearing a bra.

"Anna, I know you're in there. I can see your light."

"Hold on a sec!" I blurt. "I'll be right there." I grab my black hoodie and zip it up over the cow's face before wrenching open the door. "Hisorryaboutthat. Come in."

I open the door wide but he stands there for a moment, just staring at me. I can't read the expression on his face. Then he breaks into a mischievous smile and brushes past me.

"Nice strawberries."

"Shut up."

"No, I mean it. Cute."

And even though he doesn't mean it like I-want-to-leave-my-girlfriend-and-start-dating-you cute, something flickers inside of me. The "force of strength and destruction" Tita de la Garza knew so well. St. Clair stands in the center of my room. He scratches his head, and his T-shirt lifts up on one side, exposing a slice of bare stomach.

Foomp! My inner fire ignites.

"It's really . . . er . . . clean," he says.

Fizz. Flames extinguished.

"Is it?" I know my room is tidy, but I haven't even bought a proper window cleaner yet. Whoever cleaned my windows last had no idea how to use a bottle of Windex. The key is to only spray a little at a time. Most people spray too much and then it gets in the corners, which are hard to dry without leaving streaks or lint behind—

"Yes. Alarmingly so."

St. Clair wanders around, picking up things and examining them like I did in Meredith's room. He inspects the collection of banana and elephant figurines lined up on my dresser. He holds up a glass elephant and raises his dark eyebrows in question.

"It's my nickname."

"Elephant?" He shakes his head. "Sorry, I don't see it."

"Anna Oliphant. 'Banana Elephant.' My friend collects those for me, and I collect toy bridges and sandwiches for her. Her name is Bridgette Saunderwick," I add.

St. Clair sets down the glass elephant and wanders to my desk. "So can anyone call you Elephant?"

"Banana Elephant. And no. Definitely not."

"I'm sorry," he says. "But not for that."

"What? Why?"

"You're fixing everything I set down." He nods at my hands, which are readjusting the elephant. "It wasn't polite of me to come in and start touching your things."

"Oh, it's okay," I say quickly, letting go of the figurine. "You can touch anything of mine you want."

He freezes. A funny look runs across his face before I realize what I've said. I didn't mean it like *that*.

Not that *that* would be so bad.

But I like Toph, and St. Clair has a girlfriend. And even if the situation were different, Mer still has dibs. I'd never do that to her after how nice she was my first day. And my second. And every other day this week.

Besides, he's just an attractive boy. Nothing to get worked up over. I mean, the streets of Europe are filled with beautiful guys, right? Guys with grooming regimens and proper haircuts and stylish coats. Not that I've seen anyone even remotely as good-looking as Monsieur Étienne St. Clair. But still.

He turns his face away from mine. Is it my imagination, or does he look embarrassed? But why would he be embarrassed? I'm the one with the idiotic mouth.

"Is that your boyfriend?" He points to my laptop's wallpaper, a photo of my coworkers and me goofing around. It was taken before the midnight release of the latest fantasy-novel-to-film adaptation. Most of us were dressed like elves or wizards. "The one with his eyes closed?"

"WHAT?" He thinks I'd date a guy like *Hercules*? Hercules

is an assistant manager. He's ten years older than me and, yes, that's his real name. And even though he's sweet and knows more about Japanese horror films than anyone, he also has a ponytail.

A ponytail.

"Anna, I'm kidding. This one. Sideburns." He points to Toph, the reason I love the picture so much. Our heads are turned into each other, and we're wearing secret smiles, as if sharing a private joke.

"Oh. Uh . . . no. Not really. I mean, Toph was my almost-boyfriend. I moved away before . . ." I trail off, uncomfortable. "Before much could happen."

St. Clair doesn't respond. After an awkward silence, he puts his hands in his pockets and rocks back on his heels. "Provide for all."

"What?" I'm startled.

"*Tout pourvoir.*" He nods at a pillow on my bed. The words are embroidered above a picture of a unicorn. It was a gift from my grandparents, and the motto and crest are for the Oliphant clan. A long time ago, my grandfather moved to America to marry my grandmother, but he's still devoted to all things Scottish. He's always buying Seany and me things decorated with the clan tartan (blue-and-green-checkered, with black and white lines). For instance, my bedspread.

"Yeah, I know that's what it means. But how did you know?"

"*Tout pourvoir.* It's French."

Excellent. The Oliphant clan motto, drilled into my head since infancy, turns out to be in FRENCH, and I didn't even know it. Thanks, Granddad. As if I didn't already look like a moron. But how was I supposed to know a Scottish motto would be in French? I thought they hated France. Or is that just the English?

Argh, I don't know. I always assumed it was in Latin or some other dead language.

"Your brother?" St. Clair points above my bed to the only picture I've hung up. Seany is grinning at the camera and pointing at one of my mother's research turtles, which is lifting its neck and threatening to take away his finger. Mom is doing a study on the lifetime reproductive habits of snapping turtles and visits her brood in the Chattahoochee River several times a month. My brother loves to go with her, while I prefer the safety of our home. Snapping turtles are *mean*.

"Yep. That's Sean."

"That's a little Irish for a family with tartan bedspreads."

I smile. "It's kind of a sore spot. My mom loved the name, but Granddad—my father's father—practically died when he heard it. He was rooting for Malcolm or Ewan or Dougal instead."

St. Clair laughs. "How old is he?"

"Seven. He's in the second grade."

"That's a big age difference."

"Well, he was either an accident or a last-ditch effort to save a failing marriage. I've never had the nerve to ask which."

Wow. I can't believe I just blurted that out.

He sits down on the edge of my bed. "Your parents are divorced?"

I hover by my desk chair, because I can't sit next to him on the bed. Maybe when I'm used to his presence, I might be able to manage that particular feat. But not yet. "Yeah. My dad left six months after Sean was born."

"I'm sorry." And I can tell he means it. "Mine are separated."

I shiver and tuck my hands underneath my arms. "Then I'm sorry, too. That sucks."

"It's all right. My father's a bastard."

"So is mine. I mean, obviously he is, if he left us when Seany was a baby. Which he totally did. But it's also his fault I'm stuck here. In Paris."

"I know."

He does?

"Mer told me. But I guarantee you that my father is worse. Unfortunately, he's the one here in Paris, while my mum is alone, thousands of miles away."

"Your dad lives here?" I'm surprised. I know his dad is French, but I can't imagine someone sending their child to boarding school when they live in the same city. It doesn't make sense.

"He owns an art gallery here and another in London. He divides his time between them."

"How often do you see him?"

"Never, if I can help it." St. Clair turns sullen, and it dawns on me that I have no idea why he's even here. I say as much.

"I didn't say?" He straightens up. "Oh. Well. I knew if someone didn't come and physically drag you outside, you'd never leave. So we're going out."

A strange mix of butterflies and churning erupts in my stomach. "Tonight?"

"Tonight."

"Right." I pause. "And Ellie?"

He falls back, and now he's lying down on my bed. "Our plans fell through." He says this with a vague wave of his hand, in a way that keeps me from inquiring further.

I gesture at my pajama bottoms. "I'm not exactly dressed for it."

"Come on, Anna. Do we honestly have to go through this again?"

I give him a doubtful look, and the unicorn pillow flies at my head. I slam it back, and he grins, slides off the bed, and smacks me full force. I grab for it but miss, and he hits me again twice before letting me catch it. St. Clair doubles over in laughter, and I whack him on the back. He tries to reclaim it, but I hold on and we wrestle back and forth until he lets go. The force throws me onto the bed, dizzy and sweaty.

St. Clair flops down beside me, breathing heavily. He's lying so close that his hair tickles the side of my face. Our arms are almost touching. Almost. I try to exhale, but I no longer know how to breathe. And then I remember I'm not wearing a bra.

And now I'm paranoid.

"Okay." He's panting. "Here's the"—*pant pant*—"plan."

I don't want to feel this way around him. I want things to be normal. I want to be his friend, not another stupid girl holding out for something that will never happen. I force myself up. My hair has gone all crazy and staticky from the pillow fight, so I grab an elastic band off my dresser to pull it back.

"Put on some proper trousers," he says. "And I'll show you Paris."

"That's it? That's the plan?"

"The whole shebang."

"Wow. 'Shebang.' Fancy."

St. Clair grunts and chucks the pillow at me. My phone rings. It's probably my mom; she's called every night this week. I swipe my cell off my desk, and I'm about to silence the ringer when the name flashes up. My heart stops.

Toph.

chapter eight

$\mathcal{I}$ hope you're wearing a beret." This is how Toph greets me.

I'm already laughing. He called! Toph called!

"Not yet." I pace the short length of my room. "But I could pick one up for you, if you'd like. Get your name stitched onto it. You could wear it instead of your name tag."

"I could rock a beret." There's a grin in his voice.

"No one can rock a beret. Not even you."

St. Clair is still lying on my bed. He props up his head to watch me. I smile and point to the picture on my laptop. *Toph*, I mouth.

St. Clair shakes his head.

Sideburns.

Ah, he mouths back.

"So your sister came in yesterday." Toph always refers to Bridge as my sister. We're the same height with the same slender build, and we both have long, stick-straight hair, although hers is blond and mine is brown. And, as people who spend tons of time together are prone to do, we talk the same. Though she uses bigger words. And her arms are sculpted from the drumming. And I have the gap between my teeth, while she had braces. In other words, she's like me, but prettier and smarter and more talented.

"I didn't know she was a drummer," he says. "She any good?"

"The best."

"Are you saying that because she's your friend, or because she's actually decent?"

"She's the best," I repeat. From the corner of my eye, I see St. Clair glance at the clock on my dresser.

"My drummer abandoned ship. Think she'd be interested?"

Last summer Toph started a punk band, the Penny Dreadfuls. Many member changes and arguments over lyrical content have transpired, but no actual shows. Which is too bad. I bet Toph looks good behind a guitar.

"Actually," I say, "I think she would. Her jerkwad percussion instructor just passed her up as section leader, and she has some rage to funnel." I give him her number. Toph repeats it back as St. Clair taps an imaginary wristwatch. It's only nine, so I'm not sure what his rush is. Even I know that's early for Paris. He clears his throat loudly.

"Hey, I'm sorry. I need to go," I say.

"Is someone there with you?"

"Uh, yeah. My friend. He's taking me out tonight."

A beat. *"He?"*

"He's just a friend." I turn my back to St. Clair. "He has a girlfriend." I squeeze my eyes shut. Should I have said that?

"So you're not gonna forget about us? I mean . . ." He slows down. "Us here in Atlanta? Ditch us for some Frenchie and never return?"

My heart thrums. "Of course not. I'll be back at Christmas."

"Good. Okay, Annabel Lee. I should get back to work anyway. Hercules is probably pissed I'm not covering the door. *Ciao.*"

"Actually," I say. "It's *au revoir.*"

"Whatever." He laughs, and we hang up.

St. Clair gets up from the bed. "Jealous boyfriend?"

"I told you. He's not my boyfriend."

"But you like him."

I blush. "Well . . . yeah."

St. Clair's expression is unreadable. Maybe annoyed. He nods toward my door. "You still want to go out?"

"What?" I'm confused. "Yeah, of course. Lemme change first." I let him out, and five minutes later, we're headed north. I've thrown on my favorite shirt, a cute thrift-store find that hugs me in the right places, and jeans and black canvas sneakers. I know sneakers aren't very French—I should be wearing pointy boots or scary heels—but at least they aren't white. It's true what they say about white sneakers. Only American tourists wear them, big ugly things made for mowing grass or painting houses.

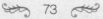

It's a beautiful night. The lights of Paris are yellow and green and orange. The warm air swirls with the chatter of people in the streets and the clink of wineglasses in the restaurants. St. Clair has brightened back up and is detailing the more gruesome aspects of the Rasputin biography he finished this afternoon.

"So the other Russians give him this dose of cyanide in his dinner, lethal enough to kill five men, right? But it's not doing *anything*, so Plan B—they shoot him in the back with a revolver. Which *still* doesn't kill him. In fact, Rasputin has enough energy to strangle one of them, so they shoot him *three more times*. And he's still struggling to get up! So they beat the bloody crap out of him, wrap him in a sheet, and throw him into an icy river. But get this—"

His eyes shimmer. It's the same look Mom gets when she's talking about turtles, or Bridge gets when she's talking about cymbals.

"During the autopsy, they discovered the actual cause of death was hypothermia. From the river! Not the poisoning or the shooting or the beating. Mother Nature. And not only that, but his arms were found frozen upright, like he'd tried to *claw his way out* from underneath the ice."

"What? No—"

Some German tourists are posing in front of a storefront with peeling golden letters. We scoot around them, so as not to wreck their picture. "It gets better," he says. "When they cremated his body, he *sat up*. No, he did! Probably because the bloke who prepared his body forgot to snip the tendons, so they shrank up when he burned—"

I nod my head in appreciation. "Ew, but cool. Go on."

"—which made his legs and body bend, but still." St. Clair smiles triumphantly. "Everyone went mad when they saw it."

"And who says history is boring?" I smile back, and everything is perfect. Almost. Because this is the moment we pass the entrance to SOAP, and now I'm farther from the school than I've ever been before. My smile wavers as I revert to my natural state of being: nervous and weird.

"You know, thanks for that. The others always shut me up long before—" He notices the change in my demeanor and stops. "Are you all right?"

"I'm fine."

"Yes, and has anyone ever told you that you are a terrible liar? Horrid. The worst."

"It's just—" I hesitate, embarrassed.

"Yeeesss?"

"Paris is so . . . foreign." I struggle for the right word. "Intimidating."

"Nah." He quickly dismisses me.

"Easy for you to say." We step around a dignified gentleman stooping over to pick up after his dog, a basset hound with a droopy stomach. Granddad warned me that the sidewalks of Paris were littered with doggie land mines, but it hasn't been the case so far. "You've been acquainted with Paris your whole life," I continue. "You speak fluent French, you dress European . . ."

"Pardon?"

"You know. Nice clothes, nice shoes."

He holds up his left foot, booted in something scuffed and clunky. *"These?"*

"Well, no. But you aren't in sneakers. I totally stick out. And I don't speak French and I'm scared of the *métro* and I should probably be wearing heels, but I hate heels—"

"I'm glad you're not wearing heels," St. Clair interrupts. "Then you'd be taller than me."

"I *am* taller than you."

"Barely."

"Please. I've got three inches on you. And you're wearing boots."

He nudges me with his shoulder, and I crack a smile. "Relax," he says. "You're with me. I'm practically French."

"You're English."

He grins. "I'm American."

"An American with a English accent. Isn't that, like, twice as much for the French to hate?"

St. Clair rolls his eyes. "You ought to stop listening to stereotypes and start forming your own opinions."

"I'm not stereotyping."

"Really? Please, then, enlighten me." He points to the feet of a girl walking ahead of us. She's yakking in French on a cell phone. "What *exactly* are those?"

"Sneakers," I mumble.

"Interesting. And the gentlemen over there, on the other side of the pavement. Would you care to explain what the one on the left is wearing? Those peculiar contraptions strapped to his feet?"

They're sneakers, of course. "But hey. See that guy over there?" I nod toward a man in jean shorts and a Budweiser T-shirt. "Am *I* that obvious?"

St. Clair squints at him. "Obviously what? Balding? Overweight? Tasteless?"

"American."

He sighs melodramatically. "Honestly, Anna. You must get over this."

"I just don't want to offend anyone. I hear they offend easily."

"You're not offending anyone except me right now."

"What about her?" I point to a middle-aged woman in khaki shorts and a knit top with stars and stripes on it. She has a camera strapped to her belt and is arguing with a man in a bucket hat. Her husband, I suppose.

"Completely offensive."

"I mean, am I as obvious as her?"

"Considering she's wearing the *American flag*, I'd venture a no on that one." He bites his thumbnail. "Listen. I think I have a solution to your problem, but you'll have to wait for it. Just promise you'll stop asking me to compare you to fifty-year-old women, and I'll take care of everything."

"How? With what? A French passport?"

He snorts. "I didn't say I'd make you French." I open my mouth to protest, but he cuts me off. "Deal?"

"Deal," I say uncomfortably. I don't care for surprises. "But it better be good."

"Oh, it's good." And St. Clair looks so smug that I'm about to call him on it, when I realize I can't see our school anymore.

I don't believe it. He's completely distracted me.

It takes a moment for me to recognize the symptoms, but my heels are bouncing and my stomach is fluttering. I'm finally excited to be out! "So where are we going?" I can't keep the eagerness from my voice. "The Seine? I know it's up here somewhere. Are we going to sit on the riverbank?"

"Not telling. Keep walking."

I let this pass. What's wrong with me? That's the second time in one minute I've let him keep me in suspense. "Oh! You have to see this first." He grabs my arm and pulls me across the street. An angry scooter honks its puny horn, and I laugh.

"Wait, what—" And then I'm knocked breathless.

We're standing in front of an absolute beast of a cathedral. Four thick columns hold up a Gothic facade of imposing statues and rose windows and intricate carvings. A skinny bell tower stretches all the way into the inky blackness of the night sky. "What *is* it?" I whisper. "Is it famous? Should I know it?"

"It's my church."

"You go here?" I'm surprised. He doesn't seem like the church-going type.

"No." He nods to a stone placard, indicating I read it.

"Saint Etienne du Mont. Hey! Saint Etienne."

He smiles. "I've always been a bit proprietary about it. Mum used to bring me here when I was young. We'd take a picnic lunch and eat it right here on the steps. Sometimes she'd bring her sketchbook, and she'd draw the pigeons and the taxis."

"Your mother is an artist?"

"A painter. Her work is in the New York MoMA." He sounds proud, and I remember what Meredith once said—that St. Clair admires Josh because he can draw so well. And that St. Clair's father owns two art galleries. And that St. Clair is taking studio art this semester. I wonder aloud if he's also an artist.

He shrugs. "Not really. I wish I were. Mum didn't pass on that particular talent, just the appreciation. Josh is much better. So is Rashmi, for that matter."

"You get along well with her, don't you? Your mom?"

"I love me mum." He says this matter-of-factly, with no trace of teenage shame.

We stand before the cathedral's double doors and look up, and up, and up. I picture my own mom, typing snapping turtle data into our home computer, her usual evening activity. Except it's not nighttime in Atlanta. Maybe she's grocery shopping. Wading in the Chattahoochee River. Watching *The Empire Strikes Back* with Sean. I have no idea, and it bothers me.

At last, St. Clair breaks the silence. "Come along, then. Loads to see."

The farther we go, the more crowded Paris gets. He talks about his mom, how she makes chocolate chip pancakes for dinner and tuna noodle casserole for breakfast. How she painted every room of her flat a different color of the rainbow. How she collects misspellings of her name on junk mail. He says nothing of his father.

We pass another enormous structure, this one like the ruins of a medieval castle. "God, there's history everywhere," I say. "What *is* that place? Can we go in?"

"It's a museum, and sure. But not tonight. I believe it's closed," he adds.

"Oh. Yeah, of course." I try not to let my disappointment show.

St. Clair is amused. "It's only the first week of school. We have all the time in the world to visit your museum."

We. For some reason, my insides squirm. St. Clair and me. Me and St. Clair.

Soon we enter an area even more touristy than our own neighborhood, crammed with bustling restaurants and shops and hotels. Street vendors everywhere shout in English, "Couscous! You like couscous?" and the roads are so narrow that cars can't drive on them. We walk down the middle of the street and through the jostling crowd. It feels like a carnival. "Where are we?" I wish I didn't have to ask so many questions.

"In between the rue St. Michel and the rue St. Jacques."

I shoot him a look.

"*Rue* means 'street.' And we're still in the Latin Quarter."

"Still? But we've been walking for—"

"Ten? Fifteen minutes?" he teases.

Hmph. Obviously Londoners or Parisians or whatever he is aren't used to the glory of car ownership. I miss mine, even if it does have trouble starting. And no air-conditioning. And a busted speaker. I say this, and he smiles. "Wouldn't do you any good even if you did have one. It's illegal to drive here if you're under eighteen."

"You could drive us," I say.

"No, I couldn't."

"You said you had a birthday! I *knew* you were lying, no one—"

"That's not what I meant." St. Clair laughs. "I don't know how to drive."

"You're serious?" I can't help the evil grin that spreads across my face. "You mean there's something I know how to do that you don't?"

He grins back. "Shocking, isn't it? But I've never had a reason. The transit systems here, in San Francisco, in London—they're all perfectly sufficient."

"Perfectly sufficient."

"Shut up." He laughs again. "Hey, you know why they call this the Latin Quarter?"

I raise an eyebrow.

"Centuries ago, the students at La Sorbonne—it was back there." He gestures with his hand. "It's one of the oldest universities in the world. Anyway, the students were taught in, and spoke to each other in, Latin. And the name stuck."

A moment of reserve. "That was it? The whole story?"

"Yes. God, you're right. That was pants."

I sidestep another aggressive couscous vendor. "Pants?"

"Rubbish. Crap. Shite."

Pants. Oh heavens, that's cute.

We turn a corner and—there it is—the River Seine. The lights of the city bob in the ripples of the water. I suck in my breath. It's gorgeous. Couples stroll along the riverbank, and booksellers have lined up dirty cardboard boxes of paperback books and old magazines for browsing. A man with a red beard strums a guitar and sings a sad song. We listen for a minute, and St. Clair tosses a few euros into the man's guitar case.

And then, as we're turning our attention back toward the river, I see it.

Notre-Dame.

I recognize it from photographs, of course. But if St-Etienne is a cathedral, then it is nothing, NOTHING compared to Notre-Dame. The building is like a great ship steaming downriver. Massive. Monstrous. Majestic. It's lit in a way that absurdly reminds me of Disney World, but it's so much more magical than anything Walt could have dreamed up. Mounds of green vines spill down the walls and into the water, completing the fairy tale.

I slowly exhale. "It's beautiful."

St. Clair is watching me.

"I've never seen anything like it." I don't know what more to say.

We have to cross a bridge to get to it. I hadn't realized it was built on an island. St. Clair tells me we're walking to the Île de la Cité, the Island of the City, and it's the oldest district in all of Paris. The Seine twinkles below us, deep and green, and a long boat strung with lights glides underneath the bridge. I peer over the edge. "Look! That guy is so trashed. He's totally gonna fall off the bo—" I glance back and find St. Clair toddling on the road, several feet away from the edge of the bridge.

For a moment, I'm confused. Then it hits me. "What? You aren't afraid of heights?"

St. Clair keeps his eyes forward, on the illuminated figure of Notre-Dame. "I just can't fathom why anyone would stand on a ledge when there's a respectable amount of walking space right next to it."

"Oh, it's about walking space, is it?"

"Drop it, or I'll quiz you about Rasputin. Or French verb conjugation."

I lean over the side of the bridge and pretend to wobble. St. Clair turns pale. "No! Don't!" He stretches out his arms like he wants to save me, then clutches his stomach like he's about to vomit instead.

"Sorry!" I jump away from the ledge. "I'm sorry, I didn't realize it was so bad."

He shakes a hand, motioning for me to stop talking. The other hand still clings to his queasy stomach.

"I'm sorry," I say again, after a moment.

"Come on." St. Clair sounds peeved, as if I was the one holding us back. He gestures to Notre-Dame. "That's not why I brought you here."

I can't fathom anything better than Notre-Dame. "We're not going inside?"

"Closed. Plenty of time to see it later, remember?" He leads me into the courtyard, and I take the opportunity to admire his backside. Callipygian. There *is* something better than Notre-Dame.

"Here," he says.

We have a perfect view of the entrance—hundreds and hundreds of tiny figures carved into three colossal archways. The statues look like stone dolls, each one separate and individualized. "They're incredible," I whisper.

"Not there. *Here*." He points to my feet.

I look down, and I'm surprised to find myself standing in the middle of a small stone circle. In the center, directly between my feet, is a coppery-bronze octagon with a star. Words are engraved in the stone around it: *POINT ZÉRO DES ROUTES DE FRANCE*.

"Mademoiselle Oliphant. It translates to 'Point zero of the roads of France.' In other words, it's the point from which all other distances in France are measured." St. Clair clears his throat. "It's the beginning of everything."

I look back up. He's smiling.

"Welcome to Paris, Anna. I'm glad you've come."

chapter nine

*S*t. Clair tucks the tips of his fingers into his pockets and kicks the cobblestones with the toe of his boots. "Well?" he finally asks.

"Thank you." I'm stunned. "It was really sweet of you to bring me here."

"Ah, well." He straightens up and shrugs—that full-bodied French shrug he does so well—and reassumes his usual, assured state of being. "Have to start somewhere. Now make a wish."

"Huh?" I have such a way with words. I should write epic poetry or jingles for cat food commercials.

He smiles. "Place your feet on the star, and make a wish."

"Oh. Okay, sure." I slide my feet together so I'm standing in the center. "I wish—"

"Don't say it aloud!" St. Clair rushes forward, as if to stop my words with his body, and my stomach flips violently. "Don't you know anything about making wishes? You only get a limited number in life. Falling stars, eyelashes, dandelions—"

"Birthday candles."

He ignores the dig. "Exactly. So you ought to take advantage of them when they arise, and superstition says if you make a wish on *that* star, it'll come true." He pauses before continuing. "Which is better than the other one I've heard."

"That I'll die a painful death of poisoning, shooting, beating, and drowning?"

"Hypothermia, not drowning." St. Clair laughs. He has a wonderful, boyish laugh. "But no. I've heard anyone who stands here is destined to return to Paris someday. And as I understand it, one year for you is one year too many. Am I right?"

I close my eyes. Mom and Seany appear before me. Bridge. Toph. I nod.

"All right, then. So keep your eyes closed. And make a wish."

I take a deep breath. The cool dampness of the nearby trees fills my lungs. What do I want? It's a difficult question.

I want to go home, but I have to admit I've enjoyed tonight. And what if this is the only time in my entire life I visit Paris? I know I just told St. Clair that I don't want to be here, but there's a part of me—a teeny, tiny part—that's curious. If my father called tomorrow and ordered me home, I might be disappointed. I still haven't seen the *Mona Lisa*. Been to the top of the Eiffel Tower. Walked beneath the Arc de Triomphe.

So what else do I want?

I want to feel Toph's lips again. I want him to wait. But there's another part of me, a part I really, *really* hate, that knows even if we do make it, I'd still move away for college next year. So I'd see him this Christmas and next summer, and then . . . would that be it?

And then there's the other thing.

The thing I'm trying to ignore. The thing I shouldn't want, the thing I can't have.

And he's standing in front of me right now.

So what do I wish for? Something I'm not sure I want? Someone I'm not sure I need? Or someone I know I can't have?

Screw it. Let the fates decide.

I wish for the thing that is best for me.

How's that for a generalization? I open my eyes, and the wind is blowing harder. St. Clair pushes a strand of hair from his eyes. "Must have been a good one," he says.

On the way back, he leads me to a walk-up sandwich stand for a late-night snack. The yeasty smell is mouthwatering, and my stomach growls in anticipation. We order panini, sandwiches pressed flat on a hot grill. St. Clair gets his stuffed with smoked salmon and ricotta cheese and chives. I order Parma ham and Fontina cheese and sage. He calls it fast food, but what we're handed looks nothing like the limp sandwiches from Subway.

St. Clair helps with the euro situation. Thankfully, euros are easy to understand. Bills and cents come in nice, even denominations. We pay and stroll down the street, enjoying the night. Crunching through the crusty bread. Letting the warm, gooey cheese run down our chins.

I moan with pleasure.

"Did you just have a foodgasm?" he asks, wiping ricotta from his lips.

"Where have you been all my life?" I ask the beautiful panini. "How is it possible I've never had a sandwich like this before?"

He takes a large bite. "Mmmph grmpha mrpha," he says, smiling. Which I'm assuming translates to something like, "Because American food is crap."

"Mmmph mrga grmpha mmrg," I reply. Which translates to, "Yeah, but our burgers are pretty good."

We lick the paper our sandwiches were wrapped in before throwing them away. Bliss. We're almost back to the dormitory, and St. Clair is describing the time he and Josh received detention for throwing chewing gum at the painted ceiling—they were trying to give one of the nymphs a third nipple—when my brain begins to process something. Something odd.

We have just passed the third movie theater in one block.

Granted, these are small theaters. One-screeners, most likely. But *three* of them. In one block! How did I not notice this earlier?

Oh. Right. The cute boy.

"Are any of those in English?" I interrupt.

St. Clair looks confused. "Pardon?"

"The movie theaters. Are there any around here that play films in English?"

He cocks an eyebrow. "Don't tell me you don't know."

"What? Don't know what?"

He's gleeful to know something I don't. Which is annoying considering we're both aware that he knows everything about Parisian life, whereas I have the savvy of a chocolate croissant. "And I was under the impression that you were some kind of cinema junkie."

"What? Know *what*?"

St. Clair gestures around in an exaggerated circle, clearly loving this. "Paris . . . is the film appreciation . . . capital . . . of the world."

I stop dead. "You're kidding."

"I'm not. You'll never find a city that loves film more. There are hundreds, maybe even thousands, of theaters here."

My heart feels like it's falling inside my chest. I'm dizzy. It can't be true.

"More than a dozen in our neighborhood alone."

"What?"

"You honestly didn't notice?"

"No, I didn't notice! How come no one told me?" I mean, this should have been mentioned Day One, Life Skills Seminars. This is very important information here! We resume walking, and my head strains in every direction to read the posters and marquees. *Please be in English. Please be in English. Please be in English.*

"I thought you knew. I would have said something." He finally looks apologetic. "It's considered pretty high art here. There are loads of first-run theaters, but even more—what do you call them?—revival houses. They play the classics and run programs

devoted to different directors or genres or obscure Brazilian actresses or whatever."

Breathe, Anna, breathe. "And are they in English?"

"At least a third of them, I suppose."

A third of them! Of a few hundred—maybe even thousand!—theaters.

"Some American films are dubbed into French, but mainly those are the ones for children. The rest are left in English and given French subtitles. Here, hold on." St. Clair plucks a magazine called *Pariscope* from the racks of a newsstand and pays a cheerful man with a hooked nose. He thrusts the magazine at me. "It comes out every Wednesday. 'VO' means *version originale*. 'VF' means *version française*, which means they're dubbed. So stick to VO. The listings are also online," he adds.

I tear through the magazine, and my eyes glaze over. I've never seen so many movie listings in my life.

"Christ, if I'd known that's all it took to make you happy, I wouldn't have bothered with the rest of this."

"I love Paris," I say.

"And I'm sure it loves you back."

He's still talking, but I'm not listening. There's a Buster Keaton marathon this week. And another for teen slasher flicks. And a whole program devoted to 1970s car chases.

"What?" I realize he's waiting for an answer to a question I didn't hear. When he doesn't reply, I glance up from the listings. His gaze is frozen on a figure that has just stepped out of our dorm.

The girl is about my height. Her long hair is barely styled, but in a fashionable, Parisian sort of way. She's wearing a short silver dress that sparkles in the lamplight, and a red coat. Her leather boots snap and click against the sidewalk. She's looking back over her shoulder toward Résidence Lambert with a slight frown, but then she turns and notices St. Clair. Her entire *being* lights up.

The magazine slackens in my hands. She can only be one person.

The girl breaks into a run and launches herself into his arms. They kiss, and she laces her fingers through his hair. His beautiful, perfect hair. My stomach drops, and I turn from the spectacle.

They break apart, and she starts talking. Her voice is surprisingly low—*sultry*—but she speaks rapidly. "I know we weren't gonna see each other tonight, but I was in the neighborhood and thought you might want to go to that club I was telling you about. You know, the one Matthieu recommended? But you weren't there, so I found Mer and I've been talking to her for the last hour, and where were you? I called your cell three times but it went straight to voice mail."

St. Clair looks disoriented. "Er. Ellie, this is Anna. She hadn't left the dorm all week, so I thought I'd show her—"

To my amazement, Ellie breaks into an ear-to-ear smile. Oddly enough, it's this moment I realize that despite her husky voice and Parisian attire, she's sort of . . . plain. But friendly-looking.

That still doesn't mean I like her.

"Anna! From Atlanta, right? Where'd you guys go?"

She knows who I am? St. Clair describes our evening while I contemplate this strange development. Did he tell her about me? Or was it Meredith? I hope it was him, but even if it was, it's not like he said anything she found threatening. She doesn't seem alarmed that I've spent the last three hours in the company of her very attractive boyfriend. Alone.

Must be nice to have that kind of confidence.

"Okay, babe." She cuts him off. "You can tell me the rest later. You ready to go?"

Did he say he'd go with her? I don't remember, but he nods his head. "Yeah. Yeah, let me grab my, er—" He glances at me, and then toward the entrance of our dorm.

"What? You're already dressed to go out. You look great. C'mon." She tugs his arm, linking it to hers. "It was nice to meet you, Anna."

I find my voice. "Yeah. Nice to meet you, too." I turn to St. Clair, but he won't look at me properly. Fine. Whatever. I give him my best I-don't-care-that-you-have-a-girlfriend smile and a cheerful "Bye!"

He doesn't react. Okay, time to go. I bolt away and pull out my building key. But as I unlock the door, I can't help but glance back. St. Clair and Ellie are striding into the darkness, arms still linked, her mouth still chattering.

As I pause there, St. Clair's head turns back to me. Just for a moment.

chapter ten

It's better this way. It is.

As the days pass, I realize that I'm glad I met his girlfriend. It's actually a relief. There are few things worse than having feelings for someone you shouldn't, and I don't like where my thoughts were headed. And I certainly don't want to be another Amanda Spitterton-Watts.

St. Clair is just friendly. The whole school likes him—the *professeurs*, the popular kids, the unpopular kids—and why wouldn't they? He's smart and funny and polite. And, yes, ridiculously attractive. Although, for being so well liked, he doesn't hang out with many people. Just our little group. And since his best friend is usually distracted by Rashmi, he's taken to hanging out with, well . . . *me*.

Since our night out, he's sat next to me at every meal. He teases me about sneakers, asks about my favorite films, and conjugates my French homework. And he defends me. Like last week in physics when Amanda called me *la moufette* in a nasty way and held her nose as I walked by her desk, St. Clair told her to "bugger off" and threw tiny wads of paper into her hair for the rest of class.

I looked up the word later, and it means "skunk." So original.

But then, just as I feel those twinges again, he disappears. I'll be staring out my window after dinner, watching the sanitation workers tidy the street in their bright green uniforms, when he'll emerge from our dorm and vanish toward the *métro*.

Toward Ellie.

Most nights I'm studying in the lobby with our other friends when he comes home. He'll plop down beside me and crack a joke about whatever drunken junior is hitting on the girl behind the front desk. (There's always a drunken junior hitting on the girl behind the front desk.) And is it my imagination, or is his hair more disheveled than usual?

The thought of St. Clair and Ellie doing—*things*—makes me more jealous than I care to admit. Toph and I email, but the messages have never been more than friendly. I don't know if this means he's still interested or if it means he's not, but I do know that emailing is not the same as kissing. Or *things*.

The only one who understands the St. Clair situation is Mer, but I can't say anything to her. Sometimes I'm afraid *she* might be jealous of *me*. Like I'll catch her watching the two of us at lunch, and when I ask her to pass me a napkin, she'll kind of chuck it at me instead. Or when St. Clair doodles bananas and elephants into the margins of my homework, she'll grow rigid and silent.

Maybe I'm doing her a favor. I'm stronger than she is, since I haven't known him as long. Since he's always been off-limits. I mean, poor Mer. Any girl faced with daily attention from a gorgeous boy with a cute accent and perfect hair would be hard-pressed not to develop a big, stinking, painful, all-the-time, all-consuming crush.

Not that that's what's happening to me.

Like I said. It's a relief to know it won't happen. It makes things easier. Most girls laugh too hard at his jokes and find excuses to gently press his arm. To touch him. Instead, I argue and roll my eyes and act indifferent. And when I touch his arm, I shove it. Because that's what friends do.

Besides, I have more important things on my mind: movies.

I've been in France for a month, and though I have ridden the elevators to the top of La Tour Eiffel (Mer took me while St. Clair and Rashmi waited below on the lawn—St. Clair because he's afraid of falling and Rashmi because she refuses to do anything touristy), and though I have walked the viewing platform of L'Arc de Triomphe (Mer took me again, of course, while St. Clair stayed below and threatened to push Josh and Rashmi into the insane traffic circle), I still haven't been to the movies.

Actually, I have yet to leave campus alone. Kind of embarrassing.

But I have a plan. First, I'll convince someone to go to a theater with me. Shouldn't be too difficult; everyone likes the movies. And then I'll take notes on everything they say and do, and then I'll be comfortable going back to that theater alone. And one theater is better than no theaters.

"Rashmi. What are you doing tonight?"

We're waiting for La Vie to begin. Last week we learned about the importance of eating locally grown food, and before that, how to write a college application essay. Who knows what they'll drag out today? Meredith and Josh are the only ones not here, Josh because he's a junior, and Mer because she's taking that extra language class, advanced Spanish. For fun. Craziness.

Rashmi taps her pen against her notebook. She's been working on her essay to Brown for two weeks now. It's one of the only universities to offer an Egyptology degree, and the only one she wants to attend. "You don't understand," she said, when I'd asked why she hadn't finished it yet. "Brown turns away *eighty percent* of its applicants."

But I doubt she'll have any problems. She hasn't received less than an A on anything this year, and the majority were perfect scores. I've already mailed in my college applications. It'll be a while before I hear back, but I'm not worried. They weren't Ivy League.

I'm trying to be friendly, but it's tricky. Last night, while I was petting her rabbit, Isis, Rashmi reminded me twice not to tell anyone about her, because animals are against dorm rules.

As if I'd tattle. Besides, it's not like Isis is a secret. The smell of bunny pee outside her door is unmistakable.

"Nothing, I guess," she says, in response to my question about her evening.

I take a deep breath to steady my nerves. It's ridiculous how difficult a question can be when the answer means so much. "Wanna go to the movies? They're showing *It Happened One Night* at Le Champo." Just because I haven't gone out doesn't mean I haven't pored over the glorious *Pariscope*.

"They're showing what? And I'm not gonna tell you how badly you just butchered that theater's name."

"*It Happened One Night*. Clark Gable and Claudette Colbert. Won five Academy Awards. It was a big deal."

"In what century?"

"Ha ha. Honestly, you'll like it. I hear it's great."

Rashmi rubs her temples. "I don't know. I don't really like old movies. The acting is so, 'Hey buddy, ol' pal. Let's go wear our hats and have a big misunderstanding.'"

"Aw, come off it." St. Clair looks up from a thick book about the American Revolution. He sits on my other side. It's weird to think he knows more American history than I do. "Isn't that the charm? The hats and the misunderstandings?"

"So why don't *you* go with her?" Rashmi asks.

"Because he's going out with Ellie," I say.

"How do you know what I'm doing tonight?" he asks.

"Please?" I beg her. "Pretty please? You'll like it, I swear. So will Josh and Mer."

Rashmi opens her mouth to protest just as the teacher arrives. Every week it's someone new—sometimes administration, sometimes a *professeur*. This time, I'm surprised to see Nate. I guess all staff members are forced to take a turn. He rubs his shaved head and smiles pleasantly at our class.

"How do you know what I'm doing tonight?" St. Clair repeats.

"Pleeeeease," I say to her.

She gives a resigned grimace. "Fine. But I'm picking the next movie."

Yippee!

Nate clears his throat, and Rashmi and St. Clair look up. That's one thing I like about my new friends. They respect the teachers. It drives me nuts to see students talk back or ignore them, because my mom is a teacher. I wouldn't want anyone being rude to her. "All right, people, enough. Amanda, *enough*." In his quiet but firm way, Nate shuts her up. She flips her hair and sighs, with a glance toward St. Clair.

He ignores her. Ha.

"I have a surprise for you," Nate says. "Since the weather is turning, and there aren't many warm days left, I've arranged for you guys to spend the week outdoors."

We're going outside for class credit. I love Paris!

"I've organized a scavenger hunt." Nate holds up a stack of papers. "There are two hundred items on this list. You'll be able to find them all in our neighborhood, but you may have to ask the locals for help."

Oh hell no.

"You'll be taking pictures of the items, and you'll be working in two teams."

Phew! Someone else can talk to the locals.

"The winning team will be determined by the total number of items found, but I'll need to find photos on *everyone's* phone or camera, if you expect to earn credit."

NOOOOOOOOOOO.

"There's a prize." Nate smiles again, now that he finally has everyone's attention. "The team that finds the most items by the end of Thursday's class . . . gets to skip class on Friday."

Now *that* might be worth it. The classroom erupts in whistles and clapping. Nate picks captains based on who begs for it the loudest. Steve Carver—the guy with the faux-surfer hair—and Amanda's best friend, Nicole, are chosen. Rashmi and I groan in a rare moment of camaraderie. Steve pumps a fist in the air. What a meathead.

The selecting begins, and Amanda is chosen first. Of course. And then Steve's best friend. Of course. Rashmi elbows me. "Bet you five euros I'm picked last."

"I'll take that bet. Because it's totally me."

Amanda turns in her seat toward me and lowers her voice. "That's a safe bet, Skunk Girl. Who'd want *you* on their team?"

My jaw unhinges stupidly.

"St. Clair!" Steve's voice startles me. It figures that St. Clair would be picked early. Everyone looks at him, but he's staring down Amanda. "Me," he says, in answer to her question. "I want Anna on my team, and you'd be lucky to have her."

She flushes and quickly turns back around, but not before shooting me another dagger. What have I ever done to her?

More names are called. More names that are NOT mine. St. Clair tries to get my attention, but I pretend I don't notice. I can't bear to look at him. I'm too humiliated. Soon the selection is down to me, Rashmi, and a skinny dude who, for whatever reason, is called Cheeseburger. Cheeseburger is always wearing this expression of surprise, like someone's just called his name, and he can't figure out where the voice is coming from.

"Rashmi," Nicole says without hesitation.

My heart sinks. Now it's between me and someone named *Cheeseburger*. I focus my attention down on my desk, at the picture of me that Josh drew earlier today in history. I'm dressed like a medieval peasant (we're studying the Black Plague), and I have a fierce scowl and a dead rat dangling from one hand.

Amanda whispers into Steve's ear. I feel her smirking at me, and my face burns.

Steve clears his throat. "Cheeseburger."

chapter eleven

Y ou owe me five bucks," I say.

Rashmi smiles. "I'll buy your movie ticket."

At least we're on the same team. Nicole divided up Nate's list, so Rashmi and I went out on our own. The week shouldn't be *too* bad. Because of Rashmi, I'll actually earn class credit. She let me take some of the pictures—a statue of some guy named Budé and a group of kids playing football in the street—even though she was the one who found both items.

"I miss football." Meredith pouts as we tell her our story. Even her springy curls look limp and sad tonight.

A breeze whips down the broad avenue, and we hold our jackets tight and shiver. A dusting of brown leaves crunches underneath our feet as Paris hovers on the edge of autumn. "Isn't

there some league you can join or something?" Josh asks, putting his arm around Rashmi. She burrows into him. "I see people playing around here all the time."

"Boo!" A familiar disheveled head pops between Mer and me, and we jump like startled cats.

"Jeez," Mer says. "Give me a heart attack. What are you doing here?"

"*It Happened One Night,*" St. Clair says. "Le Champo, right?"

"Don't you have plans with Ellie?" Rashmi asks.

"Am I not invited?" He wedges his way between Meredith and me.

"Of course you're invited," Mer says. "We just assumed you'd be busy."

"You're always busy," Rashmi says.

"I'm not *always busy*."

"You are," she says. "And you know what's weird? Mer's the only one who's even seen *Ellen* this year. Is she too good for us now?"

"Aw, get off it. Not this again."

She shrugs. "I'm just saying."

St. Clair shakes his head, but it doesn't escape our notice that he doesn't deny it. Ellie may be friendly enough in person, but it's clear she no longer needs her SOAP friends. Even I can see that.

"What do you guys even do every night?" The words slip out before I can stop them.

"It," Rashmi says. "They do it. He's ditching us to screw."

St. Clair blushes. "You know, Rash, you're as crude as those stupid juniors on my floor. Dave what's-his-name and Mike Reynard. God, they're arses."

Mike Reynard is Dave-from-French-and-history's best friend. I didn't know they lived next to him.

"Watch it, St. Clair," Josh says. There's an edge in his normally relaxed demeanor.

Rashmi whips into St. Clair's face. "Are you calling me an ass?"

"No, but if you don't back off, I bloody might."

Their bodies are tense, like they're about to bash antlers in a nature documentary. Josh tries to pull Rashmi back, but she shakes him away. "God, St. Clair, you can't be all chummy during the day and blow us off every night! You can't come back whenever you feel like it and pretend like everything's fine."

Mer tries to cut them off. "Hey, hey, hey—"

"Everything *is* fine! What the hell is wrong with you?"

"HEY!" Mer uses her considerable height and strength to force her way between them. To my surprise, she begins pleading with Rashmi. "I know you miss Ellie. I know she was your best friend, and it stinks that she's moved on, but you still have us. And St. Clair . . . she's right. It hurts not to see you anymore. I mean, away from school." She sounds like she's about to cry. "We used to be so close."

Josh puts his arm around her, and she hugs him tightly. He glares at St. Clair through her curls. *This is your fault. Fix it.*

St. Clair deflates. "Yeah. Okay. You're right."

It's not quite an apology, but Rashmi nods. Mer exhales in relief. Josh delicately pries her off and moves beside his girlfriend

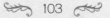

again. We tread in awkward silence. So Rashmi and Ellie used to be best friends. It's hard enough being temporarily separated from Bridge, but I can't imagine how awful it would be if she ditched me completely. I feel guilty. No wonder Rashmi's bitter.

"Sorry, Anna," St. Clair says after another muted block. "I know you were excited about the film."

"It's okay. It's not my business. My friends fight, too. I mean . . . my friends back home. Not that you guys aren't my friends. I'm just saying . . . all friends fight."

Argh. How distressing.

Gloom cloaks us like a thick fog. We resume silence, and my thoughts circle around. I wish Bridge were here. I wish St. Clair wasn't with Ellie, and Ellie hadn't hurt Rashmi, and Rashmi were more like Bridge. I wish Bridge were here.

"Hey," Josh says. "You. Check it out."

And then the darkness gives way to white neon. An Art Deco font, burning into the night, announces our arrival at the CINEMA LE CHAMPO. The letters dwarf me. *Cinema.* Has there ever been a more beautiful word? My heart soars as we pass the colorful film posters and walk through the gleaming glass doors. The lobby is smaller than what I'm used to, and though it's missing the tang of artificially buttered popcorn, there's something in the air I recognize, something both musty and comforting.

True to her word, Rashmi pays for my ticket. I take the opportunity to slip out a scrap of paper and a pen that I'd hidden in my jacket for this very purpose. Mer is next in line, and I transcribe her speech phonetically.

Oon ploss see voo play.

St. Clair leans over my shoulder and whispers. "You've spelled it wrong."

My head jerks up in embarrassment, but he's smiling. I drop my face, so that my hair shields my cheeks. They blush more for his smile than anything else.

We follow blue rope lights down the aisle of the theater. I wonder if they're blue everywhere here, rather than the golden glow of American cinemas. My heart beats faster. Everything else is the same.

Same seats. Same screen. Same walls.

For the first time in Paris, I feel at home.

I smile at my friends, but Mer and Rashmi and Josh are distracted, arguing about something that happened over dinner. St. Clair sees me and smiles back. "Good?"

I nod. He looks pleased and ducks into the row after me. I always sit four rows up from the center, and we have perfect seats tonight. The chairs are classic red. The movie begins, and the title screen flashes up. "Ugh, we have to sit through the credits?" Rashmi asks. They roll first, like in all old films.

I read them happily. I love credits. I love everything about movies.

The theater is dark except for the flicker of blacks and whites and grays on-screen. Clark Gable pretends to sleep and places his hand in the center of an empty bus seat. After a moment of irritation, Claudette Colbert gingerly plucks it aside and sits down. Gable smiles to himself, and St. Clair laughs.

It's odd, but I keep finding myself distracted. By the white of his teeth through the darkness. By a wavy bit of his hair that sticks straight out to the side. By the soft aroma of his laundry detergent. He nudges me to silently offer the armrest, but I decline and he takes it. His arm is close to mine, slightly elevated. I glance at his hands. Mine are tiny compared to his large, knuckly boy hands.

And, suddenly, I want to touch him.

Not a push, or a shove, or even a friendly hug. I want to feel the creases in his skin, connect his freckles with invisible lines, brush my fingers across the inside of his wrist. He shifts. I have the strangest feeling that he's as aware of me as I am of him. I can't concentrate. The characters on the screen are squabbling, but for the life of me, I don't know what about. How long have I not been paying attention?

St. Clair coughs and shifts again. His leg brushes against mine. It stays there. I'm paralyzed. I should move it; it feels too unnatural. How can he not notice his leg is touching my leg? From the corner of my eye, I see the profile of his chin and nose, and—oh, dear God—the curve of his lips.

There. He glanced at me. I know he did.

I bore my eyes into the screen, trying my best to prove that I am Really Interested in this movie. St. Clair stiffens but doesn't move his leg. Is he holding his breath? I think he is. I'm holding mine. I exhale and cringe—it's so loud and unnatural.

Again. Another glance. This time I turn, automatically, just as he's turning away. It's a dance, and now there's a feeling in the air like one of us should say something. Focus, Anna. Focus. "Do you like it?" I whisper.

He pauses. "The film?"

I'm thankful the shadows hide my blush.

"I like it very much," he says.

I risk a glance, and St. Clair stares back. Deeply. He has not looked at me like this before. I turn away first, then feel him turn a few beats later.

I know he is smiling, and my heart races.

chapter twelve

To: Anna Oliphant <bananaelephant@femmefilmfreak.net>
From: James Ashley <james@jamesashley.com>
Subject: Gentle Reminder

Hello, honey. It's been a while since we've spoken. Have
you checked your voice mail? I've called several times,
but I assume you're busy exploring Paree. Well, this is
just a gentle reminder to call your dear old dad and
tell him how your studies are going. Have you mastered
French yet? Tasted foie gras? What exciting museums
have you visited? Speaking of exciting, I'm sure you've
heard the good news. *The Incident* debuted at number

one on the *NY Times*! Looks like I've still got the magic touch. I'm leaving for a southeastern tour next week, so I'll see your brother soon and give him your best. Keep laser-focused on school, and I'll see YOU at Christmas.

Josh leans his lanky body over my shoulder and peers at my laptop. "Is it just me, or is that 'YOU' sort of threatening?"

"No. It's not just YOU," I say.

"I thought your dad was a writer. What's with the 'laser-focused' 'gentle reminder' shit?"

"My father is fluent in cliché. Obviously, you've never read one of his novels." I pause. "I can't believe he has the nerve to say he'll 'give Seany my best.'"

Josh shakes his head in disgust. My friends and I are spending the weekend in the lounge because it's raining again. No one ever mentions this, but it turns out Paris is as drizzly as London. According to St. Clair, that is, our only absent member. He went to some photography show at Ellie's school. Actually, he was supposed to be back by now.

He's running late. As usual.

Mer and Rashmi are curled up on one of the lobby couches, reading our latest English assignment, *Balzac and the Little Chinese Seamstress*. I turn back to my father's email.

Gentle reminder . . . your life sucks.

Memories from earlier this week—sitting next to St. Clair in the dark theater, his leg against mine, the look that passed between us—flood back in and fill me with shame. The

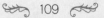

more I've thought about it, the more I'm convinced nothing happened.

Because nothing DID happen.

When we left the movie, Rashmi announced, "The ending was too abrupt. We didn't get to see any of the good stuff." And by the time I'd finished defending it, we were already back inside the dorm. I wanted to talk to St. Clair, get a sign that *something* between us had changed, but Mer broke in and hugged him good night. And since I couldn't hug him without exposing my thudding heart, I lingered behind.

And then we had this lame wave goodbye.

And then I went to bed, confused as ever.

What happened? As thrilling as it was, I must have exaggerated it in my mind, because he didn't act any differently at breakfast the next day. We had a friendly conversation, as always. Besides, he has Ellie. He doesn't need me. All I can guess is that I must have projected my own frustrated feelings about Toph onto St. Clair.

Josh is examining me carefully. I decide to ask him a question before he can ask me one. "How's your assignment going?" My team in La Vie actually won (no thanks to me), so Rashmi and I didn't have to go on Friday. Josh ditched his last class to spend the hour with us. It earned him detention and several pages of additional homework.

"Eh." He flops down in the chair beside me and picks up his sketchbook. "I have better things to do."

"But . . . won't you get in more trouble if you don't do it?"

I've never ditched. I don't understand how he can just shrug everything off.

"Probably." Josh flexes his hand and winces.

I frown. "What's the matter?"

"It's cramped," he says. "From drawing. It's okay, it's always like this."

Strange. I'd never considered art injuries before. "You're really talented. Is that what you want to do? For a living, I mean?"

"I'm working on a graphic novel."

"Really? That's cool." I push my laptop away. "What's it about?"

The corner of his mouth rises in a sly smile. "A guy forced to attend a snobby boarding school, because his parents don't want him around anymore."

I snort. "I've heard that one before. What do your parents do?"

"My dad's a politician. They're working on his reelection campaign. I haven't talked to 'Senator Wasserstein' since school started."

"Senator? As in a *senator* senator?"

"Senator as in *senator* senator. Unfortunately."

Again. What was my dad thinking? Sending me to school with the children of U.S. SENATORS? "Does everyone have a terrible father?" I ask. "Is it a requirement for attendance?"

He nods toward Rashmi and Mer. "They don't. But St. Clair's dad is a piece of work."

"So I hear." Curiosity gets the best of me, and I lower my voice. "What's his deal?"

Josh shrugs. "He's just a jerk. He keeps a tight leash on St. Clair and his mom, but he's really friendly to everyone else. Somehow that makes it worse."

I'm suddenly distracted by an odd purple-and-red knitted stocking cap walking into the lobby. Josh turns to see what I'm staring at. Meredith and Rashmi notice his movement, and they look up from their books.

"Oh God," Rashmi says. "He's wearing The Hat."

"I like The Hat," Mer says.

"You would," Josh says.

Meredith gives him a dirty look. I turn to get a better look at The Hat, and I'm startled to realize it's right behind me. And it's sitting atop St. Clair's head.

"So The Hat is back," Rashmi says.

"Yup," he says. "I know you missed it."

"Is there a story behind The Hat?" I ask.

"Only that his mother made it for him last winter, and we all agreed it was the most hideous accessory in Paris," Rashmi says.

"Oh, yeah?" St. Clair pulls it off and yanks it down over her head. Her two black braids stick out comically from underneath. "Looks great on you. Really fetching."

She scowls and tosses it back, then smoothes her part. He shoves it over his messy hair again, and I find myself agreeing with Mer. It's actually pretty cute. He looks warm and fuzzy, like a teddy bear.

"How was the show?" Mer asks.

He shrugs. "Nothing spectacular. What have you been up to?"

"Anna's been sharing her father's 'gentle reminder,'" Josh says.

St. Clair makes a yuck face.

"I'd rather not go there again, thank you." I shut my laptop.

"If you're done, I have something for you," St. Clair says.

"What? Who, me?"

"Remember how I promised I'd make you feel less American?"

I smile. "You have my French passport?" I hadn't forgotten his promise but figured he had—that conversation was weeks ago. I'm surprised and flattered he remembered.

"Better. Came in the mail yesterday. Come on, it's in my room." And, with that, he puts his hands in his coat pockets and struts into the stairwell.

I shove my computer into my bag, sling it over my shoulder, and shrug at the others. Mer looks hurt, and for a moment I feel guilty. But it's not like I'm stealing him from her. I'm his friend, too. I chase him up five flights of stairs, and The Hat bobs ahead of me. We get to his floor, and he leads me down the hallway. I'm nervous and excited. I've never seen his room before. We always meet in the lobby or on my floor.

"Home sweet home." He pulls out an "I Left My ♥ in San Francisco" key chain. Another gift from his mother, I suppose. Taped to his door is a sketch of him wearing Napoleon's hat. Josh's work.

"Hey, 508! Your room is right above mine. You never said."

St. Clair smiles. "Maybe I didn't want you blaming me for keeping you up at night with my noisy stomping boots."

"Dude. You *do* stomp."

"I know. I'm sorry." He laughs and holds the door open for me. His room is neater than I expected. I always picture guys with disgusting bedrooms—mountains of soiled boxer shorts and sweat-stained undershirts, unmade beds with sheets that haven't been changed in weeks, posters of beer bottles and women in neon bikinis, empty soda cans and chip bags, and random bits of model airplanes and discarded video games.

That's what Matt's room looked like. It always grossed me out. I never knew when I might sit on a sauce packet from Taco Bell.

But St. Clair's room is tidy. His bed is made, and there's only one small pile of clothing on the floor. There are no tacky posters, just an antique world map tacked above his desk and two colorful oil paintings above his bed. And books. I've never seen so many books in one bedroom. They're stacked along his walls like towers—thick history books and tattered paperbacks and . . . an *OED*. Just like Bridge.

"I can't believe I know two people crazy enough to own the *OED*."

"Oh, yeah? Who's the other?"

"Bridge. God, is yours *new*?" The spines are crisp and shiny. Bridgette's is a few decades old, and her spines are cracked and splintering.

St. Clair looks embarrassed. *The Oxford English Dictionary* is a thousand bucks new, and even though we've never talked about it, he knows I don't have spending money like the rest of our classmates. It's pretty clear when I order the cheapest thing on the menu every time we eat out. Dad may have wanted to give me a fancy education, but he isn't concerned about my daily expenses. I've asked him twice for a raise in my weekly allowance, but he's refused, saying I need to learn to live within my means.

Which is difficult when he doesn't give me enough means to begin with.

"Whatever happened with her and that band?" he asks, changing the subject. "Is she going to be their drummer?"

"Yeah, their first practice is this weekend."

"It's that one guy's band—Sideburns, right?"

St. Clair knows Toph's name. He's trying to get a rise out of me, so I ignore it. "Yeah. So what do you have for me?"

"It's right here." He hands me a yellow padded envelope from his desk, and my stomach dances like it's my birthday. I rip the package open. A small patch falls to the floor. It's the Canadian flag.

I pick it up. "Um. Thanks?"

He tosses his hat onto his bed and rubs his hair. It flies up in all different directions. "It's for your backpack, so people won't think you're American. Europeans are much more forgiving of Canadians."

I laugh. "Then I love it. Thank you."

"You aren't offended?"

"No, it's perfect."

"I had to order it online, that's why it took so long. Didn't know where I could find one in Paris, sorry." He fishes through a desk drawer and pulls out a safety pin. He takes the tiny maple leaf flag from my hands and carefully pins it to the pocket of my backpack. "There. You're officially Canadian. Try not to abuse your new power."

"Whatever. I'm totally going out tonight."

"Good." He slows down. "You should."

We're both standing still. He's so close to me. His gaze is locked on mine, and my heart pounds painfully in my chest. I step back and look away. Toph. I like Toph, not St. Clair. Why do I have to keep reminding myself of this? St. Clair is taken.

"Did you paint these?" I'm desperate to change the mood. "These above your bed?" I glance back, and he's still staring at me.

He bites his thumbnail before replying. His voice is odd. "No. My mum did."

"Really? Wow, they're good. Really, really . . . good."

"Anna . . ."

"Is this here in Paris?"

"No, it's the street I grew up on. In London."

"Oh."

"Anna . . ."

"Hmm?" I stand with my back to him, trying to examine the paintings. They really are great. I just can't seem to focus. Of course it's not Paris. I should've known—

"That guy. Sideburns. You like him?"

My back squirms. "You've asked me that before."

"What I meant was," he says, flustered. "Your feelings haven't changed? Since you've been here?"

It takes a moment to consider the question. "It's not a matter of how *I* feel," I say at last. "I'm interested, but . . . I don't know if he's still interested in me."

St. Clair edges closer. "Does he still call?"

"Yeah. I mean, not often. But yes."

"Right. Right, well," he says, blinking. "There's your answer."

I look away. "I should go. I'm sure you have plans with Ellie."

"Yes. I mean, no. I mean, I don't know. If you aren't doing any—"

I open his door. "So I'll see you later. Thank you for the Canadian citizenship." I tap the patch on my bag.

St. Clair looks strangely hurt. "No problem. Happy to be of service."

I take the stairs two at a time to my floor. What just happened? One minute we were fine, and the next it was like I couldn't leave fast enough. I need to get out of here. I need to leave the dorm. Maybe I'm not a brave American, but I think I can be a brave Canadian. I grab the *Pariscope* from inside my room and jog downstairs.

I'm going to see Paris. Alone.

chapter thirteen

"*Un place s'il vous plaît.*"

One place, please. I double-checked my pronunciation before stepping up to the box office and sliding over my euros. The woman selling tickets doesn't blink, just rips my ticket in half and hands me the stub. I accept it graciously and stammer my thanks. Inside the theater, an usher examines my stub. She tears it slightly, and I know from watching my friends that I'm supposed to give her a small tip for this useless tradition. I touch the Canadian patch for luck, but I don't need it. The handoff is easy.

I did it. I did it!

My relief is so profound that I hardly notice my feet carve their way into my favorite row. The theater is almost empty. Three girls around my age are in the back, and an elderly couple sits in front of me, sharing a box of candy. Some people are

finicky about going to the theater alone, but I'm not. Because when the lights go down, the only relationship left in the room is the one between the movie and me.

I sink into the springy chair and lose myself in the previews. French commercials are interspersed between them, and I have fun trying to guess what they're for before the product is shown. Two men chase each other across the Great Wall of China to advertise clothing. A scantily clad woman rubs herself against a quacking duck to sell furniture. A techno beat and a dancing silhouette want me to what? Go clubbing? Get drunk?

I have no idea.

And then *Mr. Smith Goes to Washington* begins. James Stewart plays a naive, idealistic man sent into the Senate, where everyone believes they can take advantage of him. They think he'll fail and be driven out, but Stewart shows them all. He's stronger than they gave him credit for, stronger than they are. I like it.

I think about Josh. I wonder what kind of senator his father is.

The dialogue is translated across the bottom of the screen in yellow. The theater is silent, respectful, until the first gag. The Parisians and I laugh together. Two hours speed by, and then I'm blinking in a streetlamp, lost in a comfortable daze, thinking about what I might see tomorrow.

"Going to the movies again tonight?" Dave checks my page number and flips his French textbook open to the chapter about family. As usual, we've paired up for an exercise in conversational skills.

"Yup. *The Texas Chain Saw Massacre.* You know, to get into the holiday spirit." Halloween is this weekend, but I haven't seen any decorations here. That must be an American thing.

"The original or the remake?" Professeur Gillet marches past our desks and Dave quickly adds, *"Je te présente ma famille. Jean-Pierre est . . . l'oncle."*

"Um. What?"

"Quoi," Professeur Gillet corrects. I expect her to linger, but she moves on. Phew.

"Original, of course." But I'm impressed he knew it was remade.

"That's funny, I wouldn't have taken you for a horror fan."

"Why not?" I bristle at the implication. "I appreciate any well-made film."

"Yeah, but most girls are squeamish about that sort of thing."

"What's that supposed to mean?" My voice rises, and Madame Guillotine jerks her head up from across the room. *"Marc est mon . . . frère,"* I say, glancing down at the first French word I see. Brother. Marc is my brother. Whoops. Sorry, Sean.

Dave scratches his freckled nose. "You know. The chick suggests a horror movie to her boyfriend so she can get all scared and cling onto him."

I groan. "Please. I've seen just as many scared boyfriends leave halfway through a movie as scared girlfriends—"

"And how many movies will this make this week anyway, Oliphant? Four? Five?"

Six actually. I saw two on Sunday. I've settled into a routine: school, homework, dinner, movie. I'm slowly making my way across the city, theater by theater.

I shrug, not willing to admit this to him.

"When are you gonna invite me along, huh? Maybe I like scary movies, too."

I pretend to study the family tree in my textbook. This isn't the first time he's hinted at this sort of thing. And Dave is cute, but I don't like him that way. It's hard to take a guy seriously when he still tips over backward in his chair, just to annoy a teacher.

"Maybe I like going alone. Maybe it gives me time to think about my reviews." Which is true, but I refrain from mentioning that usually I'm *not* alone. Sometimes Meredith joins me, sometimes Rashmi and Josh. And, yes, sometimes St. Clair.

"Right. Your reviews." He yanks my spiral notebook out from underneath *Level One French*.

"Hey! Give that back!"

"What's your website again?" Dave flips through the pages as I try to grab it. I don't take notes while watching the films; I'd rather hold off until I've had time to think about them. But I like to jot down my first impressions afterward.

"Like I'd tell you. Give it back."

"What's the deal with these, anyway? Why don't you go to the movies for fun, like a normal person?"

"It *is* fun. And I've told you before, it's good practice. And I can't see classics like these on the big screen back home." Not to mention I can't see them in such glorious silence. In Paris, no one talks during a movie. Heaven help the person who brings in a crunchy snack or crinkly cellophane.

"Why do you need to practice? It's not like it's hard or something."

"Yeah? I'd like to see you write a six-hundred-word review about one. 'I liked it. It was cool. There were explosions.'" I snatch again at my notebook, but he holds it above his head.

He laughs. "Five stars for explosions."

"Give. That. BACK!"

A shadow falls over us. Madame Guillotine hovers above, waiting for us to continue. The rest of the class is staring. Dave lets go of the notebook, and I shrink back.

"Um . . . *très bien, David,*" I say.

"When you 'ave finished zis fascinating dee-scussion, plizz return to ze task at 'and." Her eyes narrow. "And *deux* pages about *vos familles, en français, pour lundi matin.*"

We nod sheepishly, and her heels clip away. "For *lundi matin?* What the heck does that mean?" I hiss to Dave.

Madame Guillotine doesn't break stride. "Monday morning, Mademoiselle Oliphant."

At lunch, I slam my food tray down on the table. Lentil soup spills over the side of my bowl, and my plum rolls away. St. Clair catches it. "What's eating you?" he asks.

"French."

"Not going well?"

"Not going well."

He places the plum back on my tray and smiles. "You'll get the hang of it."

"Easy for you to say, Monsieur Bilingual."

His smile fades. "Sorry. You're right, that was unfair. I forget sometimes."

I stir my lentils aggressively. "Professeur Gillet always makes me feel stupid. I'm not stupid."

"Of course you aren't. It'd be mad for anyone to expect fluency. It takes time to learn anything, especially a language."

"I'm just so tired of going out there"—I gesture at the windows— "and being helpless."

St. Clair is surprised at my suggestion. "You aren't helpless. You go out every night, often on your own. That's a far cry from when you arrived. Don't be so hard on yourself."

"Hmph."

"Hey." He scoots closer. "Remember what Professeur Cole said when she was talking about the lack of translated novels in America? She said it's important to expose ourselves to other cultures, other situations. And that's exactly what you're doing. You're going out, and you're testing the waters. You ought to be proud of yourself. Screw French class, that means sod-all."

I crack a smile at his Briticism. Speaking of translation. "Yeah, but Professeur Cole was talking about books, not real life. There's a big difference."

"Is there? What about film? Aren't you the one who's always going on about cinema as a reflection of life? Or was that some other famous film critic I know?"

"Shut up. That's different."

St. Clair laughs, knowing he's caught me. "See? You ought to spend less time worrying about French, and more time . . ." He trails off, attention snagged by something behind me. His expression is of growing revulsion.

I turn to find Dave, kneeling on the cafeteria floor behind

us. His head is bowed, and he thrusts a small plate in the air before me. "Allow me to present this éclair with my humblest apologizes."

My face burns. "What are you doing?"

Dave looks up and grins. "Sorry about the extra assignment. That was my fault."

I'm speechless. When I don't take the dessert, he rises and delivers it in front of me with a grand flourish. Everyone is staring. He nabs a chair from the table behind us and wedges himself between St. Clair and me.

St. Clair is incredulous. "Make yourself at home, David."

Dave doesn't seem to hear him. He dips his finger in the sticky chocolate icing and licks it off. Are his hands clean? "So. Tonight. *Texas Chain Saw Massacre*. I'll never believe you aren't afraid of horror films if you don't let me take you."

Oh my God. Dave is NOT asking me out in front of St. Clair. St. Clair hates Dave; I remember him saying it before we saw *It Happened One Night*. "Uh . . . sorry." I grasp for an excuse. "But I'm not going. Anymore. Something came up."

"Come on. Nothing could be *that* important on a Friday night." He pinches my arm, and I glance desperately at St. Clair.

"Physics project," he cuts in, glaring at Dave's hand. "Last minute. Loads to do. We're partners."

"You have all weekend to do homework. Loosen up, Oliphant. Live a little."

"Actually," St. Clair says, "it sounds like Anna has quite a bit of additional work to do this weekend. Thanks to you."

Dave finally turns around to face St. Clair. They exchange scowls.

"I'm sorry," I say. And I mean it. I feel awful for turning him down, especially in front of everyone. He's a nice guy, despite what St. Clair thinks.

But Dave looks at St. Clair again. "It's cool," he says after a moment. "I get it."

"What?" I'm confused.

"I didn't realize . . ." Dave motions between St. Clair and me.

"No! No. There's nothing. There. I mean it, we'll see something soon. I'm just busy tonight. With the physics thing."

Dave looks annoyed, but he shrugs his shoulders. "No biggie. Hey, you going to the party tomorrow night?"

Nate is throwing a Halloween bash for Résidence Lambert. I wasn't planning to attend, but I lie to make him feel better. "Yeah, probably. I'll see you there."

He stands up. "Cool. I'm holding you to that."

"Right. Sure. Thanks for the éclair!" I call after him.

"You're welcome, beautiful."

Beautiful. He called me beautiful! But wait. I don't like Dave.

Do I like Dave?

"Wanker," St. Clair says, the moment he's out of earshot.

"Don't be rude."

He stares at me with an unfathomable expression. "You weren't complaining when I made an excuse for you."

I push the éclair away. "He put me on the spot, that's all."

"You ought to thank me."

"*Thank you*," I say sarcastically. I'm aware of the others staring at us. Josh clears his throat and points at my finger-smudged dessert. "You gonna eat that?" he asks.

"Be my guest."

St. Clair stands so suddenly that his chair clatters over.

"Where are you going?" Mer asks.

"Nowhere." He stalks away, leaving us in surprised silence. After a moment, Rashmi leans forward. She raises her dark eyebrows. "You know, Josh and I saw them fighting a couple nights ago."

"Who? St. Clair and Dave?" Mer asks.

"No, St. Clair and Ellie. That's what this is about, you know."

"It is?" I ask.

"Yeah, he's been on edge all week," Rashmi says.

I think about it. "That's true. I've heard him pacing his room. He never used to do that." It's not like I make a point of listening, but now that I know that St. Clair lives above me, I can't *help* but notice his comings and goings.

Josh gives me a weird look.

"Where did you see them?" Mer asks Rashmi.

"In front of the Cluny *métro*. We were gonna say hi, but when we saw their expressions, we went the other way. Definitely not a conversation I wanted to interrupt."

"What were they fighting about?" Mer asks.

"Dunno. Couldn't hear them."

"It's *her*. She's so different now."

Rashmi frowns. "She thinks she's so much better than us, now that she's at Parsons."

"And the way she dresses," Mer says, with an unusual bitter streak. "Like she thinks she's actually Parisian."

"She was always that way." Rashmi huffs.

Josh is still quiet. He polishes off the éclair, wipes the white fluff from his fingers, and pulls out his sketchbook. The way he focuses on it, deflecting Meredith and Rashmi's conversation, is . . . purposeful. I get the feeling he knows more about St. Clair's situation than he's letting on. Do guys talk about things like that with each other? Could it be possible?

Are St. Clair and Ellie breaking up?

chapter fourteen

*D*on't y'all think it's kind of a cliché to have a picnic in a graveyard on Halloween?"

The five of us—Mer, Rashmi, Josh, St. Clair, and I—are traipsing through the Cimetière du Père-Lachaise, located on a hillside overlooking Paris. It's like a miniature city itself. Wide pathways act as roads through neighborhoods of elaborate tombs. They remind me of tiny Gothic mansions with their arched doorways and statuary and stained-glass windows. A stone wall with guardsmen and iron gates runs the perimeter. Mature chestnuts stretch their branches overhead and wave their last remaining golden leaves.

It's a quieter city than Paris, but no less impressive.

"Hey, did y'all hear Anna say 'y'all'?" Josh asks.

"Oh my God, I so did not."

"You so did," Rashmi says. She adjusts the pack on her shoulders and follows Mer down yet another path. I'm glad my friends know their way around, because I'm lost. "I told you you've got an accent."

"It's a cemetery, not a graveyard," St. Clair says.

"There's a difference?" I ask, thankful for an opportunity to ignore The Couple.

"A cemetery is a plot of land set specifically aside for burial, while a graveyard is always located in a churchyard. Of course, now the words are practically interchangeable, so it doesn't *really* matter—"

"You know more useless crap, St. Clair. Good thing you're so darn cute," Josh says.

"I think it's interesting," Mer says.

St. Clair smiles. "At least 'cemetery' sounds classier. And you must admit—this place is pretty classy. Or, I'm sorry." He turns back to me. "Would you rather be at the Lambert bash? I hear Dave Higgenbottom is bringing his beer bong."

"Higgenbaum."

"That's what I said. Higgenbum."

"Oh, leave him alone. Besides, by the time this place closes, we'll still have plenty of time to party." I roll my eyes at this last word. None of us have plans to attend, despite what I told Dave yesterday at lunch.

St. Clair nudges me with a tall thermos. "Perhaps you're upset because he won't have the opportunity to woo you with his astonishing knowledge of urban street racing."

I laugh. "Cut it out."

"And I hear he has exquisite taste in film. Maybe he'll take you to a midnight showing of *Scooby-Doo 2*."

I whack St. Clair with my bag, and he dodges aside, laughing.

"Aha! Here it is!" Mer calls out, having located the appropriate patch of greenery. She unrolls a blanket onto the small lawn while Rashmi and I unpack tiny apples and prosciutto sandwiches and stinky cheeses from our backpacks. Josh and St. Clair chase each other around the nearby monuments. They remind me of the little French schoolboys I see in our neighborhood. All they need are the matching woolen sweaters.

Mer pours everyone coffee from St. Clair's thermos, and I sip happily, enjoying the pleasant warmth that spreads throughout my body. I used to think coffee was bitter and disgusting, but like everyone else, I'm up to several cups a day. We tear into the food and, like magic, the guys are back. Josh sits cross-legged next to Rashmi, while St. Clair scoots between Meredith and me.

"You have leaves in your hair." Mer giggles and pulls one of the brown skeletons from St. Clair's locks. He takes it from her, crunches it to dust, and blows it into her curls. They laugh, and my gut twinges.

"Maybe you should put on The Hat," I say. He asked me to carry it before we left. I chuck my bag into his lap, perhaps a little too hard. St. Clair *oofs* and jerks forward.

"Watch it." Josh bites into a pink apple and talks through a full mouth. "He has parts down there you don't have."

"Ooo, parts," I say. "Intriguing. Tell me more."

Josh smiles sadly. "Sorry. Privileged information. Only people with parts can know about said parts."

St. Clair shakes the rest of the leaves from his hair and puts on The Hat. Rashmi makes a face at him. "Really? Today? In public?" she asks.

"*Every* day," he says. "As long as you're with me."

She snorts. "So what's Ellen doing tonight?"

"Ugh. Ellie's attending some terrible costume party."

"You don't like costume parties?" Mer asks.

"I don't do costumes."

"Just hats," Rashmi says.

"I didn't realize anyone outside of SOAP was celebrating Halloween," I say.

"Few people are," Josh says. "The shopkeepers tried to turn it into a commercial thing years ago. It didn't catch on. But give a college chick the chance to dress up like a slutty nurse, and she's gonna take it."

St. Clair lobs a chunk of *chèvre* at Josh's head, and it smacks his cheek. "Arse. She's *not* going as a slutty nurse."

"Just a regular one?" I ask innocently. "With a low-cut dress and really big breasts?"

Josh and Rashmi crack up, and St. Clair tugs The Hat down over his eyes. "Ughhh, I hate you all."

"Hey." Meredith sounds hurt. "I didn't say anything."

"Ughhh, I hate you all but Mer."

A small group of American tourists hovers behind us. They look confused. A bearded guy in his twenties opens his mouth to speak, but Rashmi interrupts him. "Jim Morrison is that way."

She points down the path. Bearded guy smiles in relief, thanks her, and they move on.

"How'd you know what they wanted?" I ask.

"It's what they always want."

"When they *should* be looking for Victor Noir," Josh says. Everyone else laughs.

"Who?" It's frustrating being in the dark.

"Victor Noir. He was a journalist shot by Pierre Bonaparte," St. Clair says, as if that explains anything. He pulls The Hat up off his eyes. "The statue on his grave is supposed to help . . . fertility."

"His wang is rubbed shiny," Josh elaborates. "For luck."

"Why are we talking about parts again?" Mer asks. "Can't we ever talk about anything else?"

"Really?" I ask. "Shiny wang?"

"Very," St. Clair says.

"Now that's something I've gotta see." I gulp my coffee dregs, wipe the bread crumbs from my mouth, and hop up. "Where's Victor?"

"Allow me." St. Clair springs to his feet and takes off. I chase after him. He cuts through a stand of bare trees, and I crash through the twigs behind him. We're both laughing when we hit the pathway and run smack into a guard. He frowns at us from underneath his military-style cap. St. Clair gives an angelic smile and a small shrug. The guard shakes his head but allows us to pass.

St. Clair gets away with everything.

We stroll with exaggerated calm, and he points out an area

occupied with people snapping pictures. We hang back and wait our turn. A scrawny black cat darts out from behind an altar strewn with roses and wine bottles, and rushes into the bushes.

"Well. That was sufficiently creepy. Happy Halloween."

"Did you know this place is home to three *thousand* cats?" St. Clair asks.

"Sure. It's filed away in my brain under 'Felines, Paris.' "

He laughs. The tourists move on to the next photo opportunity, and we're both smiling as we approach Victor Noir. His statue is life-size and lying flat on the ground above his tomb. His eyes are closed, his top hat beside him. And despite the fact that his gray-green patina is clothed, his pants have a remarkable bulge that has, indeed, been stroked to a shiny bronze.

"If I touch it, do I get another wish?" I ask, remembering Point Zéro.

"Nope. Victor deals strictly in fertility."

"Go on. Rub it."

St. Clair backs into another grave. "No, thank you." He laughs again. "I don't need that kind of problem." My own laughter catches in my throat as I get his meaning. Shake it off, Anna. That shouldn't bother you. Don't let him see how it bothers you.

"Well. If you won't touch him, I will. I'm not in any danger of *that*." I lower my voice to a mock whisper. "You know, I've heard you *actually have to have sex* to get pregnant."

I see the question immediately pop into his head. Crap. Maybe I was too hasty with my joke. St. Clair looks half embarrassed, half curious. "So, er, you're a virgin, then?"

ARGH! ME AND MY BIG MOUTH.

My overwhelming desire is to lie, but the truth comes out. "I've never met anyone I cared about that much. I mean, I've never *dated* anyone I cared about that much." I blush and pet Victor. "I have a rule."

"Elaborate."

The statue is still warm from the previous visitors. "I ask myself, if the worst happened—if I *did* get knocked up—would I be embarrassed to tell my child who his father was? If the answer is anywhere even remotely close to yes, then there's no way."

He nods slowly. "That's a good rule."

I realize I'm resting my hand on Victor's victor and yank it away.

"Wait wait wait." St. Clair pulls out his phone. "One more time, for posterity."

I stick out my tongue and hold the ridiculous pose. He takes a picture. "Brilliant, that'll be what I see every time you call—" His cell rings, and he starts. "Spooky."

"It's Victor's ghost, wanting to know why you won't touch him."

"Just me mum. Hold on."

"*Woooooo, stroke me, St. Clair.*"

He answers, trying to keep a straight face, as Meredith and Rashmi and Josh trudge up behind us. They're lugging the remains of our picnic.

"Thanks for ditching us," Rashmi says.

"It's not like we didn't tell you where we were going," I say.

Josh grabs the statue's privates. "I think this is seven years' bad luck."

Mer sighs. "Joshua Wasserstein, what would your mother say?"

"She'd be proud that the Fine Institute of Learning she's sent me to is teaching me such refined manners." He leans over and licks Victor.

Mer and Rashmi and I squeal.

"You are *so* getting oral herpes." I whip out my hand sanitizer and squeeze a glob into my hands. "Seriously, you should put some of this on your lips."

Josh shakes his head. "You are so neurotic. Do you take that everywhere?"

"You know," Rashmi says. "I've heard if you use too much of that stuff, you can actually desensitize yourself to germs and get *more* sick."

I freeze. "What? No."

"HA!" Josh says.

"Ohmygod, are you okay?"

At the sound of Mer's alarm, I quickly turn my head.

St. Clair has fallen against a tomb. It's the only thing keeping him from collapsing to the ground. The four of us rush to his side. He's still holding the phone to his ear, but he's not listening anymore. We talk over each other. "What happened? Are you okay? What is it?"

He won't answer us. He won't look up.

We exchange worried glances. No, terrified. Something is *really* wrong. Josh and I lower him to the ground before he falls.

St. Clair looks up, surprised to find us holding on to him. His face is white.

"My mum."

"What happened?" I ask.

"She's dying."

chapter fifteen

St. Clair is drunk.

His face is buried between my thighs. Under favorable circumstances, this would be quite exciting. Considering he's minutes away from vomiting, it's less than attractive. I push his head toward my knees into a slightly less awkward position, and he moans. It's the first time I've touched his hair. It's soft, like Seany's when he was a baby.

Josh and St. Clair showed up fifteen minutes ago, stinking of cigarettes and alcohol. Since neither of them smoke, they'd obviously been to a bar. "Sorry. He said wehadtuh comeup 'ere." Josh dragged his friend's limp body inside my room. "Wouldn't shuttup about tit. Tit. Ha ha."

St. Clair burbled in heavy, slurred British. "Me dad issa

bastard. I'm gonna kill 'im. Gonna kill 'im, I'm sooo pissed."
Then his head rolled, and his chin smacked violently against his
chest. Alarmed, I guided him to my bed and propped him up
against the side for support.

Josh stared at the picture of Seany on my wall. "Tit," he said.

"Ahhh-nuhhh, he's an arse. I'm *serious*." St. Clair widened his
eyes for emphasis.

"I know, I know he is." Even though I didn't know. "Will you
stop that?" I snapped at Josh. He stood on my bed with his nose
pressed against Sean's picture. "Is he okay?"

"His mom is dying. I dontthinkhe's OKAY." Josh stumbled
down and reached for my phone. "Told Rashmi I'd call her."

"His mother is not *you-know-what*. How can you say that?" I
turned back to St. Clair. "She'll be fine. Your mom is fine, you
hear me?"

St. Clair belched.

"Jesus." I was so not equipped for this type of situation.

"Cancer." He hung his head. "She can't have cancer."

"Rashmi iss me," Josh said into my phone. "Mer? Put Rashmi
on. Iss emergency."

"It's not an emergency!" I yelled. "They're just drunk."

Seconds later, Meredith pounded on my door, and I let her
in. "How'd you know we're here?" Josh's forehead creased in
bewilderment. "Where's Rashmi?"

"I heard you through the wall, idiot. And you called my
phone, not hers." She held up her cell and then dialed Rashmi,
who arrived a minute later. They just stood there staring, while

St. Clair babbled and Josh continued to look shocked by their sudden appearance. My small room felt even smaller stuffed with five bodies.

Finally, Mer knelt down. "Is he okay?" She felt St. Clair's forehead, but he smacked her hand away. She looked hurt.

"I'm fine. My father's an arse, and my mum is dying and—oh my God, I'm so pissed." St. Clair looked at me again. His eyes were glassy like black marbles. "Pissed. Pissed. Pissed."

"We know you're pissed at your dad," I said. "It's okay. You're right, he's a jerk." I mean what was I supposed to say? He just found out his mother has cancer.

"*Pissed* is British for 'drunk,'" Mer said.

"Oh," I said. "Well. You're definitely that, too."

Meanwhile, The Couple was fighting. "Where have you been?" Rashmi asked. "You said you'd be home three hours ago!"

Josh rolled his eyes. "Out. We've been out. Someone had to help him—"

"And you call that helping? He's completely wasted. Catatonic. And you! God, you smell like car exhaust and armpits—"

"He couldn't drink alone."

"You were supposed to be watching out for him! What if something happened?"

"Beer. Liquor. Thatsswhat happened. Don't be such a prude, Rash."

"Fuck you," Rashmi said. "Seriously, Josh. Go fuck yourself."

He lunged, and Mer shoved him back onto my bed. The weight

of his body hitting the mattress rattled St. Clair, and his head fell forward again, chin hitting chest with another disturbing *smack*. Rashmi stormed out. A small crowd had gathered outside in the hallway, and she shouted further obscenities as she fought her way through them. Mer chased behind—"Rashmi! RASHMI!"— and my door slammed shut.

And that was the moment St. Clair's head landed between my thighs.

Breathe, Anna. Breathe.

Josh appears to be passed out. Fine. Good. One less boy for me to deal with.

I should probably get St. Clair some water. Isn't that what you're supposed to give drunk people? So they don't get alcohol poisoning or something? I ease him off my legs, and he grabs my feet. "I'll be right back," I say. "I promise."

He snuffles. Oh, no. He's not going to cry, is he? Because even though it's sweet when guys cry, I am so not prepared for this. Girl Scouts didn't teach me what to do with emotionally unstable drunk boys. I grab a bottle of water from my fridge and squat down. I hold up his head—the second time I've touched his hair—and angle the bottle in front of his lips. "Drink."

He shakes his head slowly. "If I drink any more, I'll puke."

"It's not alcohol. It's water." I tilt the bottle, and it spills into his mouth and dribbles down his chin. He takes the bottle and then drops it. Water pours across my floor.

"Ohhh no," he whispers. "I'm sorry, Anna. I'm sorry."

"It's okay." And he looks so sad that I lie down next to

him. The puddle soaks into the butt of my jeans. *Ack.* "What happened?"

St. Clair sighs. It's deep and exhausted. "He's not letting me visit my mum."

"What? What do you mean?"

"It's what my father does, what he's always done. It's his way of staying in control."

"I don't und—"

"He's jealous. That she loves me more than she loves him. So he's not letting me visit her."

My mind spins. That doesn't make any sense, none at all. "How can he do that? Your mom is sick. She'll need chemo, she *needs* you there."

"He doesn't want me to see her until Thanksgiving break."

"But that's a month away! She could be—" I stop myself. The moment I finish the sentence in my head, I feel sick. But there's no way. People my age do not have parents who die. She'll have chemotherapy, and of course it'll work. She'll be fine. "So what are you gonna do? Fly to San Francisco anyway?"

"My father would murder me."

"So?" I'm outraged. "You'd still get to see her!"

"You don't understand. My father would be very, very angry." The deliberate way he says this sends a chill down my spine.

"But . . . wouldn't she ask your dad to send for you? I mean, he couldn't say no to her, could he? Not when she's . . . sick?"

"She won't disobey my father."

Disobey. Like she's a child. It's rapidly becoming clear why

St. Clair never talks about his father. Mine might be self-absorbed, but he'd never keep me away from Mom. I feel awful. Guilty. My problems are so insignificant in comparison. I mean, my dad sent me to France. Boo-freaking-hoo.

"Anna?"

"Yeah?"

He pauses. "Never mind."

"What?"

"Nothing."

But his tone is definitely not *nothing*. I turn to him, and his eyes are closed. His skin is pale and tired. "What?" I ask again, sitting up. St. Clair opens his eyes, noticing I've moved. He struggles, trying to sit up, too, and I help him. When I pull away, he clutches my hand to stop me.

"I like you," he says.

My body is rigid.

"And I don't mean as a friend."

It feels like I'm swallowing my tongue. "Uh. Um. What about—?" I pull my hand away from his. The weight of her name hangs heavy and unspoken.

"It's not right. It hasn't been right, not since I met you." His eyes close again, and his body sways.

He's drunk. He's just drunk.

Calm down, Anna. He's drunk, and he's going through a crisis. There is NO WAY he knows what he's talking about right now. So what do I do? Oh my God, what am I supposed to do?

"Do you like me?" St. Clair asks. And he looks at me with those big brown eyes—which, okay, are a bit red from the drinking and maybe from some crying—and my heart breaks.

Yes, St. Clair. I like you.

But I can't say it aloud, because he's my friend. And friends don't let other friends make drunken declarations and expect them to act upon them the next day.

Then again . . . it's St. Clair. Beautiful, perfect, wonderful—

And great. That's just great.

He threw up on me.

chapter sixteen

$\mathcal{G}$'m mopping up his mess with a towel when there's a knock on my door. I open it with my elbows to keep the vomit from touching my doorknob.

It's Ellie. I nearly drop my towel. "Oh."

Slutty nurse. I don't believe it. Tiny white button-up dress, red crosses across the nipples. Cleavage city.

"Anna, I'm soooo sorry," St. Clair moans behind me, and she rushes to his side.

"Ohmygod, St. Clair! Are you okay?" Again, her husky voice startles me. As if the nurse getup weren't enough to make me feel completely juvenile and inadequate.

"'Course he's not okay," Josh grumbles from the bed. "He just puked on Anna."

Josh is awake?

Ellie smacks Josh's feet, which hang over the edge of my bed. "Get up. Help me move him to his room."

"I can get up by my bloody self." St. Clair tries to push himself up, and Ellie and I reach out to steady him. She glares at me, and I back up.

"How'd you know he was here?" I ask.

"Meredith called, but I was already on my way. I'd just gotten his message. He called a few hours ago, but I didn't get it, because I was getting ready for this stupid party." She gestures at her costume, upset with herself. "I should have been here." She brushes St. Clair's hair from his forehead. "It's okay, babe. I'm here now."

"Ellie?" St. Clair sounds confused, as if he's just noticed her. "Anna? Why is Ellen here? She's not supposed to be here."

His girlfriend shoots me a hateful look, and I shrug with embarrassment. "He's really, *really* drunk," I say.

She thwacks Josh again, and he rolls off the bed. "All right, all right!" Amazingly, he stands and pulls St. Clair off the floor. They balance him between their shoulders. "Get the door," she says sharply. I open it, and they stagger out.

St. Clair looks back. "Anna. Anna, I'm sorry."

"It's okay. I've already cleaned it up. It's fine, it's not a big deal."

"No. About everything else."

Ellie's head jerks back to me, angry and confused, but I don't care. He looks so awful. I wish they'd put him down. He could sleep in my bed tonight; I could stay with Mer. But they're already maneuvering him into the rickety elevator. They push aside the metal grate and squish inside. St. Clair stares at me sadly as the door shuts.

"She'll be fine! Your mother will be fine!"

I don't know if he hears me. The elevator creaks upward. I watch it until it disappears.

Sunday, November 1, All Saints' Day. Oddly enough, this is the actual day that Parisians visit cemeteries. I'm told people are dropping by the graves of loved ones and leaving flowers and personal tokens.

The thought makes me ill. I hope St. Clair doesn't remember today is a holiday.

When I wake up, I stop by Meredith's. She's already been to his room, and either he's out cold or he's not accepting visitors. Most likely both. "It's best to let him sleep," she says. And I'm sure she's right, but I can't help but tune my ear to the floor above. The first movements begin in the late afternoon, but even these are muffled. Slow shuffles and laborious thuds.

He wouldn't come out for dinner. Josh, who is cross and bleary, says he checked in with him on his way here—a pizza place, where we always eat on Sunday night—and St. Clair didn't want company. Josh and Rashmi have patched things up. She looks smug to see him suffering through a hangover.

My emotions are conflicted. I'm worried for St. Clair's mother, and I'm worried for St. Clair, but I'm also furious with his father. And I can't focus on anything for more than a second before my mind whirls back to this:

St. Clair likes me. As more than a friend.

I felt truth behind his words, but how can I overlook the fact that he was drunk? Absolutely, positively, one hundred and ten percent smashed. And as much as I want to see him, to be assured with my own eyes that he's still alive, I don't know what I'd say. Do we talk about it? Or do I act like it never happened?

He needs friendship right now, not relationship drama. Which is why it's *really* crappy that it's become a lot harder to kid myself that St. Clair's attention hasn't been as flattering—or as welcome—as it has.

Toph calls around midnight. We haven't talked on the phone in weeks, but with everything happening here, I'm distracted the entire time. I just want to go back to bed. It's too confusing. Everything is too confusing.

St. Clair was absent again at breakfast. And I think he's not even coming to class today (and who could blame him?), when he appears in English, fifteen minutes late. I worry that Professeur Cole will yell at him, but the faculty must have been notified of the situation, because she doesn't say a word. She just gives him a pitying look and pushes ahead with our lesson. "So why aren't Americans interested in translated novels? Why are so few foreign works published in English every year?"

I try to meet St. Clair's gaze, but he stares down at his copy of *Balzac and the Little Chinese Seamstress*. Or rather, stares through it. He's pale, practically translucent.

"Well," she continues. "It's often suggested that as a culture, we're only interested in immediate gratification. Fast food. Self-checkout. Downloadable music, movies, books. Instant coffee, instant rebates, instant messaging. Instant weight loss! Shall I go on?"

The class laughs, but St. Clair is quiet. I watch him nervously. Dark stubble is beginning to shadow his face. I hadn't realized he needed to shave so often.

"Foreign novels are less action-oriented. They have a different pace; they're more reflective. They challenge us to *look* for the story, find the story *within* the story. Take *Balzac*. Whose story is this? The narrator's? The little seamstress's? China's?"

I want to reach out and squeeze his hand and tell him everything will be okay. He shouldn't be here. I can't imagine what I'd do if I were in his situation. His dad should have pulled him from school. He should be in California.

Professeur Cole taps the novel's cover. "Dai Sijie, born and raised in China. Moved to France. He wrote *Balzac* in French, but set the story in his homeland. And then it was translated into English. So how many steps away from us is that? Is it the one, French to English? Or do we count the first translation, the one the author only made in his mind, from Chinese to French? What do we lose each time the story is reinterpreted?"

I'm only half listening to her. After class, Meredith and Rashmi and I walk silently with St. Clair to calculus and exchange worried glances when he's not looking. Which I'm sure he knows we're doing anyway. Which makes me feel worse.

My suspicions about the faculty are confirmed when Professeur Babineaux takes him aside before class begins. I can't follow the entire conversation, but I hear him ask if St. Clair would rather spend the hour in the nurse's office. St. Clair accepts. As soon as he leaves, Amanda Spitterton-Watts is in my face. "What's with *St. Clair?*"

"Nothing." Like I'd tell her.

She flips her hair, and I notice with satisfaction that a strand gets stuck to her lip gloss. "Because Steve said he and Josh were *totally* wasted Saturday night. He saw them staggering through the Halloween party, and St. Clair was *freaking out* about his dad."

"Well, he heard wrong."

"Steve said St. Clair wanted to *kill* his father."

"Steve is full of shit," Rashmi interrupts. "And where were you on Saturday, Amanda? So trashed you had to rely on Steve for the play-by-play?"

But this shuts her up only temporarily. By lunch, it's clear the whole school knows. I'm not sure who spilled—if it was the teachers, or if Steve or one of his bonehead friends remembered something else St. Clair said—but the entire student body is buzzing. When St. Clair finally arrives in the cafeteria, it's like a scene from a bad teen movie. Conversation screeches to a halt. Drinks are paused halfway to lips.

St. Clair stops in the doorway, assesses the situation, and

marches back out. The four of us chase after him. We find him pushing through the school doors, heading to the courtyard. "I don't want to talk about it." His back is to us.

"Then we won't talk about it," Josh says. "Let's go out for lunch."

"Crêpes?" Mer asks. They're St. Clair's favorite.

"That sounds amazing," Rashmi chimes in.

"I'm starving," Josh says. "Come on." We move forward, hoping he'll follow. He does, and it's all we can do not to sigh in relief. Mer and Rashmi lead the way, while Josh falls back with St. Clair. Josh talks about little nothings—a new pen he bought for their art class, the rap song his neighbor keeps blasting about sweaty rumps—and it helps. At least, St. Clair shows minimal signs of life. He mumbles something in reply.

I hover between the groups. I know it's goody-goody of me, but as concerned as I am about St. Clair, I'm also worried about ditching. I don't want to get in trouble. I glance back at SOAP, and Josh shoots me a look that says, *The school won't care today.*

I hope he's right.

Our favorite *crêperie* is only minutes away, and my fear of skipping school eases as I watch the crêpe man ladle the batter onto the griddle. I order mine the way I always do here, by pointing at the picture of a banana and Nutella crêpe and saying please. The man pours the warm chocolate-hazelnut spread over the thin, pancakelike crêpe, folds the banana in, and then drizzles more Nutella on top. As a final flourish, he adds a scoop of vanilla ice cream. Real vanilla, which is tan with black flecks.

I moan as I sink into the first bite. Warm and gooey and chocolaty and perfect.

"You have Nutella on your chin," Rashmi says, pointing with her fork.

"Mmm," I reply.

"It's a good look," Josh says. "Like a little soul patch."

I dip my finger in the chocolate and paint on a mustache. "Better?"

"Maybe if you didn't just give yourself a Hitler," Rashmi says.

To my surprise, St. Clair gives a snort. I'm encouraged. I redip and paint one side up in a swirl.

"You're getting it wrong," Josh says. "Come here." He dabs his finger in the edge of my sauce and adds the other half carefully, with his steady artist's hand, and then touches up my half. I look at my reflection in the restaurant's glass and find myself with a massive, curly mustache. They laugh and clap, and Mer snaps a picture.

The men in elaborately tied scarves sitting at the table beside us look disgusted, so I pretend to twirl the ends of my Nutella mustache. The others are cracking up, and finally, *finally* St. Clair gives the teeniest of teeny smiles.

It's a wonderful sight.

I wipe the chocolate from my face and smile back. He shakes his head. The others launch into a discussion of weird facial hair—Rashmi has an uncle who once shaved off all of his hair except what grew around the edge his face—and St. Clair leans over to speak with me. His face is close to mine, and his eyes are hollow. His voice is scratchy. "About the other night——"

"Forget about it, it wasn't a big deal," I say. "It cleaned right up."

"What cleaned right up?"

Whoops. "Nothing."

"Did I break something?" He looks confused.

"No! You didn't break anything. You just, kind of, you know . . ." I mime it.

St. Clair hangs his head and groans. "I'm sorry, Anna. I know how clean you keep your room."

I look away, embarrassed to be called out on this. "It's okay. Really."

"Did I at least hit the sink? Your shower?"

"It was on the floor. And my legs. Just a little bit!" I add, seeing the horrified expression on his face.

"I vomited *on your legs?*"

"It's okay! I'd totally have done the same if I were in your situation." The words are out before I have a chance to stop them. And I was trying so hard not to mention it. His face is pained, but he passes by this subject to one equally excruciating.

"Did I . . ." St. Clair glances at the others, ensuring they're still distracted by facial hair. They are. He scoots his chair even closer and lowers his voice. "Did I say anything peculiar to you? That night?"

Uh-oh. "Peculiar?"

"It's just . . . I only vaguely remember being in your room. But I could have sworn we had a conversation about . . . something."

My heart beats faster, and it's hard to breathe. He remembers. Sort of. What does that mean? What should I say? As anxious as I am for answers, I'm not prepared for this conversation. I bide for more time. "About what?"

He's uncomfortable. "Did I say anything odd about . . . our friendship?"

And there it is.

"Or my girlfriend?"

And there that is. I take a long look at him. Dark undereye circles. Unwashed hair. Defeated shoulders. He's so unhappy, so unlike himself. I won't be the one to add to his misery, no matter how badly I want the truth. I can't ask him. Because if he likes me, he's not in any state to begin a relationship. Or deal with the breakup of an old one. And if he *doesn't* like me, then I'd probably lose his friendship. Things would be too weird.

And right now St. Clair needs friendship.

I keep my face blank but sincere. "No. We talked about your mom. That's all."

It's the right answer. He looks relieved.

chapter seventeen

he *pâtisserie* has thick planks of creaky hardwood and a chandelier draped with tinkly strings of topaz crystals. They glow like drops of honey. The women behind the counter lay extravagant cakes into brown-and-white-striped boxes and tie each package with turquoise ribbon and a silver bell. There's a long line, but everyone here is patiently basking in the ambience.

Mer and I wait between tiered displays as tall as we are. One is a tree made from *macarons*, round sandwich cookies with crusts as fragile as eggshells and fillings so moist and flavorful that I swoon on sight. The other is an arrangement of miniature cakes, *gâteaux*, glazed with almond frosting and pressed with sugared pansies.

Our conversation is back on St. Clair. He's all we talk about anymore. "I'm just afraid they'll kick him out," I say, on tiptoe. I'm trying to peek inside the glass case at the front of the line, but a man in pinstripes carrying a wiggling puppy blocks my view. There are several dogs inside the shop today, which isn't unusual for Paris.

Mer shakes her head, and her curls bounce from underneath her knitted hat. Unlike St. Clair's, hers is robin's egg blue and very respectable.

I like St. Clair's better.

"He won't be kicked out," she says. "Josh hasn't been expelled, and he's been skipping classes for a lot longer. And the head would never expel someone whose mother is . . . you know."

She's not doing well. Cervical cancer. Stage 2B. An advanced stage.

Words I never want to hear associated with someone I love— external radiation therapy, chemotherapy—are now a daily part of St. Clair's life. Susan, his mother, started treatments one week after Halloween. His father is in California, driving her five days a week to radiation therapy and once a week to chemo.

St. Clair is here.

I want to kill his father. His parents have lived separately for years, but his father won't let his mother get a divorce. And he keeps mistresses in Paris and in London, while Susan lives alone in San Francisco. Every few months, his father will visit her. Stay for a few nights. Reestablish dominance or whatever it is he holds over her. And then he leaves again.

But now *he's* the one watching her, while St. Clair suffers six thousand miles away. The whole situation makes me so sick I can hardly bear to think about it. Obviously, St. Clair hasn't been himself these last few weeks. He's ditching school, and his grades are dropping. He doesn't come to breakfast anymore, and he eats every dinner with Ellie. Apart from class and lunch, where he sits cold and stonelike beside me, the only times I see him are the mornings I wake him up for school.

Meredith and I take turns. If we don't pound on his door, he won't show up at all.

The *pâtisserie* door opens and a chilly wind whips through the shop. The chandelier sways like gelatin. "I feel so helpless," I say. "I wish there was something I could do."

Mer shivers and rubs her arms. Her rings are made of fine glass today. They look like spun sugar. "I know. Me too. And I still can't believe his dad isn't letting him visit her for Thanksgiving."

"He's not?" I'm shocked. "When did this happen?" And why did Mer know about it and not me?

"Since his dad heard about his dropping grades. Josh told me the head called his father—because she was concerned about him—and instead of letting him go home, he said St. Clair couldn't fly out there until he started 'acting responsibly' again."

"But there's no way he'll be able to focus on *anything* until he sees her! And she needs him there; she needs his support. They should be together!"

"This is so typical of his dad to use a situation like this against him."

Gnawing curiosity gets the best of me again. "Have you ever met him? His father?" I know he lives near SOAP, but I've never seen him. And St. Clair certainly doesn't own a framed portrait.

"Yeah," she says cautiously. "I have."

"And?"

"He was . . . nice."

"NICE? How can he be nice? The man is a monster!"

"I know, I know, but he has these . . . impeccable manners in person. Smiles a lot. Very handsome." She changes the subject suddenly. "Do you think Josh is a bad influence on St. Clair?"

"Josh? No. I mean, maybe. I don't know. No." I shake my head, and the line inches forward. We're almost in viewing range of the display case. I see a hint of golden apple *tarte tatins*. The edge of a glossy chocolate-and-raspberry *gâteau*.

At first everything seemed too sophisticated for my tastes, but three months into this, and I understand why the French are famous for their cuisine. Meals here are savored. Restaurant dinners are measured in hours, not minutes. It's so different from America. Parisians swing by the markets every day for the ripest fruit and vegetables, and they frequent specialty shops for cheese, fish, meat, poultry, and wine. And cake.

I like the cake shops the best.

"It just seems like Josh is telling him it's okay to stop caring," Mer presses. "I feel like I'm always the bad guy. 'Get up. Go to school. Do your homework.' You know? While Josh is like, 'Screw it, man. Just leave.'"

"Yeah, but I don't think he's telling St. Clair not to care. He just knows St. Clair can't deal with things right now." But I squirm a bit. I do wish Josh would be supportive in a more encouraging way.

She opens her mouth to argue when I interrupt. "How's soccer?"

"Football," she says, and her face lights up. Meredith joined a local girls' league last month, and she practices most afternoons. She updates me on her latest adventures in soccer drills until we reach the front case. It shimmers with neat rows of square-shaped *tarte citrons*, spongy cakes swelling with molten chocolate, caramel éclairs like ballet slippers, and red fruity cakes with wild strawberries dusted in powdery sugar.

And more *macarons*.

Bin after bin of *macarons* in every flavor and color imaginable. Grass greens and pinky reds and sunshine yellows. While Mer debates over cakes, I select six.

Rose. Black currant. Orange. Fig. Pistachio. Violet.

And then I notice cinnamon and hazelnut praline, and I just want to die right there. Crawl over the counter and crunch my fingers through their delicate crusts and lick out the fragrant fillings until I can no longer breathe. I am so distracted it takes a moment to realize the man behind me is speaking to me.

"Huh?" I turn to see a dignified gentleman with a basset hound. He's smiling at me and pointing at my striped box. The man looks familiar. I swear I've seen him before. He talks in friendly, rapid French.

"Uhh." I gesture around feebly and shrug my shoulders. *"Je ne parle pas . . ."*

I don't speak . . .

He slows down, but I'm still clueless. "Mer? Help? Mer?"

She comes to the rescue. They chat for a minute, and his eyes are shining until she says something that makes him gasp. *"Ce n'est pas possible!"* I don't need to speak the language to recognize an "Oh, no!" when I hear it. He considers me sadly, and then they say goodbye. I add in my own shaky farewell. Mer and I pay for our treats—she's selected *un millefeuille*, a puff pastry with custard—and she steers me from the shop.

"Who was that? What did he want? What were you talking about?"

"You don't recognize him?" She's surprised. "It's the man who runs that theater on rue des Écoles, the little one with the red-and-white lights. He walks Pouce in front of our dorm all the time."

We pick our way through a flock of pigeons, who don't care we're about to step on them. They rumble with coos and beat their wings and jostle the air. "Pouce?"

"The basset hound."

A lightbulb goes off. Of course I've seen them around. "But what did he want?"

"He was wondering why he hasn't seen your boyfriend in a while. St. Clair," she adds, at my confused expression. Her voice is bitter. "I guess you guys have seen a few films there together?"

"We watched a spaghetti-western retrospective there last month." I'm baffled. He thought St. Clair and I were dating?

She's quiet. Jealous. But Meredith has no reason for envy. There's nothing—*nothing*—going on between St. Clair and me. And I'm okay with it, I swear. I'm too worried about St. Clair to think about him in that *other* way. He needs the familiar right now, and Ellie is familiar.

I've been thinking about the familiar, too. I miss Toph again. I miss his green eyes, and I miss those late nights at the theater when he'd make me laugh so hard I'd cry. Bridge says he asks about me, but I haven't talked to him lately, because their band is so busy. Things are good for the Penny Dreadfuls. They've finally scheduled their first gig. It's just before Christmas, and I, Anna Oliphant, will be in attendance.

One month. I can hardly wait.

I should be seeing them next week, but Dad doesn't think it's worth the money to fly me home for such a short holiday, and Mom can't afford it. So I'm spending Thanksgiving here alone. Except . . . I'm not anymore.

I recall the news Mer dropped only minutes ago. St. Clair isn't going home for Thanksgiving either. And everyone else, his girlfriend included, is traveling back to the States. Which means the two of us will be here for the four-day weekend. Alone.

The thought distracts me all the way back to the dorm.

chapter eighteen

Happy Thanksgiving to you! Happy Thanksgiving to yoouuu! Happy Thanks-giv-ing, St. Cla-airrr—"

His door jerks open, and he glares at me with heavy eyes. He's wearing a plain white T-shirt and white pajama bottoms with blue stripes. "Stop. Singing."

"St. Clair! Fancy meeting you here!" I give him my biggest gap-toothed smile. "Did you know today is a holiday?"

He shuffles back into bed but leaves his door open. "I heard," he says grumpily. I let myself in. His room is . . . messier than the first time I saw it. Dirty clothes and towels in heaps across the floor. Half-empty water bottles. The contents of his schoolbag spill from underneath his bed, crinkled papers and blank worksheets. I take a hesitant sniff. Dank. It smells dank.

"Love what you've done with the place. Very college-chic."

"If you're here to criticize, you can leave the way you came in," he mumbles through his pillow.

"Nah. You know how I feel about messes. They're ripe with such *possibility*."

He sighs, a long-suffering noise.

I move a stack of textbooks off his desk chair and several sketches fall from between the pages. They're all charcoal drawings of anatomical hearts. I've only seen his doodles before, nothing serious. And while it's true Josh is the better technical artist, these are beautiful. Violent. Passionate.

I pick them off the floor. "These are amazing. When did you make them?"

Silence.

Delicately, I place the hearts back inside his government book, careful not to smudge them any more than they already are. "So. We're celebrating today. You're the only person I know left in Paris."

A grunt. "Not many restaurants are serving stuffed turkey."

"I don't need turkey, just an acknowledgment that today is important. No one out there"—I point out his window, even though he's not looking—"has a clue."

He tugs his covers tight. "I'm from London. I don't celebrate it either."

"Please. You said on my first day you were an American. Remember? You can't switch nationalities as suits your needs. And today our country is gorging itself on pie and casseroles, and we need to be a part of that."

"Hmph."

This isn't going as planned. Time to switch tactics. I sit on the edge of his bed and wiggle his foot. "Please? Pretty please?"

Silence.

"Come on. I need to do something fun, and you need to get out of this room."

Silence.

My frustration rises. "You know, today sucks for both of us. You aren't the only one stuck here. I'd give anything to be at home right now."

Silence.

I take a slow, deep breath. "Fine. You wanna know the deal? I'm worried about you. We're *all* worried about you. Heck, this is the most we've talked in weeks, and I'm the only one moving my mouth! It sucks what happened, and it sucks even harder that there's nothing any of us can say or do to change it. I mean there's *nothing* I can do, and that pisses me off, because I hate seeing you like this. But you know what?" I stand back up. "I don't think your mom would want you beating yourself up over something you can't control. She wouldn't want you to stop trying. And I think she'll want to hear as many good things as possible when you go home next month—"

"IF I go home next month—"

"WHEN you go home, she'll want to see you happy."

"Happy?" Now he's mad. "How can I—"

"Okay, not happy," I say quickly. "But she won't want to see you like this either. She won't want to hear you've stopped attending class, stopped trying. She wants to see you graduate, remember? You're so close, St. Clair. Don't mess this up."

Silence.

"Fine." It's not fair, not rational, for me to be this angry with him, but I can't help it. "Be a lump. Drop out. Enjoy your miserable day in bed." I head for the door. "Maybe you aren't the person I thought you were."

"And who is that?" comes the acid reply.

"The kind of guy who gets out of bed, even when things are crap. The kind of guy who calls his mother to say 'Happy Thanksgiving' instead of avoiding talking to her because he's afraid of what she might say. The kind of guy who doesn't let his asshole father win. But I guess I'm wrong. This"—I gesture around his room, even though his back is to me; he's very still— "must be working for you. Good luck with that. Happy holidays. I'm going out."

The door is clicking shut when I hear it. "Wait—"

St. Clair cracks it back open. His eyes are blurry, his arms limp. "I don't know what to say," he finally says.

"So don't say anything. Take a shower, put on some warm clothes, and come find me. I'll be in my room."

I let him in twenty minutes later, relieved to find his hair is wet. He's bathed.

"Come here." I sit him on the floor in front of my bed and grab a towel. I rub it through his dark hair. "You'll catch a cold."

"That's a myth, you know." But he doesn't stop me. After

a minute or two, he gives a small sigh, some kind of release. I work slowly, methodically. "So where are we going?" he asks when I finish. His hair is still damp, and a few curls are forming.

"You have great hair," I say, resisting the urge to finger-comb it. He snorts.

"I'm serious. I'm sure people tell you all the time, but it's really good hair."

I can't see his expression, but his voice grows quiet. "Thanks."

"You're welcome," I say with formality. "And I'm not sure where we're going. I thought we'd just leave and . . . we'll know when we get there."

"What?" he asks. "No plan? No minute-by-minute itinerary?"

I wallop the back of his head with the towel. "Careful. I'll make one."

"God, no. Anything but *that*." I think he's serious until he turns around with half a grin on his face. I swat him again, but truthfully, I'm so relieved for that half grin that I could cry. It's more than I've seen in weeks.

Focus, Anna. "Shoes. I need shoes." I throw on my sneakers and grab my winter coat, hat, and gloves. "Where's your hat?"

He squints at me. "Mer? Is that you? Do I need my scarf? Will it be cold, Mummy?"

"Fine, freeze to death. See if I care." But he pulls his knitted stocking cap out of his coat pocket and yanks it over his hair. This time his grin is full and dazzling, and it catches me off guard. My heart stops.

I stare until his smile drops, and he looks at me questioningly.

This time, it's my voice that's grown quiet. "Let's go."

chapter nineteen

 here it is! That's my plan."

St. Clair follows my gaze to the massive dome. The violet gray sky, the same sky Paris has seen every day since the temperature dropped, has subdued it, stripped away its golden gleam, but I am no less intrigued.

"The Panthéon?" he asks warily.

"You know, I've been here three months, and I still have no idea what it is." I jump into the crosswalk leading toward the gigantic structure.

He shrugs. "It's a pantheon."

I stop to glare, and he pushes me forward so I'm not run over by a blue tourist bus. "Oh, right. A pantheon. Why didn't I think of that?"

St. Clair glances at me from the corner of his eyes and smiles. "A pantheon means it's a place for tombs—of famous people, people important to the nation."

"Is that all?" I'm sort of disappointed. It looks like it should've at least crowned a few kings or something.

He raises an eyebrow.

"I mean, there are tombs and monuments everywhere here. What's different about this one?" We climb the steps, and the full height of the approaching columns is overwhelming. I've never been this close.

"I don't know. Nothing, I suppose. It's a bit second rate, anyway."

"Second rate? You've gotta be kidding." Now I'm offended. I like the Panthéon. No, I LOVE the Panthéon. "Who's buried here?" I demand.

"Er. Rousseau, Marie Curie, Louis Braille, Victor Hugo—"

"The *Hunchback of Notre-Dame* guy?"

"The very one. Voltaire. Dumas. Zola."

"Wow. See? You can't say that's not impressive." I recognize the names, even if I don't know what they all did.

"I didn't." He reaches for his wallet and pays our admission charge. I try to get it—since it was my idea in the first place—but he insists. "Happy Thanksgiving," he says, handing me my ticket. "Let's see some dead people."

We're greeted by an unimaginable number of domes and columns and arches. Everything is huge and round. Enormous frescoes of saints, warriors, and angels are painted across the walls. We stroll across the marble in awed silence, except for when he points out someone important like Joan of Arc or Saint Geneviève, the patron saint of Paris. According to him, Saint Geneviève saved the city from famine. I think she was a real person, but I'm too shy to ask. When I'm with him, I'm always aware of how much I don't know.

A swinging brass sphere hangs from the highest point in the center dome. Okay, now I can't help it. "What's that?"

St. Clair shrugs and looks around for a sign.

"I'm shocked. I thought you knew everything."

He finds one. "Foucault's pendulum. Oh. Sure." He looks up in admiration.

The sign is written in French, so I wait for his explanation. It doesn't come. "Yes?"

St. Clair points at the ring of measurements on the floor. "It's a demonstration of the earth's rotation. See? The plane of the pendulum's swing rotates every hour. You know, it's funny," he says, looking all the way up at the ceiling, "but the experiment didn't have to be this big to prove his point."

"How French."

He smiles. "Come on, let's see the crypt."

"Crypt?" I freeze. "Like, a *crypt* crypt?"

"Where'd you think the dead bodies were?"

I cough. "Right. Sure. The crypt. Let's go."

"Unless you're scared."

"I didn't have a problem at the cemetery, did I?" He stiffens, and I'm mortified. I can't *believe* I brought up Père-Lachaise.

Distraction. Quick, I need a distraction! I blurt out the first thing that comes to mind. "Race you!" And I run toward the closest crypt entrance. My pounding feet echo throughout the building, and the tourists are all staring.

I. Am. Going. To. Die. Of. Embarrassment.

And then—he shoots past me. I laugh in surprise and pick up speed. We're neck and neck, almost there, when an angry guard leaps in front of us. I trip over St. Clair trying to stop. He steadies me as the guard shouts at us in French. My cheeks redden, but before I can try to apologize, St. Clair does it for us. The guard softens and lets us go after a minute of gentle scolding.

It *is* like Père-Lachaise again. St. Clair is practically strutting.

"You get away with everything."

He laughs. He doesn't argue, because he knows it's true. But his mood changes the moment the stairs come into view. The spiral staircase down to the crypt is steep and narrow. My irritation is replaced by worry when I see the terror in his eyes. I'd forgotten about his fear of heights.

"You know . . . I don't really wanna see the crypt," I say.

St. Clair shoots me a look, and I shut my mouth. Determined, he grips the rough stone wall and moves slowly downward. *Step. Step. Step.* It's not a long staircase, but the process is *excruciating*. At last we reach the bottom, and an impatient herd of tourists stampedes out behind us. I start to apologize—it was so stupid to bring him here—but he talks over me. "It's bigger than I thought. The crypt." His voice is strained and rushed. He won't look at me.

Deflection. Okay. I take his cue. "You know," I say carefully, "I just heard someone say that the crypt covers the entire area underneath the building. I was picturing endless catacombs decorated with bones, but this isn't so bad."

"No skulls or femurs, at least." A fake laugh.

In fact, the crypt is well lit. It's freezing down here, but it's also clean and sparse and white. Not exactly a dungeon. But St. Clair is still agitated and embarrassed. I lunge toward a statue. "Hey, look! Is that Voltaire?"

We move on through the hallways. I'm surprised by how bare everything is. There's a lot of empty space, room for future tombs. After exploring for a while, St. Clair relaxes again, and we talk about little things, like the test last week in calculus and the peculiar leather jacket Steve Carver has been wearing lately. We haven't had a normal conversation in weeks. It almost feels like it did . . . before. And then we hear a grating American voice behind us. "Don't walk behind *him*. We'll be stuck here all day."

St. Clair tenses.

"He shoulda stayed home if he was so afraid of a couple stairs."

I start to spin around, but St. Clair grips my arm. "Don't. He's not worth it." He steers me into the next hallway, and I'm trying to read a name chiseled into the wall, but I'm so furious that I'm seeing spots. St. Clair is rigid. I have to do something.

I squint at the name until it comes into focus. "Emily Zola. That's only the second woman I've seen down here. What's up with that?"

But before St. Clair can answer, the grating voice says, "It's *Émile*." We turn around to find a smug guy in a Euro Disney sweatshirt. "Émile Zola is a *man*."

My face burns. I reach for St. Clair's arm to pull us away again, but St. Clair is already in his face. "Émile Zola *was* a man," he corrects. "And *you're* an arse. Why don't you mind your own bloody business and leave her alone!"

Leave her alone, alone, alone! His shout echoes through the crypt. Euro Disney, startled by the outburst, backs into his wife, who yelps. Everyone else stares, mouths open. St. Clair yanks my hand and drags me to the stairs, and I'm nervous, so scared of what will happen. Adrenaline carries him an entire spiral up, but then it's as if his body has realized what's happening, and he abruptly halts and dangerously sways backward.

I steady him from behind. "I'm here."

He squeezes my fingers in a death grip. I gently march him upward until we're back under the domes and columns and arches, the open space of the main floor. St. Clair lets go of me and collapses onto the closest bench. He hangs his head, like he's about to be sick. I wait for him to speak.

He doesn't.

I sit on the bench beside him. It's a memorial for Antoine de Saint-Exupéry, who wrote *The Little Prince*. He died in a plane crash, so I suppose there aren't any remains for a tomb downstairs. I watch people take pictures of the frescoes. I watch the guard who yelled at us earlier. I don't watch St. Clair.

At last, he raises his head. His voice is calm. "Shall we look for a turkey dinner?"

—

It takes hours of examining menus before we find something suitable. The search turns into a game, a quest, something to lose ourselves in. We need to forget the man in the crypt. We need to forget that we aren't home.

When we finally discover a restaurant advertising an "American Thanksgiving Dinner," we whoop, and I perform a victory dance. The maître d' is alarmed by our enthusiasm but seats us anyway. "Brilliant," St. Clair says when the main course arrives. He raises his glass of sparkling water and smiles. "To the successful locating of a proper turkey dinner in Paris."

I smile back. "To your mom."

His smile falters for a moment, and then is replaced with one that's softer. "To Mum." We clink glasses.

"So, um. You don't have to talk about it if you don't want to, but how's she doing?" The words spill from my mouth before I can stop them. "Is the radiation therapy making her tired? Is she eating enough? I read that if you don't put on lotion every night, you can get burns, and I was just wondering . . ." I trail off, seeing his expression. It's as if I've sprouted tusks. "I'm sorry. I'm being nosy, I'll shut—"

"No," he interrupts. "It's not that. It's just . . . you're the first person who's known any of that. How . . . how did . . . ?"

"Oh. Um. I was just worried, so I did some research. You know, so I'd . . . know," I finish lamely.

He's quiet for a moment. "Thank you."

I look down at the napkin in my lap. "It's nothing——"

"No, it *is* something. A big something. When I try talking to Ellie about it, she has no bloody clue——" He cuts himself off, as if he's said too much. "Anyway. Thank you."

I meet his gaze again, and he stares back in wonder. "You're welcome," I say.

We spend the rest of dinner talking about his mother. And when we leave the restaurant, we keep talking about her. We walk along the Seine. The moon is full and the lamps are on, and he talks until it's as if he weighs an entire person lighter.

He stops. "I didn't mean to do that."

I breathe deeply, inhaling the pleasant river smell. "I'm glad you did."

We're at the street we'd turn on to go back to the dorm. He looks down it hesitantly, and then blurts, "Let's see a film. I don't want to go back yet."

He doesn't have to ask *me* twice. We find a theater showing a new release, a slacker comedy from the States, and stay for the double feature. I don't remember the last time I laughed so hard, and beside me, St. Clair laughs even harder. It's two in the morning before we get back to the dorm. The front desk is empty, and Nate's light is off.

"I think we're the only ones in the building," he says.

"Then no one will mind when I do this!" I jump onto the desk and parade back and forth. St. Clair belts out a song, and I shimmy to the sound of his voice. When he finishes, I bow with a grand flourish.

"Quick!" he says.

"What?" I hop off the desk. Is Nate here? Did he see?

But St. Clair runs to the stairwell. He throws open the door and screams. The echo makes us both jump, and then together we scream again at the top of our lungs. It's exhilarating. St. Clair chases me to the elevator, and we ride it to the rooftop. He hangs back but laughs as I spit off the side, trying to hit a lingerie advertisement. The wind is fierce, and my aim is off, so I race back down two flights of stairs. Our staircase is wide and steady, so he's only a few feet behind me. We reach his floor.

"Well," he says. Our conversation halts for the first time in hours.

I look past him. "Um. Good night."

"See you tomorrow? Late breakfast at the *crêperie*?"

"That'd be nice."

"Unless—" he cuts himself off.

Unless what? He's hesitant, changed his mind. The moment passes. I give him one more questioning look, but he turns away.

"Okay." It's hard to keep the disappointment out of my voice. "See you in the morning." I take the steps down and glance back. He's staring at me. I lift my hand and wave. He's oddly statuesque. I push through the door to my floor, shaking my head. I don't understand why things always go from perfect to weird with us. It's like we're incapable of normal human interaction. *Forget about it, Anna.*

The stairwell door bursts open.

My heart stops.

St. Clair looks nervous. "It's been a good day. This was the *first* good day I've had in ages." He walks slowly toward me. "I don't want it to end. I don't want to be alone right now."

"Uh." I can't breathe.

He stops before me, scanning my face. "Would it be okay if I stayed with you? I don't want to make you uncomfortable—"

"No! I mean . . ." My head swims. I can hardly think straight. "Yes. Yes, of course, it's okay."

St. Clair is still for a moment. And then he nods.

I pull off my necklace and insert my key into the lock. He waits behind me. My hand shakes as I open the door.

chapter twenty

*S*t. Clair is sitting on my floor. He tosses his boots across my room, and they hit my door with a loud *smack*. It's the first noise either of us has made since coming in here.

"Sorry." He's embarrassed. "Where shall I put those?"

But before I can reply, he's blabbering. "Ellie thinks I ought to go to San Francisco. I've almost bought the plane ticket loads of times, but it's not what Mum would want. If my father doesn't want it, she doesn't want it. It'd put too much additional stress on the situation."

I'm startled by the outburst.

"Sometimes I wonder if she—Ellie—if she, you know . . ." His voice grows quiet. "Wants me gone."

He never talks about his girlfriend. Why now? I can't *believe*

I have to defend her. I line his boots beside my door to avoid looking at him. "She's probably just tired of seeing you miserable. Like we all are," I add. "I'm sure . . . I'm sure she's as crazy about you as ever."

"Hmm." He watches me put away my own shoes and empty the contents of my pockets. "What about you?" he asks, after a minute.

"What about me?"

St. Clair examines his watch. "Sideburns. You'll be seeing him next month."

He's reestablishing . . . what? The boundary line? That he's taken, and I'm spoken for? Except I'm not. Not really.

But I can't bear to say this now that he's mentioned Ellie. "Yeah, I can't wait to see him again. He's a funny guy, you'd like him. I'm gonna see his band play at Christmas. Toph's a great guy, you'd really like him. Oh. I already said that, didn't I? But you would. He's really . . . funny."

Shut up, Anna. Shut. Up.

St. Clair unbuckles and rebuckles and unbuckles his watchband.

"I'm beat," I say. And it's the truth. As always, our conversation has exhausted me. I crawl into bed and wonder what he'll do. Lie on my floor? Go back to his room? But he places his watch on my desk and climbs onto my bed. He slides up next to me. He's on top of the covers, and I'm underneath. We're still fully dressed, minus our shoes, and the whole situation is *beyond* awkward.

He hops up. I'm sure he's about to leave, and I don't know whether to be relieved or disappointed, but . . . he flips off my light. My room is pitch-black. He shuffles back toward my bed and smacks into it.

"Oof," he says.

"Hey, there's a bed there."

"Thanks for the warning."

"No problem."

"It's freezing in here. Do you have a fan on or something?"

"It's the wind. My window won't shut all the way. I have a towel stuffed under it, but it doesn't really help."

He pats his way around the bed and slides back in. "Ow," he says.

"Yes?"

"My belt. Would it be weird . . ."

I'm thankful he can't see me blush. "Of course not." And I listen to the slap of leather as he pulls it out of his belt loops. He lays it gently on my hardwood floor.

"Um," he says. "Would it be weird—"

"*Yes.*"

"Oh, piss off. I'm not talking trousers. I only want under the blankets. That breeze is horrible." He slides underneath, and now we're lying side by side. In my narrow bed. Funny, but I never imagined my first sleepover with a guy being, well, a sleepover.

"All we need now are *Sixteen Candles* and a game of Truth or Dare."

He coughs. "Wh-what?"

"The movie, pervert. I was just thinking it's been a while since I've had a sleepover."

A pause. "Oh."

"..."

"..."

"St. Clair?"

"Yeah?"

"Your elbow is murdering my back."

"Bollocks. Sorry." He shifts, and then shifts again, and then again, until we're comfortable. One of his legs rests against mine. Despite the two layers of pants between us, I feel naked and vulnerable. He shifts again and now my entire leg, from calf to thigh, rests against his. I smell his hair. Mmm.

NO!

I swallow, and it's so loud. He coughs again. I'm trying not to squirm. After what feels like hours but is surely only minutes, his breath slows and his body relaxes. I finally begin to relax, too. I want to memorize his scent and the touch of his skin—one of his arms, now against mine—and the solidness of his body. No matter what happens, I'll remember this for the rest of my life.

I study his profile. His lips, his nose, his eyelashes. He's so beautiful.

The wind rattles the panes, and the lights buzz softly in the hall. He sleeps soundly. How long has it been since he's had a decent night's rest? There's another uncomfortable tug on my heart. Why do I care so much about him, and why do I wish I didn't? How can one person make me so confused all of the time?

What is that? Is it lust? Or something else altogether? And is it even possible for me to feel this way about him without these feelings being reciprocated? He said that he liked me. He did. And even though he was drunk, he wouldn't have said it if there wasn't at least *some* truth to it. Right?

I don't know.

Like every time I'm with him, I don't know anything. He scoots closer to me in his sleep. His breath is warm against my neck. I don't know anything. He's so beautiful, so perfect. I wonder if he . . . if I . . .

A ray of light glares into my eyes, and I squint, disoriented. Daylight. The red numbers on my clock read 11:27. Huh. Did I mean to sleep in? What day is it? And then I see the body in bed next to me. And I nearly jump out of my skin.

So it wasn't a dream.

His mouth is parted, and the sheets are kicked off. One of his hands rests on his stomach. His shirt has hiked up, and I can see his abdomen. My gaze is transfixed.

Holy crap. I just slept with St. Clair.

chapter twenty-one

I mean I didn't SLEEP sleep with him. Obviously. But I slept with him.

I slept with a boy! I burrow back down into my sheets and grin. I can't WAIT to tell Bridge. Except . . . what if she tells Toph? And I can't tell Mer, because she'd get jealous, which means I can't tell Rashmi or Josh either. It dawns on me that there is *nobody* I can tell about this. Does that mean it's wrong?

I stay in bed for as long as possible, but eventually my bladder wins. When I come back from the bathroom, he's looking out my window. He turns around and laughs. "Your hair. It's sticking up in all different directions." St. Clair pronounces it *die-rections* and illustrates his point by poking his fingers up around his head like antlers.

"You're one to speak."

"Ah, but it looks purposeful on me. Took me ages to realize the best way to get that mussed look was to ignore it completely."

"So you're saying it looks like crap on me?" I glance in the mirror, and I'm alarmed to discover I do resemble a horned beast.

"No. I like it." He grins and picks his belt up off the floor. "Breakfast?"

I hand him his boots. "It's noon."

"Thanks. Lunch?"

"Lemme shower first."

We part for an hour and meet back in his room. His door is propped open, and French punk rock is blaring down his hall. I'm shocked when I step inside and discover he's straightened up. The heaps of clothing and towels have been organized for laundry purposes, and the empty bottles and chip bags have been thrown out.

He looks at me hopefully. "It's a start."

"It looks great." And it *does* look better. I smile.

We spend the day walking around again. We catch part of a Danny Boyle film festival and take another stroll beside the Seine. I teach him how to skip stones; I can't believe he doesn't know how. It starts drizzling, so we pop into a bookshop across from Notre-Dame. The yellow-and-green sign reads SHAKESPEARE AND COMPANY.

Inside, we're struck by chaos. A horde of customers crowds the desk, and everywhere I turn there are books, books, and more books. But it's not like a chain, where everything is neatly organized on shelves and tables and end caps. Here books totter in wobbly stacks, fall from the seats of chairs, and spill from sagging shelves. There are cardboard boxes overflowing with books, and a black cat naps beside a pile on the stairs. But the most astonishing thing is that all of the books are in *English*.

St. Clair notices my awed expression. "You've never been here before?"

I shake my head, and he's surprised. "It's quite famous. Hey, look—" He holds up a copy of *Balzac and the Little Chinese Seamstress*. "This is familiar, eh?"

I wander in a daze, half thrilled to be surrounded by my own language, half terrified to disturb anything. One wrong touch might break the entire store. It could collapse, and we'd be buried in an avalanche of yellowed pages.

The rain patters against the windows. I push my way through a group of tourists and examine the fiction section. I don't know why I'm looking for him, but I can't help it. I work backward. Christie, Cather, Caldwell, Burroughs, Brontë, Berry, Baldwin, Auster, Austen. Ashley. James Ashley.

A line of my father's books. Six of them. I pull a hardcover copy of *The Incident* from the shelf, and I cringe at the familiar sunset on the cover.

"What's that?" St. Clair asks. I startle. I didn't realize he was standing beside me.

He takes the novel from me, and his eyes widen with recognition. He flips it over, and Dad's author photo grins back at us. My father is overly tan, and his teeth gleam fake white.

He's wearing a lavender polo shirt, and his hair blows gently in the wind.

St. Clair raises his eyebrows. "I don't see the relation. He's *much* better looking."

I sputter with nervousness, and he taps my arm with the book. "It's worse than I thought." He laughs. "Does he always look like this?"

"Yes."

He flips it open and reads the jacket. I watch his face anxiously. His expression grows puzzled. I see him stop and go back to read something again. St. Clair looks up at me. "It's about cancer," he says.

Oh. My. God.

"This woman has cancer. What happens to her?"

I can't swallow. "My father is an idiot. I've told you, he's a complete jackass."

An excruciating pause. "He sells a lot of these, does he?"

I nod.

"And people enjoy this? They find it entertaining, do they?"

"I'm sorry, St. Clair." Tears are welling in my eyes. I've never hated my father as much as I do right now. How could he? How dare he make money off something so horrible? St. Clair shuts the book and shoves it back on the shelf. He picks up another, *The Entrance*. The leukemia novel. My father wears a dress shirt with the first few buttons casually undone. His arms are crossed, but he has that same ridiculous grin.

"He's a freak," I say. "A total . . . goinky freak."

St. Clair snorts. He opens his mouth to say something, but then sees me crying. "No, Anna. Anna, I'm sorry."

"*I'm* sorry. You shouldn't have seen this." I snatch the book and thrust it back onto the shelf. Another stack of novels tumbles off and crashes to the floor between us. We drop to pick them up and bash heads.

"Ow!" I say.

St. Clair rubs his head. "Are you all right?"

I wrench the books from his hands. "I'm fine. Just fine." I pile them back on the bookcase and stumble to the back of the store, as far from him, as far from my father, as possible. But a few minutes later, St. Clair is back at my side.

"It's not your fault," he says quietly. "You don't pick your parents. I know that as well as anyone, Anna."

"I don't want to talk about it."

"Fair enough." He holds up a collection of poetry. Pablo Neruda. "Have you read this?"

I shake my head.

"Good. Because I just bought it for you."

"What?"

"It's on our syllabus for next semester in English. You'd need to buy it anyway. Open it up," he says.

Confused, I do. There's a stamp on the front page. SHAKESPEARE AND COMPANY, *Kilometer Zero Paris*. I blink. "Kilometer Zero? Is that the same thing as Point Zéro?" I think about our first walk around the city together.

"For old times' sake." St. Clair smiles. "Come on, the rain's stopped. Let's get out of here."

—

I'm still quiet on the street. We cross the same bridge we did that first night—me on the outside again, St. Clair on the inside—and he keeps up the conversation for the both of us. "Did I ever tell you I went to school in America?"

"What? No."

"It's true, for a year. Eighth grade. It was terrible."

"Eighth grade is terrible for everyone," I say.

"Well, it was worse for me. My parents had just separated, and my mum moved back to California. I hadn't been since I was an infant, but I went with her, and I was put in this horrid public school—"

"Oh, no. *Public* school."

He nudges me with his shoulder. "The other kids were ruthless. They made fun of everything about me—my height, my accent, the way I dressed. I vowed I'd never go back."

"But American girls love English accents." I blurt this without thinking, and then pray he doesn't notice my blush.

St. Clair picks up a pebble and tosses it into the river. "Not in middle school, they don't. Especially when it's attached to a bloke who comes up to their kneecaps."

I laugh.

"So when the year was over, my parents found a new school for me. I wanted to go back to London, where my mates were, but my father insisted on Paris so he could keep an eye on me. And that's how I wound up at the School of America."

"How often do you go back? To London?"

"Not as often as I'd like. I still have friends in England, and my grandparents—my father's parents—live there, so I used to split my summers between London and San—"

"Your grandparents are English?"

"Grandfather is, but Grandmère is French. And my other grandparents are American, of course."

"Wow. You really are a mutt."

St. Clair smiles. "I'm told I take after my English grandfather the most, but it's only because of the accent."

"I don't know. I think of you as more English than anything else. And you don't just sound like it, you look like it, too."

"I do?" He's surprised.

I smile. "Yeah, it's that . . . pasty complexion. I mean it in the best possible way," I add, at his alarmed expression. "Honestly."

"Huh." St. Clair looks at me sideways. "Anyway. Last summer I couldn't bear to face my father, so it was the first time I spent the whole holiday with me mum."

"And how was it? I bet the girls don't tease you about your accent anymore."

He laughs. "No, they don't. But I can't help my height. I'll always be short."

"And I'll always be a freak, just like my dad. Everyone tells me I take after him. He's sort of . . . *neat*, like me."

He seems genuinely surprised. "What's wrong with being neat? I wish I were more organized. And, Anna, I've never met your father, but I guarantee you that you're nothing like him."

"How would you know?"

"Well, for one thing, he looks like a Ken doll. And you're beautiful."

I trip and fall down on the sidewalk.

"Are you all right?" His eyes fill with worry.

I look away as he takes my hand and helps me up. "I'm fine. Fine!" I say, brushing the grit from my palms. Oh my God, I AM a freak.

"You've seen the way men look at you, right?" he continues.

"If they're looking, it's because I keep making a fool of myself." I hold up my scraped hands.

"That guy over there is checking you out right now."

"Wha—?" I turn to find a young man with long dark hair staring. "Why is he looking at me?"

"I expect he likes what he sees."

I flush, and he keeps talking. "In Paris, it's common to acknowledge someone attractive. The French don't avert their gaze like other cultures do. Haven't you noticed?"

St. Clair thinks I'm attractive. He called me beautiful.

"Um, no," I say. "I hadn't noticed."

"Well. Open your eyes."

But I stare at the bare tree branches, at the children with balloons, at the Japanese tour group. Anywhere but at him. We've stopped in front of Notre-Dame again. I point at the familiar star and clear my throat. "Wanna make another wish?"

"You go first." He's watching me, puzzled, like he's trying to figure something out. He bites his thumbnail.

Stephanie Perkins

This time I can't help it. All day long, I've thought about it. Him. Our secret.

I wish St. Clair would spend the night again.

He steps on the coppery-bronze star after me and closes his eyes. I realize he must be wishing about his mother, and I feel guilty that she didn't even cross my mind. My thoughts are only for St. Clair.

Why is he taken? Would things be different if I'd met him before Ellie? Would things be different if his mom wasn't sick?

He said I'm beautiful, but I don't know if that was flirty, friends-with-everyone St. Clair, or if it came from someplace private. Do I see the same St. Clair everyone else does? No. I don't think so. But I could be mistaking our friendship for something more, because I *want* to mistake it for something more.

The worrying gradually slips away at dinner. Our restaurant is covered with ivy and cozy with wood-burning fireplaces. Afterward, we stroll in a comfortable, full-bellied chocolate mousse trance. "Let's go home," he says, and the word makes my heart drum.

Home. My home is his home, too.

There's still no one behind the front desk when we get back, but Nate peeks his head out his door. "Anna! Étienne!"

"Hey, Nate," we say.

"Did you have a nice Thanksgiving?"

"Yeah. Thanks, Nate," we say.

"Do I need to check up on you guys later? You know the rules. No sleeping in opposite-sex rooms."

My face flames, and St. Clair's cheeks grow blotchy. It's true. It's a rule. One that my brain—my rule-loving, rule-abiding brain—conveniently blocked last night. It's also one notoriously ignored by the staff.

"No, Nate," we say.

He shakes his shaved head and goes back in his apartment. But the door opens quickly again, and a handful of something is thrown at us before it's slammed back shut.

Condoms. Oh my God, how humiliating.

St. Clair's entire face is now bright red as he picks the tiny silver squares off the floor and stuffs them into his coat pockets. We don't speak, don't even look at each other, as we climb the stairs to my floor. My pulse quickens with each step. Will he follow me to my room, or has Nate ruined any chance of that?

We reach the landing, and St. Clair scratches his head. "Er . . ."

"So . . ."

"I'm going to get dressed for bed. Is that all right?" His voice is serious, and he watches my reaction carefully.

"Yeah. Me too. I'm going to . . . get ready for bed, too."

"See you in a minute?"

I swell with relief. "Up there or down here?"

"Trust me, you don't want to sleep in my bed." He laughs, and I have to turn my face away, because I *do*, holy crap do I *ever*. But I know what he means. It's true my bed is cleaner. I hurry to my room and throw on the strawberry pajamas and an Atlanta Film Festival shirt. It's not like I plan on seducing him.

Like I'd even know how.

St. Clair knocks a few minutes later, and he's wearing his white bottoms with the blue stripes again and a black T-shirt with a logo I recognize as the French band he was listening to earlier. I'm having trouble breathing.

"Room service," he says.

My mind goes . . . blank. "Ha ha," I say weakly.

He smiles and turns off the light. We climb into bed, and it's absolutely positively completely awkward. As usual. I roll over to my edge of the bed. Both of us are stiff and straight, careful not to touch the other person. I must be a masochist to keep putting myself in these situations. I need help. I need to see a shrink or be locked in a padded cell or straitjacketed or *something*.

After what feels like an eternity, St. Clair exhales loudly and shifts. His leg bumps into mine, and I flinch. "Sorry," he says.

"It's okay."

" . . . "

" . . . "

"Anna?"

"Yeah?

"Thanks for letting me sleep here again. Last night . . ."

The pressure inside my chest is torturous. What? What what *what*?

"I haven't slept that well in ages."

The room is silent. After a moment, I roll back over. I slowly, slowly stretch out my leg until my foot brushes his ankle. His intake of breath is sharp. And then I smile, because I know he can't see my expression through the darkness.

chapter twenty-two

$\mathcal{S}$aturday is another day of wandering, food, and movies, followed by an awkward conversation in the stairwell. Followed by a warm body in my bed. Followed by hesitant touches. Followed by sleep.

Even with the uncomfortable bits, I've never had a better school break.

But Sunday morning, things change. When we wake up, St. Clair stretches and accidentally smacks my boobs. Which not only *hurts* but also mortifies us both equally. Then at breakfast, he grows distant again. Checks his phone for messages while I'm talking. Stares out the café windows. And instead of exploring Paris, he says he has homework to do in the dorm.

And I'm sure he does. He hasn't exactly kept up with it. But his tone strikes me as off, and I know the real reason for his departure. Students are arriving back. Josh and Rashmi and Mer will be here this evening.

And so will Ellie.

I try not to take it personally, but it hurts. I consider going to the movies, but I work on my history homework instead. At least that's what I tell myself I'm doing. My ears are tuned to the movements above me in his room, tuned to distraction. He's so close, yet so far away. As students arrive back, Résidence Lambert gets louder, and it becomes difficult to pick out individual noises. I'm not even sure if he's there anymore.

Meredith bursts in around eight, and we go to dinner. She chatters about her holiday in Boston, but my mind is elsewhere. *He's probably with her right now.* I remember the first time I saw them together—their kiss, her hands tangled in his hair—and I lose my appetite.

"You're awfully quiet," Mer says. "How was your break? Did you get St. Clair out of his room?"

"A little." I can't tell her about our nights, but for some reason, I don't want to tell her about our days either. I want to keep the memories for myself, hidden. They're mine.

Their kiss. Her hands tangled in his hair. My stomach churns.

She sighs. "And I was hoping he might come back out of his shell. Take a walk, get some fresh air. You know, something craa-zy like that."

Their kiss. Her hands tangled—

"Hey," she says. "You guys didn't do anything crazy while we were gone, did you?"

I nearly choke on my coffee.

The next few weeks are a blur. Classes pick up with the *professeurs* anxious to get to the halfway point in their lesson plans. We pull all-nighters to keep up, and we cram to prepare for their finals. For the first time, it strikes me how competitive this school is. Students here take studying seriously, and the dormitory is almost as quiet as it was when they were gone for Thanksgiving.

Letters arrive from universities. I've been accepted into all of the schools I applied to, but there's hardly time to celebrate. Rashmi gets into Brown, and Meredith gets into her top picks, too—one in London, one in Rome. St. Clair doesn't talk about college. None of us know where he's applied or *if* he's applied, and he changes the subject whenever we bring it up.

His mother is done with chemo, and it's her last week of external radiation. Next week, when we're home, she'll have her first internal radiation treatment. It requires a three-day hospital stay, and I'm thankful St. Clair will be there for it. He says her spirits are up, and she claims she's doing well—as well as can be expected under the circumstances—but he's impatient to see it with his own eyes.

Today is the first day of Hanukkah and, in its honor, the school has given us a break from homework assignments and tests.

Well, in honor of Josh.

"The only Jew in SOAP," he says, rolling his eyes. He's understandably annoyed, because jerks like Steve Carver were punching his arm and thanking him at breakfast.

My friends and I are in a department store, trying to get some shopping done while we have an actual afternoon off. The store is beautiful in a familiar way. Shiny red and gold ribbons hang from dangling wreaths. Green garlands and white twinkle lights are draped down the escalator and across the perfume counters. And American musicians sing from the speakers.

"Speaking of," Mer says to Josh. "Should you even be here?"

"Sundown, my little Catholic friend, sundown. But actually"—he looks at Rashmi—"we need to go, if we want to catch dinner in the Marais in time. I'm craving latkes like no one's business."

She glances at the clock on her phone. "You're right. We better scoot."

They say goodbye, and then it's just the three of us. I'm glad Meredith is still here. Since Thanksgiving, things have regressed between St. Clair and me. Ellie is his girlfriend, and I'm his friend-who-is-a-girl, and I think he feels guilty for overstepping those boundaries. I feel guilty for encouraging him. Neither of us has mentioned anything about that weekend, and even though we still sit next to each other at meals, there's now this *thing* between us. The ease of our friendship is gone.

Thankfully, no one has noticed. I think. Once I caught Josh mouthing something to St. Clair and then motioning toward me. I don't know what he said, but it made St. Clair shake his head in a "shut up" manner. But it could have been about anything.

Something catches my attention. "Is that . . . the *Looney Tunes* theme?"

Mer and St. Clair cock their ears.

"Why, yes. I believe it is," St. Clair says.

"I heard 'Love Shack' a few minutes ago," Mer says.

"It's official," I say. "America has finally ruined France."

"So can we go now?" St. Clair holds up a small bag. "I'm done."

"Ooo, what'd you get?" Mer asks. She takes his bag and pulls out a delicate, shimmery scarf. "Is it for Ellie?"

"Shite."

Mer pauses. "You didn't get anything for Ellie?"

"No, it's for Mum. Arrrgh." He rakes a hand through his hair. "Would you mind if we pop over to Sennelier before we go home?" Sennelier is a gorgeous little art supply store, the kind that makes me wish I had an excuse to buy oil paints and pastels. Mer and I went with Rashmi last weekend. She bought Josh a new sketchbook for Hanukkah.

"Wow. Congratulations, St. Clair," I say. "Winner of today's Sucky Boyfriend award. And I thought Steve was bad—did you see what happened in calc?"

"You mean when Amanda caught him dirty-texting Nicole?" Mer asks. "I thought she was gonna stab him in the neck with her pencil."

"I've been busy," St. Clair says.

I glance at him. "I was just teasing."

"Well, you don't have to be such a bloody git about it."

"I wasn't being a *git*. I wasn't even being a twat, or a wanker, or any of your other *bleeding* Briticisms—"

"Piss off." He snatches his bag back from Mer and scowls at me.

"HEY!" Mer says. "It's Christmas. Ho-ho-ho. Deck the halls. Stop fighting."

"We weren't fighting," he and I say together.

She shakes her head. "Come on, St. Clair's right. Let's get out of here. This place gives me the creeps."

"I think it's pretty," I say. "Besides, I'd rather look at ribbons than dead rabbits."

"Not the hares again," St. Clair says. "You're as bad as Rashmi."

We wrestle through the Christmas crowds. "I can see why she was upset! The way they're hung up, like they'd died of nosebleeds. It's horrible. Poor Isis." All of the shops in Paris have outdone themselves with elaborate window displays, and the butcher is no exception. I pass the dead bunnies every time I go to the movies.

"In case you hadn't noticed," he says. "Isis is perfectly alive and well on the sixth floor."

We burst through the glass doors and onto the street. Shoppers rush by, and for a moment, it feels like I'm visiting my father in Manhattan. But the familiar lampposts and benches and boulevards appear, and the illusion disappears. The sky is white gray. It looks like it's about to snow, but it never does. We pick our way through the throngs and toward the *métro*. The air is cold, but not bitter, and tinged with chimney smoke.

St. Clair and I continue bickering about the rabbits. I know he doesn't like the display either, but for whatever reason, he wants to argue. Mer is exasperated. "Will you guys cut it out? You're killing my holiday buzz."

"Speaking of buzzkills." I look pointedly at St. Clair before addressing Mer. "I still want to ride one of those Ferris wheels they set up along the Champs-Élysées. Or that big one at the Place de la Concorde with all the pretty lights."

St. Clair glares at me.

"I'd ask you," I say to him, "but I know what your answer would be."

It's like I slapped him. Oh God. What's wrong with me?

"Anna," Mer says.

"I'm sorry." I look down at my shoes in horror. "I don't know why I said that."

A red-cheeked man in front of a supermarket swears loudly. He's selling baskets filled with oysters on ice. His hands must be freezing, but I'd trade places with him in a second. *Please, St. Clair. Please say something.*

He shrugs, but it's forced. " 'S all right."

"Anna, have you heard from Toph lately?" Mer asks, desperate for a subject change.

"Yeah. Actually, I got an email last night." To be honest, for a while I'd stopped thinking about Toph. But since St. Clair has moved clearly, definitively out of the picture again, my thoughts have drifted back to Christmas break. I haven't heard much from Toph or Bridge, because they've been so busy with the band, and we've all been busy with finals, so it was surprising—and exciting—to get yesterday's email.

"So what'd it say?" Mer asks.

sorry i haven't written. its been insane with the
practicing. that was funny about the french pigeons
being fed contraceptive seeds. those crazy parisians.
they should put it in the school pizza here, there've been
at least six preggos this year. bridge says ur coming to
our show. lookin forward to it, annabel lee. later. toph.

"Not much. But he's looking forward to seeing me," I add.
Mer grins. "You must be so psyched."

We startle at the sound of breaking glass. St. Clair has kicked
a bottle into the gutter.

"You okay?" she asks him.

But he turns to me. "Have you had a chance to look at that
poetry book I got you?"

I'm so surprised, it takes a moment to answer. "Uh, no. We
don't have to read it until next semester, right?" I turn to Mer
and explain. "He bought me the Neruda book."

She whips her head toward St. Clair, who adjusts his face
away from her scrutiny. "Yeah, well. I was just wondering. Since
you hadn't mentioned it . . ." He trails off, dejected.

I give him a funny look and return to Mer. She's upset, too,
and I'm afraid I've missed something. No, I *know* I've missed
something. I babble to cover the peculiar silence. "I'm so happy
to be going home. My flight leaves at, like, six in the morning
this Saturday, so I have to get up insanely early, but it's worth it.
I should make it in plenty of time to see the Penny Dreadfuls.

"Their show is that night," I add.

St. Clair's head shoots up. "When does your flight leave?"

"Six a.m.," I repeat.

"So does mine," he says. "My connecting flight is through Atlanta. I bet we're on the same plane. We ought to share a taxi."

Something twinges inside me. I don't know if I want to. It's all so weird with the fighting and the not-fighting. I'm searching for an excuse when we pass a homeless man with a scraggly beard. He's lying in front of the *métro*, cardboard propped around him for warmth. St. Clair roots around his pockets and places all of his euros into the man's cup. *"Joyeux Noël."* He turns back to me. "So? A taxi?"

I glance back at the homeless man before replying. He's marveling, dumbfounded, at the amount in his hands. The frost coating my heart cracks.

"What time should we meet?"

chapter twenty-three

A fist pounds against my door. My eyes jolt open, and my first coherent thought is this: *-ai, -as, -a, -âmes, -âtes, -èrent.* Why am I dreaming about past-tense -er verb endings? I'm exhausted. So tired. Sooo sle—WHAT WHAT WHAT? Another round of rapid-fire knocking jerks me awake, and I squint at my clock. Who the heck is beating down my door at four in the morning?

Wait. Four o'clock? Wasn't there something I was supposed to—?

Oh, no. NO NO NO.

"Anna? Anna, are you there? I've been waiting in the lobby for fifteen minutes." A scrambling noise, and St. Clair curses from the floorboards. "And I see your light's off. Brilliant. Could've mentioned you'd decided to go on without me."

I explode out of bed. I overslept! I can't believe I overslept! How could this happen?

St. Clair's boots clomp away, and his suitcase drags heavily behind him. I throw open my door. Even though they're dimmed this time of night, the crystal sconces in the hall make me blink and shade my eyes.

St. Clair twists into focus. He's stunned. "Anna?"

"Help," I gasp. "Help me."

He drops his suitcase and runs to me. "Are you all right? What happened?"

I pull him in and flick on my light. The room is illuminated in its disheveled entirety. My luggage with its zippers open and clothes piled on top like acrobats. Toiletries scattered around my sink. Bedsheets twined into ropes. And me. Belatedly, I remember that not only is my hair crazy and my face smeared with zit cream, but I'm also wearing matching flannel Batman pajamas.

"No way." He's gleeful. "*You* slept in? I woke *you* up?"

I fall to the floor and frantically squish clothes into my suitcase.

"You haven't packed yet?"

"I was gonna finish this morning! WOULD YOU FREAKING HELP ALREADY?" I tug on a zipper. It catches a yellow Bat symbol, and I scream in frustration.

We're going to miss our flight. We're going to miss it, and it's my fault. And who knows when the next plane will leave, and we'll be stuck here all day, and I'll never make it in time for Bridge and Toph's show. And St. Clair's mom will cry when

she has to go to the hospital without him for her first round of internal radiation, because he'll be stuck in an airport on the other side of the world, and it's ALL. MY. FAULT.

"Okay, okay." He takes the zipper and wiggles it from my pajama bottoms. I make a strange sound between a moan and a squeal. The suitcase finally lets go, and St. Clair rests his arms on my shoulders to steady them. "Get dressed. Wipe your face off. I'll take care of the rest."

Yes, one thing at a time. I can do this. I can do this.

ARRRGH!

He packs my clothes. Don't think about him touching your underwear. Do NOT think about him touching your underwear. I grab my travel outfit—thankfully laid out the night before—and freeze. "Um."

St. Clair looks up and sees me holding my jeans. He sputters. "I'll, I'll step out—"

"Turn around. Just turn around, there's no time!"

He quickly turns, and his shoulders hunch low over my suitcase to prove by posture how hard he is Not Looking. "So what happened?"

"I don't know." Another glance to ensure his continued state of Not Looking, and then I rip off my clothes in one fast swoop. I am now officially stark naked in the room with the most beautiful boy I know. Funny, but this isn't how I imagined this moment.

No. Not funny. One hundred percent the exact opposite of funny.

"I think I maybe, possibly, vaguely remember hitting the snooze button." I jabber to cover my mortification. "Only I guess it was the off button. But I had the alarm on my phone set, too, so I don't know what happened."

Underwear, on.

"Did you turn the ringer back on last night?"

"What?" I hop into my jeans, a noise he seems to determinedly ignore. His ears are apple red.

"You went to see a film, right? Don't you set your mobile to silent at the theater?"

He's right. I'm so stupid. If I hadn't taken Meredith to *A Hard Day's Night*, a Beatles movie I know she loves, I would have never turned it off. We'd already be in a taxi to the airport. "The taxi!" I tug my sweater over my head and look up to find myself standing across from a mirror.

A mirror St. Clair is facing.

"It's all right," he says. "I told the driver to wait when I came up here. We'll just have to tip him a little extra." His head is still down. I don't think he saw anything. I clear my throat, and he glances up. Our eyes meet in the mirror, and he jumps. "God! I didn't . . . I mean, not until just now . . ."

"Cool. Yeah, fine." I try to shake it off by looking away, and he does the same. His cheeks are blazing. I edge past him and rinse the white crust off my face while he throws my toothbrush and deodorant and makeup into my luggage, and then we tear downstairs and into the lobby.

Thank goodness, the driver has waited, cigarette dangling from his mouth and annoyed expression on his face. He yammers angrily at us in French, and St. Clair says something bossy back, and soon we're flying across the streets of Paris, whizzing through red lights and darting between cars. I grip the seat in terror and close my eyes.

The taxi jerks to a stop and so do we. "We're here. You all right?" St. Clair asks.

"Yes. Great," I lie.

He pays the driver, who speeds off without counting. I try to hand St. Clair a few bills, but he shakes his head and says the ride is on him. For once, I'm so freaked out that I don't argue. It's not until we've raced to the correct terminal, checked our luggage, passed through security, and located our gate that he says, "So. Batman, eh?"

Effing St. Clair.

I cross my arms and slouch into one of the plastic seats. I am so not in the mood for this. He takes the chair next to me and drapes a relaxed arm over the back of the empty seat on his other side. The man across from us is engrossed in his laptop, and I pretend to be engrossed in his laptop, too. Well, the back of it.

St. Clair hums under his breath. When I don't respond, he sings quietly. "'Jingle bells, Batman smells, Robin flew away . . .'"

"Yes, great, I get it. Ha ha. Stupid me."

"What? It's just a Christmas song." He grins and continues a bit louder. "'Batmobile lost a wheel, on the M1 motorway, hey!'"

"Wait." I frown. "What?"

"*What* what?"

"You're singing it wrong."

"No, I'm not." He pauses. "How do you sing it?"

I pat my coat, double-checking for my passport. Phew. Still there. "It's 'Jingle bells, Batman smells, Robin laid an egg'—"

St. Clair snorts. "Laid an egg? Robin didn't *lay an egg*—"

"'Batmobile lost a wheel, *and the Joker got away*.'"

He stares at me for a moment, and then says with perfect conviction, "No."

"Yes. I mean, seriously, what's up with the motorway thing?"

"M1 motorway. Connects London to Leeds."

I smirk. "Batman is American. He doesn't take the *M1 motorway*."

"When he's on holiday he does."

"Who says Batman has time to vacation?"

"Why are we arguing about Batman?" He leans forward. "You're derailing us from the real topic. The fact that you, Anna Oliphant, slept in today."

"Thanks."

"You." He prods my leg with a finger. "Slept in."

I focus on the guy's laptop again. "Yeah. You mentioned that."

He flashes a crooked smile and shrugs, that full-bodied movement that turns him from English to French. "Hey, we made it, didn't we? No harm done."

I yank out a book from my backpack, *Your Movie Sucks*, a

collection of Roger Ebert's favorite reviews of bad movies. A visual cue for him to leave me alone. St. Clair takes the hint. He slumps and taps his feet on the ugly blue carpeting.

I feel guilty for being so harsh. If it weren't for him, I would've missed the flight. St. Clair's fingers absentmindedly drum his stomach. His dark hair is extra messy this morning. I'm sure he didn't get up that much earlier than me, but, as usual, the bed-head is more attractive on him. With a painful twinge, I recall those *other* mornings together. Thanksgiving. Which we still haven't talked about.

A bored woman calls out rows for boarding, first in French and then in English. I decide to play nice and put away my book. "Where are we sitting?"

He inspects his boarding pass. "Forty-five G. Still have your passport?"

I feel my coat once more. "Got it."

"Good." And then his hand is inside my pocket. My heart spazzes, but he doesn't notice. He pulls out my passport and flicks it open.

WAIT. WHY DOES HE HAVE MY PASSPORT?

His eyebrows shoot up. I try to snatch it back, but he holds it out of my reach. "Why are your eyes crossed?" He laughs. "Have you had some kind of ocular surgery I don't know about?"

"Give it back!" Another grab and miss, and I change tactics and lunge for his coat instead. I snag his passport.

"NO!"

I open it up, and it's . . . baby St. Clair. "Dude. How old is this picture?"

He slings my passport at me and snatches his back. "I was in *middle school*."

Before I can reply, our section is announced. We hold our passports against our chests and enter the line. The bored flight attendant slides his ticket through a machine that rips it, and he moves forward. I hand mine over. "Zis iz boarding rows forty through fifty. Plizz sit until I call your row." She hands back my ticket, and her lacquered nails click against the paper.

"What? I'm in forty-five—"

But I'm not. There, printed in bold ink, is my row. Twenty-three. I forgot we wouldn't be sitting together, which is dumb, because it's not like we made our reservations together. It's a coincidence we're on the same flight. St. Clair waits for me down the walkway. I shrug helplessly and hold up the boarding pass. "Row twenty-three."

His expression is surprised. He forgot, too.

Someone growls at me in French. A businessman with immaculate black hair is trying to hand his ticket to the flight attendant. I mutter my apologies and step aside. St. Clair's shoulders sag. He waves goodbye and disappears around the corner.

Why can't we sit together? What's the point of seat reservations, anyway? The bored woman calls my section next, and I think terrible thoughts about her as she slides my ticket through her machine. At least I have a window seat. The middle and aisle are occupied with more businessmen. I'm reaching for my book again—it's going to be a long flight—when a polite English accent speaks to the man beside me.

"Pardon me, but I wonder if you wouldn't mind switching seats. You see, that's my girlfriend there, and she's pregnant. And since she gets a bit *ill* on airplanes, I thought she might need someone to hold back her hair when . . . well . . ." St. Clair holds up the courtesy barf bag and shakes it around. The paper crinkles dramatically.

The man sprints off the seat as my face flames. His *pregnant girlfriend*?

"Thank you. I was in forty-five G." He slides into the vacated chair and waits for the man to disappear before speaking again. The guy on his other side stares at us in horror, but St. Clair doesn't care. "They had me next to some horrible couple in matching Hawaiian shirts. There's no reason to suffer this flight alone when we can suffer it together."

"That's flattering, thanks." But I laugh, and he looks pleased—until takeoff, when he claws the armrest and turns a color disturbingly similar to key lime pie. I distract him with a story about the time I broke my arm playing Peter Pan. It turned out there was more to flying than thinking happy thoughts and jumping out a window. St. Clair relaxes once we're above the clouds.

Time passes quickly for an eight-hour flight.

We don't talk about what waits on the other side of the ocean. Not his mother. Not Toph. Instead, we browse *SkyMall*.

We play the if-you-had-to-buy-one-thing-off-each-page game. He laughs when I choose the hot-dog toaster, and I tease him about the fogless shower mirror and the world's largest crossword puzzle.

"At least they're practical," he says.

"What are you gonna do with a giant crossword poster? 'Oh, I'm sorry, Anna. I can't go to the movies tonight. I'm working on two thousand across, *Norwegian Birdcall*.'"

"At least I'm not buying a Large Plastic Rock for hiding 'unsightly utility posts.' You realize you have no lawn?"

"I could hide other stuff. Like . . . failed French tests. Or illegal moonshining equipment." He doubles over with that wonderful boyish laughter, and I grin. "But what will *you* do with a motorized swimming-pool snack float?"

"Use it in the bathtub." He wipes a tear from his cheek. "Ooo, look! A Mount Rushmore garden statue. Just what you need, Anna. And only forty dollars! A bargain!"

We get stumped on the page of golfing accessories, so we switch to drawing rude pictures of the other people on the plane, followed by rude pictures of Euro Disney Guy. St. Clair's eyes glint as he sketches the man falling down the Panthéon's spiral staircase.

There's a lot of blood. And Mickey Mouse ears.

After a few hours, he grows sleepy. His head sinks against my shoulder. I don't dare move. The sun is coming up, and the sky is pink and orange and makes me think of sherbet. I sniff his hair. Not out of weirdness. It's just . . . there.

He must have woken earlier than I thought, because it smells shower-fresh. Clean. Healthy. Mmm. I doze in and out of a peaceful dream, and the next thing I know, the captain's voice is crackling over the airplane. We're here.

I'm home.

chapter twenty-four

I'm jittery. It's like the animatronic band from Chuck E. Cheese is throwing a jamboree in my stomach. I've always hated Chuck E. Cheese. Why am I thinking about Chuck E. Cheese? I don't know why I'm nervous. I'm just seeing my mom again. And Seany. And Bridge! Bridge said she'd come.

St. Clair's connecting flight to San Francisco doesn't leave for another three hours, so we board the train that runs between terminals, and he walks me to the arrivals area. We've been quiet since we got off the plane. I guess we're tired. We reach the security checkpoint, and he can't go any farther. Stupid TSA regulations. I wish I could introduce him to my family. The Chuck E. Cheese band kicks it up a notch, which is weird, because I'm not nervous about leaving *him*. I'll see him again in two weeks.

"All right, Banana. Suppose this is goodbye." He grips the straps of his backpack, and I do the same.

This is the moment we're supposed to hug. For some reason, I can't do it.

"Tell your mom hi for me. I mean, I know I don't know her. She just sounds really nice. And I hope she's okay."

He smiles softly. "Thanks. I'll tell her."

"Call me?"

"Yeah, whatever. You'll be so busy with Bridge and what's-his-name that you'll forget all about your English mate, St. Clair."

"Ha! So you *are* English!" I poke him in the stomach.

He grabs my hand and we wrestle, laughing. "I claim . . . no . . . nationality."

I break free. "Whatever, I totally caught you. Ow!" A gray-haired man in sunglasses bumps his red plaid suitcase into my legs.

"Hey, you! Apologize!" St. Clair says, but the guy is already too far away to hear.

I rub my shins. "It's okay, we're in the way. I should go."

Time to hug again. Why can't we do it? Finally, I step forward and put my arms around him. He's stiff, and it's awkward, especially with our backpacks in the way. I smell his hair again. Oh heavens.

We pull apart. "Have fun at the show tonight," he says.

"I will. Have a good flight."

"Thanks." He bites his thumbnail, and then I'm through

security and riding down the escalator. I look back one last time. St. Clair jumps up and down, waving at me. I burst into laughter, and his face lights up. The escalator slides down.

He's lost from view.

I swallow hard and turn around. And then—there they are. Mom has a gigantic smile, and Seany is jumping and waving, just like St. Clair.

"For the last time, Bridgette said she was sorry." Mom pays the grumpy woman in the airport parking deck's tollbooth. "She had to practice for the show."

"Right. Because it's not like we haven't seen each other in four months."

"Bridge is a ROCK STAR," Seany says from the backseat. His voice is filled with adoration.

Uh-oh. Someone has a crush. "Oh, yeah?"

"She says her band is gonna be on MTV someday, but not the lame one, one of the cool ones you can only get with a special cable package."

I turn around. My brother looks strangely smug. "And how do you know about special cable packages?"

Seany swings his legs. One of his freckled kneecaps is covered with *Star Wars* Band-Aids. Like, seven or eight of them. "Duh. Bridge told me."

"Ah. I see."

"She also told me about praying mantises. How the girl mantis eats the boy mantis's head. And she told me about Jack the

Ripper and NASA, and she showed me how to make macaroni and cheese. The good kind, with the squishy cheese packet."

"Anything else?"

"*Lots* of other things." There is an edge to this. A threat.

"Oh. Hey, I have something for you." I unzip my backpack and pull out a plastic shell. It's an original *Star Wars* Sand Person. The purchase on eBay ate my entire meal fund one week, but it was worth it. He really wants this. I was saving it for later, but he clearly needs coaxing back to my side.

I hold up the package. The angry little figurine glares into the backseat. "Merry early Christmas!"

Seany crosses his arms. "I already have that one. Bridge got him for me."

"Sean! What did I say about thanking people? Tell your sister thank you. She must have gone through a lot of trouble to get that for you."

"It's okay," I mumble, placing the toy back in my bag. It's amazing how small a resentful seven-year-old can make me feel.

"He just missed you, that's all. He's talked about you nonstop. He just doesn't know how to express it now that you're here. Sean! Stop kicking the seat! What have I told you about kicking my seat while I'm driving?"

Seany scowls. "Can we go to McDonald's?"

Mom looks at me. "Are you hungry? Did they feed you on the plane?"

"I could eat."

We pull off the interstate and hit the drive-through. They aren't serving lunch yet, and Seany throws a fit. We decide on hash browns. Mom and Seany get Cokes, and I order coffee. "You drink coffee now?" Mom hands it to me, surprised.

I shrug. "Everyone at school drinks coffee."

"Well, I hope you're still drinking milk, too."

"Like Sean's drinking milk right now?"

Mom grits her teeth. "It's a special occasion. His big sister is home for Christmas." She points to the Canadian flag on my backpack. "What's that?"

"My friend St. Clair bought it for me. So I wouldn't feel out of place."

She raises her eyebrows as she pulls back onto the road. "Are there a lot of Canadians in Paris?"

My face warms. "I just felt, you know, stupid for a while. Like one of those lame American tourists with the white sneakers and the cameras around their necks? So he bought it for me, so I wouldn't feel . . . embarrassed. American."

"Being American is nothing to be ashamed of," she snaps.

"God, Mom, I know. I just meant—forget it."

"Is this the English boy with the French father?"

"What does that have anything to do with it?" I'm angry. I don't like what she's implying. "Besides, he's American. He was born here? His mom lives in San Francisco. We sat next to each other on the plane."

We stop at a red light. Mom stares at me. "You like him."

"OH GOD, MOM."

"You do. You like this boy."

"He's just a friend. He has a girlfriend."

"Anna has a boooy-friend," Seany chants.

"I do not!"

"ANNA HAS A BOOOY-FRIEND!"

I take a sip of coffee and choke. It's disgusting. It's sludge. No, it's worse than sludge—at least sludge is organic. Seany is still taunting me. Mom reaches around and grabs his legs, which are kicking her seat again. She sees me making a face at my drink.

"My, my. One semester in France, and suddenly we're Miss Sophisticated. Your father will be thrilled."

Like it was my choice! Like I asked to go to Paris! And how *dare* she mention Dad.

"ANNNN-A HAS A BOOOY-FRIEND!"

We merge back onto the interstate. It's rush hour, and the Atlanta traffic has stopped moving. The car behind ours shakes us with its thumping bass. The car in front sprays a cloud of exhaust straight into our vents.

Two weeks. Only two more weeks.

chapter twenty-five

*S*ofia is dead. Because Mom only took her out three times since I left, now she's stuck in some repair shop on Ponce de Leon Avenue. My car may be a hunk of red scrap metal, but she's *my* hunk of red scrap metal. I paid for her with my own money, earned with the stench of theater popcorn in my hair and artificial butter on my arms. She's named after my favorite director, Sofia Coppola. Sofia creates these atmospheric, impressionistic films with this quiet but *impeccable* style. She's also one of only two American women to have been nominated for the Best Director Oscar, for *Lost in Translation*.

She should have won.

"Why don't you carpool with your friends?" Mom asks, when I complain about driving her minivan to the Penny Dreadfuls show.

"Because Bridge and Toph will already be there. They have to set up." Captain Jack *wheek wheek wheeks* for guinea pig treats, so I pop an orange pellet into his cage and scratch the fuzz behind his ears.

"Can't Matt drive you?"

I haven't talked to him in months. I guess he's going, but ugh, that means *Cherrie Milliken* is also going. No thanks. "I'm not calling Matt."

"Well, Anna. It's Matt or the minivan. I'm not making the choice for you."

I choose my ex. We used to be good friends, so I'm sort of looking forward to seeing him again. And maybe Cherrie isn't as bad as I remember. Except she is. She *totally* is. After only five minutes in her company, I cannot fathom how Bridge stands sitting with her at lunch every day. She turns to look at me in the backseat, and her hair swishes in a vitamin-enriched, shampoo-commercial curtain. "So. How are the guys in Paris?"

I shrug. "Parisian."

"Ha ha. You're funny."

Her lifeless laugh is one of her lesser attributes. What does Matt see in her?

"No one special?" Matt smiles and glances at me through the rearview mirror. I'm not sure why, but I forgot that he has brown eyes. Why do they make some people look *amazing* and others completely average? It's the same with brown hair. Statistically speaking, St. Clair and Matt are quite similar. Eyes: Brown. Hair: Brown. Race: Caucasian. There's a significant difference in height, but still. It's like comparing a gourmet truffle to a Mr. Goodbar.

I think about the gourmet truffle. And his girlfriend. "Not exactly."

Cherrie pulls Matt into a story about something that happened in chorus, a conversation she knows I can't contribute to. Mr. Goodbar fills me in on the who-is-who details, but my mind drifts away. Bridgette and Toph. Will Bridge look the same? Will Toph and I jump in where we left off?

It's really hitting me now. I'm about to see Toph.

The last time we were together, *we kissed*. I can't help but fantasize about our reunion. Toph picking me out of the crowd, being unable to pry his eyes from me, dedicating songs to me. Meeting him backstage. Kissing him in dark corners. I could be on the verge of an *entire winter break* spent making out with Toph. By the time we arrive at the club, my stomach is in knots, but in such a good way.

Except when Matt opens my door, I realize we aren't at a club. More like . . . a bowling alley. "Is this the right place?"

Cherrie nods. "All of the best underage bands play here."

"Oh." Bridge hadn't mentioned she was playing in a bowling alley. But that's okay, it's still a huge deal. And I'd forgotten about the whole underage thing. Which is silly, because it's not like I've lived in France that long.

Inside, we're told we have to buy a lane in order to stay for the show. This also means we have to rent bowling shoes. Um, no. There's no way I'm wearing *bowling shoes*. Hundreds of people

use those things and, what, one spritz of Lysol is supposed to kill all of their nasty stinky feet germs? I don't think so.

"That's okay," I say when the man drops them on the counter. "You can keep them."

"Lady. You ain't allowed to play without shoes."

"I'm not playing."

"Lady. Take the shoes. You're holdin' up the line."

Matt grabs them. "Sorry." He shakes his head. "I forgot how you are with stuff like this." And then Cherrie huffs, so he carries her shoes, too. He hides them underneath some plastic orange shell chairs, and we stroll over to the stage, which is pushed against the far wall. A small crowd has gathered. Bridge and Toph aren't anywhere to be seen, and I don't recognize anyone else.

"I think they're going first," Matt says.

"You mean they're the opening act in an underage bowling alley?" I ask.

He cuts his eyes at me, and I feel about two feet tall. Because he's right. This is still awesome! It's their first show! But the sinking feeling returns as we mill around. Giveaway T-shirts stretched over monstrous beer bellies. Puffy NFL jackets and porky jowls. Granted, I'm in a bowling alley, but the differences between Americans and Parisians are shocking. I'm ashamed to see my country the way the French must see us. Couldn't these people have at least brushed their hair before leaving their houses?

"I need a licorice rope," Cherrie announces. She marches toward the snack stand, and all I can think is *these people are your future.*

The thought makes me a little happier.

When she comes back, I inform her that just one bite of her Red Dye #40–infused snack could kill my brother. "God, *morbid*," she says. Which makes me think of St. Clair again. Because when I told him the same thing three months ago, instead of accusing me of morbidity, he asked with genuine curiosity, "Why?"

Which is the polite thing to do when someone offers you such an interesting piece of conversation.

I wonder if St. Clair has seen his mom yet. Hmm, he's been in California for two hours. His father was going to pick him up and drive him straight to the hospital. He's probably with her right now. I should send him a text, some well-wishes. I pull out my phone just as the tiny crowd erupts with cheers.

I forget about the text.

The Penny Dreadfuls emerge, pulsating with excitement and energy, from . . . the staff room. Okay. So it's not as glamorous as emerging from a backstage, but they do look GREAT. Well, two of them do.

The bassist is the same as always. Reggie used to come into work, mooching free tickets off Toph for the latest comic book movies. He has these long bangs that droop over half his face and cover his eyes, and I could never tell what he thought about anything. I'd be like, "How was the new *Iron Man?*" And he'd say, "Fine," in this bored voice. And because his eyes were hidden, I didn't know if he meant a good fine, or a so-so fine, or a bad fine. It was irritating.

But Bridgette is radiant. She's wearing a tank top that shows off her toned arms, and her blond hair is in Princess Leia buns with chopsticks through them. I wonder if that was Seany's idea. She finds me immediately, and her face lights up like a Christmas tree. I wave as she lifts the sticks above her head, counts off the song, and then she's *flying*. Reggie drives out a matching bass line, and Toph—I save him for last, because I know that once my eyes lock on him, they aren't moving.

Because Toph. Is still. Totally. Hot.

He's slashing at his guitar like he wants to use it for kindling, and he has that angry punk rock scream, and his forehead and sideburns are already glistening with sweat. His pants are tight and bright blue plaid, something that NO ONE else I know could pull off, and it reminds me of his Blue Raspberry Mouth, and it's so dead sexy I could die.

And then . . . he spots me.

Toph raises his eyebrows and smiles, this lazy grin that makes my insides explode. Matt and Cherrie and I thrash and jump around, and it's so exhilarating that I don't even care that I'm dancing with *Cherrie Milliken*. "Bridge is fantastic!" she says.

"I know!" My heart bursts with pride. Because she's *my* best friend, and I've always known how talented she was. Now everyone else does, too. And I don't know what I was expecting—maybe that Reggie's bangs would get in the way of his playing—but he's also pretty great. His hand tears over the strings, pushing a wicked bass line that whips us into a frenzy. The only teeny tiny minor weakness in the whole thing is . . . Toph.

Don't get me wrong. His antiestablishment, I'm-a-loser lyrics are perfect. Catchy. There's so much rage and passion that even the redneck behind the shoe counter is bobbing his head. And, of course, Toph looks the part.

It's his actual guitar playing that's weak. But it's not like I know that much about guitars. I'm sure it's a difficult instrument, and he'll totally get better with practice. It's hard to master something if you're always stuck behind a snack counter. And he plays loud, and it riles us up. I forget I'm in a bowling alley, and I forget I'm rocking out with my ex-boyfriend and his girlfriend, and it's all over way too quickly.

"We're the Penny Dreadfuls, thanks for coming out to see us. My name is Toph, that's Reggie on bass, and the hottie in the back is Bridge."

I whoop and holler.

She beams at Toph. He waggles his eyebrows back and then turns to the crowd and leers. "And, oh yeah. Don't screw her, 'cause I already am. SUCK IT, ATLANTA. GOOD NIGHT!"

chapter twenty-six

Wait. What?

I'm sorry, what did he just say?

Toph kicks over the microphone stand in a grand, asshole gesture, and the three of them jump off the stage. It's a little less dramatic when they have to come right back to take apart their stuff before the next band comes on. I try to catch Bridge's eye, but she won't look at me. Her gaze is locked on her cymbal stands. Toph takes a swig of bottled water, gives me a wave, then grabs his amp and heads for the parking lot.

"Woo! They were great!" Cherrie says.

Matt claps me on the back. "What'd ya think? She played me some of their stuff a few weeks ago, so I knew it'd be awesome."

I'm blinking back tears. "Um. What did he just say?"

"He said she played some of their songs for us a few weeks ago," Cherrie says, too close to my face.

I back up. "No. What did *Toph* just say? Before the Atlanta part?"

"What, 'Don't screw my girlfriend'?" Cherrie asks.

I can't breathe. I'm having a heart attack.

"Are you okay?" Matt asks.

Why won't Bridge look at me? I stumble forward, but Matt grabs me. "Anna. You knew she and Toph were dating, right?"

"I've gotta talk to Bridge." My throat is closing. "I don't understand—"

Matt swears. "I can't believe she didn't tell you."

"How . . . how long?"

"Since Thanksgiving," he says.

"*Thanksgiving?* But she didn't say . . . she never said . . ."

Cherrie is gleeful. "You didn't know?"

"NO, I DIDN'T KNOW."

"Come on, Anna." Matt tries to lead me away, but I push him aside and jump onstage. I open my mouth, but no words come out.

Bridge finally looks at me. "I'm sorry," she whispers.

"You're sorry? You've been dating Toph for the last month, and you're *sorry?*"

"It just happened. I meant to tell you, I wanted to tell you—"

"But you lost control over your mouth? Because it's easy, Bridge. Talking is easy. Look at me! I'm talking right—"

"You know it wasn't that easy! I didn't mean for it to happen, it just did—"

"Oh, you didn't mean to wreck my life? It just 'happened'?"

Bridge stands up from behind her drums. It's impossible, but she's taller than me now. "What do you mean, *wreck your life?*"

"Don't play dumb, you know exactly what I mean. How could you do this to me?"

"Do what? It's not like you were dating!"

I scream in frustration. "We certainly won't be now!"

She sneers. "It's kind of hard to date someone who's not interested in you."

"LIAR!"

"What, you ditch us for Paris and expect us to put our lives on hold for you?"

My jaw drops. "I didn't ditch you. They sent me away."

"Ooo, yeah. To Paris. Meanwhile, I'm stuck here in Shitlanta, Georgia, at the same shitty school, doing shitty babysitting jobs—"

"If babysitting my brother is so shitty, why do you do it?"

"I didn't mean—"

"Because you want to turn him against me, too? Well. Congratulations, Bridge. It worked. My brother loves you and hates me. So you're welcome to move in when I leave again, because that's what you want, right? My life?"

She shakes with fury. "Go to hell."

"Take my life. You can have it. Just watch out for the part where my BEST FRIEND SCREWS ME OVER!" I knock over a cymbal stand, and the brass hits the stage with an earsplitting

crash that reverberates through the bowling alley. Matt calls my name. Has he been calling it this entire time? He grabs my arm and leads me around the electrical cords and plugs and onto the floor and away, away, away.

Everyone in the bowling alley is staring at me.

I duck my head so my hair covers my face. I'm crying. This would have never happened if I hadn't given Toph her number. All of those late-night practices and . . . he said they've had sex! What if they've had it at my house? Does he come over when she's watching Seany? Do they go in my bedroom?

I'm going to be sick. I'm going to be sick. I'm going to be—

"You're not going to be sick," Matt says, and I didn't know I was talking out loud, but I don't care because my best friend is dating Toph. She's dating Toph. She's dating Toph. She's dating—Toph.

Toph's here.

Right in front of me, in the parking lot. His slender body is relaxed, and he leans his blue plaid hips against his car. "What's up, Annabel Lee?"

He was never interested in me. She said that.

Toph opens his arms for a hug, but I'm already bolting for Matt's car. I hear his peeved, "What's with her?" and Matt replying something in disgust, but I don't know what, and I'm running and running and running, and I want to be as far away from them, as far away from this night, as possible. I wish I were in bed. I wish I were *home*.

I wish I were in Paris.

chapter twenty-seven

"Anna. Anna, slow down. Bridgette's dating Toph?"
St. Clair asks over the phone.

"Since Thanksgiving. She's been ly-lying to me this whole
time!"

The Atlanta skyline is a blur outside the car window. The towers
are illuminated in blue and white lights. They're more disjointed
than the buildings in Paris; they have no relationship. They're just
stupid rectangles designed to be taller, better than the others.

"I need you to take a deep breath," he says. "All right? Take a
deep breath and start from the beginning."

Matt and Cherrie watch me in the rearview mirror as I relate
the story again. The line grows quiet. "Are you there?" I ask. I'm
startled when a pink tissue appears in my face. It's attached to
Cherrie's hand. She looks guilty.

I accept the tissue.

"I'm here." St. Clair is angry. "I'm just sorry I'm not *there*. With you. I wish there was something I could do."

"Wanna come beat her up for me?"

"I'm packing my throwing stars right now."

I sniffle and wipe my nose. "I'm such an idiot. I can't believe I thought he liked me. That's the worst part, knowing he was never even interested."

"Bollocks. He was interested."

"No, he wasn't," I say. "Bridge said so."

"Because she's jealous! Anna, I was there that first night he called you. I've seen how he looked at you in pictures." I protest, but he interrupts. "Any bloke with a working prick would be insane not to like you."

There's a shocked pause, on both ends of the line.

"Because, of course, of how intelligent you are. And funny. Not that you aren't attractive. Because you are. Attractive. Oh, bugger . . ."

I wait.

"Are you still there, or did you hang up because I'm such a bleeding idiot?"

"I'm here."

"God, you made me work for that."

St. Clair said I'm attractive. That's the second time.

"You're so easy to talk to," he continues, "that sometimes I forget you're not one of the guys."

Scratch that. He thinks I'm Josh. "Just drop it. I can't take being compared to a guy right now—"

"That's not what I meant—"

"How's your mom? I'm sorry, I've hogged our entire conversation, and this was supposed to be about her, and I didn't even ask—"

"You did ask. It was the first thing you said when you answered. And technically I called you. And I was calling to see how the show went, which is what we've been talking about."

"Oh." I fiddle with the stuffed panda on Matt's floorboard. It's carrying a satin heart that reads I WUV U. A gift from Cherrie, no doubt. "But how is she? Your mom?"

"Mum's . . . all right." His voice is suddenly tired. "I don't know if she's better or worse than I expected. In some ways, she's both. I pictured the worst—bruised and skeletal—and I'm relieved it's not the case, but seeing her in person . . . she's still lost loads of weight. And she's exhausted, and she's in this *lead-lined* hospital room. With all of these plastic tubes."

"Are you allowed to stay with her? Are you there now?"

"No, I'm at her flat. I'm only allowed a short visit because of the radiation exposure."

"Is your dad there?"

He doesn't say anything for a moment, and I'm afraid I've crossed a line. But finally he speaks. "He's here. And I'm dealing with him. For Mum's sake."

"St. Clair?"

"Yeah?"

"I'm sorry."

"Thank you." His voice is quiet as Matt's car pulls into my neighborhood.

I sigh. "I need to go. We're almost home. Matt and Cherrie are giving me a ride."

"Matt? Your ex-boyfriend, Matt?"

"Sofia's in the shop."

A pause. "Mmph."

We hang up as Matt parks in my driveway. Cherrie turns around and stares. "That was interesting. Who was that?"

Matt looks unhappy. "What?" I ask him.

"You'll talk to that guy, but you won't talk to us anymore?"

"Sorry," I mumble, and climb out of his car. "He's just a friend. Thanks for the ride."

Matt gets out, too. Cherrie starts to follow, but he throws her a sharp look. "So what does that mean?" he calls out. "We aren't friends anymore? You're bailing on us?"

I trudge toward the house. "I'm tired, Matt. I'm going to bed."

He follows anyway. I dig out my house key, but he grabs my wrist to stop me from opening the door. "Listen, I know you don't want to talk about it, but I just have this one thing to say before you go in there and cry yourself to sleep—"

"Matt, please—"

"Toph isn't a nice guy. He's never been a nice guy. I don't know what you ever saw in him. He talks back to everyone, he's completely unreliable, he wears those stupid fake clothes—"

"Why are you telling me this?" I'm crying again. I pull my wrist from his grasp.

"I know you didn't like me as much as I liked you. I know you would have rather been with him, and I dealt with that a long time ago. I'm over it."

The shame is overwhelming. Even though I *knew* Matt was aware that I liked Toph, it's awful to hear him say it aloud.

"But I'm still your friend." He's exasperated. "And I'm sick of seeing you waste your energy on that jerk. You've spent all this time afraid to talk about what was going on between you two, but if you'd ever bothered to just *ask him*, you would have discovered that he wasn't worth it. But you didn't. You never asked him, did you?"

The weight of hurt is unbearable. "Please leave," I whisper. "Please just leave."

"Anna." His voice levels, and he waits for me to look at him. "It was still wrong of him and Bridge not to tell you. Okay? You deserve better than that. And I sincerely hope whomever you were just talking to"—Matt gestures toward the phone in my purse—"is better than that."

chapter twenty-eight

To: Anna Oliphant <bananaelephant@femmefilmfreak.net>
From: Étienne St. Clair <etiennebonaparte@soap.fr>
Subject: HAPPY CHRISTMAS

Have you gotten used to the time difference? Bloody
hell, I can't sleep. I'd call, but I don't know if you're
awake or doing the family thing or what. The bay fog is
so thick that I can't see out my window. But if I could,
I am quite certain I'd discover that I'm the only person
alive in San Francisco.

To: Anna Oliphant <bananaelephant@femmefilmfreak.net>
From: Étienne St. Clair <etiennebonaparte@soap.fr>
Subject: I forgot to tell you.

Yesterday I saw a guy wearing an Atlanta Film Festival shirt at the hospital. I asked if he knew you, but he didn't. I also met an enormous, hairy man in a cheeky Mrs. Claus getup. He was handing out gifts to the cancer patients. Mum took the attached picture. Do I always look so startled?

To: Anna Oliphant <bananaelephant@femmefilmfreak.net>
From: Étienne St. Clair <etiennebonaparte@soap.fr>
Subject: Are you awake yet?

Wake up. Wake up wake up wake up.

To: Étienne St. Clair <etiennebonaparte@soap.fr>
From: Anna Oliphant <bananaelephant@femmefilmfreak.net>
Subject: Re: Are you awake yet?

I'm awake! Seany started jumping on my bed, like, three hours ago. We've been opening presents and eating sugar cookies for breakfast. Dad gave me a gold ring shaped like a heart. "For Daddy's sweetheart," he said. As if I'm the type of girl who'd wear a heart-shaped ring.

FROM HER FATHER. He gave Seany tons of *Star Wars* stuff
and a rock polishing kit, and I'd much rather have those.
I can't believe Mom invited him here for Christmas. She
says it's because their divorce is amicable (um, no) and
Seany and I need a father figure in our lives, but all they
ever do is fight. This morning it was about my hair. Dad
wants me to dye it back, because he thinks I look like
a "common prostitute," and Mom wants to re-bleach
it. Like either of them has a say. Oops, gotta run. My
grandparents just arrived, and Granddad is bellowing for
his bonnie lass. That would be me.

P.S. Love the picture. Mrs. Claus is totally checking out
your butt. And it's *Merry* Christmas, weirdo.

To: Anna Oliphant <bananaelephant@femmefilmfreak.net>
From: Étienne St. Clair <etiennebonaparte@soap.fr>
Subject: HAHAHA!

Was it a PROMISE RING? Did your father give you a
PROMISE RING?

To: Étienne St. Clair <etiennebonaparte@soap.fr>
From: Anna Oliphant <bananaelephant@femmefilmfreak.net>
Subject: Re: HAHAHA!

I am so not responding to that.

To: Anna Oliphant <bananaelephant@femmefilmfreak.net>
From: Étienne St. Clair <etiennebonaparte@soap.fr>
Subject: Uncommon Prostitutes

I have nothing to say about prostitutes (other than you'd make a terrible prostitute, the profession is much too unclean), I only wanted to type that. Isn't it odd we both have to spend Christmas with our fathers? Speaking of unpleasant matters, have you spoken with Bridge yet? I'm taking the bus to the hospital now. I expect a full breakdown of your Christmas dinner when I return. So far today, I've had a bowl of muesli. How does Mum eat that rubbish? I feel as if I've been gnawing on lumber.

To: Étienne St. Clair <etiennebonaparte@soap.fr>
From: Anna Oliphant <bananaelephant@femmefilmfreak.net>
Subject: Christmas Dinner

MUESLI? It's Christmas, and you're eating CEREAL?? I'm mentally sending you a plate from my house. The turkey is in the oven, the gravy's on the stovetop, and the mashed potatoes and casseroles are being prepared as I type this. Wait. I bet you eat bread pudding and mince pies or something, don't you? Well, I'm mentally sending you bread pudding. Whatever that is. No, I haven't talked to Bridgette. Mom keeps bugging me to answer her calls, but winter break sucks enough already. (WHY is

my dad here? SERIOUSLY. MAKE HIM LEAVE. He's wearing this giant white cable-knit sweater, and he looks like a pompous snowman, and he keeps rearranging the stuff in our kitchen cabinets. Mom is about to kill him. WHICH IS WHY SHE SHOULDN'T INVITE HIM OVER FOR HOLIDAYS.) Anyway. I'd rather not add to the drama.

P.S. I hope your mom is doing better. I'm so sorry you have to spend today in a hospital. I really do wish I could send you both a plate of turkey.

To: Anna Oliphant <bananaelephant@femmefilmfreak.net>
From: Étienne St. Clair <etiennebonaparte@soap.fr>
Subject: Re: Christmas Dinner

YOU feel sorry for ME? I am not the one who has never tasted bread pudding. The hospital was the same. I won't bore you with the details. Though I had to wait an hour to catch the bus back, and it started raining. Now that I'm at the flat, my father has left for the hospital. We're each making stellar work of pretending the other doesn't exist.

P.S. Mum says to tell you "Merry Christmas." So Merry Christmas from my mum, but *Happy* Christmas from me.

To: Étienne St. Clair <etiennebonaparte@soap.fr>
From: Anna Oliphant <bananaelephant@femmefilmfreak.net>
Subject: SAVE ME

Worst. Dinner. Ever. It took less than five minutes
for things to explode. My dad tried to force Seany to
eat the green bean casserole, and when he wouldn't,
Dad accused Mom of not feeding my brother enough
vegetables. So she threw down her fork, and said that
Dad had no right to tell her how to raise her children.
And then he brought out the "I'm their father" crap,
and she brought out the "You abandoned them"
crap, and meanwhile, the WHOLE TIME my half-deaf
Nanna is shouting, "WHERE'S THE SALT! I CAN'T TASTE
THE CASSEROLE! PASS THE SALT!" And then Granddad
complained that Mom's turkey was "a wee dry," and she
lost it. I mean, Mom just started *screaming*.

And it freaked Seany out, and he ran to his room crying,
and when I checked on him, he was UNWRAPPING A
CANDY CANE!! I have no idea where it came from. He
knows he can't eat Red Dye #40! So I grabbed it from
him, and he cried harder, and Mom ran in and yelled at
ME, like I'd given him the stupid thing. Not, "Thank you
for saving my only son's life, Anna." And then Dad came
in and the fighting resumed, and they didn't even notice

that Seany was still sobbing. So I took him outside and fed him cookies, and now he's running around in circles, and my grandparents are still at the table, as if we're all going to sit back down and finish our meal.

WHAT IS WRONG WITH MY FAMILY? And now Dad is knocking on my door. Great. Can this stupid holiday get any worse??

To: Anna Oliphant <bananaelephant@femmefilmfreak.net>
From: Étienne St. Clair <etiennebonaparte@soap.fr>
Subject: SAVING YOU

I'm teleporting to Atlanta. I'm picking you up, and we'll go someplace where our families can't find us. We'll take Seany. And we'll let him run laps until he tires, and then you and I will take a long walk. Like Thanksgiving. Remember? And we'll talk about everything BUT our parents . . . or perhaps we won't talk at all. We'll just walk. And we'll keep walking until the rest of the world ceases to exist.

I'm sorry, Anna. What did your father want? Please tell me what I can do.

To: Étienne St. Clair <etiennebonaparte@soap.fr>
From: Anna Oliphant <bananaelephant@femmefilmfreak.net>
Subject: Sigh. I'd love that.

Thank you, but it was okay. Dad wanted to apologize. For a split second, he was almost human. Almost. And then Mom apologized, and now they're washing dishes and pretending like nothing happened. I don't know. I didn't mean to get all drama queen, when your problems are so much worse than mine. I'm sorry.

To: Anna Oliphant <bananaelephant@femmefilmfreak.net>
From: Étienne St. Clair <etiennebonaparte@soap.fr>
Subject: Are you mad?

My day was boring. Your day was a nightmare. Are you all right?

To: Étienne St. Clair <etiennebonaparte@soap.fr>
From: Anna Oliphant <bananaelephant@femmefilmfreak.net>
Subject: Re: Are you mad?

I'm okay. I'm just glad I have you to talk to.

To: Anna Oliphant <bananaelephant@femmefilmfreak.net>
From: Étienne St. Clair <etiennebonaparte@soap.fr>
Subject: So . . .

Does that mean I can call you now?

chapter twenty-nine

$\mathcal{I}$n the history of terrible holidays, this ranks as the worst ever. Worse than the Fourth of July when Granddad showed up to see the fireworks in a kilt and insisted on singing "Flower of Scotland" instead of "America the Beautiful." Worse than the Halloween when Trudy Sherman and I both went to school dressed as Glinda the Good Witch, and she told everyone her costume was better than mine, because you could see my purple "Monday" panties through my dress AND YOU TOTALLY COULD.

I'm not talking to Bridgette. She calls every day, but I ignore her. It's over. The Christmas gift I bought her, a tiny package wrapped in red-and-white-striped paper, has been shoved into the bottom of my suitcase. It's a model of Pont Neuf, the oldest bridge in Paris. It was part of a model train set, and because of my poor language skills, St. Clair spent fifteen minutes convincing the shopkeeper to sell the bridge to me separately.

I hope I can return it.

I've only been to the Royal Midtown 14 once, and even though I saw Hercules, Toph was there, too. And he was like, "Hey, Anna. Why won't you talk to Bridge?" and I had to run into the restroom. One of the new girls followed me in and said she thinks Toph is an insensitive douchebag motherhumping assclown, and that I shouldn't let him get to me. Which was sweet, but didn't really help.

Afterward, Hercules and I watched the latest cheesy Christmas movie and made fun of the actors' matching holiday sweaters. He told me about the mysterious package of roast beef he found in theater six, and he said he's been enjoying my website. He thinks my reviews are getting better. At least that was nice.

It was also nice when Dad left. He kept grilling me about French monuments and making these irritating calls to his publicist. We were all relieved to see him go. The only consistent bright spot has been St. Clair. We talk every day—calls, emails, texts. It doesn't escape my attention that when Toph and I were separated, our communications fizzled out, but now that I'm not seeing St. Clair every day, we talk even more.

Which makes me feel worse about Toph. If we'd been better friends, we *would* have kept in contact. It was dumb to think there was a chance we might make it. I can't believe Matt, of all people, was the one to point out how poorly I handled it. And, honestly, now that I've had time to reflect on it, Toph isn't even that huge of a loss. It only hurts so much to think about him because of Bridgette. How could she keep this a secret from me? Her betrayal is infinitely more painful.

I didn't have anywhere to go this New Year's, so Seany and I are staying in. Mom went out with some work friends. I order a cheese pizza, and we watch *The Phantom Menace*. This is how much I want to prove to my brother I love him—I'll sit through Jar Jar–freaking–Binks. Afterward, he drags out the action figures while we watch the Times Square countdown on television. *"Pkschoo! Pkschoo!"* Han Solo fires at my Storm Trooper before ducking behind a sofa cushion for cover.

"It's a good thing I wore my laser-proof jacket," I say, marching forward.

"There's no such thing as a laser-proof jacket! You're DEAD!" Han goes running across the back of the couch. "YEHH-AHHHH!"

I pick up Queen Amidala. "Han, you're in danger! Go the other way! The Storm Trooper is wearing his laser-proof jacket."

"An-nuhhhh, stop! *Pkschoo pkschoo!*"

"Fine," Amidala says. "Leave it to a woman to do a man's work." She bashes the Storm Trooper's head with her own. "GHHNNOOOO!" He falls off the couch.

Han jumps down to the carpet and begins shooting again.

I pick up young Obi-Wan. "Ooo, Amidala. You look radiant. *Kiss kiss kiss.*"

"No!" Seany snatches Obi-Wan from my hand. "No kissing."

I pull another figure from Seany's toy box. It's a Sand Person, the one Bridgette must have bought him. Oh, well. "Ooo, Amidala. *Kiss kiss kiss*."

"Sand People don't kiss! They ATTACK! RARRRRR!" He steals this one, too, but then pauses to examine its bumpy little head. "Why aren't you talking to Bridge?" he asks suddenly. "Did she hurt your feelings?"

I'm startled. "Yes, Sean. She did something that wasn't very nice."

"Does that mean she's not going to babysit me anymore?"

"No, I'm sure she will. She likes you."

"I don't like her."

"Sean!"

"She made you cry. You cry all the time now." He throws the Sand Person in the bottom of his box. "Do you still have the one you bought me?"

I smile. I get my backpack and start to hand the toy over, but something nags at me. *Sigh*. "You can have this on one condition. You have to be nice to her. It's either Bridgette or Granddad, those are Mom's only babysitting options. And Granddad's getting too old for this." I gesture toward the pile of discarded action figures.

"Okay," he says shyly. I give him the package, and he cradles it. "Thank you."

The kitchen phone rings. Mom checking up on us, no doubt. Seany gets up to answer it while I look for a suitable new boyfriend for Amidala. "I don't understand you," he says. "Please speak English."

"Sean? Who is it? Just hang up." Aha! Luke Skywalker! The one missing a hand, but oh well. Amidala and Luke kiss. Wait. Isn't she his mom? I toss Luke aside, as if he's personally offended me, and dig through the box again.

"Your voice is weird. Yeah, she's here."

"Sean?"

"Is this her BOYFRIEND?" My brother laughs maniacally.

I lunge into the kitchen and grab the phone. "Hello? St. Clair?" There's laughter on the other end of the line. Seany sticks out his tongue, and I push him away by his head. "GO. AWAY."

"Sorry?" the voice on the phone says.

"I was talking to Sean. Is that you?"

"Yeah, it's me."

"How'd you get this number?"

"Well, you see, there's this book. It has white pages. And it has all of these phone numbers listed inside it. It's also online."

"Is that your booooy-friend?" Seany asks directly over the receiver.

I push him away again. "He's a boy who's a friend. Go watch the countdown."

"What happened to your mobile?" St. Clair asks. "Did you forget to charge it?"

"I can't believe it! That's so unlike me."

"I know, I was shocked to be sent to voice mail. But I'm glad to have your real number now. Just in case."

The extra effort it took for him to call me makes me happy. "What are you up to? Shouldn't you be out celebrating?"

"Eh. Mum wasn't feeling well, so I'm staying in tonight. She's sleeping, so I suppose I'll be watching the countdown alone." His mom came home from the hospital a few days ago. The situation has been up and down.

"What about Ellie?" The words fall out before I can stop them.

"I, er . . . talked to her earlier. It's the New Year in Paris, after all. She went back the day after Christmas," he adds.

I picture them making Amidala kissing noises over the phone. My heart sinks.

"She's out partying." His voice is sort of glum.

"Sorry to be your second choice."

"Don't be stupid. Third choice. Mum's asleep, remember?" He laughs again.

"Thanks. Well, maybe I should hang up before *my* first choice falls asleep." I glance at Seany, who has become quiet in the other room.

"Nonsense, I've only just called. But how is your man? He sounded good, even if he didn't understand a word I said."

"You do talk funny." I smile. I love his voice.

"Speak for yourself, Atlanta. I've heard the southern accent slip out—"

"No!"

"Yes! Several times this week."

I hmph, but my smile grows bigger. I've spoken with Meredith a few times over the break, too, but she's never as much fun as St. Clair. I walk the phone into the living room, where Seany is curled up with my Sand Person. We watch the countdown together. I'm three hours ahead of St. Clair, but we don't care. When my midnight hits, we toot imaginary horns and throw imaginary confetti.

And three hours later, when his midnight hits, we celebrate again.

And for the first time since coming home, I'm completely happy. It's strange. Home. How I could wish for it for so long, only to come back and find it gone. To be here, in my technical *house*, and discover that home is now someplace different.

But that's not quite right either.

I miss Paris, but it's not home. It's more like . . . I miss this. This warmth over the telephone. Is it possible for home to be a person and not a place? Bridgette used to be home to me. Maybe St. Clair is my new home.

I mull this over as our voices grow tired and we stop talking. We just keep each other company. My breath. His breath. My breath. His breath.

I could never tell him, but it's true.

This is home. The two of us.

chapter thirty

$\mathcal{I}$t saddens me how relieved I feel to be going back to France. The plane ride is quiet and long. It's my first flight alone. By the time the plane lands at Charles de Gaulle, I'm anxious to get back to the School of America, even if it means navigating the *métro* by myself. It's almost as if I'm not afraid of riding it anymore.

That can't be right. Can it?

But the train ride back to the Latin Quarter is smooth and easy, and before I know it, I'm unlocking my door and unpacking my suitcase. Résidence Lambert rumbles pleasantly with the sound of other students arriving. I peek through my curtains at the restaurant across the street. No opera singer, but it's only the afternoon. She'll be back tonight. The thought makes me smile.

I call St. Clair. He arrived last night. The weather is unseasonably warm, and he and Josh are taking advantage of it. They're hanging out on the steps of the Panthéon, and he says I should join them. Of course I will.

I can't explain it, but as I stroll down my street, I'm suddenly racked with nerves. Why am I shaking? It's only been two weeks, but what a peculiar two weeks. St. Clair has morphed from this confusing *thing* into my closest friend. And he feels the same way. I don't have to ask him; I know it like I know my own reflection.

I stall and take the long way to the Panthéon. The city is beautiful. The gorgeous St-Etienne-du-Mont appears, and I think about St. Clair's mother packing picnic lunches and drawing the pigeons. I try to picture him racing around here in a young schoolboy's uniform, shorts and scabby knees, but I can't. All I see is the person I know—calm and confident, hands in his pockets, strut in his step. The kind of person who radiates a natural magnetic field, who everyone is drawn to, who everyone is dazzled by.

The January sun peeks out and warms my cheeks. Two men carrying what can only be described as man-purses stop to admire the sky. A trim woman in stilettos halts in wonder. I smile and move past them. And then I turn another corner, and my chest constricts so tightly, so painfully, that I can no longer breathe.

Because there he is.

He's engrossed in an oversize book, hunched over and completely absorbed. A breeze ruffles his dark hair, and he bites his nails. Josh sits a few feet away, black sketchbook open and brush pen scribbling. Several other people are soaking up the rare sunshine, but as soon as they're registered, they're forgotten. Because of him.

I grip the edge of a sidewalk café table to keep from falling. The diners stare in alarm, but I don't care. I'm reeling, and I gasp for air.

How can I have been so stupid?

How could I have ever for a moment believed I wasn't in love with him?

chapter thirty-one

I study him. He bites his left pinkie nail, so his book must be good. Pinkie means excited or happy, thumb means thinking or worried. I'm surprised I know the meaning of these gestures. How closely have I been paying attention to him?

Two elderly women in fur coats and matching hats shuffle past. One of them pauses and turns back around. She asks me a question in French. I can't make the direct translation, but I know she's concerned if I'm okay. I nod and tell her thank you. She flashes me another look of unease but moves on.

I can't walk. What am I supposed to say? Fourteen consecutive days of telephone conversations and now that he's here in person, I doubt I can stammer a hello. One of the diners at the café stands up to help me. I let go of the round table and stumble across the street. I'm weak in the knees. The closer I get, the more overwhelming it gets. The Panthéon is huge. The steps seem so far away.

He looks up.

Our eyes lock, and he breaks into a slow smile. My heart beats faster and faster. Almost there. He sets down his book and stands. And then this—the moment he calls my name—is the real moment everything changes.

He is no longer St. Clair, everyone's pal, everyone's friend.

He is Étienne. Étienne, like the night we met. He is Étienne; he is *my* friend.

He is so much more.

Étienne. My feet trip in three syllables. É-ti-enne, É-ti-enne, É-ti-enne. His name coats my tongue like melting chocolate. He is so beautiful, so perfect.

My throat catches as he opens his arms and wraps me in a hug. My heart pounds furiously, and I'm embarrassed, because I know he feels it. We break apart, and I stagger backward. He catches me before I fall down the stairs.

"Whoa," he says. But I don't think he means me falling.

I blush and blame it on clumsiness. "Yeesh, that could've been bad."

Phew. A steady voice.

He looks dazed. "Are you all right?"

I realize his hands are still on my shoulders, and my entire body stiffens underneath his touch. "Yeah. Great. Super!"

"Hey, Anna. How was your break?"

Josh. I forgot he was here. Étienne lets go of me carefully as I acknowledge Josh, but the whole time we're chatting, I wish he'd return to drawing and leave us alone. After a minute, he glances behind me—to where Étienne is standing—and gets a funny expression on his face. His speech trails off, and he buries his nose in his sketchbook. I look back, but Étienne's own face has been wiped blank.

We sit on the steps together. I haven't been this nervous around him since the first week of school. My mind is tangled, my tongue tied, my stomach in knots. "Well," he says, after an excruciating minute. "Did we use up all of our conversation over the holiday?"

The pressure inside me eases enough to speak. "Guess I'll go back to the dorm." I pretend to stand, and he laughs.

"I have something for you." He pulls me back down by my sleeve. "A late Christmas present."

"For me? But I didn't get you anything!"

He reaches into a coat pocket and brings out his hand in a fist, closed around something very small. "It's not much, so don't get excited."

"Ooo, what is it?"

"I saw it when I was out with Mum, and it made me think of you—"

"Étienne! Come on!"

He blinks at hearing his first name. My face turns red, and I'm filled with the overwhelming sensation that he knows *exactly* what I'm thinking. His expression turns to amazement as he says, "Close your eyes and hold out your hand."

Still blushing, I hold one out. His fingers brush against my palm, and my hand jerks back as if he were electrified. Something goes flying and lands with a faint *dink* behind us. I open my eyes. He's staring at me, equally stunned.

"Whoops," I say.

He tilts his head at me.

"I think . . . I think it landed back here." I scramble to my feet, but I don't even know what I'm looking for. I never felt what he placed in my hands. I only felt *him*. "I don't see anything! Just pebbles and pigeon droppings," I add, trying to act normal.

Where is it? What is it?

"Here." He plucks something tiny and yellow from the steps above him. I fumble back and hold out my hand again, bracing myself for the contact. Étienne pauses and then drops it from a few inches above my hand. As if he's avoiding touching me, too.

It's a glass bead. A banana.

He clears his throat. "I know you said Bridgette was the only one who could call you 'Banana,' but Mum was feeling better last weekend, so I took her to her favorite bead shop. I saw that and thought of you. I hope you don't mind someone else adding to your collection. Especially since you and Bridgette . . . you know . . ."

I close my hand around the bead. "Thank you."

"Mum wondered why I wanted it."

"What did you tell her?"

"That it was for you, of course." He says this like, *duh*.

I beam. The bead is so lightweight I hardly feel it, except for the teeny cold patch it leaves in my palm. Speaking of cold . . .

I shiver. "Has the temperature dropped, or is it just me?"

"Here." Étienne unwraps the black scarf that had been tied loosely around his neck, and hands it to me. I take it, gently, and wrap it around mine. It makes me dizzy. It smells like freshly scrubbed *boy*. It smells like him.

"Your hair looks nice," he says. "You bleached it again."

I touch the stripe self-consciously. "Mom helped me."

"That breeze is wicked, I'm going for coffee." Josh snaps his sketchbook closed. I'd forgotten he was here again. "You coming?"

Étienne looks at me, waiting to see how I answer.

Coffee! I'm dying for a real cup. I smile at Josh. "Sounds perfect."

And then I'm heading down the steps of the Panthéon, cool and white and glittering, in the most beautiful city in the world. I'm with two attractive, intelligent, funny boys and I'm grinning ear to ear. If Bridgette could see me now.

I mean, who needs *Christopher* when Étienne St. Clair is in the world?

But as soon as I think of Toph, I get that same stomach churning I always do when I think about him now. Shame that I ever thought he might wait. That I wasted so much time on him. Ahead of me, Étienne laughs at something Josh said. And the sound sends me spiraling into panic as the information hits me again and again and again.

What am I going to do? I'm in love with my new best friend.

chapter thirty-two

$\mathcal{I}$t's a physical sickness. Étienne. How much I love him.

I *love* Étienne.

I love it when he cocks an eyebrow whenever I say something he finds clever or amusing. I love listening to his boots clomp across my bedroom ceiling. I love that the accent over his first name is called an acute accent, and that he *has* a cute accent.

I love that.

I love sitting beside him in physics. Brushing against him during labs. His messy handwriting on our worksheets. I love handing him his backpack when class is over, because then my fingers smell like him for the next ten minutes. And when Amanda says something lame, and he seeks me out to exchange an eye roll—I love that, too. I love his boyish laugh and his

wrinkled shirts and his ridiculous knitted hat. I love his large brown eyes, and the way he bites his nails, and I love his hair so much I could die.

There's only one thing I don't love about him. *Her*.

If I didn't like Ellie before, it's nothing compared to how I feel now. It doesn't matter that I can count how many times we've met on one hand. It's that first image, that's what I can't shake. Under the streetlamp. Her fingers in his hair. Anytime I'm alone, my mind wanders back to that night. I take it further. She touches his chest. I take it further. His bedroom. He slips off her dress, their lips lock, their bodies press, and—oh my God—my temperature rises, and my stomach is sick.

I fantasize about their breakup. How he could hurt her, and she could hurt him, and all of the ways I could hurt her back. I want to grab her Parisian-styled hair and yank it so hard it rips from her skull. I want to sink my claws into her eyeballs and *scrape*.

It turns out I am not a nice person.

Étienne and I rarely discussed her before, but she's completely taboo now. Which tortures me, because since we've gotten back from winter break, they seem to be having problems again. Like an obsessed stalker, I tally the evenings he spends with me versus the evenings he spends with her. I'm winning.

So why won't he give her up? Why why why?

It torments me until I cave, until the pressure inside is so unbearable that I have to talk to someone or risk explosion. I choose Meredith. The way I see it, she's probably obsessing over the situation as much as I am. We're in her bedroom, and she's helping me write an essay about my guinea pig for French class. She's wearing soccer shorts with a cashmere sweater, and even though it's silly-looking, it's endearingly Meredith-appropriate. She's also doing crunches. For fun.

"Good, but that's present tense," she says. "You aren't feeding Captain Jack carrot sticks *right now*."

"Oh. Right." I jot something down, but I'm not thinking about verbs. I'm trying to figure out how to casually bring up Étienne.

"Read it to me again. Ooo, and do your funny voice! That faux-French one you ordered *café crème* in the other day, at that new place with St. Clair."

My bad French accent wasn't on purpose, but I jump on the opening. "You know, there's something, um, I've been wondering." I'm conscious of the illuminated sign above my head, flashing the obvious—I! LOVE! ÉTIENNE!—but push ahead anyway. "Why are he and Ellie are still together? I mean they hardly see each other anymore. Right?"

Mer pauses, mid-crunch, and . . . I'm caught. She knows I'm in love with him, too.

But then I see her struggling to reply, and I realize she's as trapped in the drama as I am. She didn't even notice my odd tone of voice. "Yeah." She lowers herself slowly back to the floor. "But it's not that simple. They've been together *forever*. They're practically an old married couple. And besides, they're both really . . . cautious."

"Cautious?"

"Yeah. You know. St. Clair doesn't rock the boat. And Ellie's the same way. It took her ages to choose a university, and then she still picked one that's only a few neighborhoods away. I mean, Parsons is a prestigious school and everything, but she chose it because it was familiar. And now with St. Clair's mom, I think he's afraid to lose anyone else. Meanwhile, she's not gonna break up with him, not while his mom has cancer. Even if it isn't a healthy relationship anymore."

I click the clicky-button on top of my pen. *Clickclickclickclick.* "So you think they're unhappy?"

She sighs. "Not unhappy, but . . . not happy either. Happy enough, I guess. Does that make sense?"

And it does. Which I hate. *Clickclickclickclick.*

It means I can't say anything to him, because I'd be risking our friendship. I have to keep acting like nothing has changed, that I don't feel anything more for him than I feel for Josh. Who, the next day, is ignoring our history lecture for the billionth class in a row. He has a graphic novel, Craig Thompson's *Goodbye, Chunky Rice,* hidden on his lap. Josh scrawls something into the sketchbook beneath it. He's taking notes, but not about the storming of the Bastille.

Josh and Rashmi had another blowup at lunch. No one is worried about Étienne dropping out anymore, but Josh is ditching with an alarming frequency. He's stopped doing homework altogether. And the more Rashmi pushes him, the more he pulls away.

Professeur Hansen paces the front of the classroom. He's a short man with thick glasses and wispy hair that flies out whenever he bangs our desks for emphasis. He teaches the dirty parts of history and never makes us memorize dates. I can see why Étienne is interested in the subject when he's had a teacher like this for four years.

I wish I could stop bringing everything back to Étienne.

I look at the juniors surrounding me, and discover I'm not the only one ravaged by hormones. Emily Middlestone bends over to pick up a dropped eraser, and Mike Reynard leers at her breasts. Gross. Too bad for him she's interested in his best friend, Dave. The eraser drop was deliberate, but Dave is oblivious. His eyes glaze over as they follow Professeur Hansen's pacing.

Dave notices me staring and sits up. I quickly turn away. Emily glares at me, and I smile blandly back. She returned to school with a stripe in her hair. It's pink and the rest is blond, so it's not *quite* like mine. Still.

Professeur Hansen relays the details of Marie Antoinette's execution. I can't concentrate. Étienne and I are going to the movies after school. And, okay, Josh and Rashmi are also coming—Mer can't because she has soccer practice—but that still makes this week's score: Anna 4, Ellie 1. The teacher bangs another desk, and the redhead to my left jumps and drops her papers.

I lean over to help her pick them up, and I'm startled to discover an entire page of doodles of a familiar skull tattoo. I look up in surprise, and her face burns as red as her hair. I glance toward Josh and then raise my eyebrows at her. Her eyes widen in horror, but I shake my head and smile. I won't tell.

What's her name? Isla. Isla Martin. She lives on my floor, but she's so quiet I often forget about her. She'll have to be louder if she likes Josh. They're both shy. It's a shame, because they'd look cute together. Probably fight less than he and Rashmi, too. Why is it that the right people never wind up together? Why are people so afraid to leave a relationship, even if they know it's a bad one?

I'm still contemplating this later, while Étienne and I wait outside Josh's room on the first floor, ready for the movies. Étienne presses his ear against Josh's door but then shoots back like it's on fire.

"What is it?"

He grimaces. "They've made up again."

I follow him outside. "Rashmi's in there?"

"They're having it off," he says bluntly. "I'd rather not interrupt."

I'm glad he's ahead of me, so he can't see my face. It's not like I'm ready to sleep with anyone—I'm not—but it's still this stupid wall between us. I'm always *aware* of it. And now I'm thinking about Étienne and Ellie again. His fingertips stroking her bare shoulder. Her lips parted against his naked throat. *Stop thinking about it, Anna.*

Stop it, stop it, STOP IT.

I switch the conversation to his mother. She's finished treatments, but we won't know if the disease is gone until March.

The doctors have to wait until the radiation leaves her system before they can test her. Étienne is always trapped between worry and hope, so I steer him toward hope whenever possible.

She's feeling well today, so he is, too. He tells me something about her medication, but my attention wavers as I study his profile. I'm jolted back to Thanksgiving. Those same eyelashes, that same nose, silhouetted against the darkness in my bedroom.

God, he's beautiful.

We walk to our favorite cinema, the one we've dubbed the "Mom and Pop Basset Hound Theater." It's only a few blocks away, and it's a comfortable one-screener run by the gentleman who walks Pouce, the dog from the *pâtisserie*. I don't actually think there's a "Mom" around—Pouce's owner is more likely a "Pop and Pop" kind of guy—but it's still a fitting nickname. We walk in and the friendly, dignified man behind the counter calls out, *"Jo-ja! Atlanna, Jo-ja!"*

I smile back. I've been practicing my French with him, and he's been practicing his English. He remembers I'm from Atlanta, Georgia (Jo-ja!), and we have another brief chat about the weather. Then I ask him if Pouce is a happy dog and if he, the gentleman, likes to eat good food. At least I'm trying.

The movie this afternoon is *Roman Holiday,* and the rest of the theater is empty. Étienne stretches his legs and relaxes back into his seat. "All right, I have one. Being bad has . . ."

"Never looked so good."

"Yes!" His eyes sparkle. This is one of our favorite games,

where one of us creates the beginning of a clichéd tagline and the other finishes it.

"With friends like these . . ."

He matches my darkened voice, *"Who needs enemies?"*

As my laughter bounces off the curtained walls, Étienne struggles to keep his expression straight. He fails and grins wider because of it. The sight makes my heart skip a beat, but I must make an odd face, because he covers his mouth. "Stop staring."

"What?"

"My teeth. You're staring at my bottom teeth."

I laugh again. "Like I have the right to make fun of anyone's teeth. I can shoot water incredible distances through this gap, you know. Bridge used to tease me all the ti——" I cut myself off, feeling ill. I still haven't talked to Bridgette.

Étienne lowers his hand from his mouth. His expression is serious, maybe even defensive. *"I* like your smile."

I like yours, too.

But I don't have the courage to say it aloud.

chapter thirty-three

The front-desk girl smiles when she sees me. "I 'ave package for you!"

Résidence Lambert's door opens again, and my friends troop in behind me. The girl hands over a large brown box, and I happily sign for it. "From your mom?" Mer asks. Her cheeks are pink from the cold.

"Yes!" Today is my birthday. And I know exactly what's inside. I carry the box eagerly to the lobby sofas and dig for something to open it with. Josh pulls out his room key and slices through the tape.

"AHH!" he screams.

Rashmi, Mer, and Étienne peek inside, and I gloat trium-phantly.

"No!" Mer says.

"Yes," I say.

Étienne picks up a slender green box. "Cookies?"

Josh snatches it from him. "Not just any cookies, my fine English fellow. *Thin Mints*." He turns to me. "Can I open this?"

"Of course!" Every year, my family celebrates my birthday with a feast of Girl Scout cookies instead of cake. The timing is always perfect.

Rashmi pulls out a box of Lemon Chalet Cremes. "Your mom is the best."

"What's so special about . . . Tagalongs?" Étienne says, inspecting another box.

"TAGALONGS?" Mer rips them from his hands.

"They're only the tastiest morsels on the entire planet," I explain to Étienne. "They only sell them this time of year. Haven't you ever had a Girl Scout cookie?"

"Did someone say *Girl Scout* cookies?"

I'm surprised to find Amanda Spitterton-Watts peering over my shoulder. Her eyes bulge when she sees my stash.

"Girl Scout cookies?" Another face appears behind us, wearing a familiar expression of confusion. It's Cheeseburger. Amanda curls her lip in disgust and turns back to me.

"You *have* to give me a Thin Mint," she says.

"Uh, yeah. Sure," I say. Josh makes a face, but I hand one over anyway. Amanda sinks her teeth into the chocolate wafer and grips Étienne's arm. She groans with pleasure. He tries to pull away, but her grasp is tight. She licks her lips. I'm amazed she doesn't have crumbs on her mouth. How does she do that?

"Have you ever *tasted* one of these?" she asks him.

"Yes," he lies.

Rashmi snorts.

There's a cough behind me, and I find Cheeseburger staring anxiously at my box. I glare at Amanda, the Arm-Toucher, and pull out an entire sleeve of Thin Mints. "Here you go, Cheeseburger."

He looks at me in surprise, but then again, that's how he always looks. "Wow. Thanks, Anna." Cheeseburger takes the cookies and lumbers toward the stairwell.

Josh is horrified. *"Whyareyougivingawaythecookies?"*

"Seriously." Mer gives Amanda an irritated glance. "Let's go someplace private." She grabs my package and carries it upstairs. Always prepared, she has fresh milk in her mini-fridge. They wish me happy birthday, and we clink glasses. And then we stuff ourselves until bursting.

"Mmm." Étienne moans from the floor. "Tagalongs."

"Told you," Mer says, licking chocolaty peanut butter from her rings.

"Sorry we didn't get you anything." Rashmi collapses. "But thanks for sharing."

I smile. "I'm happy to."

"Actually"—Étienne sits up—"I was planning to give this to you at dinner, but I suppose now is as good a time as any." He reaches into his backpack.

"But you hate birthdays!" I say.

"Don't thank me yet. And I don't hate them, I just don't

celebrate my own. Sorry it's not wrapped." He hands me a spiral notebook.

I'm confused. "Um . . . thanks."

"It's left-handed. See?" He flips it the other way. "Your old one is almost filled with notes and film reviews, so I thought you'd need a new one soon."

No one ever remembers I'm left-handed. A lump rises in my throat. "It's perfect."

"I know it's not much—"

"No. It's perfect. Thank you."

He bites his pinkie nail, and we smile at each other.

"Aw, St. Clair. That's sweet," Josh says.

Étienne chucks one of Mer's pillows at his head.

"So you've never explained it to me," Rashmi says. "What's the deal with that? The reviews?"

"Oh." I tear my gaze from Étienne. "It's just something I've always wanted to do. I like talking about movies. And it's hard to get into the business—it's kind of like a lifetime position—so I need all the practice I can get."

"Why don't you want to be a director? Or a screenwriter or an actress or something?" she asks. "No one wants to be a critic, it's weird."

"It's not weird," Étienne says. "I think it's cool."

I shrug. "I just like . . . expressing my opinion. That possibility of turning someone on to something really great. And, I dunno, I used to talk with this big critic in Atlanta—he lived in my theater's neighborhood, so he used to go there for screenings—

and he once bragged about how there hadn't been a respectable female film critic since Pauline Kael, because women are too soft. That we'll give any dumb movie four stars. I want to prove that's not true."

Mer grins. "Of course it's not true."

Étienne props himself up. "I don't think anyone who knows you would say it's easy to earn your good review."

I look at him, puzzled. "What does that mean?"

"Yawn," Josh says, not actually yawning. "So what's the plan?"

I wait for Étienne to reply, but he doesn't. I turn to Josh, distracted. "Huh?"

"Let's not sit here all evening. Let's go out."

He doesn't mean to the movies. I shift uncomfortably. "I like staying in."

Josh's eyes shine. "Anna. Haven't you ever drunk before?"

"Of course," I lie. But a blush destroys my cover. They all scream.

"How can you have gone half a school year without drinking?" Rashmi asks.

I squirm. "I just . . . don't. It still feels illegal."

"You're in France," Josh says. "You should at least try it."

And now they're all jumping up and down. You'd think they'd just turned of age. "YES! Let's get Anna drunk!" they say.

"I don't know—"

"Not drunk." Étienne smiles. He's the only one still sitting. "Just . . . happy."

"Happy birthday drunk," Josh says.

"Happy," Étienne repeats. "Come on, Anna. I know the perfect place to celebrate."

And because it's him, my mouth answers before my brain does. "Okay," I say.

We agree to meet later tonight. What was I thinking? I'd much rather stay in and hold a Michel Gondry marathon. I'm ooky with nerves, and it takes ages to find something to wear. My wardrobe isn't exactly stocked with clothes for barhopping. When I finally come down to the lobby, everyone's already there, even Étienne. I'm surprised he's on time for once. His back is to me.

"All right," I say. "Let's get this party started."

At the sound of my voice, he turns around. And his head nearly snaps off.

I'm in a short skirt. It's the first time I've worn one here, but my birthday feels like the appropriate occasion. "Woo, Anna!" Rashmi fake-adjusts her glasses. "Why do you hide those things?"

Étienne is staring at my legs. I tuck my coat around myself self-consciously, and he startles and bumps into Rashmi.

Maybe she's right. Maybe I should wear skirts more often.

chapter thirty-four

The band in the club is rocking so hard, screaming guitars and furious drumming and shouting lyrics, I can hardly hear myself think. All I know is that I feel good. Really good. Why have I never drunk before? I was such an idiot—it's not a big deal. I totally understand why people drink now. I'm not sure *what* I've been drinking, but I do know it was something fruity. It started out disgusting, but the more I drank, the better it got. Or the less I noticed it. Something like that. Man, I feel weird. Powerful.

Where is Étienne?

I scan the dark room, through the thrashing bodies of disillusioned Parisian youth, getting their anger out with a healthy dose of French punk rock. I finally find him leaning against a wall talking to Mer. Why is he talking to her? She laughs and tosses her curly hair. And then she touches his arm.

Meredith has turned into an Arm-Toucher. I don't believe it.

Before I know it, my feet are propelling the rest of my body toward them. The music thrums through my veins. I stumble over some guy's feet. He curses at me in French, and I mumble an apology as I lurch away. What's his problem?

Étienne. I need to talk to Étienne.

"Hey." I shout in his face, and he flinches.

"Jeez, Anna. Are you okay? How much have you had to drink?" Mer asks.

I wave my hand. Three fingers. Four fingers. Five. Something like that.

"Dance with me," I say to Étienne. He's surprised, but he hands Mer his beer. She fires me a dirty look but I don't care. He's more my friend than hers. I grab his hand and pull him onto the floor. The song changes to something even rowdier, and I let it take me over. Étienne follows my body with his eyes. He finds the rhythm, and we move together.

The room spins around us. His hair is sweaty. My hair is sweaty. I grab him closer, and he doesn't protest. I writhe down his body to the beat. When I come up, his eyes are closed, his mouth slightly parted.

We match each other thrust to thrust. The band launches into a new song. Louder and louder. The crowd is in a frenzy. Étienne screams the chorus with the rest of them. I don't know the words—even if I spoke French, I doubt I could make out the lyrics over the roar—all I know is this band is SO MUCH BETTER than the Penny Dreadfuls. HA!

We dance until we can't dance any longer. Until we're gasping for breath and our clothes are soaked and we can hardly stand up. He leads me to the bar, and I grip onto it with everything left in me. He falls next to me. We're laughing. I'm crying, I'm laughing so hard.

A strange girl shouts at us in French.

"Pardon?" Étienne turns around, and his eyes widen in shock when he sees her. The girl has sleek hair and a hard face. She keeps yelling, and I pick out a few choice swearwords. He replies in French, and I can tell by his stance and tone of voice that he's defending himself. The girl shouts again, gives him a final sneer, then spins away and pushes her way back through the pulsing mass.

"What was that about?" I ask.

"Shite. *Shite.*"

"Who was that? What happened?" I lift my hair to get some air on my neck. I'm hot. It's so hot in here.

Étienne pats his pockets, panicked. "Fuck. Where's my phone?"

I fumble in my purse and pull out my cell. "USE MINE!" I shout over the music.

He shakes his head. "I can't use yours. She'll know. She'll fucking know." He pulls at his hair, and before I know it, he's making his way for the door. I'm on his heels. We burst through the club into the cold night.

Snowflakes are falling. I don't believe it. It never snows in Paris! And it's snowing on my birthday! I stick out my tongue, but I don't feel them hit. I stick it out farther. He's still searching frantically for his phone. Finally, he finds it in a coat pocket. He calls someone, but they must not pick up, because he screams.

I jump backward. "What's going on?"

"What's going on? *What's going on?* I'll tell you what's going on. That girl in there, the one who wanted to kill me? That's Ellie's roommate. And she saw us dancing, and she's called her, and she's told her all about it."

"So what? We were just dancing. Who cares?"

"Who cares? Ellie's freaked out about you as it is! She hates it when we're together, and now she'll think something's going on——"

"She hates me?" I'm confused. What did I do to her? I haven't even *seen* her in months.

He screams again and kicks the wall, then howls in pain. "FUCK!"

"Calm down! God, Étienne, what's with you?"

He shakes his head, and his expression goes blank. "It wasn't supposed to end like this." He runs a hand through his damp hair.

What was supposed to end? Her or me?

"It's been falling apart for so long——"

Oh my God. Are they breaking up?

"But I'm just not ready for it," he finishes.

My heart hardens to ice. Screw him. Seriously. SCREW. HIM. "Why not, *St. Clair*? Why aren't you ready for it?"

He looks up at me when I say his name. St. Clair, not Étienne. He's hurt, but I don't care. He's St. Clair again. Flirty, friends-with-everyone St. Clair. I HATE him. Before he can answer, I'm stumbling down the sidewalk. I can't look at him anymore. I've been so stupid. I'm such an idiot.

It's Toph, all over again.

He calls after me, but I keep moving forward. One foot in front of the other. I'm focusing so hard on my steps that I bump into a streetlamp. I curse and kick it. Again and again and again and suddenly St. Clair is pulling me back, pulling me away from it, and I'm kicking and screaming and I'm so tired and I just want to go HOME.

"Anna. Anna!"

"What's happening?" someone asks. Meredith and Rashmi and Josh surround us. When did they get here? How long have they been watching us?

"It's all right," St. Clair says. "She's just a little drunk—"

"I am NOT DRUNK."

"Anna, you're drunk, and I'm drunk, and this is ridiculous. Let's just go home."

"I don't want to go home with you!"

"What the hell has gotten into you?"

"What's gotten into *me*? You've got a lot of nerve asking that." I stagger toward Rashmi. She steadies me while giving Josh an appalled look. "Just tell me one thing, St. Clair. I just want to know one thing."

He stares at me. Furious. Confused.

I pause to steady my voice. "Why are you still with her?"

Silence.

"Fine. Don't answer me. And you know what? Don't call me either. We're done. *Bonne nuit*."

I'm already stomping away when he replies.

"Because I don't want to be alone right now." His voice echoes through the night.

I turn around to face him one last time. "You *weren't* alone, asshole."

chapter thirty-five

$\mathcal{W}$ ow, Anna. You are such a mean drunk."

I pull the covers over my head. Rashmi is on the phone. My head is killing me.

"How much did you and St. Clair drink last night?"

Étienne. What happened last night? I remember the club. I remember the music and—Was there dancing? I think there was dancing—and, oh yeah, some girl was yelling at us, and then we went outside and . . . oh no.

Oh no, oh no, oh no.

I sit up quickly and ohmyfreakinggod my head is THROBBING. I close my eyes to shut out the painful light, and slowly, slowly sink back down into bed.

"You guys practically had sex on the dance floor."

We did?

I open my eyes again and regret it immediately. "I think I have the flu," I croak. I'm thirsty. My mouth is dry. Disgusting. It tastes like the bottom of Captain Jack's cage.

"More like a hangover. You should have some water. But not too much, you might puke again."

"Again?"

"Look in your sink."

I groan. "I'd rather not."

"Josh and I practically carried you home. You should be thanking me."

"Thanks." I am so not in the mood for Rashmi right now. "Is Étienne okay?"

"Haven't seen him. He went to Ellie's last night."

Just when I thought I couldn't feel any worse. I twist the corners of my pillow. "Did I, uh, say anything weird to him last night?"

"Apart from acting like a jealous girlfriend and saying you never wanted to speak to him again? No. Nothing weird at all." I moan as she recounts the night for me blow by blow. "Listen," she says when she finishes, "what's the deal with you two?"

"What do you mean?"

"You know what I mean. You two are inseparable."

"Except when he's with his girlfriend."

"Right. So what's the deal?"

I groan again. "I don't know."

"Have you guys . . . you know . . . done anything?"

"No!"

"But you like him. And he likes you, too."

I stop choking my pillow. "You think?"

"Please. The boy gets a boner every time you walk in the room."

My eyes pop back open. Does she mean that figuratively or has she actually *seen* something? No. Focus, Anna. "So why—"

"Why is he still with Ellie? He told you last night. He's lonely, or at least he's scared of being lonely. Josh says with all of this stuff with his mom, he's been too freaked out to change anything else in his life."

So Meredith was right. Étienne is afraid of change. Why haven't I talked about this with Rashmi before? It seems obvious now. Of course she has inside information, because Étienne talks to Josh, and Josh talks to Rashmi.

"You really think he likes me?" I can't help it.

She sighs. "Anna. He teases you all the time. It's classic boy-pulling-girl's-pigtail syndrome. And whenever anyone else even remotely does it, he always takes your side and tells them to shove it."

"Huh."

She pauses. "You really like him, don't you?"

I'm struggling not to cry. "No. It's not like that."

"Liar. So are you getting up today or what? You need sustenance."

I agree to meet her in the cafeteria in half an hour, but I have no idea why, because the moment I'm out of bed, I want to crawl back in. I'm nauseous, and my head feels like someone smacked it with a Wiffle ball bat. And speaking of whiffs, that's when I catch a smell of myself. My pores are boozy and sour. My hair reeks of stale cigarettes. And my clothes. Oh, *gross*. I run to my sink, dry-heaving.

And that's when I discover last night's vomit. And I puke for real. Again.

In the shower, I find weird bruises on my legs and feet. I have no idea what they're from. I slump in my tiny tiled corner and let the hot water run. And run. And run. I'm twenty minutes late for breakfast. Lunch. Whatever it is. Paris is blanketed in several inches of snow. When did that happen? How could I sleep through the first snowfall? The white glare makes me shade my eyes.

Thankfully, Rashmi is alone at our table when I stumble in. I couldn't face anyone else right now. "Morning, sunshine." She smirks at my wet hair and puffy eyes.

"What I don't understand is how people actually think drinking is fun."

"You were having fun when you were dancing last night."

"Too bad I can't remember."

Rashmi slides a plate of dry toast toward me. "Eat this. And drink some water, but not too much. You might throw up again."

"I already did."

"Well. You're off to a good start."

"Where's Josh?" I take a small bite of toast. *Yuck*. I'm not hungry.

"You'll feel better if you eat it." She nods at my plate. "He's still asleep. We don't spend every minute together, you know."

"Yeah. Right. That's why you and I hang out all the time."

Whoops.

Rashmi's brown skin reddens. "I know this'll be a shock to you, Anna, but you aren't the only one with problems. Josh and I aren't exactly on the best of terms right now."

I slink down in my seat. "I'm sorry."

She fiddles with her juice lid. "Whatever."

"So . . . what's going on?" It takes a minute of prodding, but once she starts, it's as if a dam has burst. It turns out they're fighting more often than I'd thought. Over Josh skipping school. Over her pushing him. She thinks he's upset because she's leaving next year, and he's not. We're all leaving for college, and he's not.

I hadn't thought of that before.

And she's upset about her younger sister, Sanjita, who's hanging out with Amanda's crowd, and worried about her brother, Nikhil, who's getting bullied, and angry with her parents, who won't stop comparing her to her older sister, Leela, who was the School of America's valedictorian two years ago. And Mer is always too busy with soccer to hang out, and Étienne and I are always buddy-buddy, and . . . she lost her best friend.

Ellie still hasn't called her.

And the whole time she's spilling her guts, I feel so ashamed. I never realized she didn't have anyone to talk with. I mean, I know Ellie was her best friend, and she wasn't around anymore, but somehow I forgot that meant Rashmi didn't have anyone else. Or maybe I assumed Josh was enough.

"But we'll work through it," she says about him. She's trying not to cry. "We always do. It's just hard." I hand her a napkin, and she blows her nose. "Thanks."

"Of course. Thanks for the toast."

She gives me half a smile, but it disappears as she notices something behind me. I turn in my seat to follow her gaze.

And there he is.

His hair is completely disheveled, and he's wearing his Napoleon shirt, which is more wrinkled than ever. He shuffles toward Monsieur Boutin with a plate of . . . dry toast. It looks like he hasn't slept in a week. And he's still beautiful. My heart shatters. "What do I say? What am I supposed to say to him?"

"Deep breath," Rashmi says. "Take a deep breath."

Breathing is impossible. "What if he won't talk to me? I told him not to talk to me anymore."

She reaches out and squeezes my hand. "You're fine. And he's coming over, so I'm letting go now. Act natural. You're *fine*."

Right. I'm fine. Right.

His walk to our table is excruciatingly slow. I close my eyes. I'm worried he won't sit with us, that he really WILL never speak to me again, when his tray clatters down across from me. I don't remember the last time he didn't sit beside me, but that's okay. As long as he's here.

"Hey," he says.

I open my eyes. "Hey."

"Shoot!" Rashmi says. "I gotta call Josh. I said I'd wake him before I ate, and I totally forgot. Seeyouguyslater." And she scurries away as if we're contagious.

I push my toast around my plate. Try another bite. Gag.

Étienne coughs. "You all right?"

"No. You?"

"Feel like hell."

"You look like hell."

"Says the girl with hair dripping like a wet beastie."

I sort of laugh. He kind of shrugs.

"Thanks a lot, Étienne."

He prods his toast but doesn't pick it up. "So I'm 'Étienne' again?"

"You have too many names."

"I have one name. People just split it oddly."

"Whatever. Yeah. You're Étienne again."

"Good."

I wonder if this interaction counts as an apology. "How was she?" I don't want to say her name.

"Vicious."

"I'm sorry." And I'm not, but I have an overwhelming urge to prove we can still be friends. There's an actual ache inside of me that needs him. "I didn't mean to mess things up, I don't know what got into me—"

He rubs his temples. "Please don't apologize. It's not your fault."

"But if I hadn't dragged you out to dance—"

"Anna." Étienne speaks slowly. "You didn't make me do anything I didn't want to do."

My face grows hot as the knowledge explodes inside of me like dynamite.

He likes me. Étienne really does like me.

But as soon as the information hits, it's replaced by confusion, by a notion so sickening it thrusts my emotions to the opposite end of the spectrum. "But . . . you're still with her?"

He shuts his eyes in pain.

I can't control my voice. "You spent the night with her!"

"No!" Étienne's eyes jerk back open. "No, I didn't. Anna, I haven't . . . *spent the night* with Ellie in a long time." He looks at me beseechingly. "Since before Christmas."

"I don't understand why you won't break up with her." I'm crying. The anguish of being so close to what I want, and it still being so far away.

He looks panicked. "I've been with her for a long time. We've been through loads together, it's complicated—"

"It's not complicated." I stand and shove my tray across the table. The toast bounces off the plate and hits the floor. "I put myself out there, and you rejected me. I won't make that mistake again."

I storm away.

"Anna! Anna, wait!"

"Oliphant! Feeling better?" I jump back, having nearly run into Dave. He's smiling. His friends Mike and Emily Middlestone, aka the Girl with the Pink Stripe, wait behind him with lunch trays.

"Um. What?" I look over, and Étienne is on his feet. He was about to follow me, but now that he's seen Dave, he isn't sure anymore.

Dave laughs. "I saw you in the lobby last night. Guess you don't remember. Your friends were struggling to get you in the elevator, so I helped them carry you."

 286

Rashmi didn't mention this.

"You yakked something fierce in your sink."

Dave was in my room?

"You okay today?" He tucks a shaggy lock of hair behind an ear.

Another glance at Étienne. He steps forward but then hesitates again. I turn back to Dave, something new and ugly hardening inside of me. "I'm fine."

"Cool. So we're going to this Irish pub in Montmartre tonight. Wanna come?"

I've had enough drinking for a while. "Thanks, but I'd rather stay in."

"That's cool. Maybe some other time?" He grins and nudges me. "When you're feeling better?"

I want to punish Étienne, hurt him in the way that he hurt me. "Yeah. I'd like that."

Dave's eyebrows lift, perhaps in surprise. "Cool. See you around, then." He smiles again, shyly this time, and then follows his friends to their usual table across the room.

"Cool," Étienne says behind me. "It was really cool talking to you, too."

I whirl around. "What's your problem? So you can keep dating Ellie, but I can't even talk to Dave?"

Étienne looks shamed. He stares at his boots. "I'm sorry."

I don't even know what to do with his apology.

"I'm sorry," he says again. And this time, he's looking at me. Begging me. "And I know it's not fair to ask you, but I need more time. To sort things out."

"You've had the entire year." My voice is cold.

"Please, Anna. Please be my friend."

"Your friend." I give a bitter laugh. "Right. Of course."

Étienne looks at me helplessly. I want to tell him no, but I've NEVER been able to tell him no. "Please," he says again.

I cross my arms, protecting myself. "Sure, *St. Clair*. Friends."

chapter thirty-six

9 can't believe you had lunch with David." Mer watches him swagger down the hall and shakes her head. We're headed in the opposite direction from him, toward physics.

"Dave," I correct. "What? He's a nice guy."

"If you like rodents," St. Clair says. "You'd think with those big bucked teeth, it'd be hard for him to chew."

"I know you don't like him, but you could at least try to be civil." I refrain from pointing out we've already had a conversation about our own less-than-perfect chompers. The last few weeks have been terrible. St. Clair and I are still friends—in theory—but now that *thing* is back, even larger and nastier than it was after Thanksgiving. It's so huge it feels physical, an actual weight and body keeping us from getting close.

"Why?" His voice is suspicious. "Are you two going out now?"

"Yeah, we set up our first date right after he asked me to marry him. Please. We're just friends."

Mer grins. "Dave doesn't want to be just friends."

"Hey, did you catch what our assignment was in English?" I ask.

"Subject-changer, thy name is Anna," Rashmi says. But in a friendly way. Since my postbirthday breakfast, things have been easier between us.

"I'm not changing the subject. I just didn't hear what our homework was."

"That's odd," St. Clair says. "Because I saw you write it down."

"I did?"

"Yes," he says. It's a challenge.

"Oh, come on, you guys," Mer says. Our friends are sick of us fighting, even though they still don't know the details of our current situation. Which is how I prefer it. "Anna, it's a comparative essay between the two stories in *Kitchen*. Remember?"

Of course I remember. I'm actually looking forward to this assignment. We just finished reading a book by Banana Yoshimoto, a Japanese author, and it's my favorite so far. Both of her stories are about heartache and mourning, but they're tinged with this . . . simplicity and romance. I can't help but think of my father's work.

He writes about love and death, too. But while his books are filled with sappy melodrama, Yoshimoto reflects on the healing process. Her characters are also suffering, but they're putting their lives back together. Learning to love again. Her stories are harder, but they're also more rewarding. The characters suffer in the beginning and the middle, but not the end. There's positive resolution.

I should mail my dad a copy. Circle the happy endings in red.

"Er," St. Clair says. "Shall we work on the paper together, then? Tonight?"

He's making an effort to be friendly. It sounds painful. He keeps trying, and I keep shooting him down. "I don't know," I say. "I have to get measured for my wedding dress."

St. Clair's face flickers with frustration, but for some reason this doesn't make me feel as satisfied as it should. Argh, fine. "Sure," I say. "That'd be . . . nice."

"Yeah, I need to borrow your calculus notes," Mer says. "I must have missed something. It just wasn't clicking for me today."

"Oh," St. Clair says. Like he just noticed she's standing here. "Yeah. You can borrow them. When you join us."

Rashmi smirks but doesn't say anything.

He turns back to me. "So did you enjoy the book?"

"I did." Discomfort lingers between us. "Did you?"

St. Clair considers it for a moment. "I like the author's name the best," he finally says. *"Ba-nah-na."*

"You're pronouncing it wrong," I say.

He nudges me gently. "I still like it best."

—

"Oliphant, what'd you get for number nine?" Dave whispers.

We're taking a pop quiz. I'm not doing so hot, because conjugating verbs isn't my strong point. Nouns I can handle—boat, shoelace, rainbow. *Le bateau, le lacet, l'arc-en-ciel*. But verbs? If only everything could be said in the present tense.

I go to store yesterday for milk!

Last night he ride bus for two hours!

A week ago, I sing to your cat at beach!

I make sure Professeur Gillet is distracted before replying to Dave. "No idea," I whisper. Though I actually do know the answer. I just hate cheating. He holds up six fingers, and I shake my head. And I *don't* know the answer to that one.

"Number six?" he hisses, not sure if I've understood him.

"Monsieur Higgenbaum!"

Dave tenses as Madame Guillotine advances. She rips the quiz from his hands, and I don't need to speak French to understand what she says. Busted. "And you, Mademoiselle Oliphant." She snatches my quiz as well.

That's so unfair! "But—"

"I do not tolerate chee-ting." And her frown is so severe I want to hide underneath my desk. She marches back toward the front of the classroom.

"What the hell?" Dave whispers.

I shush him, but she jerks back around. "Monsieur! Mademoiselle! I zought I made eet clear—zere iz no talking during tests."

"Sorry, *professeur*," I say as Dave protests he *wasn't* saying anything. Which is dumb, because everyone heard him.

And then . . . Professeur Gillet kicks us out.

I don't believe it. I've never been kicked out of a class. We're instructed to wait in the hall until the period is over, but Dave has other plans. He tiptoes away and motions for me to follow. "Come on. Let's just go in the stairwell so we can talk."

But I don't want to go. We're in enough trouble as it is.

"She'll never know. We'll be back before the hour is up," he says. "I promise."

Dave winks, and I shake my head but follow him anyway. Why can't I say no to cute boys? I expect him to stop once we're in the stairwell, but he descends the entire way. We go outside and onto the street. "Better, right?" he asks. "Who wants to be stuck inside on a day like today?"

It's freezing out, and I *would* rather be in school, but I hold my tongue. We sit on a chilly bench, and Dave is prattling about snowboarding or skiing or something. I'm distracted. I wonder if Professeur Gillet will let me make up the quiz points. I wonder if she's checking the hallway. I wonder if I'm about to get in more trouble.

"You know, I'm kinda glad we got kicked out," Dave says.

"Huh?" I turn my attention back to him. "Why?"

He smiles. "I never get to see you alone."

And then—just like that—Dave leans over, and we're kissing.

I. Am kissing. Dave Higgenbaum.

And it's . . . nice.

A shadow falls over us, and I break apart from his lips, which have already grown overactive. "Crap, did we miss the bell?" he asks.

"No," St. Clair says. "You have five more minutes of teeth gnashing to enjoy."

I shrink back in mortification. "What are you doing here?"

Meredith stands behind him, holding a stack of newspapers. She grins. "We should be asking you that question. But we're running an errand for Professeur Hansen."

"Oh," I say.

"Hiii, Dave," Mer says.

He nods at her, but he's watching St. Clair, whose face is cold and hard.

"Anyway! We'll let you get back to . . . what you were doing." Mer's eyes twinkle as she tugs on St. Clair's arm. "See you, Anna. Bye, Dave!"

St. Clair shoves his hands in his pockets. He won't meet my gaze as he stalks away, and my stomach turns over. "What's that guy's problem?" Dave asks.

"Who? Étienne?" I'm surprised when this name rolls out of my mouth.

"Étienne?" He raises his eyebrows. "I thought his name was St. Clair."

I want to ask, *Then why did you call him* that guy? But that's rude. I shrug.

"Why do you hang out with him, anyway? Girls are always going on and on about him, but I don't see what's so great."

"Because he's funny," I say. "He's a really nice guy."

Nice. That was how I described Dave to St. Clair the other day. What's wrong with me? As if Dave is anything like St. Clair. But he looks disgruntled, and I feel bad. It's not fair to compliment St. Clair to Dave's face. Not after kissing him.

Dave shoves his hands into his pockets. "We should get back."

We shlump upstairs, and I imagine Professeur Gillet waiting for us, smoke pouring from her nostrils like an incensed dragon. But when we get there, the hall is empty. I peek into her classroom window as she finishes up her lecture. She sees me and nods.

I don't believe it.

Dave was right. She never knew we were gone.

chapter thirty-seven

Okay, so Dave isn't as attractive as St. Clair. He's kind of gangly, and his teeth are sort of bucked, but his tan-but-freckled nose is cute. And I like how he brushes his shaggy hair from his eyes, and his flirty smile still catches me off guard. And, sure, he's a *little* immature, but he's nothing like his friend Mike Reynard, who's always talking about the Girl with the Pink Stripe's chest. Even when she's within hearing distance. And though I don't think Dave would ever get excited by a history book or wear a funny hat made by his mom, the important thing is this: Dave is available. St. Clair is not.

It's been a week since we've kissed, and we're dating now by default. Sort of. We've taken a few walks, he's paid for some meals, and we've made out in various locations around campus. But I don't hang out with his friends, and he's never hung out with mine. Which is good, because they tease me about Dave relentlessly.

I'm lounging around with them in the lobby. It's late Friday night, so there isn't a crowd. Nate is behind the front desk, because the regular workers are on strike. Someone is always striking in Paris; it was bound to happen here sooner or later. Josh sketches Rashmi, who is talking on the phone with her parents in Hindi, while St. Clair and Meredith quiz each other for a government test. I'm checking my email. I'm startled when one appears from Bridgette. She hasn't written in nearly two months.

I know you don't want to hear from me, but I thought I'd try one last time. I'm sorry I didn't tell you about Toph. I was afraid, because I knew how much you liked him. I hope someday you'll understand that I didn't mean to hurt you. And I hope your second semester in France is going well. I'm excited there are only two months until graduation, and I can't wait till prom! Does SOAP have a prom? Are you going with someone? Whatever happened to that English guy? It sounded like a more-than-friends situation to me. Anyway. I'm sorry, and I hope you're okay. And I won't bug you again. And I didn't use any big words because I know you hate that.

"Are you all right, Anna?" St. Clair asks.

"What?" I snap my laptop shut.

"You look like the Mom and Pop Basset Hound Theater closed," he says.

Bridgette and Toph are going to prom. Why am I upset? I've never cared about prom before. But they'll get those wallet-size pictures. He'll be in a tux that he's punk-rocked out with safety pins and she'll be in a fabulous vintage gown and he'll have his hands on her waist in some awkward pose and they'll be captured for all eternity together. And I am never going to prom.

"It's nothing. I'm fine." I keep my back to him and wipe my eyes.

St. Clair sits up. "It's not nothing. You're crying."

The front door opens, and the decibel level rises as Dave, Mike, and three junior girls arrive. They've been drinking, and they're laughing loudly. Emily Middlestone, the Girl with the Pink Stripe, clutches Dave's arm. One of his hands rests casually on her waist. Prom picture. The stab of jealousy surprises me.

Emily's cheeks are flushed, and she laughs harder than anyone else. Mer nudges me with the toe of her shoe. The others, even Josh and Rashmi, watch the situation with interest. I open my laptop back up, determined not to look as pissed off as I feel.

"Anna!" Dave gives me a gigantic, exaggerated wave. Emily's face sours. "You missed it!" He shakes her off and staggers toward me with limp arms. He looks like a newly hatched chick with useless wings. "You know that café with the blue window? We stole their outside tables and chairs and set them up in the fountain. You should've seen the look on the waiters' faces when they found them. It was awesome!"

I look at Dave's feet. They are, indeed, wet.

"What are you doing?" He flops down next to me. "Checking your email?"

St. Clair snorts. "Give the lad a medal for his brilliant skills in detection."

My friends smirk. I'm embarrassed again, for both Dave and myself. But Dave doesn't even look at St. Clair, he just keeps grinning. "Well, I saw the laptop, and I saw the cute frown that means she's concentrating so hard, and I put two and two together—"

"NO," I tell St. Clair, who opens his mouth to say something else. He shuts it, surprised.

"Wanna come upstairs?" Dave asks. "We're gonna chill in my room for a while."

I probably should. He *is* sort of my boyfriend. Plus, I'm annoyed with St. Clair. His hostile stare only makes me more determined. "Sure."

Dave whoops and pulls me to my feet. He trips over St. Clair's textbook, and St. Clair looks ready to commit murder. "It's just a book," I say.

He scowls in disgust.

Dave takes me to the fifth floor. St. Clair's floor. I forgot they were neighbors. His room turns out to be the most . . . American place I've seen in Paris. The walls are covered in tacky posters—99 BOTTLES OF BEER ON THE WALL, *Reefer Madness*, a woman with huge boobs in a white bikini. Her cleavage is covered with sand, and she's pouting as if to say: *Can you believe this? Sand! At the beach!*

The girls pile onto Dave's unmade bed. Mike hurls himself on top of them, and they squeal and bat at him. I hover in the doorway until Dave pulls me inside and onto his lap. We sit on his desk chair. Another guy comes in. Paul? Pete? Something like that. One of the juniors, a girl with dark hair and tight jeans, stretches in a move designed to show off her belly button ring to Paul/Pete. Oh, please.

The party divides and people make out. Emily doesn't have a partner, so she leaves, but not before shooting me another bitchy look. Dave's tongue is in my mouth, but I can't relax, because he's slobbering tonight. His hand creeps underneath my shirt and rests against the small of my back. I glance down at his other hand and realize they aren't much bigger than mine. He has little-boy hands.

"I need to take a leak." Mike Reynard stands, knocking tonight's date to the floor. I expect him to exit the room, but, instead, he does the unforgivable. He unzips his pants—right there in front of all of us—and *pees in Dave's shower.*

And no one says anything.

"Aren't you going to stop him?"

But Dave doesn't reply to my question. His head has fallen back, and his mouth is open. Is he *asleep?*

"Everyone pisses in the showers." Mike curls his lip at me. "What, you wait in line for the bathroom?"

I fight revulsion as I fly down the stairs to my floor. What was I thinking? I could've just contracted any number of life-threatening diseases. There's no way Dave has EVER cleaned his room. I think back to St. Clair's tidy, pleasant space, and I'm jealous of Ellie in an entirely new way. St. Clair would never hang up a poster of beer bottles or hold house parties in his room or use his shower as a toilet.

How did I end up with Dave? It was never a decision, it just happened. Was I only with him because I'm mad at St. Clair? The thought strikes a nerve. Now I feel ashamed as well as stupid. I reach for my necklace, and a new panic sets in.

Key. I don't have my key.

Where did I leave it? I curse, because there's no way I'm going back to Dave's room. Maybe it's downstairs. Or maybe I never grabbed it in the first place. Does this mean I have go to the front desk? Except—I swear again—they're striking. Which means I have to go to Nate's, which means I have to wake him up in middle of the night. Which means he'll get mad at me.

Mer's door flies open. It's St. Clair.

"Night," he says, clicking her door shut. She calls good night back. He glares at me, and I flinch. He knew I was out here.

"You and Higgenbaum have a nice time?" He sneers.

I don't want to talk about Dave. I want to find my freaking room key, and I want St. Clair to go away. "Yes. Great. *Thank you.*"

St. Clair blinks. "You're crying. That's the second time tonight." A new edge to his voice. "Did he hurt you?"

I wipe my eyes. "What?"

"I'll KILL that bloody—"

He's already halfway to the stairs before I can yank him back. "No!" St. Clair looks at my hand on his arm, and I hastily remove it. "I'm locked out. I'm just upset because I lost my stupid key."

"Oh."

We stand there for a moment, unsure of what to do with ourselves. "I'm going downstairs." I avoid his gaze. "Maybe I left it there."

St. Clair follows me, and I'm too exhausted to argue. His boots echo in the empty stairwell. *Clomp. Clomp. Clomp.* The lobby is dark and empty. The March wind rattles the glass on the front door. He fumbles around and switches on a light. It's a Tiffany lamp, red dragonflies with bulbous turquoise eyes. I start lifting couch cushions.

"But you were on the floor the whole time," he says. I think back, and he's right. He points to a chair. "Help me lift this. Maybe it was kicked under here."

We move it aside. No key.

"Could you have left it upstairs?" He's uncomfortable, so I know he means at Dave's.

"I don't know. I'm so tired."

"Shall we check?" He hesitates. "Or . . . shall I check?"

I shake my head no, and I'm relieved when he doesn't press me.

He looks relieved, too. "Nate?"

"I don't want to wake him."

St. Clair bites his thumbnail. He's nervous. "You could sleep in my room. I'll sleep on the floor, you can have my bed. We don't have to, er, sleep together. Again. If you don't want to."

That's only the second time, apart from one of his emails

at Christmas, either of us has mentioned that weekend. I'm stunned. The temptation makes my entire body ache with longing, but it's one hundred different kinds of a bad idea. "No. I'd— I'd better get it over with now. Because I'd still have to see Nate in the morning, and then I'd have to explain about . . . about being in your room."

Is he disappointed? He takes a moment before replying. "Then I'll go with you."

"Nate's gonna be mad. You should go to bed."

But he marches over to Nate's room and knocks. A minute later, Nate opens his door. He's barefoot and wearing an old T-shirt and boxer shorts. I look away, embarrassed. He rubs his shaved head. "Ungh?"

I stare at his diamond-patterned rug. "I locked myself out."

"Mmm?"

"She forgot her key," St. Clair says. "Can she borrow your spare?"

Nate sighs but motions us inside. His place is much larger than ours, with a private bath, a sitting room, and a full-size (though tiny by American standards) kitchen in addition to a separate bedroom. He shuffles over to a wooden cupboard in his sitting room. It's filled with brass keys hanging on nails, a painted golden number above each one. He grabs 408 and hands it to me. "I want that back before breakfast."

"Of course." I grasp the key so hard it dents my palm. "I'm sorry."

"Out," he says, and we scurry into the hall. I catch a glimpse of his condom bowl, which brings back another uneasy Thanksgiving memory.

"See?" St. Clair switches off the dragonfly lamp. "That wasn't so terrible."

The lobby is cloaked in darkness again, the only light coming from the screen saver on the front desk's computer. I stumble forward, patting the walls for guidance. St. Clair bumps into me. "Sorry," he says. His breath is warm on my neck. But he doesn't adjust his body. He stays close behind me as we stumble down the hall.

My hand hits the stairwell door. I open it, and we shield our eyes from the sudden brightness. St. Clair shuts it behind us, but we don't walk upstairs. He's still pressed against me. I turn around. His lips are only a breath from mine. My heart beats so hard it's practically bursting, but he falters and backs away. "So are you and Dave . . .?"

I stare at his hands, resting on the door. They aren't little-boy hands.

"We were," I say. "Not anymore."

He pauses, and then takes a step forward again. "And I don't suppose you'll tell me what that email earlier was about?"

"No."

Another step closer. "But it upset you. Why won't you tell me?"

I step back. "Because it's embarrassing, and it's none of your business."

St. Clair furrows his brow in frustration. "Anna, if you can't tell your best mate what's bothering you, who *can* you tell?"

And just like that, I have to fight to keep from crying for a third time. Because even with all of the awkwardness and hostility, he still considers me his best friend. The news fills me with more relief than I could have imagined. I've missed him. I hate being mad at him. Before I know it, the words spill out about Bridgette and Toph and prom, and he listens attentively, never taking his eyes from me. "And I'll never go to one! When Dad enrolled me here, he took that away from me, too."

"But . . . proms are lame." St. Clair is confused. "I thought you were glad we didn't have one."

We sit down together on the bottom step. "I was. Until now."

"But . . . Toph is a wanker. You hate him. And Bridgette!" He glances at me. "We still hate Bridgette, right? I haven't missed anything?"

I shake my head. "We still hate her."

"All right, so it's a fitting punishment. Think about it, she'll get dolled up in one of those satin monstrosities no rational girl would ever wear, and they'll take one of those awful pictures—"

"The picture," I moan.

"No. They're *awful*, Anna." And he looks genuinely revolted. "The uncomfortable poses and the terrible slogans. 'A Night to Remember.' 'This Magic Moment'—"

"'What Dreams Are Made Of.'"

"Exactly." He nudges me with his elbow. "Oh, and don't forget the commemorative photo key chain. Bridgette is bound to buy one. And it'll embarrass Toph, and he'll break up with

her, and that'll be it. The prom picture will be their complete undoing."

"They still get to dress up."

"You hate dressing up."

"And they still get to dance."

"You dance here! You danced across the lobby desk on Thanksgiving." He laughs. "There's no way Bridgette will get to dance on a desk at the prom."

I'm trying to stay upset. "Unless she's trashed."

"Exactly."

"Which she probably will be."

"No 'probably' about it. She'll be bombed out of her skull."

"So it'll be really embarrassing when she loses her dinner—"

He throws up his hands. "The terrible prom food! How could I have forgotten? Rubbery chicken, bottled barbecue sauce—"

"—on Toph's shoes."

"*Mortifying*," he says. "And it'll happen during the photo shoot, I guarantee it."

I finally crack a smile, and he grins. "That's more like it."

We hold each other's gaze. His smile softens, and he nudges me again. I rest my head on his shoulder as the stairwell light turns off. They're all on timers.

"Thanks, Étienne."

He stiffens at hearing his first name. In the darkness, I take one of his hands into my lap and squeeze it. He squeezes back. His nails are bitten short, but I love his hands.

They're just the right size.

chapter thirty-eight

$\mathcal{N}$ow I know why people are always carrying on about Paris in the springtime. The leaves are bright green with birth, the chestnut trees are clustered with pink buds, and the walkways are lined with lemon yellow tulips. Everywhere I look, Parisians are smiling. They've shed their woolen scarves for scarves that are thinner, lighter, softer. Le Jardin du Luxembourg, the Luxembourg Gardens, is busy today, but it's a pleasant crowd. Everyone is happy because it's the first warm day of the year. We haven't seen sunshine in months.

But I'm grateful for a different reason.

This morning, Étienne received a phone call. Susan St. Clair is *not* going to be the protagonist in a James Ashley novel. Her PET/CT scan was clear—no evidence of cancer. She'll still be

Stephanie Perkins

tested every three months, but as of right now, this very moment, his mother is alive in the fullest sense of the word.

We're out celebrating.

Étienne and I are sprawled before the Grand Bassin, an octagonal pool popular for sailing toy boats. Meredith is playing a league football game in an indoor field across the street, and Josh and Rashmi are watching. We watched, too, for a while. She's fantastic, but our attention to organized sports only lasts so long. Fifteen minutes into it, and Étienne was whispering in my ear and prodding me with lifted brows.

I didn't take much convincing. We'll head back in a bit, to catch the end.

It's strange that this is my first time here, because the garden rests against the Latin Quarter. I've been missing out. So far Étienne has shown me a beekeeping school, an orchard, a puppet theater, a carousel, and a courtyard of gentlemen lost in *boules*, lawn bowling. He says we're in the best park in all of Paris, but I think it's the best park in the world. I wish I could take Seany here.

A tiny sailboat breezes behind us, and I sigh happily. "Étienne?"

We're lying next to each other, propped up against the ledge of the Bassin. He shifts, and his legs find a comfortable spot against me. Our eyes are closed. "Hmm?" he asks.

"This is sooo much better than a football game."

"Mm, isn't it, though?"

"We're so rotten," I say.

He slaps me with a lazy arm, and we laugh quietly. Sometime later, I realize he's calling my name.

"Wha?" I must have drifted asleep.

"There's a sailboat in your hair."

"Huh?"

"I said, 'There's a sailboat in your hair.'"

I try to lift my head, but it snaps back, snagged. He wasn't kidding. An agitated boy about Seany's age approaches, speaking in rapid French. Étienne laughs as I try to pry the toy's sails from my head. The boat tips over, and my hair dips into the Bassin. The young boy shouts at me.

"Hello, help?" I throw an exasperated look at Étienne, whose laughter has reduced him into a fit of giggles. He struggles up as the boy reaches for my hair, tearing at the wet tangles.

"OUCH!"

Étienne snaps at him, and the boy lets go. Étienne's fingers wrap around my hair and gently work the cloth and string and wood from it. He hands the boat back to the boy and says something else, this time in a softer voice, hopefully warning him to keep the boat away from innocent bystanders. The boy clutches his toy and runs away.

I wring out my hair. "Ugh."

"That's very clean water." He grins.

"Sure it is." But I love how he knows what I'm thinking.

"Come on." He stands and offers his hand. I take it, and he helps me up. I expect him to drop it, but he doesn't. Instead, he leads me to a safe spot away from the pool.

It's nice holding hands. Comfortable.

I wish friends held hands more often, like the children I see on the streets sometimes. I'm not sure why we have to grow up and get embarrassed about it. We sit in the grass underneath a canopy of pink blossoms. I glance around for the Grass Police in their little conductor hats, always eager to remove citizens from the lawns, but I don't see them. Étienne is a good-luck charm when it comes to this sort of thing. My hair drips through the back of my shirt but, somehow, it's not so bad right now.

We are still holding hands.

Okay, we should let go. This is the point where it would be normal to let go.

Why aren't we letting go?

I force my gaze to the Grand Bassin. He does the same. We're not watching the boats. His hand is burning, but he doesn't let go. And then—he scoots closer. Just barely. I glance down and see the back of his shirt has crawled up, exposing a slice of his back. His skin is smooth and pale.

It's the sexiest thing I have ever seen.

He shifts again, and my body answers with the same. We're arm against arm, leg against leg. His hand crushes mine, willing me to look at him.

I do.

Étienne's dark eyes search mine. "What are we doing?" His voice is strained.

He's so beautiful, so perfect. I'm dizzy. My heart pounds, my pulse races. I tilt my face toward his, and he answers with an identical slow tilt toward mine. He closes his eyes. Our lips brush lightly.

"If you ask me to kiss you, I will," he says.

His fingers stroke the inside of my wrists, and I burst into flames.

"Kiss me," I say.

He does.

We are kissing like crazy. Like our lives depend on it. His tongue slips inside my mouth, gentle but demanding, and it's nothing like I've ever experienced, and I suddenly understand why people describe kissing as melting because every square inch of my body dissolves into his. My fingers grip his hair, pulling him closer. My veins throb and my heart explodes. I have never wanted anyone like this before. Ever.

He pushes me backward and we're lying down, making out in front of the children with their red balloons and the old men with their chess sets and the tourists with their laminated maps and I don't care, I don't care about any of that.

All I want is Étienne.

The weight of his body on top of mine is extraordinary. I feel him—all of him—pressed against me, and I inhale his shaving cream, his shampoo, and that extra scent that's just . . . him. The most delicious smell I could ever imagine.

I want to breathe him, lick him, eat him, drink him. His lips taste like honey. His face has the slightest bit of stubble and it rubs my skin but I don't care, I don't care at all. He feels wonderful. His hands are everywhere, and it doesn't matter that his mouth is already on top of mine, I want him closer closer closer.

And then he stops. Instinct. His body is rigid.

"How *could* you?" a girl cries.

chapter thirty-nine

My first thought is Ellie.

Ellie found us, and she's going to strangle me with her bare hands, right here, with the puppeteer and carousel horses and beekeepers all as witnesses. My throat will turn purple, and I'll stop breathing, and I'll die. And then she'll go to prison and write Étienne psychotic letters on parchment made from dried skin for the rest of his life.

But it's not Ellie. It's Meredith.

Étienne springs off me. She turns her head away, but not before I notice that she's crying. "Mer!" She runs away before I can say anything else. I look at Étienne, and he's rubbing his head in disbelief.

"Shite," he says.

"Shite is right," Rashmi says. I'm startled to discover she and Josh are here, too.

"Meredith." I moan. "Ellie." How could we let this happen? He has a girlfriend, and we both have a friend who is in love with him—the secret that isn't a secret and never has been.

Étienne jumps to his feet. His shirt is covered with dried grass. And then he's gone. He races after Meredith, shouting her name. He disappears behind a copse of trees, and Josh and Rashmi are talking, but I don't comprehend their words.

Did Étienne just leave me? For *Meredith*?

I can't swallow. My throat is closing. Not only have I been caught with someone I had no right to be kissing—and not only was it the greatest moment of my life—but he's rejecting me.

In front of everyone.

There's a hand in front of me, and in a daze, I follow it to its wrist, its elbow, its skull-and-crossbones tattoo, its shoulder, its neck, its face. Josh. He grips my hand and helps me stand. My cheeks are wet, and I don't even remember starting to cry.

Josh and Rashmi don't speak as they steer me onto a bench. They let me blubber about how I don't know how it happened, and I didn't mean to hurt anyone, and please don't tell Ellie. How I can't believe I did that to Mer, and she'll never talk to me again, and I'm not surprised Étienne ran away because I am so, so awful. The worst.

"Anna. *Anna*," Josh interrupts. "If I had a euro for every stupid thing I've done, I could buy the *Mona Lisa*. You'll be fine. You'll both be fine."

Rashmi crosses her arms. "Your lips weren't the only ones working out there."

"Meredith, she's so," I choke. "Nice." Again, that word. So inadequate. "How could I do that to her?"

"Yeah. She is," Rashmi says. "And that was pretty crappy of you guys to do that just now. What were you thinking?"

"I *wasn't* thinking, it just happened. I've ruined everything. She hates me. Étienne hates me!"

"St. Clair definitely doesn't hate you," Josh says.

"Though if I were Mer, I'd hate him." Rashmi scowls. "He's been leading her on for way too long."

Josh is indignant. "He's never once given her the impression that he liked her more than a friend."

"Yeah, but he's never discouraged her!"

"He's been dating Ellie for a year and a half. You'd think that'd be discouragement enough—oh. Sorry, Anna."

I sob harder.

They stay with me on the bench until the sunlight dips behind the trees, and then they walk me from *le jardin* back to Résidence Lambert. When we arrive, the lobby is empty. Everyone is still out enjoying the nice weather.

"I need to talk to Mer," I say.

"Oh, no, you don't," Rashmi says. "Give her time."

I slink into my room, scolded, and pull out my key. The night I lost it, I'd just left it in my room. The Beatles thump from the wall between Mer and me, and I remember my first night here. Is "Revolution" covering the sound of her crying? I tuck the key

315

back into my shirt and flop onto my bed. I pop up and pace my room, and then lie back down.

I don't know what to do.

Meredith hates me. Étienne has disappeared, and I don't know if he likes me or hates me or thinks he made a mistake or what. Should I call him? But what would I say? "Hi, this is Anna. The girl you made out with in the park and then ditched? You wanna hang out?" But I *have* to know why he left. I *have* to know what he thinks about me. My hand shakes as I put my phone to my ear.

Straight to voice mail. I look at my ceiling. Is he up there? I can't tell. Mer's music is too loud to hear footsteps, so I'll have to go up. I check my reflection. My eyes are puffy and red, and my hair looks like an owl pellet.

Breathe. One thing at a time.

Wash your face. Brush your hair. Brush your teeth, for good measure.

Breathe again. Open door. Walk upstairs. My stomach churns as I knock on his door. No one answers. I press my ear against the drawing of him in the Napoleon hat, trying to hear inside his room. Nothing. Where is he? Where IS he?

I go back to my floor, and John Lennon's scratchy voice is still blasting down the hall. My feet slow as I pass her room. I have to apologize, I don't care what Rashmi says, but Meredith is furious when she opens her door. "Great. It's you."

"Mer . . . I'm so sorry."

She gives a nasty laugh. "Yeah? You looked really sorry with your tongue lodged down his windpipe."

"I'm sorry." I feel so helpless. "It just happened."

Meredith clenches her hands, which are oddly ring-free. She's not wearing any makeup either. In fact, she's completely disheveled. I've never seen her look anything but polished before. "How could you, Anna? How could you do this to me?"

"I . . . I . . ."

"You *what?* You knew how I felt about him! I can't believe you!"

"I'm sorry," I say again. "I don't know what we were thinking—"

"Yeah, well, it doesn't matter anyway. He's not choosing either one of us."

My heart stops. "What? What do you mean?"

"He chased me down. Told me he wasn't interested." Her face reddens. "And then he went to Ellie's. He's there right now."

Everything turns hazy. "He went to Ellie's?"

"Just like he always does when there's trouble." Her voice changes to smug. "Now how does it feel? Not so hot anymore, huh?" And then she slams her door in my face.

Ellie. He's choosing Ellie. *Again.*

I run to the bathroom and yank up the toilet lid. I wait to lose my lunch, but my stomach just churns, so I put the lid back down and sit on it. What's wrong with me? Why do I always fall for the wrong guy? I didn't want Étienne to be another Toph, but he is. Only it's so much worse because I only liked Toph.

And I love Étienne.

I can't face him again. How could I possibly face him again? I want to go back to Atlanta, I want my mom. The thought shames me. Eighteen-year-olds shouldn't need their mother. I don't know how long I've been in here, but suddenly I'm aware of irritated sounds in the hallway. Someone bangs on the door.

"God, are you gonna be in there *all night?*"

Amanda Spitterton-Watts. As if things could get any worse.

I check my reflection. My eyes look like I've mistaken cranberry juice for Visine, and my lips are swollen like wasp stings. I turn the faucet marked *froid* and splash cold water on my face. A scratchy paper towel to dry, and then I hide my face with my hand as I escape to my room.

"Hello, *bulimic*," Amanda says. "I heard you, you know."

My back bristles. I turn, and her pale eyes widen in innocence over her beaky nose. Nicole is here, too, along with Rashmi's sister Sanjita, and . . . Isla Martin, the petite, red-haired junior. Isla lags behind. She's not a part of their crowd, just someone waiting in line for the bathroom.

"She was *totally* puking her dinner. Look at her face. She's *disgusting.*"

Nicole sniggers. "Anna always looks disgusting."

My face burns, but I don't react because that's what Nicole wants. I can't, however, ignore her friend. "You didn't hear anything, Amanda. I'm not bulimic."

"Did you just hear La Moufette call me a *liar?*"

Sanjita raises a manicured hand. "I did."

I want to smack Rashmi's sister, but I turn around. Ignore

them. Amanda clears her throat. "What's this about you and St. Clair?"

I freeze.

"Because while you were *puking*, I heard Rashmi talking to the dyke through her door."

I spin around. She did NOT just say that.

Her voice is like poisoned candy, sweet but deadly. "Something about the two of you hooking up, and now the *big freaky dyke* is crying her eyes out."

My jaw drops. I'm speechless.

"It's not like she ever stood a chance with him anyway," Nicole says.

"I'm not sure why *Anna* here thinks she stood a chance with him either. Dave was right. You *are* a slut. You weren't good enough for him, and you're *definitely* not good enough for St. Clair." Amanda flicks her hair. "He's *A-list*. You're D."

I cannot even begin to process that information. My voice shakes. "Don't you ever call Meredith that again."

"What, *dyke*? Meredith Chevalier is a big. Freaky. DYKE!"

I slam into her so hard that we burst through the bathroom door. Nicole is shouting and Sanjita is laughing and Isla is begging us to stop. People run from their rooms, surrounding us, egging us on. And then someone tears me off of her.

"What the hell is going on here?" Nate says, holding me back. Something drips down my chin. I wipe it and discover it's blood.

"Anna attacked Amanda!" Sanjita says.

Isla speaks up. "Amanda was goading her—"

"Amanda was defending herself!" Nicole says.

Amanda touches her nose and winces. "I think she broke it. Anna broke my nose."

Did I do that? Tears sting my cheek. The blood must have been a scratch from one of Amanda's fingernails.

"We're all waiting, Mademoiselle Oliphant," Nate says.

I shake my head as Amanda launches into a tirade of accusations. "Enough!" Nate says. She stops. We've never heard him raise his voice before. "Anna, for goodness' sake, what happened?"

"Amanda called Mer—" I whisper.

He's angry. "I can't hear you."

"Amanda called—" But I cut myself off when I see Meredith's blond curls hovering above everyone else in the crowd. I can't say it. Not after everything else I've done to her today. I look down at my hands and gulp. "I'm sorry."

Nate sighs. "All right, people." He gestures to the crowd in the hall. "Show's over, back to your rooms. You three." Nate points at me and Amanda and Nicole. "Stay."

No one moves.

"Get back to your rooms!"

Sanjita makes a hasty exit down the stairs and everyone else scrambles away. It's just Nate and the three of us. And Isla. "Isla, go back to your room," he says.

"But I was here." Her soft voice grows braver. "I saw it happen."

"Fine. All four of you, to the head's office."

"What about a doctor?" Nicole whines. "She totally broke Amanda's nose."

Nate leans over and inspects Amanda. "It's not broken," he says at last.

I exhale in relief.

"Are you sure?" Nicole asks. "I totally think she should go to a doctor."

"Mademoiselle, please refrain from speech until we get to the head's office."

Nicole shuts her mouth.

I can't believe it. I've never been sent to the principal's office! My principal at Clairemont High didn't even know my name. Amanda limps forward into the elevator, and I trudge behind with increasing dread. The moment Nate turns his back to us, she straightens up, narrows her eyes, and mouths this: *You're going down. Bitch.*

chapter forty

The head gave me detention.

ME. DETENTION.

Amanda was given one weekend, but I have detention after school for the next two weeks. "I'm disappointed in you, Anna," the head said, massaging the tension from her ballerina neck. "What will your father say?"

My *dad*? Who cares about my dad? What will Mom say? She'll kill me. She'll be so angry that she'll leave me here, imprisoned in France forever. I'll end up like one of those bums near the River Seine who smell like underarms and cabbage. I'll have to boil my own shoes for food like Charlie Chaplin in *The Gold Rush*. My life is RUINED.

The detention was divided unfairly because I refused to tell her what Amanda said. Because I hate that word. Like being gay is something to be ashamed of. Like because Mer likes sports, it automatically makes her a lesbian. The insult doesn't even make sense. If Meredith were gay, why would she be upset about Étienne and me?

I hate Amanda.

When the head asked Isla for the story, she defended me, which is the only reason I don't have detention for the rest of the year. She also took my cue; she didn't tell the head what Amanda said about Mer. I thanked her silently with my eyes.

We return to Résidence Lambert, and everyone is hanging around the lobby. Word of our fight has spread, and our class-mates are looking for bruises. They shout questions at us, as if this is a press conference for shamed celebrities, but I ignore them and push my way past. Amanda is already holding court, spreading her side of the story.

Whatever. I'm too furious to deal with that crap now.

I pass Dave and Mike in the stairwell. Mike does that dumb thing jerks do where they purposely bump your shoulder with theirs to throw you off balance.

"What the hell is your problem?" I shout.

Dave and Mike exchange surprised, self-satisfied smirks.

I stomp into my room. Everyone hates me. Étienne ditched me for his girlfriend. AGAIN. Meredith hates me, and Rashmi and Josh certainly aren't pleased. Dave and Mike hate me. And Amanda and her friends, and now everyone else downstairs, too. If only I'd taken Rashmi's advice. If only I'd stayed in my room,

Mer wouldn't have yelled at me. I wouldn't know Étienne chose Ellie. I wouldn't have attacked Amanda. And I wouldn't have detention for the next two weeks.

WHY IS ÉTIENNE CHOOSING ELLIE? WHY?

Étienne. Who has perfect lips and perfect kisses. Who tastes like honey. Who will never, ever, EVER give up his stupid girlfriend! I'm startled by a knock on my door. I'm worked into such a frenzy that I didn't hear the footsteps.

"Anna? Anna are you in there?"

My heart seizes. The voice is English.

"Are you all right? Amanda's downstairs, talking complete bollocks. She says you hit her?" He knocks again, louder. "Please, Anna. We need to talk."

I throw open the door. "*Talk?* Oh, you'd like to talk now?"

Étienne stares at me in shock. The whites of my eyes are still red, I have a two-inch scratch down my cheek, and my body is poised for attack. "*Anna?*"

"What, you didn't think I'd find out you went to Ellie's?"

He's thrown. "Wh-what?"

"Well?" I cross my arms. "Did you?"

He didn't expect me to know this. "Yes, but . . . but—"

"But *what?* You must think I'm a complete idiot, right? That I'm just some doormat who'll wait for you on the sidelines forever? That you can keep running back to her every time things get difficult, and I'll just *be okay* with it?"

"It's not like that!"

"It's ALWAYS like that!"

Étienne opens his mouth but then snaps it shut. His expression flips between hurt and fury a thousand times. And then it hardens. And then he storms away.

"I THOUGHT YOU WANTED TO TALK!" I say.

I slam my door.

chapter forty-one

*L*et's see. Yesterday, I: (1) made out with my best friend, even though I swore to myself I never would, (2) betrayed another friend by that same make-out session, (3) brawled with a girl who was already out to get me, (4) earned two weeks of detention, and (5) verbally attacked my best friend until he ran away.

Correction. Until he ran away *again.*

If there were a contest to see who could do more damage to herself in a single day, I'm pretty confident I would win. My mother spat fire when she found out about my fight with Amanda, and now I'm grounded for the entire summer. I can't even face my friends. I'm ashamed of what I've done to Meredith, and Rashmi and Josh have clearly taken her side, and St. Clair . . . he won't even look at me.

St. Clair. Once again, he's no longer Étienne, *my* Étienne.

That hurts worse than anything.

The whole morning is hideous. I skip breakfast and slip into English at the last possible second. My friends don't acknowledge my existence, but everyone else whispers and stares. I guess they're taking Amanda's side. I just hope they don't know about the St. Clair situation, which is unlikely considering how loudly I shouted at him in the hallway last night. I spend the class sneaking peeks at him. He's so exhausted that he can barely keep his eyes open, and I don't think he's showered.

But he's still beautiful. I hate that. And I hate myself for desperately wanting him to look at me, and I hate it even more when Amanda catches me staring, because then she smirks in a way that says, *See? I told you he was out of your league.*

And Mer. She doesn't have to turn her body away from me in her seat like St. Clair—although she does, they both do—because her waves of hostility crash into me, again and again, all period long. Calculus is an extension of this misery. When Professeur Babineaux hands back our homework, St. Clair passes the stack of papers behind his head without looking at me. "Thanks," I mumble. He freezes, just for a moment, before settling back into a rigid state of ignorance to my being.

I don't try talking to him again.

French is predictably bad. Dave sits as far from me as possible, but the way he ignores me is strange and purposeful. Some of the freshmen pester me about it, but I don't know what Dave's problem is, and thinking about him only makes me feel gross inside. I tell the annoying classmates to shove it, and Madame Guillotine gets mad at me. Not because I told them to shove it, but because *I didn't say it in French*. What is wrong with this school?

At lunch, I'm back in the bathroom stall, just like my first day.

I don't have an appetite anyway.

In physics, I'm grateful we don't have a lab, because I can't bear the thought of St. Clair finding a new partner. Professeur Wakefield drones on about black holes, and halfway through his lecture, Amanda gives an exaggerated stretch and drops a folded piece of paper behind her head. It lands at my feet. I read it underneath my desk.

HEY SKUNK GIRL, MESS WITH ME AGAIN & I'LL GIVE YOU MORE THAN A SCRATCH. DAVE SAYS YER A SLUTBAG.

Wow. Can't say anyone's ever called me that before. But why is Dave talking to Amanda about me? That's the second time Amanda has said something like this. And I can't believe I'm being called a slut for just *kissing* someone! I ball up the note and chuck it at the back of her head. For better or worse, my aim is so abysmal that it hits the back of her chair. It bounces and catches in her long hair. She doesn't feel it. I feel the slightest bit better. The note is still stuck in her hair.

Still there.

Still th—whoops. She shifts, and it falls to the ground, but Professeur Wakefield chooses this moment to walk down our

aisle. Oh, no. What if he finds it and reads it aloud? I really, truly don't need another nickname at this school. Next to me, St. Clair is also eyeing the note. Professeur Wakefield is almost to our table when he casually slides out his boot and steps on it. He waits until the *professeur* strolls away before retrieving the paper. I hear him uncrumple it, and my face flushes. He glances at me for the first time all day. But he still doesn't say anything.

Josh is quiet in history, but at least he doesn't switch seats. Isla smiles at me, and incredibly, this singular moment of niceness helps. For about thirty seconds. Then Dave and Mike and Emily huddle together, and I hear my name thrown around while they look back at me and laugh. This situation, whatever it is, is getting worse.

La Vie is a free period. Rashmi and St. Clair sketch for their art class while I pretend to bury my nose in homework. There's a tinkly laugh behind me. "Maybe if you weren't such a little slut, Skunk Girl, you might still have friends."

Amanda Spitterton-Watts, the biggest cliché in school. The pretty mean girl. Perfect skin, perfect hair. Icy smile, icy heart.

"What's your problem?" I ask.

"You."

"Excellent. Thank you."

She tosses her hair. "Don't you want to know what people are *saying* about you?" I don't answer, because I know she'll tell me anyway. She does. "Dave says you only *slept* with him to make St. Clair *jealous*."

"WHAT?"

Amanda laughs again and struts away. "Dave was right to *dump* your sorry ass."

I'm shocked. Like I'd ever sleep with Dave! And he told everyone that *he* broke up with *me*? How dare he? Is this what everyone thinks of me? Oh my God, is this what St. Clair thinks of me? *Does St. Clair think I slept with Dave?*

The rest of the week, I flip-flop between total despair and simmering rage. I have detention every afternoon, and every time I walk down the halls, I overhear my name spoken in hushed, gossipy tones. I look forward to the weekend, but it ends up being worse. I finished my homework in detention, so I have nothing to do. I spend my weekend at the movies, but I'm so distraught that I can't even enjoy it.

School has ruined cinema. It's official. There's nothing worth living for.

By Monday morning, my mood is so foul that I have the reckless courage to confront Rashmi in the breakfast line. "Why aren't you talking to me?"

"Excuse me?" she asks. "*You* aren't talking to *me*."

"What?"

"I never threw you from our table. You stopped coming." Her voice is tight.

"But you were mad at me! For . . . for what I did to Mer."

"All friends fight." She crosses her arms, and I realize she's quoting *me*. I said it last autumn after she fought with St. Clair about Ellie.

Ellie. I've ditched Rashmi, just like Ellie.

"I'm sorry." My heart falls. "I can't do anything right."

Rashmi's arms loosen, and she tugs one of her long braids. She's uncomfortable, an unusual emotion for her. "Just promise me next time you attack Amanda, you'll actually break something?"

"I didn't mean to!"

"Relax." She shoots me an uneasy glance. "I didn't realize you were so sensitive."

"You know, I still have another week of detention for that fight."

"That was a harsh punishment. Why didn't you just tell the head what Amanda said?"

I nearly drop my tray. "What? How do you know what she said?"

"I don't." Rashmi frowns. "But it must have been something seriously nasty to make you react like that."

I avert my eyes, relieved. "Amanda just caught me at a bad time." Which isn't entirely untrue. I place my order with Monsieur Boutin—a large bowl of yogurt with granola and honey, my favorite— and turn back to her. "You guys . . . don't believe what Amanda and Dave are saying, do you?"

"Dave is a jerk. If I thought you'd slept with him, we wouldn't be talking right now."

I'm gripping my tray so tightly that my knuckles are turning white. "So, um, St. Clair knows I never slept with him?"

"Anna. We *all* think Dave is a jerk."

I'm quiet.

"You should talk to St. Clair," she says.

"I don't think he wants to talk to me."

She pushes her tray away. "And I think he does."

I eat breakfast alone again, because I still can't face Mer. I'm five minutes late to English. Professeur Cole is sitting on top of her desk, sipping coffee. She narrows her eyes as I creep into my seat, but she doesn't say anything. Her orange sundress sways as she swings her feet. "People. Wake up," she says. "We're talking about the technical aspects of translation again. Do I have to do all the work here? Who can tell me one of the problems translators face?"

Rashmi raises her hand. "Well, most words have different meanings."

"Good," Professeur Cole says. "More. Elaborate."

St. Clair sits next to Rashmi, but he's not listening. He scribbles something fiercely in the margins of his book. "Well," Rashmi says. "It's the translator's job to determine which definition the author means. And not only that, but there could be other meanings in relation to the context."

"So what you're saying," Professeur Cole says, "is that the translator has a lot of decisions to make. That there are multiple meanings to be found in any word, in any sentence. In any situation."

"Exactly," Rashmi says. And then she cuts her eyes at me.

Professeur Cole laughs. "And I'm sure none of us have ever mistaken something someone has said or done to mean something else, right? And we're all speaking the same language. You can see how challenging this gets once things like . . . figures of speech are added. Some things just don't translate between cultures."

Misinterpretations swarm my mind. Toph. Rashmi. St. Clair?

"Or how about this?" Professeur Cole strolls over to the tall windows. "The translator, no matter how true he thinks he's staying to the text, still brings his own life experiences and opinions to the decisions he makes. Maybe not *consciously*, but every time a choice is made between one meaning of a word or another, the translator determines which one to use based on what *he believes is correct*, based on his own personal history with the subject."

Personal history. Like because St. Clair was always quick to run back to Ellie, I assumed he did it again. Is that it? And did he? I'm not sure anymore. I've spent my entire senior year suffocating between lust and heartache, ecstasy and betrayal, and it's only getting harder to see the truth. How many times can our emotions be tied to someone else's—be pulled and stretched and twisted—before they snap? Before they can never be mended again?

Class ends, and I stumble in a fog toward calculus. I'm almost there when I hear it. So quiet, it could almost be someone clearing his throat. "Slut."

I freeze.

No. Keep moving. I hug my books tighter and continue down the hall.

A little louder this time. "Slut."

And, as I turn around, the worst part is that I don't even know who it'll be. So many people hate me right now. Today, it's Mike. He sneers, but I stare past him at Dave. Dave scratches his head and looks away.

"How could you?" I ask him.

"How could *you*?" Mike says. "I always told Dave you weren't worth it."

"Yeah?" My eyes are still locked on Dave. "Well, at least I'm not a liar."

"*You're* the liar." But Dave says it under his breath.

"What was that? What did you say?"

"You heard me." Dave's voice is louder, but he's squirming, blinking at his friend. A wave of disgust rolls over me. Mike's little lapdog. Of course. Why didn't I see it before? My hands clench. One more word from him, one word . . .

"Slut," he says.

Dave slams into the floor.

But it wasn't my fist.

chapter forty-two

"Arghhh!" St. Clair cradles his hand.

Mike lurches for St. Clair, and I jump between them. "No!"

Dave moans from the floor. Mike pushes me aside, and St. Clair throws him into the wall, his voice filled with rage. "Don't touch her!"

Mike is shocked, but he bounces back. "You psycho!" And he lunges toward St. Clair just as Professeur Hansen steps between them, bracing himself for blows.

"Hey hey HEY! What is going ON out here?" Our history teacher glares at his favorite student. "Monsieur St. Clair. To the head's office. NOW." Dave and Mike simultaneously proclaim innocence, but Professeur Hansen cuts them off. "Shut it, the both of you, or follow Étienne." They shut up. St. Clair doesn't meet my eyes, he just storms away in the direction told.

"Are you okay?" Professeur Hansen asks me. "Did any of these morons hurt you?"

I'm in shock. "St. Clair was defending me. It— it wasn't his fault."

"We don't defend with our fists at this school. You know that." He gives me a wry look before departing downstairs to join St. Clair in the head's office.

What just happened? I mean, I know what happened, but . . . *what just happened*? Does this mean St. Clair doesn't hate me? I feel my first surge of hope, even though there's a chance that he just hates Dave and Mike more. I don't see him for the rest of the school day, but when I arrive in detention, he's already sitting in the back row.

St. Clair looks weary. He must have been here all afternoon. The *professeur* in charge today isn't here yet, so it's just the two of us. I take my usual seat—it's sad I have a usual seat—on the opposite side of the room. He stares at his hands. They're smudged with charcoal, so I know he's been drawing.

I clear my throat. "Thank you. For sticking up for me."

No reply. Okay. I turn back to the chalkboard.

"Don't thank me," he says a minute later. "I ought to have punched Dave ages ago." His boots kick the marble floor.

I glance over again. "How much detention did you get?"

"Two weeks. One per arsehole."

I give a small snort of laughter, and his head jerks up. My own hope flashes at me, mirrored in his expression. But it disappears almost instantly. Which hurts.

"It's not true, you know," I say bitterly. "What Dave and Amanda are saying."

St. Clair closes his eyes. He doesn't speak for several seconds. When he opens them again, I can't help but notice how relieved he looks. "I know."

His delayed reaction irks me. "You sure about that?"

"Yes. I am." He faces me for the first time in over a week. "But it's still nice to hear it from your own lips, all right?"

"Right." I turn away. "I can only imagine."

"And what, exactly, is that supposed to mean?"

"Forget it."

"No. Let's not forget it. I'm sick and tired of forgetting it, Anna."

"*You're* tired of forgetting it?" My voice shakes. "I've had to do nothing BUT forget it. Do you think it's easy sitting in my room every night, thinking about you and Ellie? Do you think *any* of this has been easy for me?"

His shoulders drop. "I'm sorry," he whispers.

But I'm already crying. "You tell me I'm beautiful, and that you like my hair and you like my smile. You rest your leg against mine in darkened theaters, and then you act as if nothing happened when the lights go up. You *slept in my bed* for three nights straight, and then you just . . . blew me off for the next month. What am I supposed to do with that, St. Clair? You said on my birthday that you were afraid of being alone, but I've been here this whole time. *This whole time*."

"Anna." He rises and edges toward me. "I am so sorry that

I've hurt you. I've made terrible decisions. And I realize it's possible that I don't deserve your forgiveness, because it's taken me this long to get here. But I don't understand why you're not giving me the chance. You didn't even let me explain myself last weekend. You just tore into me, expected the worst of me. But the *only truth I know* is what I feel when we're together. I thought you trusted those feelings, too. I thought you trusted me, I thought you *knew* me—"

"But that's just it!" I burst from my chair, and suddenly he's right on top of me. "I *don't* know you. I tell you everything, St. Clair. About my dad, about Bridgette and Toph, about Matt and Cherrie. I told you about being a *virgin*." I look away, humiliated to say it aloud. "And what have you told me? Nothing! I know nothing about you. Not about your father, not about Ellie—"

"You know me better than *anyone*." He's furious. "And if you ever bothered to pay attention, you'd understand that things with my father are beyond shite right now. And I can't believe you think so poorly of me that you'd assume I'd wait the entire year to kiss you, and then the moment it happened, I'd . . . I'd be *done* with you. OF COURSE I was with Ellie that night. I WAS BLOODY BREAKING UP WITH HER!"

The silence is deafening.

They broke up? Oh God. I can't breathe. I can't breathe. I can't—

He stares me directly in the eyes. "You say that I'm afraid of being alone, and it's true. I am. And I'm not proud of it. But you need to take a good look at yourself, Anna, because I am *not* the only one in this room who suffers this problem."

He's standing so close that I feel his chest rising and falling, quick and angry. My heart pounds against his. He swallows. I swallow. He leans in, hesitantly, and my body betrays me and mimics his in response. He closes his eyes. I close mine.

The door flies open, and we startle apart.

Josh enters detention and shrugs. "I ditched pre-calc."

chapter forty-three

I can't look at him for the rest of detention. How can I be afraid of being alone, if it's the only thing I've been lately? It's not like I've had a boyfriend all year, like he's had a girlfriend. Though I did cling to the idea of Toph. Kept him as—the thought makes me wince—a reserve. And Dave. Well. He was there, and I was there, and he was willing, so I was, too. I've been worried that I was only with Dave because I was mad at St. Clair, but perhaps . . . perhaps I *was* tired of being alone.

But is that so wrong?

Does that mean it's not wrong that St. Clair didn't want to be alone either? He's afraid of change, afraid to make big decisions, but so am I. Matt said that if I'd just talked with Toph, I could have saved myself months of anguish. But I was too scared to mess with the relationship we *might* have, to deal with what we really *did* have. And if I'd bothered to listen to what Matt was trying to tell me, maybe St. Clair and I would have had this conversation ages ago.

But St. Clair should have said something! I'm not the only one at fault.

Wait. Isn't that what he was just saying? That we're both at fault? Rashmi said I was the one who walked away from her. And she was right. She and Josh actually helped me that day at the park, and I ditched them. And Mer.

Oh my God, Meredith.

What's wrong with me? Why haven't I tried apologizing again? Am I incapable of keeping a friend? I have to talk to her. Today. Now. Immediately. When Professeur Hansen releases us from detention, I tear for the door. But something stops me when I hit the hall. I pause beneath the frescoed nymphs and satyrs. I turn around.

St. Clair is waiting in the doorway, staring at me.

"I have to talk to Meredith." I bite my lip.

St. Clair nods slowly.

Josh appears behind him. He addresses me with a peculiar confidence. "She misses you. You'll be fine." He glances at St. Clair. "You'll both be fine."

He's said that to me before. "Yeah?" I ask.

Josh lifts an eyebrow and smiles. "Yeah."

It's not until I'm walking away that I wonder if "both" means Meredith and me, or St. Clair and me. I hope both means *both.*

I return to Résidence Lambert, and I knock on her door after a quick trip to my own room. "Mer? Can we talk?"

She cracks open her door. "Hey." Her voice is gentle enough.

We stare at each other. I hold up two mugs. *"Chocolat chaud?"*

And she looks like she could cry at the sight. She lets me in, and I set down a cup on her desk. "I'm sorry. I'm so sorry, Meredith."

"No, *I'm* sorry. I've been a jerk. I had no right to be angry with you."

"That's not true, I knew how you felt about him, and I kissed him anyway. It wasn't right. I should have told you that I liked him, too."

We sit on her bed. She twists a glittery star-shaped ring around her finger. "I knew how you felt about each other. *Everyone* knew how you felt about each other."

"But—"

"I didn't want to believe it. After so long, I still had this . . . stupid hope. I knew he and Ellie were having problems, so I thought maybe—" Meredith chokes up, and it takes a minute before she can continue.

I stir my hot chocolate. It's so thick it's nearly a sauce. She taught me well.

"We used to hang out all the time. St. Clair and me. But after you arrived, I hardly saw him. He'd sit next to you in class, at lunch, at the movies. *Everywhere*. And even though I was suspicious, I knew the first time I heard you call him Étienne—I knew you loved him. And I knew by his response—the way his eyes lit up *every time* you said it—I knew he loved you, too. And I ignored it, because I didn't want to believe it."

The struggle rises inside me again. "I don't know if he loves me. I don't know if he does, or if he ever did. It's all so messed up."

"It's obvious he wants more than friendship." Mer takes my shaking mug. "Haven't you seen him? He suffers every time he looks at you. I've never seen anyone so miserable in my life."

"That's not true." I'm remembering he said the situation with his father is really terrible right now. "He has other things on his mind, more important things."

"Why aren't the two of you together?"

The directness of her question throws me. "I don't know. Sometimes I think there are only so many opportunities . . . to get together with someone. And we've both screwed up so many times"—my voice grows quiet—"that we've missed our chance."

"Anna." Mer pauses. "That is the dumbest thing I've ever heard."

"But—"

"But what? You love him, and he loves you, and you live in the most romantic city in the world."

I shake my head. "It's not that simple."

"Then let me put it another way. A gorgeous boy is in love with you, and you're not even gonna *try* to make it work?"

I've missed Meredith. I return to my room feeling both solaced and saddened. If St. Clair and I hadn't fought in detention today, would I have tried to apologize again? Probably not. School would have ended, we'd have gone our separate ways, and our friendship would have been severed forever.

Oh, no. The horrible truth knocks me over.

How could I have missed it? It's the same thing. The exact. Same. Thing.

Bridge couldn't help it. The attraction was there, and I *wasn't* there, and they got together, and *she couldn't help it*. And I've blamed her this entire time. Made her feel guilty for something beyond her control. I haven't even tried to listen to her; I haven't answered a single phone call or replied to a single email. And she kept trying anyway. I remember what Matt and Rashmi said *again*. I really do abandon my friends.

I yank out my luggage and unzip the front pocket. It's still there. A little beat-up, but a small package wrapped in red-and-white-striped paper. The toy bridge. And then I compose the most difficult letter I've ever written. I hope she forgives me.

chapter forty-four

The rest of the week is quiet. I mail Bridge's package, I rejoin my friends at our table, and I finish my detention. St. Clair and I still haven't talked. Well, we've spoken a bit, but not about anything important. Mostly we sit beside each other and fidget, which is ridiculous, because isn't that what this is all about? That we won't talk?

But breaking old habits isn't easy.

We sit a row apart in detention. I feel him watching me the entire hour, the entire week. I watch him, too. But we don't walk together to the dorm; he packs his things slowly to allow me time to leave first. I think we've arrived at the same conclusion. Even if we managed to begin *something*, there's still no hope for us. School is almost over. Next year, I'll attend San Francisco

State University for film theory and criticism, but he still won't tell me where he's going. I flat-out asked him after detention on Friday, and he stammered something about not wanting to talk about it.

At least I'm not the only one who finds change difficult.

On Saturday, the Mom and Pop Basset Hound Theater screens my favorite Sofia Coppola movie, *Lost in Translation*. I greet the dignified man and Pouce, and slide into my usual seat. It's the first time I've watched this film since moving here. The similarities between the story and my life are not lost on me.

It's about two Americans, a middle-aged man and a young woman, who are alone in Tokyo. They're struggling to understand their foreign surroundings, but they're also struggling to understand their romantic relationships, which appear to be falling apart. And then they meet, and they have a new struggle—their growing attraction to each other, when they both know that such a relationship is impossible.

It's about isolation and loneliness, but it's also about friendship. Being exactly what the other person needs. At one point, the girl asks the man, "Does it get easier?" His first reply is "no," and then "yes," and then "it gets easier." And then he tells her, "The more you know who you are, and what you want, the less you let things upset you."

And I realize . . . it's okay. It's okay if St. Clair and I never become more than friends. His friendship alone has strengthened me in a way that no one else's ever has. He swept me from my room and showed me independence. In other words, he was exactly what I needed. I won't forget it. And I certainly don't want to lose it.

When the film ends, I catch my reflection in the theater's bathroom. My stripe hasn't been retouched since my mother bleached it at Christmas. Another thing I need to learn how to do myself. Another thing I *want* to learn how to do myself. I pop into the Monoprix next door—which is kind of like a mini SuperTarget— to buy hair bleach, and I'm walking back out when I notice someone familiar across the boulevard.

I don't believe it. St. Clair.

His hands are in his pockets, and he's looking around as if waiting for someone. My heart swells. He knows Sofia is my favorite director. He knew I'd come here, and he's waiting for me to appear. It's finally time to talk. I soar over the crosswalk to his side of the street. I feel happier than I have in ages. And I'm just about to call his name, when I realize he's no longer alone.

He's been joined by an older gentleman. The man is handsome and stands in a way that's strangely familiar. St. Clair is speaking in French. I can't hear him, but his mouth moves differently in French. His gestures and his body language change, they become more fluid. A group of businessmen passes by and temporarily bars him from view, because St. Clair is shorter than them.

Wait a second. The man is short, too.

I startle as I realize I'm staring at St. Clair's father. I look closer. He's immaculately dressed, very Parisian. Their hair is the same color, although his father's is streaked with silver and is shorter, tidier. And they have that same air of confidence, although St. Clair looks unsettled right now.

I feel shamed. I did it again. Everything is not always about me. I duck behind a *métro* sign, but I've unwittingly positioned myself in hearing distance. The guilty feeling creeps back in. I should walk away, but . . . it's St. Clair's biggest mystery. Right here.

"Why haven't you registered?" his father says. "It was due three weeks ago. You're making it difficult for me to convince them to take you."

"I don't want to stay here," St. Clair says. "I want to go back to California."

"You hate California."

"I want to go to Berkeley!"

"You don't know what you want! You're just like her. Lazy and self-centered. You don't know how to make decisions. You need someone to make them for you, and I say you stay in France."

"I'm not staying in bloody France, all right?" St. Clair bursts out in English. "I'm not staying here with you! Breathing down my neck all the time!"

And that's when it hits me. I've been following their entire conversation. In French.

Oh. Holy. Crap.

"How dare you talk to me like this?" His father is enraged. "And in public! You need a smack in the head—"

St. Clair switches back to French. "I'd like to see you try.

Here, in front of everyone." He points at his cheek. "Why don't you, *Father?*"

"Why, you—"

"Monsieur St. Clair!" A friendly woman in a low-cut dress calls from across the boulevard, and St. Clair and his father both turn in surprise.

Monsieur St. Clair. She's talking to his dad. That's so weird.

She strolls over and kisses his father on both cheeks. His father returns *les bises*, smiling graciously. His whole manner is transformed as he introduces her to his son. She looks surprised at the mention of a son, and St. Clair—Étienne—scowls. His father and the woman chat, and St. Clair is forgotten. He crosses his arms. Uncrosses them. Kicks his boots. Puts his hands in his pockets, takes them out.

A lump rises in my throat.

His father keeps flirting with the woman. She touches his shoulder and leans into him. He flashes a brilliant grin, a dazzling grin—St. Clair's grin—and it's odd to see it on another person's face. And that's when I realize what Mer and Josh said is true. His father *is* charming. He has that natural charisma, just like his son. The woman continues to flirt, and St. Clair trudges away. They don't notice. Is he crying? I lean forward for a better look and find him staring right at me.

Oh, no. Oh no oh no oh NO.

He stops. "Anna?"

"Um. Hi." My face is on fire. I want to rewind this reel, shut it off, destroy it.

His expression runs from confusion to anger. "Were you listening to that?"

"I'm sorry—"

"I can't believe you were eavesdropping!"

"It was an accident. I was passing by, and . . . you were there. And I've heard so much about your father, and I was curious. I'm sorry."

"Well," he says, "I hope what you saw met your grandest expectations." He stalks past me, but I grab his arm.

"Wait! I don't even speak French, remember?"

"Do you promise," he says slowly, "that you didn't understand a single word of our conversation?"

I let go of him. "No. I heard you. I heard the whole thing."

St. Clair doesn't move. He glares at the sidewalk, but he's not mad. He's embarrassed.

"Hey." I touch his hand. "It's okay."

"Anna, there's nothing 'okay' about *that*." He jerks his head toward his father, who is still flirting with the woman. Who still hasn't noticed his son has disappeared.

"No," I say, thinking quickly. "But you once told me no one chooses their family. It's true for you too, you know."

He stares at me so hard that I'm afraid I'll stop breathing. I gather my courage and lace my arm through his. I lead him away. We walk for a block, and I ease him onto a bench beside a café with pale green shutters. A young boy, sitting inside, tugs at the curtains and watches us. "Tell me about your father."

He stiffens.

"Tell me about your father," I repeat.

"I hate him." His voice is quiet. "I hate him with every fiber of my being. I hate what he's done to my mother and what he's done to me. I hate that every time we meet, he's with a different woman, and I hate that they all think he's this wonderful, charming bloke, when really he's a vicious bastard who'd sooner humiliate me than discuss my education rationally."

"He's chosen your college for you. And that's why you didn't want to talk about it."

"He doesn't want me to be near her. He wants to keep us apart, because when we're together we're stronger than he is."

I reach over and squeeze his hand. "St. Clair, you're stronger than him *now*."

"You don't understand." He pulls his hand away from mine. "My mum and I depend on him. For everything! He has all of the money, and if we upset him, Mum is on the street."

I'm confused. "But what about her art?"

He snorts. "There's no money in that. And what money there *was*, my father has control over."

I'm silent for a moment. I've blamed so many of our problems on his unwillingness to talk, but that wasn't fair. Not when the truth is so awful. Not when his father has been bullying him his whole life. "You have to stand up to him," I say.

"It's easy for you to say—"

"No, it's *not* easy for me to say! It's not easy for me to see you like this. But you can't let him win. You have to be smarter than him, you have to beat him at his own game."

"His own game?" He gives a disgusted laugh. "No, thank you. I'd rather not play by his rules."

My mind is working in overdrive. "Listen to me, the second that woman showed up, his personality completely changed—"

"Oh, you noticed, did you?"

"Shut up and listen, St. Clair. This is what you're gonna do. You're going back there *right now*, and if she's still there, you're telling her how happy you are that he's sending you to Berkeley."

He tries to interrupt, but I push forward. "And then you're going to his art gallery, and you're telling everyone who works there how *happy* you are that he's sending you to Berkeley. Then you're calling your grandparents, and you're telling them how *happy* you are that he's sending you to Berkeley. And then you're telling his neighbors, his grocer, the man who sells him cigarettes, EVERYONE in his life how *happy* you are that he's *sending you to Berkeley*."

He's biting his thumbnail.

"And he'll be pissed as hell," I say, "and I wouldn't trade places with you for a second. But he's clearly a man who believes in keeping up appearances. So what's he gonna do? He'll send you to Berkeley to save face."

St. Clair pauses. "It's mad, but . . . it's so mad it might work."

"You don't always have to solve your problems alone, you know. This is why people talk to their friends." I smile and widen my eyes for emphasis.

He shakes his head, trying to speak.

"GO," I say. "Quick, while she's still there!"

St. Clair hesitates again, and I push him up. "Go. Go go go!"

He rubs the back of his neck. "Thank you."

"*Go.*"

He does.

chapter forty-five

I return to Résidence Lambert. I'm anxious to know what's happening, but St. Clair has to deal with his father on his own. He has to stand up for himself. The glass banana bead on my dresser snags my attention, and I cradle it in my hand. He's given me so many gifts this year—the bead, the left-handed notebook, the Canadian flag. It feels good to have finally given him something back. I hope my idea works.

I decide to pull out my homework. I'm flipping through my papers when I discover the assignment for English. Our last unit, poetry. The Neruda book. It sits on the shelf above my desk in the same place it's been since Thanksgiving. Because it was a schoolbook, right? Just another gift?

Wrong. So very, very wrong.

I mean, it *is* a schoolbook, but it's also love poetry. Really *sexy* love poetry. Why would he have given this to me if it didn't mean anything? He could have given me the Banana Yoshimoto book. Or one of our translation textbooks.

But he bought me love poetry.

I flip back to the front, and the stamp stares at me. SHAKESPEARE AND COMPANY, KILOMETER ZERO PARIS. And I'm back on the star, that first night. Falling in love with him. And I'm back on the star, over Thanksgiving break. Falling in love with him. And I'm back in my room, staring at this ill-timed book—Why didn't he just *tell* me? Why didn't I open this when he asked me about it last Christmas?—when I'm struck by a need to return to Point Zéro.

I only have a few weeks left in Paris, and I still haven't been inside of Notre-Dame. What am I doing in the dormitory on a Saturday afternoon? I yank on my shoes, run out of the building, and race down the boulevards at the speed of sound. I can't get there fast enough. I have to be there. Now. I can't explain it.

The eyes of the city are fastened to me as I shoot across the Seine and onto the Île de la Cité, but this time, I don't care. The cathedral is as breathtaking as ever. A crowd of tourists is gathered around Point Zéro, and I admire the star as I fly by, but I don't wait for a turn, I just keep pushing pushing pushing forward until I'm inside.

Once again, Paris leaves me awed.

The high-vaulted ceiling, the intricate stained glass, the gold-and-marble statuary, the delicately carved woodwork . . . Notre-

Dame is mesmerizing. Organ music and the murmurs of many languages surround me. The warm scent of burning candles fills the air. And I've never seen anything lovelier than the jewel-colored light shining through the rose windows.

An enthusiastic tour guide passes behind me, waving his hands about. "Just imagine! In the early nineteenth century, this cathedral was in such a state of disrepair that the city considered tearing it down. Luckily for us, Victor Hugo heard about the plans to destroy it and wrote *The Hunchback of Notre-Dame* to raise awareness of its glorious history. And, by golly, did it work! Parisians campaigned to save it, and the building was repaired and polished to the pristine state you find today."

I smile as I leave them, wondering what building my dad would try to save with his writing. Probably a baseball stadium. Or a Burger King. I examine the high altar and the statues of the Virgin Mary. It's peaceful, but I'm restless. I examine my visitor's guide and my attention is snagged by the words *Galerie des Chimères*.

The chimera. The gargoyles. Of course!

I need to go up, I need to see the city while I still can. The entrance to the towers—to the top of Notre-Dame—is to the left of the main doors. While I'm paying to get in, I swear I hear someone call my name. I scan the courtyard but don't see anyone familiar.

So I climb the stairs.

The first landing leads to a gift shop, so I keep going up. And up. And up. *Oof.* There sure are a lot of stairs. Holy crap, will these things ever end?

Seriously?

MORE STAIRS?

This is ridiculous. I'm never buying a house with stairs. I won't even have steps to my front door, just a gradual incline. With each step, I loathe the gargoyles more and more, until I reach the exit and—

I'm really high up. I follow the tight walkway that leads from the North Tower to the South. There's my neighborhood! And the Panthéon! Its massive dome is impressive, even from here, but the tourists around me are snapping pictures of the gargoyles.

No. Not gargoyles. Chimera.

St. Clair once told me that what most people think of when they hear the word "gargoyle" is really a chimera. And gargoyles are these skinny things that stick straight out and are used as rain gutters. I don't remember the purpose of the chimeras. Were they protecting the cathedral? A warning to demons? If he were here, he'd tell me the story again. I consider calling him, but he's probably still busy with his father. He doesn't need me bothering him with vocabulary questions.

The Galerie des Chimères is pretty cool. The statues are half man and half beast, grotesque, fantastic creatures with beaks and wings and tails. My favorite holds his head in his hands and sticks out his tongue, contemplating the city. Or maybe he's just frustrated. Or sad. I check out the belfry. And it's . . . a big bell.

What am I doing here?

A guard waits beside another set of stairs. I take a deep breath. *"Bonne soirée,"* I say. He smiles and lets me pass. I squeeze inside. It's a tight corkscrew, and the staircase grows narrower and narrower as I climb. The stone walls are cold. For the first time here, I'm paranoid about falling. I'm glad I'm alone. If someone came down, someone even a little bigger than me, I don't know how we'd pass each other. My heart beats faster, my ears prick for footsteps, and I'm worried this was a mistake when—

I'm there. I'm on top of Paris.

Like the chimera gallery, there's a protective wire structure to keep people from falling or jumping. And I'm so high up, that I'm grateful for it. I'm the only one here, so I sit on one of the quiet stone corners and watch the city.

I'm leaving soon. I wonder what Dad would say if he could see me, melancholy about saying goodbye when I fought so hard to stay in Atlanta. He meant well. Observing the steady boats gliding down the Seine and the proud Eiffel Tower stretched above the Champ de Mars, I know this now. A noise on the stairwell startles me—a screech, followed by pounding feet. Someone is running up the stairs. And I'm alone.

Relax, Anna. I'm sure it's just a tourist.

A running tourist?

I prepare for the onslaught, and it doesn't take long. A man bursts onto the viewing platform. He's wearing teeny tiny running shorts and athletic sneakers. Did he just climb those stairs *for fun*? He doesn't acknowledge me, just stretches, jogs in place for thirty seconds, and then bursts back down the stairs.

That was weird.

I'm settling back down when I hear another yell. I bolt up. Why would the running man be screaming? There's someone else there, terrified by the runner, afraid of falling. I listen for more footsteps but don't hear anything. Whoever it is has stopped. I think about St. Clair, about how frightened he is of heights. This person may be trapped. With growing dread, I realize perhaps someone *did* fall.

I peek down the stairs. "Hello? *Bonsoir? Ça va?*" No response. I climb down a few spirals, wondering why it's *me* doing this, not the guard. "Is someone there? Do you need help?"

There's a strange shifting, and I continue down cautiously. "Hello?" They must not speak English. I hear them panting. They're just below me, just around this corner—

I scream. He screams.

chapter forty-six

Wat the hell are you doing here? Jeez, St. Clair! You scared the crap out of me."

He's crouched down, gripping the stairs, and looking more freaked out than I've ever seen him before. "Then why did you come down?" he snaps.

"I was trying to *help*. I heard a scream. I thought maybe someone was hurt."

His pale skin is beet red. "No. I'm not hurt."

"What are you doing here?" I ask again, but he's silent. "At least let me help you."

He stands, and his legs wobble like a baby goat. "I'm fine."

"You're not fine. You are clearly not fine. Give me your hand."

St. Clair resists, but I grab it and start herding him down. "Wait." He glances up and swallows. "I want to see the top."

I give him a look that I hope is incredulous. "Sure you do."

"No," he says with a new determination. "I want to see the top."

"Fine, go." I release his hand.

He just stands there. I take his hand again. "Oh, come on." Our climb is painful and slow. I'm thankful no one is behind us. We don't speak, but his grip is crushing my fingers. "Almost there. You're doing good, so good."

"Piss. Off."

I should push him back down.

At last we reach the top. I let go of his hand, and he collapses to the ground. I give him a few minutes. "You okay?"

"Yes," he says miserably.

And I'm not sure what to do. I'm stuck on a tiny roof in the center of Paris with my best friend, who is scared of heights and also apparently angry with me. And I have no idea why he's even here in the first place. I take a seat, lock my eyes on the riverboats, and ask a third time. "What are you doing here?"

He takes a deep breath. "I came for you."

"And how on EARTH did you know I was up here?"

"I saw you." He pauses. "I came to make another wish, and I was standing on Point Zéro when I saw you enter the tower. I called your name, and you looked around, but you didn't see me."

"So you decided to just . . . come up?" I'm doubtful, despite the evidence in front of me. It must have taken superhuman

strength for him to make it past the first flight of stairs alone.

"I had to. I couldn't wait for you to come down, I couldn't wait any longer. I had to see you now. I have to know——"

He breaks off, and my pulse races. What what what?

"Why did you lie to me?"

The question startles me. Not what I was expecting. Nor hoping. He's still on the ground, but he stares up at me. His brown eyes are huge and heartbroken. I'm confused. "I'm sorry, I don't know what——"

"November. At the *crêperie*. I asked you if we'd talked about anything strange that night I was drunk in your room. If I had said anything about our relationship, or my relationship with Ellie. And you said no."

Oh my God. "How did you know?"

"Josh told me."

"When?"

"November."

I'm stunned. "I . . . I . . ." My throat is dry. "If you'd seen the look on your face that day. In the restaurant. How could I possibly tell you? With your mother——"

"But if you had, I wouldn't have wasted all of these months. I thought you were turning me down. I thought you weren't interested."

"But you were drunk! You had a girlfriend! What was I supposed to do? God, St. Clair, I didn't even know if you meant it."

"Of course I meant it." He stands, and his legs falter.

"Careful!"

Step. Step. Step. He toddles toward me, and I reach for his hand to guide him. We're so close to the edge. He sits next to me and grips my hand harder. "I meant it, Anna. I *mean* it."

"I don't under—"

He's exasperated. "I'm saying I'm in love with you! I've been in love with you this whole bleeding year!"

My mind spins. "But Ellie—"

"I cheated on her every day. In my mind, I thought of you in ways I shouldn't have, again and again. She was nothing compared to you. I've never felt this way about *anybody* before—"

"But—"

"The first day of school." He scoots closer. "We weren't physics partners by accident. I saw Professeur Wakefield assigning lab partners based on where people were sitting, so I leaned forward to borrow a pencil from you at just the right moment so he'd think we were next to each other. Anna, I wanted to be your partner *the first day*."

"But . . ." I can't think straight.

"I bought you love poetry! 'I love you as certain dark things are loved, secretly, between the shadow and the soul.'"

I blink at him.

"Neruda. I starred the passage. God," he moans. "Why didn't you open it?"

"Because you said it was for *school*."

"I said you were beautiful. I slept in your bed!"

"You never made a move! You had a girlfriend!"

"No matter what a terrible boyfriend I was, I wouldn't

actually cheat on her. But I thought you'd know. With me being there, I thought you'd know."

We're going in circles. "How could I know if you never said anything?"

"How could I know if *you* never said anything?"

"You had Ellie!"

"You had Toph! And Dave!"

I'm speechless. I blink at the rooftops of Paris.

He touches my cheek, pulling my gaze back to him. I suck in my breath.

"Anna. I'm sorry for what happened in Luxembourg Gardens. Not because of the kiss—I've never had a kiss like that in my life—but because I didn't tell you why I was running away. I chased after Meredith because of *you*."

Touch me again. *Please, touch me again.*

"All I could think about was what that bastard did to you last Christmas. Toph never tried to explain or apologize. How could I do that to Mer? And I ought to have called you before I went to Ellie's, but I was so anxious to just *end it*, once and for all, that I wasn't thinking straight."

I reach for him. "St. Clair—"

He pulls back. "And that. Why don't you call me Étienne anymore?"

"But . . . no one else calls you that, It was weird. Right?"

"No. It wasn't." His expression saddens. "And every time you say 'St. Clair,' it's like you're rejecting me again."

"I have *never* rejected you."

"But you have. And for Dave." His tone is venomous.

"And you rejected me for Ellie *on my birthday*. I don't understand. If you liked me so much, why didn't you break up with her?"

He gazes at the river. "I've been confused. I've been so stupid."

"Yes. You have."

"I deserve that."

"Yes. You do." I pause. "But I've been stupid, too. You were right. About . . . the alone thing."

We sit in silence. "I've been thinking lately," he says after a while. "About me mum and dad. How she gives in to him. How she won't leave him. And as much as I love her, I hate her for it. I don't understand why she won't stand up for herself, why she won't go for what *she* wants. But I've been doing the same thing. I'm just like her."

I shake my head. "You aren't like your mom."

"I am. But I don't want to be like that anymore, I want what *I* want." He turns to me again, his face anxious. "I told my father's friends that I'm studying at Berkeley next year. It worked. He's really, *really* angry with me, but it worked. You told me to go for his pride. You were right."

"So." I'm cautious, hardly daring to believe. "You're moving to California?"

"I have to."

"Right." I swallow hard. "Because of your mom."

"Because of *you*. I'll only be a twenty-minute train ride from your school, and I'll make the commute to see you every night. I'd take a commute ten times that just to be with you every night."

His words are too perfect. It must be a misunderstanding, surely I'm misunderstanding—

"You're the most incredible girl I've ever known. You're gorgeous and smart, and you make me laugh like no one else can. And I can *talk* to you. And I know after all this I don't deserve you, but what I'm trying to say is that I love you, Anna. Very much."

I'm holding my breath. I can't talk, but my eyes are filling with tears.

He takes it the wrong way. "Oh God. And I've mucked things up again, haven't I? I didn't mean to attack you like this. I mean I did but . . . all right." His voice cracks. "I'll leave. Or you can go down first, and then I'll come down, and I promise I'll never bother you again—"

He starts to stand, but I grab his arm. "No!"

His body freezes. "I'm so sorry," he says. "I never meant to hurt you."

I trail my fingers across his cheek. He stays perfectly still for me. "Please stop apologizing, Étienne."

"Say my name again," he whispers.

I close my eyes and lean forward. *"Étienne."*

He takes my hands into his. Those perfect hands, that fit mine just so. "Anna?"

Our foreheads touch. "Yes?"

"Will you please tell me you love me? I'm dying here."

And then we're laughing. And then I'm in his arms, and we're kissing, at first quickly—to make up for lost time—and then slowly, because we have all the time in the world. And his lips are soft and honey sweet, and the careful, passionate way he moves them against my own says that he savors the way I taste, too.

And in between kisses, I tell him I love him.

Again and again and again.

chapter forty-seven

Rashmi clears her throat and glares at us.

"Seriously," Josh says. "We were never like that, were we?"

Mer groans and chucks her pen at him. Josh and Rashmi have broken up. In a way, it's strange they waited this long. It seemed inevitable, but then again, so did other things. And those things took a while, too.

They've split as amicably as possible. It didn't make sense for them to keep this up long distance. They both seem relieved. Rashmi's excited about Brown, and Josh . . . well, he still has to come to terms with the fact that we're leaving and he's staying. And he *is* staying. He squeaked by again, barely. He's losing himself in his drawings, and his hands are in a constant state of cramps. Truthfully, I'm worried. I know how it feels to be alone. But Josh is an attractive, funny guy. He'll make new friends.

We're studying for exams in my room. It's dusk, and a warm breeze blows my curtains. Summer is almost here. I'll see Bridge again soon. I received a new email from her. Things are shaky, but we're trying. I'll take that.

Étienne and I are sitting side by side, feet intertwined. His fingers trace swirly patterns on my arm. I burrow into him, inhaling that scent of shampoo and shaving cream and that something else that's just *him* that I can never get enough of. He kisses my stripe. I tilt my head, and his mouth moves onto mine. I run a hand through his perfect, messy hair.

I LOVE his hair, and now I get to touch it whenever I want.

And he doesn't even get irritated. Most of the time.

Meredith has been very accepting of our relationship. Of course, it doesn't hurt that she's attending college in Rome. "Imagine," she said, after registering, "a whole city of gorgeous Italian guys. They can say anything to me, and it'll be sexy."

"You'll be so easy," Rashmi said. "*Would you like-ah to order-ah the spa-ghe-tti?* 'Oh, do me, Marco!'"

"I wonder if Marco will like football?" Mer asked dreamily.

As for us, Étienne was right. Our schools are only a twenty-minute transit ride away. He'll stay with me on the weekends, and we'll visit each other as often as possible during the week. We'll be together. We both got our Point Zéro wishes—each other. He said he wished for me every time. He was wishing for me when I entered the tower.

"Mmm," I say. He's kissing my neck.

"That's it," Rashmi says. "I'm outta here. Enjoy your hormones."

Josh and Mer follow her exit, and we're alone. Just the way I like it.

"Ha!" Étienne says. "Just the way I like it."

He pulls me onto his lap, and I wrap my legs around his waist. His lips are velvet soft, and we kiss until the streetlamps flicker on outside. Until the opera singer begins her evening routine. "I'm going to miss her," I say.

"I'll sing to you." He tucks my stripe behind my ear. "Or I'll take you to the opera. Or I'll fly you back here to visit. Whatever you want. Anything you want."

I lace my fingers through his. "I want to stay right here, in this moment."

"Isn't that the name of the latest James Ashley bestseller? *In This Moment?*"

"Careful. Someday you'll meet him, and he won't be nearly as amusing in person."

Étienne grins. "Oh, so he'll only be mildly amusing? I suppose I can handle *mildly* amusing."

"I'm serious! You have to promise me right now, this instant, that you won't leave me once you meet him. Most people would run."

"I'm not most people."

I smile. "I know. But you still have to promise."

His eyes lock on mine. "Anna, I promise that I will never leave you."

My heart pounds in response. And Étienne knows it, because he takes my hand and holds it against his chest, to show me how hard his heart is pounding, too. "And now for yours," he says.

I'm still dazed. "My what?"

He laughs. "Promise you won't flee once I introduce you to my father. Or, worse, leave me for him."

I pause. "Do you think he'll object to me?"

"Oh, I'm sure he will."

Okay. Not the answer I was looking for.

Étienne sees my alarm. "Anna. You know my father dislikes anything that makes me happy. And you make me happier than anyone ever has." He smiles. "Oh, yes. He'll hate you."

"So that's . . . a good thing?"

"I don't care what he thinks. Only what you think." He holds me tighter. "Like if you think I need to stop biting my nails."

"You've worn your pinkies to nubs," I say cheerfully.

"Or if I need to start ironing my bedspread."

"I DO NOT IRON MY BEDSPREAD."

"You do. And I love it." I blush, and Étienne kisses my warm cheeks. "You know, my mum likes you."

"She does?"

"You're the only thing I've talked about all year. She's ecstatic we're together."

I'm smiling inside and out. "I can't wait to meet her."

He smiles back, but then his expression grows worried. "So will your father object to me? Because I'm not American? I mean, not fully American? He's not one of those mad, patriotic nuts, is he?"

"No. He'll love you, *because* you make me happy. He's not always so bad."

Étienne raises his dark eyebrows.

"I know! But I said *not always*. He still is the majority of the time. It's just . . . he means well. He thought he was doing good, sending me here."

"And was it? Good?"

"Look at you, fishing for compliments."

"I wouldn't object to a compliment."

I play with a strand of his hair. "I like how you pronounce 'banana.' *Ba-nah-na*. And sometimes you trill your *r*'s. I love that."

"Bri*ll*iant," he whispers in my ear. "Because I've spent loads of time practicing."

My room is dark, and Étienne wraps his arms back around me. We listen to the opera singer in a peaceful silence. I'm surprised by how much I'll miss France. Atlanta was home for almost eighteen years, and though I've only known Paris for the last nine months, it's changed me. I have a new city to learn next year, but I'm not scared.

Because I was right. For the two of us, home isn't a place. It's a person.

And we're finally home.

acknowledgments

I would still be trapped inside the first three chapters if it weren't for Paula Davis. Paula, thanks to you, *I wrote a novel*. Thank you for being the first to believe in Anna and Étienne. Thank you for believing in me. If I could, I would name a moon or a planet or an entire galaxy after you.

Thank you to Kate Schafer Testerman, my Dream Agent who became my Real Agent. It's not often in life that we get what we wish for. I am still pinching myself.

I feel privileged to have Julie Strauss-Gabel on my side, whose editorial career I have admired for so long. Julie, thank you for your patient, extraordinary guidance. I can't believe that not only did you read my novel, but that you also wanted to work with it. I am so grateful. And lucky. And stunned. With all my heart, I extend these thanks to the rest of Penguin. Extra hugs for Lisa Yoskowitz, Lauri Hornik, and Scottie Bowditch.

Thank you to my parents, who only gave encouragement when I announced I was majoring in creative writing. Do you realize how rare you are? I love you.

Endless thanks to Laini Taylor and Sumner Smith. Laini, not only do you give brilliant advice, but you also write brilliant emails. Thank you for the guidance (and for the goinky freak). Sumner, you are the most honest reader that I could ask for. Thank you for your romantic wisdom and your contagious enthusiasm.

The Weaverville librarians were unrelentingly awesome. Thank you for looking the other way whenever I googled "Notre-Dame" on the job, and extra thanks to Lauren Biehl for letting me hold her thesis captive for an entire year.

Merci beaucoup to my sister Kara for being brave when I couldn't be.

Merci, merci, merci to Manning Krull, American Parisian superhero.

And thank you, Kiersten White, for always being there. It is this simple: I would not have survived last year without you. It's an honor to travel this strange path together.

The following people provided answers to questions and immeasurable moral support: Jim Di Bartolo, Marjorie Mesnis, the North Asheville librarians, Taiyo la Paix, Fay and Roger Perkins, Mary and Dave Prahler, The Tenners, Staci Thomas, Natalie Whipple, Thomas Witherspoon, Sara and Jeff Zentner, and everyone who reads my blog. Special thanks to Amanda Reid for keeping my hair blue, and to Ken Hanke and Justin Souther, film critics extraordinaire. Chris Prahler gave me several versions of what his acknowledgment should say. Here is the shortest: "Thanks to my favorite brother-in-law." Chris is my *only* brother-in-law, but my thanks are genuine.

This story was birthed during National Novel Writing Month. Thank you, Chris Baty and staff, for everything you've done for aspiring writers.

Finally, thank you to Jarrod Perkins. Who will always be my first reader. Who pulls me out of bed, pours coffee and tea down my throat, and pushes me into my office. Who cooks dinner, carries it to my desk, and carts away the dirty dishes. Who never doubted I would succeed. Who wipes away my tears, laughs at the funny bits, and seriously considers my most frequently asked question: "Is the boy hot enough?" I am deeply in love with you. Thank you for being you, because you are my favorite.

Discussion Questions

- What emotions does Anna experience throughout her first day at SOAP? Why does she feel so out of place?

- What qualities make St. Clair so appealing to Anna? To other members of the SOAP community (including teachers)?

- What differences between American and French schools and cultures does Anna mention? Which seems hardest for her to adapt to?

- Many characters in this novel have problems with their parents. What struggles does each character face? How do problems with your parents impact your relationships with your friends?

- Why is Anna so afraid of being seen as American by the citizens of Paris? What does St. Clair do to assuage these worries? Do his attempts work? Why or why not?

• How do Anna's relationships with people back home—Seany, Bridge, Toph—change while she is in Paris? Is it always necessary for relationships to change when conducted at a distance?

• Why does St. Clair continue to stay with Ellie, even as their relationship is clearly falling apart? Is it healthy for people to continue in their romantic relationships even when it's obvious that they're going to end?

• In what ways does Anna's betrayal of Mer mirror Bridge's betrayal of Anna? Is it ever okay to go after or become involved with a person that your best friend is interested in, too?

• At the end of the novel, Anna and St. Clair are together romantically. Do you think that this relationship will work after they leave Paris? Why or why not?

Turn the page for an excerpt from
Lola and the Boy Next Door!

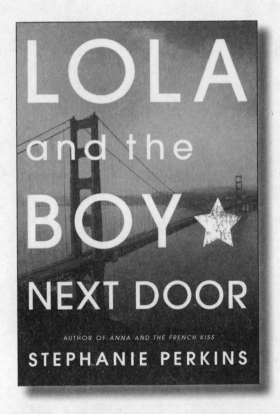

chapter one

$\mathcal{I}$ have three simple wishes. They're really not too much to ask.

The first is to attend the winter formal dressed like Marie Antoinette. I want a wig so elaborate it could cage a bird and a dress so wide I'll only be able to enter the dance through a set of double doors. But I'll hold my skirts high as I arrive to reveal a pair of platform combat boots, so everyone can see that, underneath the frills, I'm punk-rock tough.

The second is for my parents to approve of my boyfriend. They hate him. They hate his bleached hair with its constant dark roots, and they hate his arms, which are tattooed with sleeves of spiderwebs and stars. They say his eyebrows condescend, that his smile is more of a smirk. And they're sick of hearing his music blasting from my bedroom, and they're tired of fighting about my curfew whenever I watch his band play in clubs.

And my third wish?

To never ever ever see the Bell twins ever again. Ever.

But I'd much rather discuss my boyfriend. I realize it's not cool to desire parental approval, but honestly, my life would be so much easier if they accepted that Max is *the one*. It'd mean the end of embarrassing restrictions, the end of every-hour-on-the-hour phone-call check-ins on dates, and—best of all—the end of Sunday brunch.

The end of mornings like this.

"Another waffle, Max?"

My father, Nathan, pushes the golden stack across our antique farmhouse table and toward my boyfriend. This is not a real question. It's a command, so that my parents can continue their interrogation before we leave. Our reward for dealing with brunch? A more relaxed Sunday-afternoon date with fewer check-ins.

Max takes two and helps himself to the homemade raspberry-peach syrup. "Thanks, sir. Incredible, as always." He pours the syrup carefully, a drop in each square. Despite appearances, Max is careful by nature. This is why he never drinks or smokes pot on Saturday nights. He doesn't want to come to brunch looking hungover, which is, of course, what my parents are watching for. Evidence of debauchery.

"Thank Andy." Nathan jerks his head toward my other dad, who runs a pie bakery out of our home. "He made them."

"Delicious. Thank you, sir." Max never misses a beat. "Lola, did you get enough?"

I stretch, and the seven inches of Bakelite bracelets on my right arm knock against each other. "Yeah, like, twenty minutes ago. Come on," I turn and plead to Andy, the candidate most likely to let us leave early. "Can't we go now?"

He bats his eyes innocently. "More orange juice? Frittata?"

"No." I fight to keep from slumping. Slumping is unattractive.

Nathan stabs another waffle. "So. Max. How goes the world of meter reading?"

When Max isn't being an indie punk garage-rock god, he works for the City of San Francisco. It irks Nathan that Max has no interest in college. But what my dad doesn't grasp is that Max is actually brilliant. He reads complicated philosophy books written by people with names I can't pronounce and watches tons of angry political documentaries. I certainly wouldn't debate him.

Max smiles politely, and his dark eyebrows raise a titch. "The same as last week."

"And the band?" Andy asks. "Wasn't some record executive supposed to come on Friday?"

My boyfriend frowns. The guy from the label never showed. Max updates Andy about Amphetamine's forthcoming album instead, while Nathan and I exchange scowls. No doubt my father is disappointed that, once again, he hasn't found anything to incriminate Max. Apart from the age thing, of course.

Which is the real reason my parents hate my boyfriend.

They hate that I'm seventeen, and Max is twenty-two.

But I'm a firm believer in age-doesn't-matter. Besides, it's only five years, way less than the difference between my parents. Though it's no use pointing this out, or the fact that my boyfriend is the same age Nathan was when my parents started dating. This only gets them worked up. "*I* may have been his age, but Andy was thirty," Nathan always says. "Not a teenager. And we'd both had several boyfriends before, plenty of life experience. You can't jump into these things. You have to be careful."

But they don't remember what it's like to be young and in love. Of course I can jump into these things. When it's someone like Max, I'd be stupid not to. My best friend thinks it's hilarious that my parents are so strict. After all, shouldn't a couple of gay men sympathize with the temptation offered by a sexy, slightly dangerous boyfriend?

This is so far from the truth it's painful.

It doesn't matter that I'm a perfect daughter. I don't drink or do drugs, and I've never smoked a cigarette. I haven't crashed their car—I can't even drive, so they're not paying high insurance rates—and I have a decent job. I make good grades. Well, apart from biology, but I refused to dissect that fetal pig on principle. And I only have one hole per ear and no ink. Yet. I'm not even embarrassed to hug my parents in public.

Except when Nathan wears a sweatband when he goes running. Because really.

I clear my dishes from the table, hoping to speed things along. Today Max is taking me to one of my favorite places, the

Japanese Tea Garden, and then he's driving me to work for my evening shift. And hopefully, in between stops, we'll spend some quality time together in his '64 Chevy Impala.

I lean against the kitchen countertop, dreaming of Max's car.

"I'm just shocked she's not wearing her kimono," Nathan says.

"What?" I hate it when I space out and realize people have been talking about me.

"Chinese pajamas to the Japanese Tea Garden," he continues, gesturing at my red silk bottoms. "What *will* people think?"

I don't believe in fashion. I believe in costume. Life is too short to be the same person every day. I roll my eyes to show Max that I realize my parents are acting lame.

"Our little drag queen," Andy says.

"Because that's a new one." I snatch his plate and dump the brunch remains into Betsy's bowl. Her eyes bug, and she inhales the waffle scraps in one big doggie bite.

Betsy's full name is Heavens to Betsy, and we rescued her from animal control several years ago. She's a mutt, built like a golden retriever but black in color. I wanted a black dog, because Andy once clipped a magazine article—he's *always* clipping articles, usually about teens dying from overdoses or contracting syphilis or getting pregnant and dropping out of school—about how black dogs are always the last to be adopted at shelters and, therefore, more likely to be put down. Which is totally Dog Racism, if you ask me. Betsy is all heart.

"Lola." Andy is wearing his serious face. "I wasn't finished."

"So get a new plate."

"Lola," Nathan says, and I give Andy a clean plate. I'm afraid they're about to turn this into A Thing in front of Max, when they notice Betsy begging for more waffles.

"No," I tell her.

"Have you walked her today?" Nathan asks me.

"No, Andy did."

"Before I started cooking," Andy says. "She's ready for another."

"Why don't you take her for a walk while we finish up with Max?" Nathan asks. Another command, not a question.

I glance at Max, and he closes his eyes like he can't believe they're pulling this trick again. "But, Dad—"

"No buts. You wanted the dog, you walk her."

This is one of Nathan's most annoying catchphrases. Heavens to Betsy was supposed to be mine, but she had the nerve to fall in love with Nathan instead, which irritates Andy and me to no end. We're the ones who feed and walk her. I reach for the biodegradable baggies and her leash—the one I've embroidered with hearts and Russian nesting dolls—and she's already going berserk. "Yeah, yeah. Come on."

I shoot Max another apologetic look, and then Betsy and I are out the door.

There are twenty-one stairs from our porch to the sidewalk. Anywhere you go in San Francisco, you have to deal with steps and hills. It's unusually warm outside, so along with my pajama bottoms and Bakelite bangles, I'm wearing a tank top. I've also got on my giant white Jackie O sunglasses, a long brunette wig with emerald tips, and black ballet slippers. *Real* ballet slippers, not the flats that only look like ballet slippers.

My New Year's resolution was to never again wear the same outfit twice.

The sunshine feels good on my shoulders. It doesn't matter that it's August; because of the bay, the temperature doesn't change much throughout the year. It's always cool. Today I'm grateful for the peculiar weather, because it means I won't have to bring a sweater on my date.

Betsy pees on the teeny rectangle of grass in front of the lavender Victorian next door—she always pees here, which I totally approve of—and we move on. Despite my annoying parents, I'm happy. I have a romantic date with my boyfriend, a great schedule with my favorite coworkers, and one more week of summer vacation.

We hike up and down the massive hill that separates my street from the park. When we arrive, a Korean gentleman in a velveteen tracksuit greets us. He's doing tai chi between the palm trees. "Hello, Dolores! How was your birthday?" Mr. Lim is the only person apart from my parents (when they're mad) who calls me by my real name. His daughter Lindsey is my best friend; they live a few streets over.

"Hi, Mr. Lim. It was divine!" My birthday was last week. Mine is the earliest of anyone in my grade, which I love. It gives me an additional air of maturity. "How's the restaurant?"

"Very good, thank you. Everyone asking for beef galbi this week. Goodbye, Dolores! Hello to your parents."

The old lady name is because I was named after one. My

great-grandma Dolores Deeks died a few years before I was born. She was Andy's grandmother, and she was fabulous. The kind of woman who wore feathered hats and marched in civil rights protests. Dolores was the first person Andy came out to. He was thirteen. They were really close, and when she died, she left Andy her house. That's where we live, in Great-Grandma Dolores's mint green Victorian in the Castro district.

Which we'd never be able to afford without her generous bequeathal. My parents make a healthy living, but nothing like the neighbors. The well-kept homes on our street, with their decorative gabled cornices and extravagant wooden ornamentation, all come from old money. Including the lavender house next door.

My name is also shared with this park, Mission Dolores. It's not a coincidence. Great-Grandma Dolores was named after the nearby mission, which was named after a creek called *Arroyo de Nuestra Señora de los Dolores*. This translates to "Our Lady of Sorrows Creek." Because who wouldn't want to be named after a depressing body of water? There's also a major street around here called Dolores. It's kind of weird.

I'd rather be a Lola.

Heavens to Betsy finishes, and we head home. I hope my parents haven't been torturing Max. For someone so brash onstage, he's actually an introvert, and these weekly meetings aren't easy on him. "I thought dealing with one protective father was bad enough," he once said. "But two? Your dads are gonna be the death of me, Lo."

A moving truck rattles by, and it's odd, because suddenly—just that quickly—my good mood is replaced by unease. We pick up speed. Max must be beyond uncomfortable right now. I can't explain it, but the closer I get to home, the worse I feel. A terrible scenario loops through my mind: my parents, so relentless with inquiries that Max decides I'm not worth it anymore.

My hope is that someday, when we've been together longer than one summer, my parents will realize he's *the one,* and age won't be an issue anymore. But despite their inability to see this truth now, they aren't dumb. They deal with Max because they think if they forbade me from seeing him, we'd just run off together. I'd move into his apartment and get a job dancing naked or dealing acid.

Which is beyond misguided.

But I'm jogging now, hauling Betsy down the hill. Something's not right. And I'm positive it's happened—that Max has left or my parents have cornered him into a heated argument about the lack of direction in his life—when I reach my street and everything clicks into place.

The moving truck.

Not the brunch.

The moving truck.

But I'm sure the truck belongs to another renter. It has to, it always does. The last family, this couple that smelled like baby Swiss and collected medical oddities like shriveled livers in formaldehyde and oversize models of vaginas, vacated a week ago. In the last two years, there's been a string of renters, and every time someone moves out, I can't help but feel ill until the new ones arrive.

Because what if *now* is the time they move back in?

I slow down to get a better look at the truck. Is anyone outside? I didn't notice a car in the garage when we passed earlier, but I've made a habit out of not staring at the house next door. Sure enough, there are two people ahead on the sidewalk. I strain my eyes and find, with a mixture of agitation and relief, that it's just the movers. Betsy tugs on her leash, and I pick up the pace again.

I'm sure there's nothing to worry about. What are the chances?

Except . . . there's *always* a chance. The movers lift a white sofa from the back of the truck, and my heart thumps harder. Do I recognize it? Have I sat on that love seat before? But no. I don't know it. I peer inside the crammed truck, searching for anything familiar, and I'm met with stacks of severe modern furniture that I've never seen before.

It's not them. It can't be them.

It's not them!

I grin from ear to ear—a silly smile that makes me look like a child, which I don't normally allow myself to do—and wave to the movers. They grunt and nod back. The lavender garage door is open, and now I'm positive that it wasn't earlier. I inspect the car, and my relief deepens. It's something compact and silver, and I don't recognize it.

Saved. Again. It *is* a happy day.

Betsy and I bound inside. "Brunch is over! Let's go, Max."

Everyone is staring out the front window in our living room.

"Looks like we have neighbors again," I say.

Andy looks surprised by the cheer in my voice. We've never talked about it, but he knows something happened there two years ago. He knows that I worry about their return, that I fret each moving day.

"What?" I grin again, but then stop myself, conscious of Max. I tone it down.

"Uh, Lo? You didn't see them, by any chance, did you?"

Andy's concern is touching. I release Betsy from her leash and whisk into the kitchen. Determined to hurry the morning and get to my date, I swipe the remaining dishes from the table and head toward the sink. "Nope." I laugh. "What? Do they have another plastic vagina? A stuffed giraffe? A medieval suit of armor—what?"

All three of them are staring at me.

My throat tightens. "What is it?"

Max examines me with an unusual curiosity. "Your parents say you know the family."

No. NO.

Someone says something else, but the words don't register. My feet are carrying me toward the window while my brain is screaming for me to turn back. It can't be them. It wasn't their furniture! It wasn't their car! But people buy new things. My eyes are riveted next door as a figure emerges onto the porch. The dishes in my hands—*Why am I still carrying the brunch plates?*—shatter against the floor.

Because there she is.

Calliope Bell.